I0679620

The Crucible

RUBY BARNES

Print Edition

Published by Marble City Publishing

Copyright 2012 by Ruby Barnes

ISBN 10 1908943106

ISBN 13 978-1-908943-10-1

For Adrienne

Tell me what you goin' do,

when death comes creeping in.

Tell me what you goin' do,

when death comes creeping in your room.

Tell me what you goin' do,

if when he find you full o' sin.

Oh my Lord, oh my Lord

What shall I do?

Traditional Bluegrass song

Origin

Southern Cameroon, West Africa 1936

She ran fast but not as fast as she could. They were chasing her again, thinking they were hunting her, but in truth they were too slow, heavy and clumsy. Here the tribe came now, through the undergrowth, full of testosterone and shrouded in that musty odour of all male jungle dwellers.

'Red? Where are you, Red?' they shouted at her in their thick foreign accents, using their name for her tribe as an insult.

She didn't answer but ran on further. Although they could never catch her it was tiresome. She had much better things to do than play cat and mouse with a bunch of hairy, flat-footed morons. As well as that, the sickness was back and she would soon have to lie down again.

One of them caught sight of her and hurled a stick through the air. It landed harmlessly on the rain forest floor but close enough to alarm her. Looking down at the infant cradled against her breast she decided to climb to safety and wait until they would become bored and leave her alone. With a few nimble moves she reached the higher branches of a tree and, feeling secure, decided to hurl back some insults.

'You useless bunch of clowns! Go find some nuts or berries and leave me alone. Don't pretend you can catch me. You're too slow and heavy. Look at you, old hairy guy with the big fat belly. Go and rest your belly in the mud, roll around like the dirty pig that you are!'

Although the tribe had trouble understanding her jungle patois, they gathered it was serious verbal abuse and roared back. Fat Belly tried to climb the tree but was too heavy to reach the flimsy higher branches from which she safely grinned at him.

They were on the verge of turning away when the ground began to tremble. The tribe members looked at each other in alarm. Had they forgotten to appease Mother Earth? Was the end time upon them?

The tremors increased in violence and, above the troop, the jungle trees began to sway. She grasped with her free hand at the branch but, with the other arm around her infant and unable to sacrifice the child, felt her grip slip and began the fall down to the jungle floor. She landed awkwardly with a snap of bone. The infant disengaged itself and scurried off into the undergrowth.

The tribe fell upon her in a rage, shrieking, tearing, dismembering. Fat Belly held aloft the leg of his tormentor and shouted at the treetops. He bared his rotting teeth and bleeding gums, showing meaty shreds of the spot-nosed monkey they had hunted and eaten two days ago. That one had been slow, perhaps had a sickness, but he didn't care. This was Red he was eating now and the flesh was sweet.

Red-capped mangabey and spot-nosed monkey. The flesh, blood and viruses of two species mingled in the body of the third and the virus mutated.

Two weeks later Fat Belly's head was on a plate in the local village. The chimpanzee hunter had followed Fat Belly's progress as head of the local chimpanzee troop and decided to take him in his prime. The brain, heart and blood of the brave chimpanzee covered the hunter's new facial markings, specially cut into his own skin for the occasion. Consuming Fat Belly's strength and courage would increase his own prowess with women during the upcoming seasonal festivities.

At the festival the women were attracted by the self confidence and alluring facial markings of the chimpanzee hunter. He was very successful. He shared in their favours and in return they received the virus.

Slowly it moved, from town to village to town, season to season. People became ill and died but in those parts of the world with short life expectancy such deaths pass without notice.

After two generations the virus went abroad to Haiti in the blood of a migrant worker returning from seasonal work and celebration in the Congo. There, in the Americas, it found lifestyles that gave it wings. Because HIV is a lentivirus, by its nature taking a long time to produce any adverse effects upon the body, the spread of the virus had gone global by the time AIDS was recognised as the outcome.

In the soup

Thomas couldn't see his soup although he could smell it. He couldn't even see the spoon and his first attempt to eat flowed down his chin and onto the tablecloth with a soft, spattering sound.

Reto chuckled. 'Mr Thistlethwaite, I was led to understand you are a man of precision. Is that not so?'

Thomas tried again, this time with success. The texture was coarse on his lips but delicious. Potato, and something else that smelled and tasted like garlic, yet different. Reaching out with the left hand he located a piece of bread and brought it to his mouth, bouncing first lightly off the end of his nose.

There was further mirth from the other side of the table.

'Reto, you're wearing those goddamn goggles, aren't you?' Thomas leaned forward. 'Take them off and pass them over, this is impossible!'

'I have to first observe the clientele, if that's okay with you. And not until you have experienced the main course, my friend.'

A couple of minutes passed without further conversation between them, although there was a background murmur of hushed voices. Thomas, assuming Reto had completed his surveillance, reached out a hand with the intention of locating the goggles and found himself grasping a leg that hadn't been there before.

'Gentlemen, are you finished with your appetisers? May I bring the main course?' the waiter asked in heavily Swiss accented English, prising Thomas's hand from his thigh in a firm but respectful way.

'Please do,' Reto replied and they sensed rather than saw their soup dishes being removed from the table.

The meat dish arrived. They knew this only because the waiter announced it. Fillet steak with gnocchi, again that mild and herblike garlic odour and taste.

'Bärlauch. Wild garlic from the forest,' Reto said. 'Springtime speciality.'

Thomas was used to the Swiss interpretation of seasonal specialities. The Bärlauch seemed to be in every dish on the menu. It was certainly unusual but left him with an aftertaste, reminiscent of childhood experimentation with eating grass shoots and dandelions.

The fillet steak, on the other hand, was to die for and medium rare. It had a slight odour of blood, appropriate to the sanguine main event and reason for their presence. Reaching out with his right hand, half expecting to find yet another strange limb, Thomas felt for the wineglass and brought it carefully up to his lips, tasting further blood in the heavy French red wine.

'Okay, Reto. Very tasty, now let me see.'

Reto Hersperger passed the night vision goggles under the table. Thomas placed them on his head and the room lit up for him in an eerie green light. That evening's dinner guests at the Blindekuh were revealed.

The Blindekuh, an exclusive yet inexpensive restaurant in Zurich, serves its guests in complete darkness. Blindekuh is the German word for the children's game of Blind Man's Buff and the concept is intended to provide a heightened sensory experience of the culinary variety.

With the goggles Thomas could see one or two of the diners were having sensory experiences of a different sort. In the far right corner a presentable man, who Thomas recognised from his briefing documents, was holding the hand of a beautiful young blonde woman and caressing her face with his fingertips. The man, with his straight brow, pale complexion and prominent nose looked typically

English, the woman clearly Swiss. And clearly not his wife.

Across the room a middle aged gentleman of Nordic appearance was enjoying under-table attentions from a slim fellow considerably his junior.

The other guests were behaving themselves, more or less.

Reto leaned across and whispered. 'Behind and to your left, at the table of four, the one with the spectacles.'

Thomas turned and identified, a couple of tables away, four African men seated together. The bespectacled individual was having considerable trouble with some noodles in a dish. Reaching for something in his pocket, Thomas rose and took a swipe at a small pile of side plates being carried on the palm of one hand by the passing blind waiter. There was a crash of breaking crockery.

In the brief commotion that followed Thomas stepped over to the Africans' table and injected the bespectacled man in the neck with a small hypodermic needle. He caught the man's head as it slumped into the plate of Bärlauch and potato soup, and then returned to his own table, placing the goggles in a backpack.

'Shall we get the bill?' he asked Reto. 'I don't really fancy Bärlauch dessert.'

'No problem, my friend,' Reto replied. 'We pay on the way out. My treat.'

Afterwards, as they wandered down the Mühlebachstrasse, Thomas contemplated his first, and rather creative, kill of this new assignment. A diabetic man dying in his soup from an insulin and cocaine overdose was no commonplace event. It would only serve to further enhance the mystique of the Blindekuh.

Don't lift a finger

Greg Marshall could not believe someone had died in the darkened restaurant. It had ruined his clandestine dinner date with Simone Buettiker, a young work colleague. She was from a well known family in Zurich and they had specifically selected the Blindekuh to avoid recognition by other dinner guests. This had proved futile when, the dead African finally being discovered, the lights had gone on and she came face to face with friends, associates and even extended family members. Worst of all, her young brother had been discovered with an elderly Nordic gentleman beneath his table.

They drove in silence for a while, Simone favouring the local roads rather than the motorway that, together with lake Zürichsee, bordered the city of Zurich. She drove her Honda sports cabriolet sedately, the hood up, certainly not wishing to attract further attention and anyway the early spring evening was very cold. The road they took led them through the industrialised suburb of Altstetten towards the town of Dietikon. Dark hills rose up behind the linear conglomerations of offices and factories but there were no green spaces between the conjoined sprawl of lesser Zurich.

In Dietikon they came to a halt at the red lights of a major intersection. There was an approaching sound from behind of someone gunning a weedy engine and Simone glanced in her door mirror. Greg, turning round in the passenger seat, could see a dark blue Fiat driving wildly, swerving in and out of the traffic. The lights turned green and Simone moved on in her usual fashion.

The reckless driver of the Italian car was soon directly behind them and Simone started to become agitated as the other driver pulled perilously close to the rear of the Honda.

'He's trying to get you to race,' Greg said.

'Well, he's out of luck. I don't do racing.'

When this became clear to the other driver he swerved onto the wrong side of the road and swept passed them, the poor little Italian engine screaming as it was thrashed. The sound of a horn from an oncoming vehicle blared and faded but the Fiat driver was undeterred and disappeared into the distance.

Three minutes later they found themselves at another intersection, infamous for its slow changing traffic lights. The Fiat was in the right turn lane, waiting for the green filter. Reckless as he was, no amount of bravado would save him from an automatic two hundred and fifty Swiss Franc fine if he crashed the light. The traffic camera mounted up high above the road would ensure that. Even criminals observe some of the myriad rules of daily life in Switzerland.

The Honda rolled up to the lights just as they changed to green and, as they were going straight ahead, Greg came briefly face to face with the Fiat driver and committed a felony. He raised his middle finger triumphantly. Worth up to four hundred Swiss Francs if caught.

As soon as Greg did this, he realised his mistake. The driver of the Fiat looked to be a large man but, more disturbingly, his creased and broodingly dark features suggested an individual who had experienced many unspeakable things. Greg had seen such faces before amongst the former Yugoslav community in Switzerland, many of them war victims and even war crime perpetrators. The mouth of the Fiat driver twisted even further into a snarl as he pulled out of the right turn lane and charged after the Honda. There was a flash of light as the traffic camera recorded his number plate. Changing of lane in front of traffic lights, one hundred Swiss Francs.

'Shit!' Greg said , looking at their pursuer in his door mirror. 'I've just done something stupid. You'd better put your foot down, Simone!'

'I'll just let him pass,' Simone replied, cool as ever.

The Fiat did pass them, engine screaming as it did the first time a few minutes previously. This time, however, the driver pulled close in front of them and began to let his now idle engine slow them down. After a couple of hundred meters both cars came to a halt. Simone sensibly maintained a distance of several meters.

The driver's door of the dark blue Fiat opened and the driver stepped slowly out, unfurling to his full height which was considerably more than Greg's. He stood legs apart and hands held out in a beckoning gesture, a clear invitation to conflict.

Greg, no stranger to ill-advised physical confrontations, usually involving excess alcohol, would normally have stepped up to the plate and received his black eye with good grace. But when he made that incendiary 'up yours' gesture back at the Dietikon intersection he had done so half-heartedly and without any genuine anger. Now the cocoon of the Honda made him feel isolated from his potential opponent's anger and he had no appetite for a fight.

He was considering how best to explain this to Simone without losing face when she took control of the situation and, slipping the car into gear, drove straight at their aggressor. At the last second she swerved around the man, who managed to land a slap on the rear wing of Honda which then roared up the road, taking a slip onto the motorway before the next town of Spreitenbach.

'Ha!' Simone laughed as she pushed the Honda to the red line, the VTEC engine screaming up to nearly nine thousand rpm. It was the first time she had ever tested the car and she liked it. There was no sign of the Fiat. By the time they drove into the Bäregg tunnel they were both shaking with adrenaline. Simone slowed the car down to the one hundred kilometre speed limit.

But as they neared the tunnel exit the blue car appeared behind them. It must have been travelling at nearly twice the speed limit through the tunnel and was on a collision course with their rear end. Greg turned and could see the white knuckles of the driver gripping the steering wheel, closer, closer. And then his head banged against the headrest and the side window as Simone slewed the car off the carriageway unexpectedly and down a slip road. The Fiat couldn't follow and went straight ahead.

'Ha, ha!' Simone shouted, exhilarated by her new found driving skills.

They drove steadily down the slip to the junction but their elation was short lived as, across the junction, they saw the blue car turn sharply down the on slip and fly down the wrong way towards them.

'Head for work, the underground car park,' Greg said.

They raced away towards the research centre that was only a few hundred meters away. As they approached their refuge and the metal door of the subterranean car park began to roll up, they both realised what a bad idea it was. Likely as not, the car park would be empty, the door would stay up for their pursuer to follow them in and then they would be trapped with a man who now surely would only be satisfied with blood.

Simone drove, instead, around the back of the research centre before the Fiat arrived to see where they had gone. The Honda came to a halt on the tarmac surface. Greg and Simone looked at each other and then across to the wide but shallow River Limmat that ran close by.

'We could always swim for it,' Simone said.

'Well, looks like that won't be necessary, we lost him.'

'We? *I* lost him, thank you very much!'

Unfortunately they hadn't lost him. The Fiat approached from the other side of the research centre and came slowly to a halt, facing the Honda some five metres away. Out stepped the driver again, wide-eyed and fists clenched. The blue car was old and battered and the driver's clothes were cheap and not very new or clean. This was more than a road rage incident, this was a clash between the privileged and the under classes.

'Well, either I knock him down or you do,' Simone said, cool as a cucumber and revving the engine.

Greg considered. He considered his standing with Simone. He considered his job with his Swiss employer. He considered his wife and two children back in Ireland. And finally he considered the likely outcome of this impending encounter.

The adrenaline made him feel uncomfortable and vulnerable. When he had previously been in a situation of physical confrontation there had always been a hot temper, an insult received or perceived, an unaccepted push or shove and, of course, alcohol. A heated exchange and no real damage beyond a fat lip and a bruised ego. This time he sensed danger and wasn't sure his rusty karate skills would be available when he most needed them.

The man came to Greg's side of the car and began talking animatedly. Greg couldn't understand. It was Serbo-Croat or some other Slavic language.

Greg lowered the window by one centimetre and spoke to the man in German. 'I can't understand you.'

The would-be assailant changed his language and talked through gritted teeth. 'Step out of the car. I just want to talk to you for a minute.'

Greg looked the man in the eyes through the side window. Narrow, dark eyes, too wide apart. A creased face with a day's stubble as dense as a worn brush. The neck straining with tension, the shoulders bunched and seeking release, and fists clenched with white knuckles. No, this guy didn't want to have a cosy little chat with him. It would be a serious fight with maybe a knife or, even worse, a gun. Neither of which he himself carried or even knew how to use. He was an engineer, not an assassin.

'Get out of the car or I will rip open the roof!' the man shouted, grabbing the side of the Honda's fold-down roof and trying to prise it away from the frame.

'Greg,' Simone hissed, 'he's damaging my car. Do something. Be a man for God's sake!'

Greg thought very quickly what to do. *A lover, not a fighter.* Any woman would surely respect that.

'I am very sorry if I insulted you,' he shouted in German through the gap in the window. 'I apologise. Unreservedly. Very sorry. I intended no personal insult against you. It was a bad mistake. Please accept my apology.' Greg held up his hands submissively, trying to look meek and frightened. He didn't have to try too hard.

The Fiat driver's face twisted to an expression of disgust. His eyes flicked over to Simone. Then he hawked loudly, spat onto the floor next to Greg's window and turned away. In seconds he and the blue Fiat were gone from sight.

'What a man!' Simone said with a smile.

'Thanks,' Greg said. 'I turned the other cheek.'

'Not you, you worm! Get out and go home to your wife and children.'

She left him at the rear of the research centre. For a few minutes he hid, shivering, amongst the trees bordering the river in case the Fiat driver returned. Then he walked around the building until he found someone working late who could let him in to phone a taxi back to his hotel.

Method of murder

Reto Hersperger turned the walnut steering wheel with one finger and guided his Daimler through the streets of Zurich's financial district.

'I have been made complicit in a murder, my friend,' Reto said.

'You seem fairly cool about it,' Thomas replied.

'I half expect the Stadtpolizei to burst through the door at any minute. That would be embarrassing for my company.'

'Were that to occur, what would be your next course of action?'

'I would have to phone my brother and call in a favour. I have no wish to owe my brother another such favour.'

'What exactly is your main objection here, Reto?'

'Your intentions were not made plain to me in advance. A man has been assassinated in the middle of a famous restaurant full of Zurich's high society, including myself. Even the Buettiker family were there.'

Thomas recalled the beautiful blonde seated opposite a man in whom he had a professional interest. He returned to the subject of the restaurant death. 'It appears the dead man was diabetic and a cocaine addict.'

'That's true,' Reto confirmed. He had known the victim from his business dealings.

'And he died of an insulin and cocaine overdose, the drugs consumed before he entered the restaurant. There is no evidence of foul play and the restaurant's reputation remains unscathed, perhaps even slightly enhanced by the melodrama. My recommendation to them would be to be a little more select with their clientele.'

'You mean that they should refuse tables to the emissaries of African despots? Very droll, Thomas.'

'So, in principle, we don't have a problem?'

'I have no problem with the principle. But this was sailing too close to the wind for my taste. Please keep your James Bond activities away from my social circle.'

'Regarding the police, I understand there's no murder enquiry.'

'That's correct. I don't know what you did to the Kenyan, Thomas, but there's not a mark on him. Having said that, the state pathologist has been instructed not to look too closely and my brother will ensure no murder file is opened. It's clearly not just me you have involved in your subterfuge.'

'I see nothing gets past you, Reto. Switzerland is a small place when you're well connected. And the funds from the Kenyan account with your bank?'

'They were transferred today to the Central European Bank Special Development Unit, twenty billion dollars. Just promise me, Thomas, no more Agatha Christie murders at the Blindekuh or any other such venue.'

'Agreed. In which case, Reto, we need to come up with a better method for cleansing the city of Zurich.'

'I have an idea that might appeal, Thomas. But for now, some relaxation.'

This team is secure, Thomas thought to himself. The operation can proceed.

The two men opened their doors and stepped out of the fragrant and warm leather interior of the Daimler into the cold underground car park.

Reto led the way across the smooth concrete to a fire door in the far wall and gave three knocks. Thomas noticed a spy hole in the door just as it opened and Reto entered. Thomas followed without hesitation. A black suited man led them through a carpeted corridor and to a waiting elevator. Thomas noticed the slight tell-tale bulge at the lower left side of the man's jacket.

The elevator interior was sumptuous. Smoked glass mirrors flattered the complexion. Plush, deep red fabric on the other walls, more indicative of a bordello than a private bank. Thomas thought his suspicions about Swiss bad taste were being confirmed when the elevator doors slid open at their destination. These were not the premises of Reto's private bank.

A mature but beautiful woman awaited them. She was dressed as for a formal evening occasion, but with a strong touch of the risqué.

'Mr Hersperger, how nice to see you again. And such a handsome friend! We will make him most welcome at the Prince's Club.'

'Barbara, this is Thomas. We've had a most strenuous day and are seeking a little relaxation, if you and your ladies would please be so kind.'

Brazil

He was an idiot. There could be no argument about it. A failed philanderer, inept at road rage, cowardly in confrontation.

Greg nursed his bruised ego and reflected upon the recent run of events. Simone had been bored enough with life to accept his offer of dinner and amused enough to let him flatter and flirt with her. It had gone wrong after the restaurant and he should grasp this lucky escape. No one else would know at this stage except Simone and she would only go as far as to tease him occasionally, he knew her to be discreet. Anyway, he was not in Switzerland that frequently, just occasionally to check progress at the research centre. Should he make such a mistake at the Irish office then that might be more consequential, both professionally and privately.

No, at his age, nearly forty, he was too old for such complications, such mistakes. When, he wondered, would a grain of common sense enter his head and become his guiding force instead of that uncontrollable thing inhabiting his pants?

'This is KLM Flight 97 to Sao Paolo. Please ensure that your seat belt is fastened, your tray table stowed and your seat back in the upright position. All luggage must be stowed underneath the seat in front of you or in the lockers above your head. We will shortly be showing the in-flight safety video. Please sit back, relax and enjoy this flight with KLM.'

Greg was able to mime the words, they were so familiar, and it had a soporific effect upon him. Belt fastened, arms crossed and eyes closed, his breathing regulated and he drifted into a brief sleep before the aircraft even took off.

Once the aircraft had completed its ascent and levelled off at cruising altitude, the seatbelt sign turned off and the plane's occupants slowly came to life. A youngish man next to Greg was joined by two colleagues and they started to joke loudly, waking Greg out of his slumber. He recognised that the men spoke in German but a little too quickly for his full understanding. Something about billions of dollars recently discovered in Swiss bank accounts and frozen by the Central European Bank Regulators. *I could do with some of that* thought Greg, mindful of his personal bank account that always strained to accommodate the needs of him and his family.

Most of the aircraft's passengers slept successfully during the overnight flight. Greg was, perversely as usual, unable to sleep after takeoff and filled his hours with a selection of golden oldie films. He watched the first two *Matrix* films one after the other and felt his eyes turn dry and square. Refuelled by an airline meal of chicken, rice and chickpeas, he moved on to *The Day After Tomorrow* and felt the temperature drop way below zero as the ice age advanced upon America. Mexico had closed the borders to southbound USA refugees and people were massing at the border crossings. Ironic, Greg thought.

Shivering from the deadly temperatures, Greg bravely endured the story. Boy meets girl, painful death looms, dad rescues boy and girl, reunites with mum. No surprises there.

Nursing a glass of single malt on the rocks, Greg thought about his parents, now in their seventies and recently moved abroad for the first time to escape increasingly brutal winters in Scotland. And where had they chosen to move to? Kenya, of all places. So soon after the civil unrest of Christmas 2007 and not exactly accessible to the grandchildren. But low cost airlines were increasingly flying to several African destinations.

Since the recent return of Kenya to the New Commonwealth and rapid restoration of democracy, there had been a steady stream of immigrants from the UK. Greg's parents had found their new home in a town north of Nairobi and paid a very modest sum for it. The climate was temperate in the region, both weather and politics. During Greg's formative years Africa had been a byword for brutal violence and corruption, not to mention the constant global charity drives to ameliorate endless famines and droughts. How had that change come about?

A sudden noticeable increase in cabin pressure brought Greg out of his reverie as the aircraft began its descent. The flight attendants were handing out immigration cards to all USA passport holders.

The pilot's voice came over the speaker: 'Ladies and gentlemen, we are now on our final approach to Sao Paolo. Cabin crew prepare for landing.'

The steward passed by, collecting Greg's empty whisky glass on the way.

~

As the passengers of Flight KLM 97 stepped off the plane they reeled from the heat.

Progress through immigration and customs was swift. Retina recognition and e-passports had certainly speeded things up but baggage collection was the usual melee.

Brazil, the great footballing nation. A land of beautiful women and breathtaking scenery. He would see none of it, just the usual cloned factory that might be anywhere in the world, although the ride to and from the airport could be a little more exciting than elsewhere. Two visitors to the factory had been mugged in their taxis at gunpoint the previous month.

Within thirty minutes of landing Greg found himself being escorted by a driver to a parked car, a large old Opel saloon with blacked-out windows all round.

'For security reasons,' the Brazilian driver said. 'Black windows, old car, they think we are the problem and not the victims.'

They arrived at the factory gate and an armed security guard searched the car, including the luggage compartment.

'Why did they search the car on the way in?' Greg asked.

'You see, he looks for guns. We have cash machine in the factory, last week they take the money.'

The factory was as expected, the project on schedule. Greg did what he had to do, took what he needed and was on his way back to the airport by late afternoon. Confidential company business, no sightseeing, no football, no beautiful women.

Singing Stone

Mayhem in the domestic terminal at Sao Paolo. Flights had been cancelled or postponed because the state airline VARIG had collapsed financially - again. Slightly perplexed, Greg wandered up to an automated machine and eyed the retina scanner. He was impressed when it immediately printed his boarding pass and, within minutes, he was standing in a jostling pack at the entry to the security check. Gritting his teeth and trying to tolerate the personal space invasion of the jostlers, he put his computer bag through the scanner and promptly had his tweezers confiscated.

Could be worse, thought Greg, as he checked the project prototypes were still in place in the zipped inner compartment of his bag.

The domestic departure hall was a mess of swirling bodies, over-amplified announcements in Portuguese and small cups of strong coffee. Twice Greg tried to exit the wrong gate and was turned back, before he finally found the right one at the right time. Squeezed onto the crowded, sweating bus and hustled up the aircraft steps, he took his seat and tried to anticipate what lay ahead. This was not his planned tortuous return journey to Dublin, this was a short notice adventure down south. To where the borders of Brazil meet with Argentina and Paraguay.

~

The next morning at ten o'clock Greg was on his hands and knees. He lowered himself slowly and gently, it was very dark and the air was cool. He touched his lips to Itaipu, the Singing Stone.

The dust enveloped Greg's right hand. It felt cool and ancient. Like the dust that might accumulate over millennia inside the burial chamber of an Egyptian pyramid. The Singing Stone, deep below the sonorous cathedral-like vaults of the Itaipu dam on the border of Brazil and Paraguay.

'What are you doing, Mr Greg?' asked Ronaldo, the special engineering guide from the power station. 'Why do you kiss the stone, Mr Greg?'

'Oh, I thought it was customary,' Greg said, standing up and brushing the dust from his face and trousers. Better than kissing the Blarney stone, he thought, far less second hand saliva here.

Ronaldo continued with his narrative. 'Native Indians named Itaipu the Singing Stone because of amazing singing tones that sounded from the rock when the Parana River crashed over it. Sadly, the natives were all wiped out by the Smallpox brought here by the Conquistadors. Itaipu lost her voice when the dam was built but it was deemed worthy sacrifice. Itaipu power station provides twenty-five percent of Brazil's electricity needs and all that Paraguay needs. It generates more than twelve Gigawatts of power and was the largest power station in the world when we built it thirty years ago. Even now, only Three Gorges in China is bigger and that's more than one station, so we're still the biggest.' The guide smiled.

Greg looked suitably impressed. This was a privileged tour he was receiving and only thanks to his project involvement. In fact he was more impressed with being able to kiss a river bed. And, of course, with planting one of the project prototypes in the dust of the echoing foundations of the dam.

'Of course, it's unlikely the world will see again such large power as the building costs are so prohibitive,' the relentless Ronaldo continued. 'Each Gigawatt costs about one billion US dollars to build, regardless of technology.

Hydro, wind, nuclear, gas, whatever you like, it all costs a big lot of money.'

Now that would need a Swiss bank account Greg thought.

They walked back through the cavernous shadows to the elevator that took them the seventeen stories back up to the surface.

Greg absentmindedly licked his dusty lips and thought he felt the first sniffle of a cold coming on.

Back at the surface, the enormous scale of the facility was astounding. The massive auxiliary equipment supplied by Greg's employer was dwarfed by nineteen sets of gargantuan apparatus that constituted the generating power.

They entered a massive hall and Greg could see some activity across the other side. A short young man looked rather familiar. He was holding one end of a measuring tape across a massive pit and shaking his head in disbelief.

'Yes, what do we see here? Finally after thirty years the last turbine is being installed by your German competitors. Unfortunately they have today discovered they built it three millimetres too wide for the pit. This represents something of a problem for them.' Ronaldo chuckled.

Greg recognised his neighbouring passenger from KLM flight 97. So much for German precision.

'And here, Mr Greg, here is the equipment from your European company from thirty years ago.' Ronaldo indicated with a flourish. 'And over here, the new ones from five years ago made by your South African colleagues.'

Ronaldo then drove Greg along and up a service road to the top of the dam.

'Mr Greg, now please step out of the car.'

Greg obliged.

'You are now standing with that leg in Brazil,' Ronaldo said. 'And the other one in Paraguay.'

Greg handed his camera phone to Ronaldo who took the regulation tourist picture of each leg in a different country.

Ronaldo returned the camera phone and turned back to the car. Seizing the opportunity, Greg launched one of the remaining prototypes from his backpack into the air and watched it hurtle down the man-made waterfall of the dam overflow outlet, towards the huge plunge pool at the foot of the wall. He was pretty certain it would come to a stop close enough to the output of the massive hydro station to be effective.

Panorama

The Iguassu Falls tour bus left the pick-up point and headed on through the forest. Greg had a window seat and was glad he had remembered his expensive new Blue Dog sunglasses. He would have been feeling pretty smart in them but they had chafed against something hard in his suitcase during the flight from Amsterdam and there was an abraded area smack in the middle of each lens.

Rolling down the dusty track, the heavy hanging greenery was swept aside by their passing. The bus slowed to a halt and the languid passengers disembarked. Greg stepped out onto the path and immediately broke into a sweat with the humidity.

A path descended through the forest and the sound of rushing river and rapids grew louder below. Small lizards crowded rocks where the sun broke through the canopy and strange mammals occasionally stopped to watch the tourists from a safe distance. A faded warning sign was planted at the path edge.

Greg inhaled, enjoying the unfamiliar scents and savouring the moistness.

The path levelled out at river level and a few bedraggled Japanese came back against the flow of traffic, Nikons hanging dripping from their necks and spectacles steamed up, some stumbling perilously close to the edge of the water.

Greg passed through a clump of trees and paused to take in the panorama of the Iguassu Falls as it unfolded before him. A steep escarpment of rock wound its way across the river from the Brazilian bank where he stood to Argentina on the far side, and the river tumbled over the length of the drop in a mighty roar. Spray from the impact of the fallen water rose high into the air. He could taste the bitterness of ozone on his tongue.

A long wooden walkway led out from the shore across the choppy river surface, disappearing into spray at the bottom of the falls. Not everyone was taking the stroll. Greg felt no fear as he headed towards the roar – the water was not deep and the walkway looked solid enough. He stepped out a little too confidently, slipped on the wet planks and managed to regain his balance, catching his sunglasses before they fell. Several elderly tourists came towards him, clinging to the handrail, their heads swathed in some kind of plastic bag.

The spray swirled around and across the walkway in a welcome draught. Teenagers on a local school outing clustered with their mobile phones, taking videos of each other. Greg continued to the end of the walkway where an octagonal viewing area jutted out beyond the swirling mist. The cascade from the falls was close to painful, both sound and the brightness, swamping the senses. Like being on the surface of a star, Greg thought.

A sudden gust of cool air brought Greg back to earth with a chill, the mist having drenched his cotton shirt and trousers without his notice. Unloading the backpack he withdrew a black torpedo shaped object and hurled it into the foaming waters. The turbulence and flow would trigger the device without any problem. He turned his back on the great Iguassu Falls and headed back to the bus.

Fair exchange

The late autumn breeze pushed a few papery leaves down a narrow cobbled alleyway in Zurich's financial district. Reto Hersperger stepped out, anxious to ensure his punctuality for the rendezvous. There were very few people on the streets. He checked his Rado watch again, knowing the correspondent would not linger if Reto was not on point at precisely ten o'clock.

The bells of the Gross Munster began to strike the hour as Reto reached the middle of the Limmatquai bridge. A tall, elegant and dark figure strode towards him and grasped the shoulder of his coat roughly.

'Good evening, Henry. Please be so kind as to remove the hand,' Reto said.

'Be so kind as to tell me how you are going to fix this mess your famous *private* bank has created for me,' The man snarled, his eyes glistening. 'And, further, explain to me why we are not meeting in your beautiful client rooms but instead like clandestine lovers on this bridge.'

'Henry, you and your most esteemed client are highly valued both as long-standing customers and as friends. However, the events of the past week are, as you well know, beyond the control of my *famous* private bank and you would risk arrest if seen at our premises.'

'My most esteemed, but now seriously impoverished and murderously angry client is sharpening his machete,' Henry replied. His gritted teeth were dazzling in the bright moonlight. 'Thirty billion dollars frozen makes a client into an enemy.'

Reto fought down a rising feeling of alarm. Surely this large man he knew only as Henry was not going to attempt something rash in a public place. He said nothing, fighting to keep a calm expression but poised to make a run for it if necessary.

Henry's tone turned from menacing to pleading. 'Is there truly nothing that can be done?'

'I am terribly sorry, Henry. The accounts are now inaccessible to you. The funds will be transferred to the Central European Bank Special Development Unit by the end of this week.'

'There will be dire retribution, both here and back home. My family, my children.'

'I am so sorry, Henry. The matter is out of my hands. This regrettably concludes our business relationship. There remains the small matter of management fees for this quarter but we are waiving the charges, under the circumstances.'

Reto had an envelope in his pocket; a separation bonus authorised by the Central European Bank. He decided to save this little bit of good news for a few minutes to first see what might happen there on the bridge.

'Efficient to the end,' Henry hissed. 'In that case, Reto, I bid you farewell, for life ends here.'

Reto jumped back but not fast enough and Henry enveloped him in his huge arms. There was no chance to struggle. Henry must have weighed 120 kilos to Reto's 70. Reto braced himself for death. Henry's arms released him, there was a blur at the parapet of the bridge and a splash below in the Limmat river. Henry was gone.

Walking over to the parapet, Reto could see the African's inert body floating just under the surface and gathering pace downstream.

'They'll probably find him near the hydro power station, like the others,' a voice from behind said.

Reto turned and saw Thomas slip a Taser gun back inside his overcoat. 'Thomas, this lunacy cannot continue.'

'It's like the Wall Street crash. This fellow was going to jump anyway, we just helped him along.'

'But the cameras!' Reto gestured towards the CCTV cameras that scanned the bridge and quay from the roofs of buildings along the riverbanks.

'No cause for concern. Look more closely, Reto. The cameras are conveniently facing away from us.'

Reto checked. Thomas was right.

'We have an arrangement, once again, with your local police friends.'

They walked towards the financial district. Reto pressed a pre-counted wad of money into Thomas's chest, extracted from the separation bonus envelope.

'How about a little drink at the Prince's Club now you're off duty?' he asked. 'I'm paying, I insist. I have my eye on a rather tall Romanian girl from Transylvania and she's sure to have a friend with a thirst for champagne.'

'Very well.' Thomas laughed. 'Your treat.' He knew this was the only way to get an equitable division of the spoils.

At the street entrance of the Prince's Club a hulking security woman held the door open wide for them. 'Gentlemen, third time this week, what a great pleasure.'

Titillation

Inside a dark and moist corner of the Prince's Club a girl with long dark hair sat on Reto's lap and squeezed his thigh with apparent enthusiasm. Reto reached for the champagne bottle and poured another glass. She took a long draught of the golden bubbles and thrust her tongue into his mouth, sharing the tingling sensation and light, dry taste. Then, pressing her chest close to his face, she leaned towards the girl who sat on Thomas's knee.

'They're spending money like water. They must have had some good luck.'

'Looks that way,' the tall blonde replied. 'Try and get yours upstairs, he's in the mood for it. Mine is a cold fish with low blood pressure.' She gave a sideways glance at Thomas who was half-heartedly caressing her back.

'I can fix that. Jump up for a second.'

The blonde rolled off Thomas's knee and the dark haired one folded into his lap. Taking another mouthful of champagne she grabbed the blonde, pulled her down and kissed her. She could feel things firming up under her leg. Then she turned to Thomas and ran her tongue over his lips. Not bad. He had nice lips and a sharp, firm tongue. She could tell she was to his liking, he just needed a more experienced handler. Meanwhile, Reto and the blonde were getting to know each other pretty well.

Thomas started to feel a little hot under the collar. Vampire Girl was getting to him and his inhibitions were starting to slip away. The champagne was hitting the spot too. He reached for the glass and noticed another bottle had magically appeared.

'Er, Reto? Mate? I think we had better be going.'

Reto emerged from his entwining with the blonde. 'Finding it a little too much for your English reserve, Thomas?'

'Finding it a little too much for your reserve, I think. Have you seen the bill?' Thomas indicated the growing pile of papers next to the champagne bottle.

Reto did a quick accounting, as only the Swiss can, refilled all the glasses and downed his in one gulp.

'Well spotted, Thomas, right on the button. I would hate to exceed the budget.' He unfolded three thousand Swiss Francs from the envelope and placed it on the table. Pausing for a moment, he added a further two thousand. 'And a little extra for you ladies to keep us in your thoughts.'

The blonde girl sat astride Reto for a fond farewell. Thomas extricated himself from the vampire's grasp.

'Reto, you waste your money on titillation,' Thomas said as they headed for the door.

'How quaint. In any case, not my money. I'm merely redistributing the ill-gotten gains of our African friends to those in need. A socialist ideal that would meet with their own ethos. Titillation, as you put it, is merely a coincidental by-product.'

Dark eyes watched them exit.

Mistaken identity

Greg checked his watch. It was just before five a.m. and, with a flight at nine, he resolved to stay awake and sleep on the plane. Breathing the heady hotel garden fragrances in deeply, he took stock of the last couple of days. His project was on schedule and the prototype sensors were ready. As instructed, he had planted one deep in the dust of Itaipu. He was confident it would lie there undisturbed for a few weeks as the area would be closed to visitors during the commissioning of the final turbine. That would be long enough to serve the purpose of the project.

A second prototype had been dropped rather haphazardly at the outlet of the Itaipu hydro station. In this case he could not be sure the mechanism would have survived the fall, but there had been no other way to place it in the desired location.

Then there had been the trip to Iguassu Falls, launching the third sensor close to the viewing platform. That one was sure to be a success.

Ten minutes later he was at the Foz regional airport of Cataratas. A small crowd thronged around the check-in desks. There were half a dozen unoccupied electronic check-in booths and Greg approached one. Why the crowds avoided those booths was a mystery to him. Maybe they enjoyed the skirmishes at the check-in desk queues. He preferred the high-tech appeal of the non-contact retina scanner.

He waved his passport in front of the laser reader. The retina scanner was out of order so he would have to use the fingerprint scanner. So much for non-contact.

Greg pressed the pad of his right forefinger on the greasy glass and suppressed a shudder as his fingertip slid across the surface. The display screen flashed up the name Thomas Thistlethwaite and a flight destination that read like somewhere in Africa. Greg fished in his bag for a cleansing wipe, cleaning his forefinger and then wiping the scanner lens. Another press of the finger and his name and flight plan appeared on the screen. The machine printed the boarding cards for Bilbao via Paris and Rio de Janeiro. He picked them out of the chute and moved off to the security queue.

Somehow the security check didn't seem very thorough but he still felt uneasy about the remaining two project items in his hand luggage and nervously checked them through the material. They weren't revealed by the luggage scanner and a half-hearted random hand search didn't discover the long tubes attached with Velcro strips to the inner ribs of his bag.

The shopping area lay ahead. Faced with a very long journey back to Europe, he intended to buy a book and read it on the trip. Unfortunately, the airport bookstore had only a small stand of English language books. Most of them were easy airport reading of the kind he shunned. Then he saw it, a hardback with a bright yellow cover. An English translation of the Koran. He picked it up and opened a few random pages. *Dire retribution, Gardens beneath which rivers flow.* The imagery was immediate. Fascinated by the Old Testament as a child, he had to have it.

Greg endured the sweaty bustle of boarding the flight to Rio. His plane made a stopover at Curitiba but he didn't disembark and only took his eyes away from the book to order subsequent gin and tonics. At Rio he took a whistle-stop tour of the city by taxi and a stroll along the beach at Ipanema, but the girl was nowhere to be seen. Just before nightfall he assumed his allocated business class seat aboard an Air France flight to Bilbao via Charles de Gaulle.

Henry's wives

Edward Mboto's face trembled with rage. The presidential palace in Kampala was silent, exccpt for the slippered footsteps of an approaching aide carrying a white bone china teacup and saucer on a silver tray.

'Mint tea, your Excellency. Calming, it lowers the blood pressure,' the President's medical advisor said.

The teacup and saucer crashed against the wall as Mboto struck them away with his clenched fist. Jowls quivering, he tried to gather the words of expression.

'DIRE RETRIBUTION!' he bellowed. The stress at the back of his skull released slightly and he gave a shiver. The numerous staff in the room all stepped backwards. Cunningham, the medical advisor, knew only too well what this meant. It had been some time since the last occurrence but the President's frame of mind could only be assuaged by bloodshed.

'ASOBAYIRE has betrayed us all! Draw up a list of Henry Asobayire's family. All wives, brothers, sisters, sons, daughters. I want current names and addresses. Every one of them is to be at Henry Asobayire's Kampala residence by six o'clock this evening.'

Mboto's personal assistant scribbled frantically on a notepad.

'Prepare my cavalcade. Take the stretch Corniche. Obote's Boys are to tail the procession.'

There was no doubt in the mind of anybody present that Obote's Boys would enjoy an eventful evening. Those in the room who had been friends of the affable Henry Asobayire felt their palms break into a sweat. Hopefully dire retribution would be restricted to direct family.

At five-thirty the President inspected Obote and his boys in the underground car park of the palace. It had been some time since they last saw action but there are skills that, once learnt, are never forgotten. Like riding a bicycle, thought Mboto. He stepped into the Corniche limousine, lay back into the deeply upholstered leather and pressed the play button of the music system. Rimsky-Korsakov's *Flight of the Bumblebee* buzzed out of the speakers. It had been his theme tune when he was an Olympic heavyweight boxing champion and it always put him in the right frame of mind for physically demanding tasks. Tonight he had many opponents to defeat and his sting would be fatal.

Mboto's limousine slid silently through Kampala, sandwiched between two armoured cars with mounted machine canons and followed by the long dark van of Obote's Boys. People on the street stopped, turned and started to wave at the President's car. The smiles faded and the waving hands froze as Obote's van came into view. Several people made a sign of the cross and one old woman fell to her knees in supplication.

The cavalcade came to a halt at a compound in an affluent Kampala suburb. The armoured cars positioned themselves at the front and rear compound exits, training their machine canon on the gates. Mboto's limousine stopped silently in front of the canopied porch of the grandest villa in the compound and Obote's van pulled up behind. Obote's Boys stepped out of the van and Obote himself opened the door of the President's car.

Edward Mboto stepped out into the fading sunlight, a smile across his face as Obote handed him a gleaming machete. He strode fearlessly into the villa.

Inside the large hallway were gathered around twenty people of varying ages. The late Henry's relatives had no illusion as to the occasion of this presidential visit. Several of the women and younger girls whimpered in fear. The men and older boys stood proud and erect, awaiting their fate.

'Henry Asobayire is dead!' Mboto shouted. 'He has squandered the vast riches of this nation, all we have entrusted him with. You know our nation's creed and the symbol of the machete. Dire retribution must be visited on the enemies of this nation.'

The small crowd flinched visibly as Mboto brandished the machete menacingly and took a laughing swipe towards the head of the nearest child. From outside there was a series of dull thuds. Heavy men moving with executioners' intent.

'You will meet your fate here tonight at my hand and at the hands of Obote's Boys. This is my decree. Make peace now with your God.' Mboto bowed his head momentarily and then, with a gleam in his eye, called to Obote's Boys to 'go to work'.

Mboto raised his arm and a hand grasped it. He found himself restrained on all sides and disarmed. *Well*, he thought, *if this is a coup d'état by Obote then I have to endure exile*. Historically, the more ruthless the African tyrant, the quicker the exile and Mboto certainly qualified. But the uniform of those restraining him was not that of Obote's Boys and the flesh of the hands and faces was pale.

Led out onto the porch of the villa, Mboto gasped in surprise as he saw the prone bodies of Obote and his boys, each shot through the head. Mboto's hands were bound in front of him. He looked up into the pale face of Thomas Thistlethwaite.

'This man,' Thomas said loudly to the relatives of Henry Asobayire, 'has taken your country's wealth for his own pocket. It will be returned to your nation, but you must be cleansed of Edward Mboto and his kind.' Thomas turned and walked towards the limousine.

Another man, a very dark African unknown to the onlookers, stepped forward with Mboto's machete in his hand. 'Long or short sleeves?' the man asked.

Mboto began to whimper. 'No, please! I will go to exile! I have money.'

The machete whistled through the air and Edward Mboto saw his own severed hands and wrists fall to the ground, still tied together. He made an attempt to move but strong hands gripped his shoulders.

'Long trousers?' came the voice again. The machete followed.

New man

Winston Cunningham took his seat in the presidential limousine. Thomas Thistlethwaite was waiting for him.

'Was that really necessary?' Cunningham asked. 'We could have sent him to Switzerland or perhaps somewhere in the East.'

'Absolutely necessary,' Thistlethwaite replied. 'There's no longer any real sanctuary for Mboto's kind. This country's people need to see that Mboto and Obote are eradicated. It serves as a zero tolerance warning. With the investments that shall be made you'll have no subsequent need of coercion.'

'On behalf of Uganda I thank you, Thomas. What is the price we have to pay for your support in this?' Cunningham eyed Thistlethwaite cautiously.

'You will see we have extensive plans,' Thistlethwaite replied. 'I believe you will find our infrastructure investment proposals to be of great benefit. Believe me when I say we have a social duty to make recompense for our negligence in Africa since de-colonisation and our misplaced trust in recent times. This nation's riches will be returned to their rightful place and future misappropriation of funds will be impossible.'

'In that case I may be the first president of Uganda to survive solely on the presidential salary,' Cunningham joked. He took a sheaf of papers handed to him by Thistlethwaite.

'This is the composition of your cabinet and these are the draft amendments to the constitution. You will see an indigenous majority remains in the cabinet. However, that may have to change as fifty percent of them are known to be HIV positive.'

Cunningham looked through the papers as Thistlethwaite continued.

'A team of engineers will arrive next week to commence the development projects. Several of the project leaders are Ugandans and have completed their education and training in Britain over the past five years. You are assured of success and, in three years time, there will be an admirable infrastructure in place. *Tranquil rivers will run beneath verdant pastures*. I think you'll be rather pleasantly surprised.'

It all sounded very easy but Thomas Thistlethwaite knew the real costs of major infrastructure developments in similar countries. The great Suez Canal had employed nearly 1.2 million workers but more than one hundred thousand had lost their lives in the hazardous business. Comparable to the building of the Egyptian pyramids. And no one really knew the figures involved in Muhamar Gaddafi's Great Man-Made River Project but rumour had it the channelling of fossil water from beneath the Sahara to the thirsty Libyan coast in four metre diameter pipes had not been without human cost.

The Ugandan development projects could cost many lives and the true beneficiaries would not be those families left fatherless. Of course, in the scheme of things in Africa, no one would blink an eye.

Faint

Greg was having trouble sleeping on the overnight flight and envied his blindfolded and snoring neighbours. He decided to try and induce unconsciousness. Raising an eyebrow in the direction of the stewardess, Greg was rewarded with a top-up in his glass of vintage port.

On this flight the chap next to Greg was raw-boned and long-legged. He wore smart grey suit trousers and had a very square chin. Engaging him in conversation, Greg determined his neighbour was a Dutch businessman on his way to an important company board meeting. Greg was wearing T-shirt and jeans that had seen better days. Pondering whether he ought to try and compete with the Dutchman in the importance stakes, Greg felt a sudden twinge in his stomach. Perhaps it was the port. Hopefully it wasn't the king prawns in the appetiser. A trip to the bathroom might help but would have to wait until later. He didn't feel quite sober enough to avoid embarrassment.

'Thanks ever so much, felt a bit queer and just had to lie down for a bit.' Greg looked up and saw the Air France stewardess take away his untouched breakfast tray.

'Sir, you've been asleep since dinner. That was eight hours ago. We will land in ten minutes.'

The plane was making a fairly rapid descent. Greg's tongue felt strange in his mouth and he knew he was in trouble. A sharp pain ran across his stomach and he tried to stand up with the intention of using the toilet, but the stewardess signalled him to stay seated. There didn't seem to be enough air in the cabin. He leaned forward, head in hands. A sweat formed on his face, there was a smell of rubber, he felt his spine run cold and, with an apologetic glance at the Dutchman, he lurched into the darkness.

~

Greg came to his senses with a jolt and his eyes flickered open to behold a scene of devastation. A strange, foul smelling, viscous purple liquid covered the back of the seat in front of him and the window and wall at his side. He sensed the same substance was on the thighs of his jeans and down the front of his T-shirt. The worst was yet to come. His neighbour was staring in disbelief at a purple mess on one leg of his smart grey trousers.

'Sorry about the trousers. Must have been those prawns, they tasted a bit squiffy,' Greg said, still drooling slightly from the corner of his mouth. He offered the Dutchman a paper serviette.

'No, it really doesn't matter,' his neighbour said, looking at Greg's clothes. 'I think your predicament is much worse than mine.'

The passengers took several minutes to disembark, during which time Greg sat motionless, his face covered by refreshing towels the stewardess had brought to him. Once the footsteps had faded away he removed the towels and attempted to wipe down his clothes. Two stewardesses and a steward glared at him from the galley. *Why aren't they helping me*, he thought. His hands were trembling and his neck felt strangely stiff. Staggering to his feet, Greg dragged his hand luggage down from the overhead bin and wandered towards the air-bridge.

'Sir, are you okay to disembark?' the stewardess who had served him asked. 'It's likely you are dehydrated from the flight. Please take this bottle of water.'

Greg placed the water in his jacket pocket.

'Thank you. Prawns and port, not a good combination,' he said.

Once within the terminal Greg headed directly to a toilet and examined his clothes. The T-shirt had to be removed and he left it in the rubbish bin. The jeans were in an awful state but, opening his luggage, he found all the clothes inside to be too damp to wear. Buttoning up his sports jacket over gooey jeans and bare chest, he headed out to the passport control and joined the tail-end of the queue.

When the passport official looked up at Greg his eyes registered some surprise. 'May I ask the purpose of your visit to France, sir?' he asked in heavily accented English with only a hint of civility.

'Just passing through to Bilbao on business,' Greg answered, pulling the lapels of his jacket across his bare chest. The terminal was rather chilly and he wished, not for the first time, that he was a hairier man.

The official gestured towards the fingerprint reader and Greg placed a rather slimy purple forefinger on the glass. It didn't work. Frowning at the mess on the glass, the official indicated the retina scanner. Unable to keep his head still, Greg nodded stupidly into the scanner which beeped loudly.

Clicking his tongue, the official waved Greg back to the fingerprint scanner, wiping the glass with a cloth. This time it gave a reassuring chime.

A uniformed Gendarme appeared and took Greg by the elbow. 'Please step this way, sir. We won't keep you a moment.'

Head spinning, Greg found himself sitting in a mean little white room on a hard plastic chair. He grasped his hand luggage to his chest like a small child with a teddy bear.

A door opened suddenly behind him and a cultured English voice boomed out. 'Good Lord, Thomas. Back so soon? And how on earth did you get into this state and on a flight from Rio?'

Looking up in bewilderment, Greg met a cold pair of grey eyes that froze him to his seat. 'Not Thomas at all, rather embarrassing,' said the stranger in some confusion and then proceeded to fire off some rapid phrases in French at the Gendarme. Greg managed to catch something about retina and the Gendarme shook his head.

'Terribly sorry, old chap, wrong date of birth. Simple mistake, sorry to have kept you.' Greg felt himself propelled out of the chair and through the back door into the arrivals hall. He stood there shivering for a few seconds until he regained his senses and realised the time to connection to Bilbao was getting tight.

A passing Air France ground staff member took pity upon him and he was ferried through the express route to the departure gate, just in time for boarding.

The flow

Heavy melt waters rushed down from the mountains into the Lake of Zurich. On the lake's Gold Coast millionaires' yachts tugged at their anchors and mooring ropes, the strong current trying to snatch them away and on down the River Limmat to its eventual confluence with the Rhine.

A stiff breeze blew onshore at the Limmatquai and brought fresh mountain air loaded with ozone. Reto breathed deeply and watched as large perch swam against the current under the bridge, catching smaller fish that were swept into waiting jaws. He would be pleased when these African proceedings had been wrapped up.

The Frau Munster chimed nine o'clock and Reto turned towards the financial district, feeling the stiff envelope pressing against his chest inside his jacket. A strong hand grasped his right shoulder and whirled him around.

The handsome ebony of Jean Bouquet's dark face was just inches from Reto's own. He felt the familiar affinity of all his previous meetings with the Congolese man and could hardly wait to hear his melodic French phrases. They enjoyed each other's company both in business and socially.

Reto delivered his standard opening.

'Jean, we have reached an impasse with your client's account. The funds are frozen and will be transferred to the Central European Bank tomorrow. There is nothing further I can do to prevent or delay this. I am very sorry.'

'You know, Reto, this is a terrible time. All these years, the diamonds, the blood and the treachery. Fifty billion dollars! In a way I am quite happy that it's over.'

Jean had a gentle smile on his face and Reto knew he deserved an escape from this situation. To this end Reto had scheduled the rendezvous one hour earlier than requested by the Belgian agent Pierre Lafayette.

'The Central European Bank has honoured you with a separation bonus of half a million dollars.' Reto reached inside his jacket.

'Many thanks.' Jean took the envelope and placed it inside his coat. He knew Reto would have deducted a healthy personal bonus but that was their accepted way of doing business.

Jean embraced Reto and kissed his cheek. 'My good friend, I hope we have the chance to meet again.'

Reto was returning Jean's parting gesture when he saw a dark form flying across the bridge towards them. 'Jean, you must leave now, immediately!'

But it was too late. There was a blinding flash and Reto felt his body convulse. The side of his head hit the cobbles on the quay and he could only watch helplessly as Pierre Lafayette dragged Jean from his grasp and tipped the African's inert body over the edge of the bridge into the churning melt waters.

'So, you would have tricked me and enabled one of the intermediaries to escape,' Pierre snarled as he turned back towards Reto. 'Well, I guessed your little game. Everyone knows you were close friends with Bouquet. Now, where is my share of the separation bonus?'

Regaining his powers of speech but still lying on the floor, Reto pointed at the edge of the bridge. 'It's in his pocket, you idiot. You want it, you get it!'

With an oath Lafayette ran towards the edge of the bridge. There was a neat splash as he dived into the freezing cold flow of melt waters, striking out for the body of Jean Bouquet already more than one hundred meters downstream.

Trembling, Reto pulled himself to his feet and headed across the bridge. He was sad his efforts to save a friend had been unsuccessful but life goes on and he would have to celebrate at the Prince's Club on his own. And the curious side effect of the Taser gun was something he wished to discuss with Svetlana.

Later that week the Limmatpost newspaper reported on the latest river tragedy. The drowned bodies of two men, one European and one African, had been found entwined in a lover's embrace at the Limmat hydro power station. Their identities were as yet undetermined. The African had an envelope in his jacket containing two hundred and fifty thousand dollars.

Your wine, sir

Greg headed straight to the taxi rank at Bilbao airport and asked the driver to take him to the Gran Hotel Domine.

The hotel was crowded with Greg's work colleagues, all there for the conference. A few of them expressed some surprise at his bare chest under the jacket and the vomit stained jeans. One or two knew Greg a little better.

The atrium of the hotel had, as its centrepiece, a twenty six meter high tower of stones entitled the *Fossil Cypress by Mariscal*. Greg tilted his head to view the phallic structure and began to feel nauseous again. His eyes were sore, his scalp aching. So he headed up to his room, collapsed immediately onto the bed and slid into a deep sleep.

~

In a plush hotel room off the Champs-Élysées in Paris a tall, square-jawed Dutchman kicked off his Bally shoes, placed a Luis Vuitton flight bag carefully on the thick carpet and threw himself backwards onto the bed. He stood again, removed his soiled trousers and threw them in the rubbish bin. There was a knock at the door.

Sliding silently from the bed, Wim van der Hoek pulled the Luger automatic pistol from his shoulder holster and moved up to the side of the door frame.

There was another knock, double this time, accompanied by a deep voice.

'Room service, Chateau Neuf du Pape 1988 as ordered by the President.'

Van der Hoek flicked the lock open and pulled down the handle. Thomas Thistlethwaite walked in wearing a waiter's garb and carrying a tray raised upon his right hand. He certainly looked the part. The mentioned vintage was accompanied by two crystal glasses.

The Dutchman lowered and holstered his pistol.

'Thomas, such extravagance.' Van der Hoek took the bottle and proceeded with the opening ritual.

'Yes, well. A worthy password has to be correctly performed for authenticity, regardless of cost. I trust we're entitled to a celebration after your transatlantic efforts?'

Van der Hoek reached for the suitcase and opened it on the bed, revealing strange but well organised contents. There were no clothes at all but a kind of goggles with totally opaque lenses and a rubber mould that had strands of hair around the edge.

'I had to drug him heavily and clamp his head in order to keep his eyes motionless. And when I removed the mould from his face the bastard threw up all over my trousers.'

Thistlethwaite laughed. Taking hold of the goggles he inserted a small electronic chip for a few seconds until a tone sounded, and then removed it. He placed the rubber mould in a plastic zip-lock bag and stowed it in his large waiter's apron pocket.

'So much for high technology, still you can't beat latex. Those hairs will come in handy for colouring and, if there's a follicle, we might have some DNA.'

The Dutchman reclined in a padded chair across the room and savoured his wine.

'You know you can trust me to do a sound job, Thomas. I am even prepared to put my good trousers on the line.'

'Yes, most excellent, thank you. And please also thank your little friend for the fingerprints from Brazil. By the way, I suppose you heard. That bloody idiot Lafayette screwed it up with the Congo job. Got himself killed and found floating in the Limmat with a stiff.'

'About what I would have expected from poor old Pierre. He and his team see too little action to stay on the case. I'll consider Pierre's requirements as cancelled, but I think we need to watch that Swiss fellow. I know he's a friend of yours, Thomas, but everything has its price.'

'What? Do you think old Reto would turn traitor?' Thistlethwaite shook his head. 'He has sticky fingers but I would trust him with my life.'

'Well you may have to. With Pierre out of the picture you'll have to pick up his outstanding business. Your ticket and passport will be provided at the Coffee Dock midday on Wednesday.'

Thistlethwaite's brow furrowed. He had hoped to return to his family home. A detour via Kinshasa wasn't his intention.

'Okay, Thomas. I need to get some sleep. I have to appear at a board meeting in The Hague first thing tomorrow.'

'In that case, Wim, you had better buy some new trousers.'

Exchanging what was to be their last cordiality, they parted.

Fish and Hands

The Guggenheim museum in Bilbao sparkled in the warm spring sunshine. It was designed in an eccentric style intended to represent the curling, thrashing silver scales of a wet fish bought home fresh from market in a bucket of water.

Greg didn't consider himself a massive fan of contemporary art. It was something he had never given a chance so he tried to approach the museum with an open mind. There had been a brochure in his hotel room describing an exhibit entitled *Speaking Hands* and that somehow appealed to him.

He wandered through the halls, past Andy Warhol and Picasso pieces, to the Fish Room containing works by the sculptor Richard Serra. Voices could be heard from within but there seemed to be simply a twenty foot steel wall ahead. Greg found an entrance at one end and walked in a spiral towards the centre of a disorientating circular maze. As he neared the centre Greg let out a sneeze and his ears rang with the echo. Starting with a low drone and steadily raising the tone it was possible to determine a resonance he estimated to be somewhere around eighty Hertz in frequency.

Perfect, he thought, and reached inside his jacket for the ceramic project canister concealed there. He removed the sensor from the canister and secured it on the inner curl of the sculpture using a strong magnet integrated in the device. The resonant sound waves of any large crowd of visitors would be certain to trigger the sensor.

Greg found his way out. In a corner of the atrium he saw what looked at first glance to be a waterfall of red droplets, perhaps blood. He walked closer. It was a cleverly mirrored image of several red LED column displays that were running words vertically in some kind of hypnotic sequence. A number of people stood mesmerised and others leaned against the walls or sat on wooden benches. A plaque identified the artist of *Installation for Bilbao* as Jenny Holzer. The truisms displayed had originated in a work to highlight the spread of AIDS.

Greg wasn't sure quite how long he sat there. Eventually he forced himself up onto his feet and turned in the direction of the room where *Speaking Hands* should be.

Well, yes, there were very many hands. Over a hundred photographs of hands, young, old, male, female, gloved, bare, concealing faces, concealing naked bodies. He looked at each photograph and the few sculptures in sequence until something stopped him in his tracks. Titled *Short Sleeves*, an African child of perhaps twelve years of age held out recently healed wrist stumps to the camera, a look of sad admonishment in her eyes. There was a long commentary below the photograph about the UN failure to deal with genocide in Africa, citing in particular the Rwanda conflict at the end of the last century.

Rwanda. No oil, no diamonds, no gold, ergo no international intervention. He hurried away, thinking of his own ten year old daughter and trying to erase the image of *Short Sleeves* from his mind.

Outside the Guggenheim the night had turned cold and dark.

Money talks

It was a cool, fresh morning in The Hague. Members of the board had already been meeting for two hours before Wim van der Hoek's slot came up on the agenda.

The secretary came out through double walnut doors and into the corridor, expecting the tall Dutchman to be seated and waiting, but there was no one to be seen. Just as he began to turn back, the lift doors opened with a soft hiss and van der Hoek stepped out.

The stony faced secretary escorted van der Hoek into the boardroom and indicated a large black leather chair at the nearest end of the immense walnut table.

Around this table sat some of the most powerful men and women in the world, but they looked quite innocuous, many of them slight and ageing with grey hair and glasses.

'So, Wim. You are here. What do you have to report?' the man immediately to van der Hoek's right asked in a French accent.

'All the necessary components for Thistlethwaite's facsimile have been obtained and he is processing them as we speak,' the Dutchman replied. 'But I must admit to being a little confused at the choice of target and the necessity of the exercise.'

'Rest assured, it's no exercise,' a woman further down the table said. 'The facsimiles are carefully chosen for access to strategic industrial technology. It will simply help us to expedite our projects. You can be sure no material espionage is involved.'

'And the facsimile is totally unaware of this little acquisition of components?' another member asked.

'Blissfully unaware,' van der Hoek said, looking down at his trousers.

'Very well,' the Frenchman resumed. 'You will be aware the proceeds from the Congo have been transferred. There was a most unfortunate complication in Zurich, and Thistlethwaite has been delegated to complete the process by the end of this week.'

'Yes, of course, and he has accepted delegation of the process.' Van der Hoek paused and then decided to speak out on Thomas's behalf. 'I must say this is beyond the agreement. *In the event of complications, a delegate is to be provided from the same service,*' he quoted.

A small voice cleared itself at the far end of the table and all the other board members turned in respect to their long serving chairman.

'Mr van der Hoek, your memory for detail is admirable. So I need not remind you Belgium does not have a current delegate available of sufficient calibre. Mr Thistlethwaite is simply the best substitute.'

Van der Hoek bristled. He considered the best substitute to be the man currently wearing slightly short trousers, but knew he had to show respect to the board.

'Mr Chairman you are, as always, quite correct.'

'One thing further,' the Chairman continued, 'we are remunerating your organisation handsomely for your involvement. Your exceptional memory will also recall we all share a role to police and enforce transparency and accountability in the collection and subsequent distribution of these considerable funds. Every single dollar, euro, pound and Swiss franc is essential for success of the development projects. If you discern anyone deviating from this ethos then we rely upon you to make disclosure, but only in this forum.'

Wim van der Hoek had to suppress a smile. He could certainly lean on Reto and one or two others for a higher percentage. And he suspected the board would accept an increase in his fees if he handed them a miscreant.

'We share your ethos, Mr Chairman. The sole objective is repatriation of funds.' The Dutchman looked at his watch. 'May I take it that, considering the hour, we are done?'

'Thank you, Mr van der Hoek,' responded the Chairman and the rest of the board echoed his words.

As Wim van der Hoek was escorted through the walnut doors he turned and saw the board members move towards the hand basins situated at the rear of the boardroom, rolling up their sleeves to the elbow.

Loose talk costs lives

A red phone rang in the Grand Imperial Palace in Kinshasa. The hand of a servant reached out and plucked the handset from the cradle, moving it to the right ear of the man in the massage chair.

'Who wishes to speak with the chosen one, the Last True Descendant of the First King of Africa?' the massaged man asked imperiously. 'Wim van der Hoek, I recognise your breathing. Talk to me.'

The Dutchman could never work out how the President of the Congo was able to identify a caller in this way. It didn't occur to him that his supposedly encrypted mobile number had been deciphered.

'Your Royal Imperial Highness. I have news of interest.' Van der Hoek could never be sure of the mood of his sponsor and always addressed him cautiously.

'Okay, Wim. Tell me good news. Tell me you have secured my fifty billion.'

'Ah. Well, I don't have that good news, I'm afraid.' Van der Hoek heard a cry of pain from the other end of the phone. 'That idiot Pierre is dead. The Swiss guy transferred the money to the Central European Bank and Jean is also dead.'

'Jean Bouquet!' The President shouted across the room. 'Bouquet's family, round them all up immediately. No, wait!' He turned his mouth back to the phone, suddenly calm again. 'Wim, have you something more urgent to divulge?'

'Most urgent. Do not touch Bouquet's family or friends, it's a trap.'

'Go on.'

'Your life is in danger.'

This time Van der Hoek could hear the President's heavy breathing.

'I promise you will receive ten million dollars to your usual Swiss account if your information can save my life.'

The Dutchman considered his options. *Everyone has their price.*

'An English agent by the name of Thomas Thistlethwaite will come for you. His particulars are available via Interpol.' Van der Hoek paused again. 'He may be under cover. I'll send you the details immediately via email.'

'Wim, you are faithful to the Last True Descendant. Goodbye.'

Before the receiver clicked down the Dutchman heard the President shouting for his secretary to bring the royal laptop computer.

Five minutes later President Philippe Dubois stared in disbelief at the information contained in van der Hoek's email. 'What is this? Mission Impossible? Call Jean Bouquet's brothers in Switzerland, we will avenge the death of our faithful servant!'

The right bag

After a day of suppressing yawns and fighting unconsciousness at the seminar in the Gran Hotel Domine, Greg had to pack for an overnight trip to Norway.

Flying to Oslo via Charles de Gaulle needed to be done with small hand luggage. The last of the project canisters was needed in Norway and couldn't be checked in with the risk of being mishandled or lost. He would have to use his backpack. Socks and underwear would have to go in his jacket pockets.

Downstairs in the lobby Greg was approached by a smiling African who addressed him in Spanish but soon changed to English when he saw Greg's dress style and backpack.

'You are wishing a taxi to the airport, sir? We are always waiting for our customers. Please, let me take your bag.'

'Yes, to the airport. No, thank you, I'll keep the bag with me.'

The taxi driver held open the rear car door for Greg and then got in behind the wheel. He sent a text message on his mobile phone before starting the engine and pulling away.

It was a tortuous drive to the airport. Once out of the scenic city centre the brown apartment blocks looked dour and cramped. The motorway wound up through the suburbs and around the mountains surrounding Bilbao port. A persistent drizzle compounded the heavy traffic. The driver seemed loathe to switch on the air conditioning and Greg sweated in his seat.

Bilbao airport was a stark contrast to the dreary suburbs. Bright, airy and modern, the only thing it lacked was customers. Greg was able to quickly check-in, pass through security and browse the departures area for a little shopping. The project canister fitted snugly into one of the semi-rigid carry straps on the backpack and was undetectable.

There were only a few shops. One store had a selection of small children's toys and he bought some presents for his return home at the end of the week. The next store had a wide choice of Samsonite luggage and there was a special offer on a compact navy coloured suitcase that could be taken as hand luggage. Greg snapped up the bargain. Finding a row of empty seats nearby, he emptied the backpack and the contents of his pockets into the bag.

In the next row of seats a swarthy man puffed heavily on a Gitanes. The smell of the unfiltered cigarette was exotic but Greg wasn't sure if public smoking was permitted in Spain. A glance at the smoker's narrowed eyes and twisted mouth suggested confrontation wouldn't be a good idea. So Greg moved with his new bag further down the departure hall.

~

Interpol had been made aware of Greg's movements. In response to a specially coded request from Zurich, the registration of Greg at check-in had triggered an automatic email which arrived within seconds at the Interpol desk of the Zurich Kantonal Police. Striding up to the computer, a tall officer read the message thoroughly, printed a copy and deleted the email from the system. He pulled a packet of Marlboro cigarettes and his mobile phone from a pocket and headed for the exit. There was plenty of time and this had to be done right.

The wrong bag

Greg had been assured at check-in that he could carry on his bag but most of the hand luggage on Air France flight AF762 from Bilbao to Charles de Gaulle ended up checked into the hold. The overhead lockers were too small for anything bigger than a sandwich and all bags were taken from the passengers at the foot of the aircraft stairs.

The heavens opened on arrival at CDG and rain fell as though the sky were a sieve under an ocean. Greg could see his new bag with several others getting drenched on a trolley on the tarmac. At least, it looked like his. Every second business traveller had the same Samsonite bag. The navy coloured bag second from the end looked to be his. Most of the others were black or else more worn looking.

The Gitanes smoker pulled Greg's bag off the trolley and sprinted through the torrential rain to board a waiting bus. Greg's stomach flipped. To lose the last canister would be a disaster but seated in the tail of the plane he could do nothing but wait for the other passengers to move.

Finally he managed to get off the plane. Standing in the downpour, Greg looked at the black bag on the trolley and then at the waiting buses. There were around a hundred people crammed onto two buses.

He reached down for the black bag and saw his own luggage fly through the rain and land with a thump on the trolley. The black bag was wrenched from his hands and Monsieur Gitanes fled back to the first bus, uttering French oaths.

Soaked to the skin, Greg picked up his own bag. It didn't look very new any more. His copy of the Koran was protruding from the front pocket of the case, so he unzipped the main compartment and stuffed the soggy book inside with some difficulty.

The AF232 connection to Oslo was not due to take off for another three and a half hours. An earlier flight to Oslo had been delayed so he enquired at the Air France information desk about getting onto that one. The girl at the desk arranged the change and made some handwritten notes on his boarding card.

~

When he landed in Oslo Greg took the train to Lissafjord, arriving some three hours ahead of schedule. He called the factory from his room and found they were preparing for their annual works outing. The manager invited him to join them.

Ten minutes later Greg was staring at the inside of his suitcase. Nestled under the crinkled Koran was an unfamiliar brown paper package. He removed folded back an edge of the paper to see a slab of something wrapped in cling film. The Gitanes man. He started to pace the room, running a hand through his hair and expecting a knock on the door any second from the Norwegian police drug squad or some local drug baron. Greg reckoned he was in for either a long enforced holiday or a bit of a beating, or both.

He returned to the suitcase and picked up the package, removing the wrapper. The block looked like yellow Play-Doh. He turned it over in his hands and nearly dropped it when he saw what was on the other side. Several wires emerged from within the block of substance and were attached to some compact electronics with a small display unit. The display showed 00:55 and, as he watched, it changed to 00:54.

Greg had seen things like this on the Internet. *A semtex bomb, in my suitcase? Why would anyone do this to me?* In fifty-four minutes he was supposed to be up in the air above the Baltic Sea. Someone wanted to blow-up the plane he should have been on.

Before he could think any further there was a knock on the door. He shoved the device and some other items into the backpack and shouldered it before opening the door. Britt, the factory manager, stood there smiling, her short blonde hair and athletic figure breathtaking as ever.

'Come on, Englishman. We have to show you how Norwegians have fun.'

'Wait, I have something important to tell you,' Greg said as he was propelled out of the door and downstairs by his hostess. Within seconds they were seated in Britt's Volvo. 'Britt, I have a bomb in my bag.'

'Yes, of course you do. That's an English joke, right? You're so funny, Greg, if I could only understand your humour. You are being Mr Bean for me? How nice.'

Greg went silent, considering the best next step. A plane was not going to be blown out of the sky; that was one good thing. He should inform the police immediately so the matter could be investigated. Then there was the small problem of an unexploded time-bomb in his rucksack.

Deactivating bombs was not amongst his otherwise extensive skills, so it either had to be deactivated by someone else or abandoned in a safe place. There were some fifty minutes left to dispose of the thing safely.

By the time Greg had thought all this through, Britt had driven the Volvo into a car park and ushered Greg onto a walkway. He saw the other seventy factory workers onboard the boat, already raising their glasses to each other. Before he could try and explain again to Britt the seriousness of the situation, ropes were thrown and the steps drawn up onto the quayside, casting them adrift. Britt stuffed a bunch of vouchers for beer and food into Greg's shirt pocket with a smile. They had invited him onboard their annual fjord cruise with a bomb.

He took a look inside the backpack. The display panel of the device was reading 50. Time to keep his cool. Surrounded by beer drinking Norwegians in genial mood, he figured there was time enough to wait for deeper, more isolated water to dispose of the device. So he placed the backpack in an unoccupied area towards the stern of the boat, took a beer voucher from his shirt and headed for the bar.

The wooden boat chugging slowly past quaint moored boats, and couples, young and old, could be seen taking an early spring evening stroll on the footpaths that flanked the fjord.

Norwegians are a very sociable people, extremely fond of social gatherings and subject to animated conversation when the beer starts to flow. Greg found himself in one conversation after another and vouched for another beer.

There was a loud shout from the far end of the boat followed by several exclamations in Norwegian from a huddle of people. *Looks like the food is served, I'd better stake my claim*, Greg thought. He grabbed a paper plate and some cutlery and worked his way through the crowd. What he found was his backpack standing open and someone holding a thin yellow block aloft with one hand.

'For God's sake, don't touch it!' he shouted.

Everyone turned and stared.

'Everyone stand back! I brought this problem onboard, it's my responsibility and I will handle it alone.'

Britt reached for the upheld hand, took the yellow item and placed it on Greg's paper plate.

'Greg, what's the matter? Is this yours? Why are you shouting, do you want more beer or do you need something to eat? You English are so funny.'

It was his yellow hardback copy of the Koran. He took it from his plate and returned it to the backpack, both relieved and embarrassed.

'A little light reading for air travel,' he said. 'But I've finished it now.'

He turned to place the backpack on a wooden bench that ran around the stern but collided with the elbow of one of the other guests. The backpack slipped over the rail, into the water and sank immediately.

Well, bomb or not, at least the damn thing is gone now, Greg thought. It should be safe, some seven hundred meters deep at the bottom of a fjord. So was the project canister, which was a bit of a disaster.

The boat tour continued regardless of Greg's antics. Chicken, potato salad and beer were consumed and the strange behaviour of the Englishman was all but forgotten.

'Why are there so many fishing boats moored up near the town?' Greg asked one of the factory workers.

'It's spawning season for the herring,' the man said. 'No fishing, they have to be allowed to spawn.'

The boat sounded a bell and made a tight turn to commence the return journey.

After a few minutes Greg was drawn into another conversation, this time about football. The Norwegians assumed he shared their enthusiasm for the sport. A young man produced a digital camera with over a hundred pictures of the recently constructed Arsenal stadium. Greg had almost zero interest in football and, to his enormous relief, the camera batteries ran out at photo number eleven. He was trying to get out of meeting the next day to view the rest of the photos when there was a shower of seawater, the boat lurched and Greg found himself sprawled on top of the Arsenal supporter.

Almost everyone on the boat had lost their footing and was soaking wet. A few dead fish lay on the deck and, through the rails, he could see a couple of small boats had capsized. Their crews were already starting to right the vessels.

'Donner en blitz!' came a shout from the front of the boat and everyone rushed forward.

The revellers turned silent as they viewed the scene of devastation. Herring floated on the surface of the water all around, their silver scales glimmering in the rays of the setting sun. One glance at his watch told Greg everything he needed to know. It had been intended for him and the rest of flight AF232 to be floating dead in the sea.

Out of hours

The boat returned to berth and Greg declined an offer of a lift back to the hotel. He wandered slowly back towards the town centre on foot. How many flights had he taken in the past year? About eighty. He couldn't believe what had nearly happened and was unsure what to do next. If he called the Norwegian police they might arrest him for single-handedly destroying the local fishing industry.

The receptionist at the Hotel Tollgaten attempted to engage in her usual flirtatious banter but, for once, Greg was having none of it. He went straight up the stairs, marched to his room and took the phone book out of the desk drawer. He tried to formulate what to say whilst waiting for someone to pick up at the British Embassy in Oslo. An answering machine informed him in BBC English that office hours were closed but it did give an emergency number. He jotted it down on the notepad next to the phone.

Greg started to dial the emergency number but paused to reconsider the story he had to tell and realised how improbable it sounded. Someone may have planted a bomb in his bag at CDG, he had hand-carried this through customs and then onto a train to Lissafjord where it was disposed of and detonated at the bottom of a fjord, destroying all evidence and a lot of herring. He hadn't even had the presence of mind to take any photos of the device.

The phone emitted a disconnect tone in his ear. He put the receiver down and decided to see what fresh ideas the morning would bring. Then he opened the mini-bar.

~

In Zurich a confused Patrique Bouquet was scanning the information sources in the Interpol office of the Zurcher Kantonalpolizei. How could it have gone wrong? He had been assured the device was foolproof and the operative had confirmed delivery. So, he and his brother would have to take matters into their own hands. Stepping outside into the evening rain for a cigarette, he made a few phone calls from his mobile to secure two visas for the early morning.

~

Across the River Limmat two familiar men languished in the plush surroundings of the Prince's Club.

'This big one is putting up some resistance,' the blonde said in Romanian, leaning over to Svetlana. 'I need more time to get his enthusiasm up.'

'Don't worry,' Svetlana replied. 'I have a firm promise from Reto that we'll have some fun and games upstairs tomorrow night.'

Reto extricated himself and sent the girls away. He didn't trust this Dutchman with his square jaw and lack of social skills. Reto's sixth sense told him something bad was in the air, but he had to play along until he could work it out.

'So, Wim. Tomorrow night you want to have a big celebration. We could have it here. Okay?'

'Perfect,' van der Hoek replied. 'I have to dispose of some assets and I wish to share the outcome with you, my friend. You deserve it.'

The wrong man

At seven a.m. Norwegian time there was a sharp knock on the door. Greg took a bleary look through the peephole and saw the spiky blonde head of Britt. He opened the door.

'Britt, are you ever going to sleep with me?' he asked, absentmindedly scratching his stomach.

'When you ask nicely, have had a shave and a shower and haven't just slept in your clothes,' she replied.

Greg rubbed his jaw and smiled.

'How long do you need, twenty minutes? I'll see you downstairs.'

'Okay.' Greg closed the door and shuffled into the shower room.

Half an hour later he arrived at the dining room and had a quick breakfast of roll mop herring, yoghurt and orange juice. The fish reminded Greg of the events of the previous evening and he half imagined it must have been a dream. However, on the way to the train station in Britt's car she broached the subject.

'I suppose you blew up all the herring in the fjord with your bomb?'

'Yes, I'm afraid so. Can you ever forgive me?' he replied.

Greg couldn't tell if she was laughing or crying.

For the rest of the journey Britt alternated between surmising it must have been a wartime mine in the fjord and breaking out again into laughter.

Greg exchanged a fond farewell with his old friend at the train station. He found a quiet carriage and dialled the British Embassy emergency number. A brusque female voice answered and Greg gave his name. He heard a muffled conversation at the other end then a well educated English male voice came onto the line.

'Yes, hello, Mr Marshall? Mr Greg Marshall? We are informed you may have been unwittingly involved in an attempt to smuggle drugs. Don't be alarmed, we'll take up contact with you again on your return to Bilbao. Thanks ever so much for keeping us informed. Goodbye.'

Greg stared at the phone in confusion and looked blankly around the carriage. The matter appeared to be under control and out of his hands.

The rest of the train journey passed by unremarkably. Greg had little to do except daydream, having thrown his reading material into the fjord. At Oslo airport he checked in his luggage all the way through CDG to Bilbao for safety's sake and dozed on the plane, hoping for a few quiet days ahead.

When he reached Bilbao Greg made a visit to the rest room. He stepped out of the cubicle and was confronted by a tall African who grabbed him by the wrists.

Another man approached from the right. Greg saw a glint of metal

'For my brother!' the man shouted, wielding a big blade towards Greg's exposed arms. A terrible image from the Guggenheim *Hands* exhibition in Bilbao flashed into his mind.

Greg acted on instinct and let his knees collapse, dropping his bodyweight and pulling the first man down with him.

The machete glanced off the African's bowed head and blood splashed across the sink behind. Greg saw a flash of movement in the mirror as a man in a suit ran in through the door.

Greg jumped up and let loose a front kick, catching the bleeding man in the chest and sending him flying backwards into the stone surround of the sink.

He turned, expecting the guy with the blade to attack again.

'I have him,' the suited man said from between clenched teeth as he tightened a cord around the neck of the machete wielder. The blade dropped to the floor and the African slumped.

The first attacker got up off the floor and ran at the suited man. Greg aimed a kick with his left leg and took the guy right off his feet.

The suited man leapt across and punched Greg's opponent hard in the throat. The African let out a brief, hoarse rasping sound and lay still.

'Who the hell are you?' Greg asked the suited man.

'Greg, old chap. I *am you.*'

The wrong place

Thomas Thistlethwaite led Greg by the arm to the rest room exit. He picked up a sign that said *closed for cleaning* in Spanish and placed it across the doorway.

They went over to the stationary luggage conveyor belt where Greg's navy Samsonite lay. Greg picked it up and they walked out of the airport.

Greg took a longer look at Thistlethwaite and recalled where he had seen him before. This man had helped serve food onboard the fjord cruise.

Thistlethwaite opened the driver's door of a Ford and gestured for Greg to get in but Greg hesitated.

'Listen, Greg. I just saved your life in there. Trust me. I'll explain everything once we get some good Spanish wine inside us.'

Thistlethwaite pulled a mobile phone out of his pocket.

'You drive. I need to make three phone calls to smooth things out, then I'm all yours.'

The first call was in Spanish. All Greg could make out was his name mentioned once or twice but the tone of the conversation was definitely ingratiating.

A second call was in English, technical jargon concerning email traffic. He heard the word *Congo* and assumed it was some kind of code or acronym. Thistlethwaite had appeared to be stunned by the call and covered his face with his hands. It seemed Greg's new guardian angel might be cracking up.

The third call was in German and, from the slow rural style of speech and strange turns of phrase, it was clear to Greg the person on the other end was a Swiss German speaker. He was able to understand considerably more of that conversation, although it made little sense. Interpol would advise that Thomas Thistlethwaite was found dead in Bilbao airport this morning, bearing facsimile traces of Greg Marshall. The industrial plan should be put into action before end of business today and Tulip would enjoy a trip to the mountains.

Thistlethwaite finished the call and replaced the phone in his pocket.

There was no further exchange of words in the car during the twenty minute drive.

Greg parked underground at the Gran Hotel Domine and sat staring at his hands on the steering wheel.

'Let's go on up,' Thistlethwaite said and stepped out of the car.

They took the lift to Greg's room on the fourth floor.

Greg went straight to the bathroom and showered. His skin felt sensitive to the hot water and the shower gel stung his face. The steamy mirror showed a long shallow cut down his right cheek.

Twenty minutes later the two Englishmen sat in a tapas bar with glasses of Rioja in front of them.

'So, Greg. I'd like to explain a few of the things that have happened in the last few days,' Thistlethwaite said.

Greg nodded. He half expected Spanish police to burst into the bar at any minute, brandishing pistols and ruining his life even further.

'The bomb planted in your hand luggage on the Paris to Oslo flight. You were the target for that bomb.'

'Why would someone want to do that?'

'Greg, you're a very important person in the view of my employers. Your project is invaluable to us and, in order to provide ourselves with some access to details, we had to borrow your identity.'

'Identity theft? How and what does this have to do with murder? And anyway the project is the property of my employer.'

'To cut a long story short, we have your fingerprints from Brazil and a good friend scanned your retinas while you slept on a transatlantic flight. I needed your identity to gain access to the project. Unfortunately, some other activities of mine made me a target and someone assumed I was travelling under your identity.'

'So they were trying to kill you and not me? Well, thanks a lot!' Greg knocked back his glass of red wine and poured more from the bottle.

'You wouldn't have come to harm. I was in the process of defusing that bomb on the boat. And the toilet incident would have been dealt with differently had you not decided to join in. Where did you learn to fight like that anyway?'

'Karate classes, years ago.' Greg laughed, raised his glass and toasted Thistlethwaite. 'I guess I owe you some thanks, and I guess you owe me the return of my identity.'

'You'll be called to Zurich tomorrow and all this subterfuge will come to an end. It'll turn out well for you, I promise.'

After a second bottle of wine had been drunk the two Englishmen headed back to the hotel.

Up in his hotel room Greg reflected on what he had learned that evening. He had a feeling of being on the edge of greatness. Thistlethwaite's employers considered his life and his project worth protecting. He had participated in the murder of two men. It was both horrifying and thrilling. Just before succumbing to sleep, Greg had a drowsy recollection that he had forgotten to quiz Thistlethwaite on the Congo issue.

The right time

'My firm recommendation to the Research and Development Council will be this project is no longer a core area of interest. There are other areas of focus more key to strategic success. We'll ensure all strings are cut and he's free to move forward by the end of the month.'

The bottle of champagne gurgled as the waiter topped up their glasses.

Reto groaned at the simpering adoration of his dinner colleague for the undeniably handsome Croatian waiter.

'And how is your dear wife Solwig, Andreas?'

'Oh, you know. She still misses Scandinavia. In fact, she spends much of her time in the summer cottage and I'm often left alone.'

The piano player struck up *Summertime* on the baby grand in the corner of the room.

'And the living is easy,' Andreas crooned. He opened the wine list and deftly pocketed a slim white envelope that lay within.

The Piano Bar in Zurich Altstadt wasn't one of Reto's regular haunts. Entertainment there was tailored to a different taste than his, more in the direction of rich foreign businessmen left to their own devices by wives who had long ago discovered them cringing in the closet.

'Andreas, a great pleasure doing business with you, as always.' Reto stood and offered his hand.

Andreas took the hand and clasped Reto's upper arm. Reto could feel the fingers testing his muscle tone.

'Must you leave so early? I thought you might join me this evening.'

'No, thank you. I never mix business with pleasure. Á la prochaine.' Reto headed straight out of the door, down the street towards his next meeting at the Prince's Club.

Van der Hoek was already waiting outside the club. The security staff on the door eyed the big Dutchman.

'You're early. Eager to get stuck in tonight?' Reto said.

Van der Hoek gave Reto a cool look.

'Come on, relax, you're going to have a really good time. I have a big surprise for you. Let's go in.' Reto took the Dutchman by the arm and led him inside the club.

Svetlana and another girl were waiting in the bar area and took the men straight to a corner booth where a bottle of champagne was waiting in a bucket of ice. The new girl was introduced and Reto felt his pulse quicken. She was tall, nearly as tall as van der Hoek, and her skin was the colour and texture of ebony. Van der Hoek was clearly interested too. The girl's name was Sophie and she could speak Afrikaans, which was close enough to Dutch for van der Hoek to feel at home.

After initial pleasantries and champagne, Sophie leaned over to Reto.

'Hey, skinny boy, your big friend here doesn't like champagne and wants a beer.'

'I'll take care of it,' Reto replied. He walked over to the bar and ordered a glass of Heineken. When the barman had served the drink and turned away, Reto let three droplets of liquid fall into it from a small bottle concealed in his palm, then added another two to be sure. He slipped a small pill into his own mouth and returned to their booth.

Van der Hoek guzzled the Heineken and began to relax. He seemed very tired.

Reto proposed a move to more private quarters upstairs. Sophie had to support van der Hoek in climbing the steps but it was no problem for her tall athletic frame.

Upstairs, Svetlana led Reto by the tie into a room with a massive bed covered in light blue silk sheets. Sophie followed with van der Hoek and was just able to get the Dutchman onto the bed before he collapsed with a snore. She elbowed him onto the floor and turned to the other two. Reto was glad he had taken the little pill. His natural stamina was not what it used to be.

Some sixty minutes later two hefty security men schlepped the Dutchman by the armpits to a hired Mercedes parked behind the club. Reto slipped them a few notes and liftcd one of van der Hoek's eyelids with his thumb. The pupil was dilated. Not taking any chances, he clicked the seatbelt across his passenger's lap and fastened a couple of heavy duty tie-wraps around the Dutchman's wrists and ankles. Then he draped a blanket over the legs and body up to the waist, just in case any traffic police might take a look.

Reto found what he was looking for inside van der Hoek's jacket; a number of documents indicated money transfers from the Congo to a private account in Reto's name. Others were printed copies of email correspondence between Reto and the President of the Congo relating to Thomas Thistlethwaite and someone named Greg Marshall. The emails advised that Thistlethwaite / Marshall was eliminated, giving the President a few days grace to flee from the Congo into exile.

The documents were carefully forged. With his expert eye, Reto could just see the lack of authenticity. Others might not have done so. He had come very close to being set up by the Dutchman.

Twenty minutes later the Mercedes was heading across the tarmac of Zurich airport toward a small single-engined Cessna hired in van der Hoek's name. A hydraulic wheelchair lift was positioned next to the passenger side of the aircraft.

Reto dragged the Dutchman's body out of the car and into a folding wheelchair he had removed from the boot of the Mercedes. The hydraulic lift took van der Hoek up parallel with the passenger door of the plane. Reto folded down the arm of the wheelchair, slid him across onto the grey leather of the aircraft seat and repositioned the blanket for warmth. He wanted his charge to stay comfortably unconscious for a little while longer.

He parked the Mercedes in a hire car pick-up bay next to the private aircraft hangar and strolled back to the Cessna carrying a large holdall and a military style backpack. Inside the plane he changed his clothes to something more suitable for the adventure. Then he cut the tie-wrap on the Dutchman's feet with a knife and placed it in his pocket, put the backpack behind the pilot's seat and proceeded with the pre-take off formalities.

They were soon airborne and climbing up through the clear night sky. The lights of Zurich were visible below and Reto could make out the general area of the Prince's Club. He sent a telepathic note of gratitude to Svetlana and Sophie.

Past Zurich the landscape changed from rolling valleys bathed in moonlight to the frosty foothills of the Alps. Setting a heading for the Eiger, Reto reached behind his seat for the backpack and put it on over his army issue alpine clothes. The Dutchman stirred in his seat.

'Where are we, what happened and why is it so goddamn cold?' van der Hoek said, shifting beneath his blanket.

Reto set the plane into a steep climb and pulled on a balaclava and goggles.

'Don't worry, you won't have to put up with the cold for long. Thomas and I wish you bon voyage and a happy landing. Goodbye, Wim.'

Reto turned the key, pulled it from the ignition and threw it over his shoulder into the back of the plane. The engine spluttered and died. The steep climb of the plane levelled off and the indicator on the air speed gauge began to drop. He opened the pilot's door, swung his feet out and launched himself out into the dark night. A few moments later the military parachute on his back opened and Reto started to steer himself in the direction of a snowy slope.

Back in the cockpit of the plane van der Hoek gulped the freezing air and shook off the blanket. He grabbed the loose end of the tie-wrap in his teeth, trying to loosen it but only succeeding in pulling it tighter. The coroner at the inquest would later report these teeth marks indicated the deceased had fastened the tie-wrap on his own wrists and over-tightened it in this fashion, cutting through the skin. The plane stalled, the nose dipped and the aircraft turned in a spin towards the north face of the Eiger.

Time to pray

'Thomas, for God's sake tell me what is happening and what I should do! The military is putting my government under increasing pressure. Enemy armies are massing on our borders with Rwanda and the Congo. It's all going pear shaped. How did I get into this? I'm a medical advisor, not a president!' Winston Cunningham paced the length of his office in the presidential palace in Kampala.

Thistlethwaite reclined in the President's chair, sipping on a gin and tonic. 'Winston, try to relax. There's been a slight hiccup with the process in the Congo and Philippe Dubois is still holding the reins. We know he plans to go into exile before the week is out. Everything will change after that and Rwanda will follow suit.'

'But the military in this new Uganda of ours, they're nearly out of control,' the Scotsman said, putting the palm of one hand to his forehead.

'No cloud without a silver lining, Winston. The only opposition to your government now is the military and the ringleaders have shown their hands. Once the borders have calmed down we'll have your troublemakers transferred to UN peacekeeping duties, somewhere far afield with a high mortality rate.'

Cunningham stopped pacing and Thistlethwaite rose from the chair.

'Dubois is a truly dangerous man, Thomas. Exile won't be comfortable for him and he has vast wealth. The people of the Congo won't sleep well at night unless he and his aides are appropriately despatched.'

'You know, Winston, I won't make you complicit in the affairs of the Congo. It's not my business either. But I've been assured all loose ends will be tied up. Let's just leave it at that and look forward to the future.' Thistlethwaite moved to the drinks cabinet and fixed himself another drink. 'In the meantime, we have twenty-four hour surveillance on your military friends. They're being tracked by satellite. Our snipers could eliminate them at any time and will do if things start to get out of hand. But that's not the way your government is to operate. This country is to be a true democracy. Once we've weeded the garden we'll be able to enjoy the fruits of our labour.'

~

Across the border the Congolese troops were nervous in their camps. A strong rumour was circulating that the President was planning to flee the country. Philippe Dubois had ruled the Congo with an iron fist for a generation. His personal wealth, squeezed relentlessly from the country's natural resources, was legendary. Every man, woman and child lived in fear of his displeasure. It was a one man show. Dubois' cohorts showed no free will, merely following decrees that could be unpredictable, irrational and terrifyingly brutal. The irony was that, although a tyrant, if he left the Congo there would be a dangerous vacuum.

Fifty miles to the east a disciplined Ugandan army was still confined to barracks. They had a strong British army advisor contingent and were recently re-equipped with the latest battle technology. If Dubois fled then the Ugandans would be able to march straight across the border without fear of recrimination. The only options for the unpaid and poorly nourished Congolese soldiers would be capitulation or slaughter. All that prevented the invasion was the vicious reputation of Dubois and a threatening mass of Rwandan forces on the southern border of Uganda. These Rwandans were mercenaries paid for by the blood diamonds Dubois had cheated from the nation. Many in the Rwandan force had been a party to the genocide at the end of the previous century. Uganda would try to avoid a confrontation with them.

But, unbeknown to the desperate Congolese army, the Rwandan forces were already disbanding. Dubois' funds had dried up and they were not going to wait around unpaid in the fashion of Congolese conscripts.

At three-thirty p.m. Radio Kinshasa put out a broadcast across the country and beyond its borders. His Royal Highness, the Last True Descendant of the First King of Africa, had announced a self imposed exile for spiritual reasons. In the interim, a United Nations peacekeeping force had stepped into the power vacuum, led by a Belgian commander whose name was familiar from other operations in Africa.

Two Lear jets stood on the tarmac at Dubois Royal International Airport in Kinshasa. Philippe Dubois was escorted up the small aircraft steps by a blue helmeted UN soldier. Seven other senior aides followed and a party of eight key members of the Dubois family boarded the second jet.

Within minutes the jets were airborne. Guided by Dubois' pilots and heading north, they streaked over diamond mines that had been the source of untold riches and unspeakable exploitation.

In the deserted open cast mine, known as Dubois Quinze, tarpaulins were removed from the rear of two large trucks. The Belgian Elite Forces were swift and precise. It took just three seconds for the surface-to-air missiles to connect with their Lear jet targets. The Dubois exile was of the most permanently spiritual kind.

At four p.m. precisely Commander Claude Piquet announced the sad news. A small rebel group from the north of the country had attacked and downed the aircraft carrying the President, his family and his aides. The entire presidential party had met their fate. UN forces in the area investigating the apparent missile launch site had been fired upon by the rebels. Within their peacekeeping mandate, and assisted by Belgian Elite Forces, they had returned fire. There were no rebel survivors.

At four-thirty Commander Piquet made a personal broadcast. He had been asked by the church and civil service leaders in Kinshasa to take the role of interim president and had been released by the UN for this important function. On return to barracks, all Congolese military personnel would receive the six months back pay owed to them. All soldiers suffering from HIV and onset AIDS would be honourably discharged and care provided. As this category constituted more than seventy percent of the conscripted armed forces it would effectively demilitarise the country. In addition, the Central European Bank and the Belgian Government had announced a national investment programme that would bring the country's infrastructure into the twenty first century. Diplomatic missions were being despatched to neighbouring countries and an official partnership invitation had been extended to President Cunningham of Uganda.

In Kampala, Winston Cunningham listened in amazement to the radio broadcast.

'You see, Winston,' Thistlethwaite said, 'all things move towards their end.'

Released

Greg Marshall's last day at the seminar in Bilbao was hijacked by a short notice trip to Switzerland, at the request of his boss. The steering committee governing his project had unexpectedly brought forward toll gate five.

A toll gate was a go / no-go decision point and the timing was all wrong. The project pilots in Brazil and Spain were not yet complete and the third prototype had been lost in the Norwegian fjord. Greg had dedicated the last five years of his working life to development of those prototypes and launch of the project. He felt a grinding sensation in his stomach as he headed up into the clouds above Bilbao on the early morning flight to Zurich.

On arrival at the Swiss research centre Greg entered the foyer of the spa-like building with some trepidation. The computerised recognition system acknowledged his fingerprint and retina scan, displaying a message confirming his fifth visit of the month. It was in fact his first. So Thomas Thistlethwaite had clearly been making good use of his credentials.

Greg found his boss already in the meeting room. Lars Melkstam gave him a firm handshake.

'Thanks for coming at such short notice. It rather caught me out myself. Astrid and I had planned a few days hill walking but I had to cut it short. I'll get this fixed and regain adequate time for the project pilot.'

It was clear to Greg that Melkstam had no more idea of what was going on than he did.

The steering committee members filed into the room. This was a rare honour for Greg as he had previously attended all toll gate meetings via conference call.

'Gentlemen, and lady,' Lars commenced with a smile at the female representative of Finance, 'as chair of this project I welcome you to toll gate 5. But I have to tell you I'm surprised by the request to bring the meeting forward. Frankly put, we are not ready for this toll gate and I propose we reschedule for two months hence.' Lars raised his eyebrows at the committee members. They had always followed his previous recommendations.

'I requested that the toll gate be brought forward,' Andreas Bjornsund said.

Greg felt a cold shiver run across his shoulders. Bjornsund always gave him the creeps with his dapper appearance and silky tones.

Lars' eyebrows fell and knitted into a frown that spread right across his forehead. Bjornsund and he were historical adversaries.

Bjornsund continued. 'As you may be aware, our executive has been conducting a strategic review of operations and projects. The firm view of the Research and Development Council is this project is no longer an area of core interest. There are other areas of focus more essential to strategic success. This means the steering committee is giving a no-go at this toll gate 5 and the project will close by the end of the month.'

The other committee members were nodding their heads during this information and muttering their assent.

From the corner of his eye Greg could see Lars run a hand through his hair, always a sign his boss was losing control. The atmosphere in the meeting room suddenly seemed rarefied.

'Andreas, this is rather sudden. I'm not aware of a new strategic review,' Lars retorted. 'The executive authorised a patent application for the prototype only three weeks ago. We have invested twenty man years and millions of dollars in the project. It offers us the potential for a clear competitive advantage within the next twelve months.

What is the rationale for this assessment of our work as non-core?'

Greg knew Lars was doing what he did best, applying pressure upwardly through unassailable logic.

'Lars, it takes considerable courage to focus on core strategic developments and to stop exciting but non-core projects such as this. Our company no longer wants to be in the business of rendering existing power generation solutions redundant with the invention of revolutionary new technology. The Executive is advised by the best minds in industry and we all respect the decision. The patent application is withdrawn.' Bjornsund turned to the other steering committee members and they nodded agreement.

Greg decided to intervene. 'Mr Bjornsund, with due respect to the executive's judgement, there has been massive human investment in this project. I have personally dedicated the last five years of my life to what I am certain would be a hugely successful technology of great commercial value. To throw away a potential patent for this is incomprehensible.'

Greg knew the patent ethic in his company was paramount. It had to be his best chance of a stay of execution for the project.

Bjornsund looked at Greg with the manner of a grandfather coming to the final part of a familiar bedtime story. 'That is recognised and the company discharges all proprietary claim upon the potential patent. Should you wish to do so, you are free to pursue this patent privately. Although, in that case, you would have to leave our employ. Under the circumstances the company is prepared to make a reasonable settlement such that you may continue seamlessly with your work, commencing next month. Alternatively, we can offer you a start-up project based in New Delhi.'

Greg and Lars looked at each other in confusion. The company had never, ever released its proprietary claim on a patent, whether established or under application. This was more astonishing than the decision to close the project. Furthermore, Greg was clearly no longer required by the company. It was no secret he had become desperately ill for six months following a previous trip to India and a posting to New Delhi might as well be on the dark side of the moon as far as he and his family were concerned. So this was their thanks for five years of devotion. The corporate suits obviously perceived him to be about as useful as a decorative toilet bowl. He stood up.

'Let me have your proposal in writing and I'll give it due consideration.' Greg could hear the tremble in his own voice. 'I thank the committee and Lars for supporting the project up to this point.'

'Colleagues, this meeting has concluded. Thank you for your openness and your valuable time. The project is closed.' Bjornsund clasped his hands and sat back in his chair.

Lars stood to join Greg and they both left the room.

~

Greg and Lars raised their fifth glasses of golden beer for a toast in the Zeughauskeller in Zurich. Greg scanned the ancient armoury of weapons decorating the walls of the medieval beer hall and fantasised he was laying about the project steering committee members with a double-headed axe.

'Decapitation is one alternative, it's true,' Lars said. He was definitely the worse for wear, not being a habitual beer drinker. 'In the cold light of day I think you might see a golden future ahead of you. It could be a rare business opportunity if you can find some start-up capital.'

'Well, let the cold light of day show me that, but tonight we're going to get pissed.' Greg laughed, raising his glass again.

Food finally arrived in the shape of the house speciality, a meter long sausage with a bucket of potato salad.

'Not a bad idea to get something in the stomach, Greg. I believe we have a long night ahead of us.'

An hour later the two friends staggered across Bahnhofstrasse, past the famous boutiques and expensive jewellers and on towards the banking district.

'What's this?' Greg asked, looking at a poster of a scantily clad woman. 'The Prince's Club? Would you believe it, I've never been in here.'

'Me neither,' Lars said, pushing the Englishman through the door.

Nowhere to go

At nine-thirty a.m. the buzzing of a mobile phone alarm caused a slight stirring beneath the deluxe duvet of the Swissotel executive bedroom.

Greg tried to focus on the time display and dragged a hand across his aching face. Bed at four in the morning and a skinful of alcohol were not a combination conducive to work, but he had some small satisfaction in the knowledge his boss would be in an even worse condition.

He threw on some clothes and made his way down to breakfast, heading for a quiet corner where he hoped his unsavoury condition would not offend other diners.

Someone hovered by the table and Greg mumbled in German that a cup of hot chocolate would be really rather nice.

'Certainly, sir, and would you also like some Alka Seltzer for your impending hangover?'

Greg looked up to see the cheery face of Thomas Thistlethwaite.

'So, you've been having a little celebration with your Swedish friend, by the state of you.' Thistlethwaite pulled out a chair and sat.

'I thought you said all the subterfuge would come to an end.'

'And so it has. The world is now officially your oyster. But first you'll have to point out to me the obvious flaw in this golden opportunity you've been presented with.'

'You mean the fact I'm free to patent an invention my employer has rejected, one no competitor will purchase because it threatens their existing established technology?

And I therefore have no chance of financial backing and no market for the product?'

'Yes, that's the one. However, you've forgotten some of what I told you in Bilbao. Your project has immense potential value to my employer. The financial resources at our disposal for your project are, I hesitate to say, almost limitless. As a next step we're inviting you to The Hague to discuss terms and conditions. You're going to be very busy but there will be rewards. If you're religious then now is the time to thank your God.'

Greg stared at Thistlethwaite.

'I would suggest you head for the research centre this afternoon to check on project progress and I'll email you with a proposed date for our next meeting.'

'Okay. Right.' Greg put a hand to his head and let his eyes close.

Thistlethwaite stood to leave. 'If I was in your shoes I'd go back to bed for a couple of hours, old chap.'

~

Greg took the advice and grabbed a further two hours sleep before checking out soon after noon. On the train to the research centre he tried to collect his thoughts. A beep and a buzz from his phone indicated email. The HR department had initiated negotiations for his departure or transfer to India.

Greg could not seriously believe Thistlethwaite represented the solution to his future but he would keep the option open. In the meantime plan A would be to maximise the severance package and gain financial breathing time until he found a suitable job. Perhaps something a bit closer to home this time. The novelty of international travel had seriously worn off for both him and his family.

The tranquillity of the research centre surroundings was, as usual, sublime. Greg was welcomed by the computerised recognition system on his seventh visit.

Thistlethwaite obviously had some interim business to conduct. Greg wasn't too concerned as he knew the real project results were inaccessible to anyone except himself.

In the project lab Greg closed a glass door and logged onto the system. User name: Copacabana. Password: Ipanema.

A map of the world appeared on the screen in the normal Magellan projection. There were five flashing green beacons. Three in Brazil, one in Spain and, surprisingly, one in Norway.

He zoomed in on Brazil and could make out the topography of the Itaipu Dam. Switching to three dimensional view, the contour lines disappeared and a virtual landscape on the screen showed the exact location of the two prototypes, one deep in the foundations of the dam and the other at the base of the hydro station overflow outlet. Both were flashing, indicating the systems were triggered and the satellite positioning systems operative.

The third prototype at the Iguassu Falls was also active, about ten metres from the octagonal end of the viewing walkway. In Brazil it would be early evening. Greg could almost hear the white noise and smell the ozone charged air of the falls.

He changed the display to move across the Atlantic to Spain where the fourth prototype was active in the Guggenheim museum. He closed his eyes to try and recall the strange resonance of the curling walls of steel but visions of *Hands* flashed through his mind.

Up into Scandinavia and the final resting place of the fifth and final prototype could be seen in the Lissafjord. It had sunk to nearly seven hundred metres and was miraculously still transmitting despite the detonation.

All was much as he had expected, with the exception of Lissafjord. Now to the results. The software showed magnitude and frequency of transmission from each device.

A weak and erratic signal from the dusty depths of Itaipu's foundations was produced from the resonance occasioned by engineers and privileged tourists. Not such an inspired location after all. By comparison, both the hydro station overflow and the foot of the falls had produced constant transmissions from the turbulent water flow. Their signals were of a magnitude that inspired optimism for the project. He realised at this point the project would continue.

In Bilbao the Guggenheim prototype had generated emissions of significant magnitude from the special resonance of the sculpture but they were intermittent.

Greg had thought to ignore the Lissafjord prototype but a desire for thoroughness led him to review those results. For the first thirty minutes of the positioning system being activated by contact with water there was a continuous medium level transmission. This suggested the unit had fallen from the backpack as it entered the water and sunk several hundred meters, the velocity of the fall generating the signal. At the time of the bomb's detonation there had been several transmission waves of enormous magnitude. Once the shock waves of the detonation had settled down the prototype had continued a steady, low level transmission that might indicate either a slow steady current at the bottom of the fjord or damage to the unit. Greg was amazed the prototype had withstood the explosion.

Initial results are promising, wrote Greg in the project log. Resonance and flow both act as transmission triggers in the field. The design also appears extremely robust.

He logged off the system and left the office, failing to notice a discreet new security camera in the corner.

To wrap up the visit Greg called an impromptu meeting of the project team. He informed them the project would close at the end of the month. There were groans of dismay. They weren't placated by his vague suggestions that the project might continue externally with venture capital backing. But he was sure their professionalism would commit them to the project during the remaining month. Promising them feedback within one week, he took his leave and headed back to the corporate HR offices for negotiation, fortified by the firm belief that only he knew the real value and potential of this project. After the HR meeting there was an early evening connection to Dublin and Greg was looking forward to getting home.

Nowhere like home

He pulled up in his Saab at the front of their house.

The place was quiet and looked very clean. Someone had been busy preparing it for his homecoming. A quick look in the fridge showed all the essentials for the weekend were already there. Fresh milk, some chicken fillets and a few nice looking vegetables. No need for any last minute shopping. There were even a couple of bottles of good red wine in the rack. Now time to take a turn around the grounds.

The trees were leafing out nicely. White blossom had come and gone on the plum and the apple trees were full with red petals. It gave early promise of some good fruit. The kids loved to take plums to school in their lunchboxes and to make apple pies with him at the weekend.

In a corner of the garden the swing looked to be in a bit of a sorry state. The metal frame was faded and rusty, the rope tangled and the weathered wooden seat at an angle. On the patio the children's garden furniture was in a similar condition. He should really replace the stuff, but what was the point. He didn't want to get rid of them. There was still some sentimental value as they had all chosen the garden playthings together.

He fixed a pasta dish of penne with chicken, sun dried tomatoes and mushrooms, and took it through to the dining room together with a large mug of tea. Always a good habit for the family to eat together at the table and a habit he found difficult to break, even when eating on his own.

The children should be home from school soon but, wait, it was a Saturday. They would be at a party. Natalie would bring the kids home in the Volkswagen. Hannah would insist on Natalie fitting her seatbelt even though she could easily do it herself. Matt would take his time getting into his child seat and drive Natalie to distraction with the five little action hero figures that had to be carried everywhere. When they finally arrived home he would have to take immediate duty of care to give Natalie the break she deserved.

By nine o'clock it was adult time and one of the bottles of red wine was brought out with two Waterford crystal glasses. Today was their anniversary and it was a small celebration, fifteen years married. Upstairs under Natalie's pillow he had placed a surprise present, an unusual pendant with matching earrings of Brazilian Azure.

Rather unwisely the second bottle of red was also opened and dispatched with due ceremony. An old film on the TV was followed through to the end. They had both seen it before but he couldn't quite remember the ending, which turned out rather tragic.

'I'll clear up,' he said to himself. Natalie must have already gone. He took the empty bottles through to the recycling bin in the kitchen and washed both glasses, although only one showed traces of wine.

He locked the doors front and back, headed slowly up the oak staircase, watching shadows thrown through the windows by the yellow moonlight.

Hannah's room was immaculate, not a pin out of place. It really never used to be like that. 'Goodnight, princess.'

Matt's room was the smallest, a box room really. A typical boy's room with cars and planes and action figures. 'Goodnight, my prince.'

There was no noise from the children. The night breeze sighed through the trees and into the open windows. They all slept more comfortably with their windows open, although Natalie had a morbid fear of the kids accidentally falling to their deaths.

Ablutions completed in a slightly drunken manner, he sat on his side of the bed, furthest from the door. Reaching under Natalie's pillow he pulled out a box, opened it and gazed at the azure jewellery. They were quite unusual pieces and he knew Nat would have liked them; they came from her home country. He closed the box, gave it a light kiss and placed it on Natalie's bedside table.

'Happy anniversary, Natalie. I will love you always.'

She was there in spirit, as were the children. Wife and children, murdered in a field under a hot African sun with many others. Tomorrow he would visit the family grave in a nearby Bedfordshire village. It would be the seventh anniversary of their passing but to Thomas Thistlethwaite it felt like an eternity.

From the Land of the Delta

The fetid deltas of the River Niger disgorged black gold from their depths. Nigeria was established as one of the world's top ten oil producers. Predictably, a succession of corrupt rulers had pocketed most of the proceeds and maintained a state of chaos that gave Lagos an unenviable reputation as the world's most dangerous city.

The combined accumulated personal wealth amassed by the top five presidents in the last two decades was enormous. Conservative estimates placed the sum at three hundred billion dollars. One previous leader had failed to make the big list, having only extracted six billion dollars to his Swiss bank account.

Such fabulous wealth and institutionalised lawlessness combined to make Reto's mission for the evening somewhat daunting. He stood next to an extravagantly dressed African in flowing robes reminiscent of Joseph's biblical coat of many colours. The man spoke with a supremely confident voice that oozed menace.

'Mr Reto, thank you for joining us here this evening.' They stood together on a viewing platform at the top of the Uetliberg Tower above Zurich. 'Your wife and children are enjoying a most pleasurable evening at our embassy. Their hospitality is, of course, assured by me personally.'

Reto's family had been guests at the Nigerian embassy, if indeed that was where they really were, for three days now.

Reto clenched and unclenched his fists. His knuckles ached. 'I have the financial instruments here in my case.' He indicated the titanium briefcase attached to his wrist by a chain and handcuff. 'The Central European Bank agrees to your terms. You have fifty billion in negotiable bonds and bullion receipts.'

At last the African cracked a smile. 'And you, Reto, my friend, you will have breakfast with your family tomorrow.' He pulled a mobile phone from the folds of his robes and barked several commands into it. 'Now let us enjoy the view, it's really great up here at night. You know, I will miss Switzerland.'

Reto was in no mood for small talk. The next ten minutes were spent in silence until Reto's phone issued a shrill ring. A friend from the Swiss military advised him his family were indeed safe and sound.

'Let us complete our business,' Reto said. He put his hand inside a jacket pocket for the handcuff key but found his arms in the grasp of two black suited bodyguards.

They forced him to the floor and held out his arm with the handcuff. There was a glint of starlight reflecting on metal and Reto saw a heavy machete raised high in the air.

'My God, no!' he shouted in desperation but it was too late. The machete sailed in an arc through the air towards his wrist and deftly cut through the chain.

'You know what, Reto? You are a very scared man. What did you think we would do? Cut off your hand in front of these cameras?' Edward Johnson waved his fingers at the CCTV system installed on the viewing platform.

Reto got to his feet and watched as the Nigerians rapidly descended seven flights of metal steps to the ground. The helicopter next to the tower started its engines and within one minute the fifty billion dollars were airborne. Reto took his phone again in a trembling hand and made a call to Thomas Thistlethwaite. It would take more than a Taser to stop these guys.

In just ten minutes the helicopter reached Zurich airport. A waiting limousine slid across the apron and pulled to a stop next to the chopper. The driver got out and held open one of the back doors for the party to enter. As they did so, each of them assumed an air of deference to the occupant of the rear seat. The long, dark, muscular car then sped out of the security gate.

Reaching speeds of up to two hundred kilometres per hour, the Nigerians headed north. A number of speed cameras flashed in the limousine's wake but diplomatic card holders are not in the habit of paying their fines.

The time was close to midnight and the Switzerland-Germany border post was normally unmanncd at such an hour. However, on this occasion, there was a heavy contingent of Swiss and German border police exchanging pleasantries. The limousine came to a halt and the driver let down his window, showing a diplomatic passport.

'Step out of the car,' the German officer said. The driver opened his door, stood out on the tarmac and opened his hands in a gesture of appeal. He was a big man but he fell like a sack of potatoes when the policeman's stick hit his knee.

The colourfully robed Edward Johnson emerged from the car, moving angrily towards the border guard who immediately dealt Johnson a stinging blow to the head. Four bodyguards burst out of the limousine, one brandishing a machine pistol.

On cue, a dozen Swiss soldiers jumped from the back of two parked military trucks. The commanding Swiss officer shouted a warning and the bodyguard started to replace his weapon in its holster. Without further dialogue the Swiss opened fire at close quarters, the commanding officer taking careful aim through the open rear door.

Thistlethwaite watched from behind the mirrored and bullet-proof glass of the border post. On a signal from the Swiss he came out into the night air and walked over to the car. Taking care not to get blood on his shoes, he reached inside the vehicle for the titanium briefcase. He had to prise it from the grasp of the late Nigerian President, Joseph Kano.

Thistlethwaite turned to the soldiers. 'Congratulations, you have intercepted one of the greatest bank thefts in history.'

By one a.m. he was lying on his executive bed in the Swissotel. He couldn't sleep. Once or twice he closed his eyes briefly but all he could see were pools of blood spreading across the tarmac.

Now it really was time to sleep. With concentration, he was able to apply discipline and invoke his mantra. He inhaled slowly and deeply, savouring the fresh fragrance of spring flowers that grew in the garden. On his tongue he could detect the tang of freshly mown lawn. Birds chattered in the branches of newly leafed trees, petals of blossom released onto the breeze. He walked down the gentle slope of the grass. A pebble bank came into view across which the river flowed, burbling like a brook. A few feet out from the edge the current was slower and large fish swam lazily, effortlessly. *Gardens beneath which rivers flow*. He fell into a deep and fulfilling slumber.

I'm only sleeping

The grass had grown long in the hot summer sun and seeds were spread at the top of the stems, ready to fall. It was a river meadow.

Greg lay on his back and gazed at the wispy clouds hanging high in the sapphire sky. Joe took another drag and passed the joint over.

Their portable cassette tape player pushed out a Beatles song. Wake up in the middle of a dream... close your eyes, drift downstream.

Down at the riverbank their boat tugged lightly at the mooring stakes the boys had driven down deep into the soft earth. A traditional narrow-boat chugged by, occupants exchanging a friendly wave of the hand with Greg and Joe.

Neither of the lads were regular smokers but they pulled long and steady on the carefully prepared smoke; this was a moment to savour for life.

A while later, it could have been half an hour or half a day, they moored up again just around a long, sandy bend in the river. Greg cooked up some rice and tinned stew on a small stove while Joe played skimming stones with a couple of children who had appeared on the small beach.

The little blonde girl had taken a shine to Joe. He told her she would break a few hearts when she was bigger but she didn't understand. After extracting a promise from the little girl to meet again in ten years, Joe rejoined Greg and they ate their meal, washed down with a few cans of Strongbow cider, the fashionable summer drink of choice.

A sudden hard blow struck Greg square on the forehead, shattering one of his favourite dream sequences.

He opened his eyes and found himself face to face with three year old Pete.

'I lie with you on your pillow?' the toddler asked.

'Yep, Daddy's pillow is best,' Greg said, encircling his son with his right arm.

A patter of small footsteps and Kate burst in through the door.

'Not fair, Pete always gets first cuddle!'

'Come and lie between us,' Rose said. 'Just for a few minutes. Daddy will bring you down to breakfast soon.' She threw a sleepy glance and a lopsided grin at Greg.

One hour later the kids were outside on their bikes, terrorising the neighbourhood. Rose came downstairs and joined Greg at the breakfast island in their kitchen. She was about to place her order when a mug of tea and a fried egg sandwich appeared as if by magic.

'Thanks for the lie-in. Your turn tomorrow.'

'You're welcome,' Greg said. 'You deserve it with such a runaway husband.' He gave a wide smile and ran a hand down Rose's back, over her silk nightdress.

'Tell me again what you told me last night. I seem to have forgotten bits of it together with that last glass of wine.'

'Well. My work project is dead in the water. I can stay with the company and we move to India. Alternatively I can strike out on my own and there's a potential financial backer in the form of some dodgy guy I keep bumping into.'

Rose recalled Greg's terrible illness from his last trip to India. He had lost about ten kilos within a few weeks. Not that it didn't have some benefits. He had fit into his wedding suit for the first time in years. But no, there had been some kind of parasitic infection and India was not for him or the family.

'Would you seriously consider branching out on your own again?' Rose asked. 'It didn't last very long last time. What would be different this time?'

'I really don't know. It depends on the financial security. There's a mortgage to pay, not to mention an extravagant wife and two starving kids.'

The children came flying into the garden on their bikes, followed by the neighbour's large hairy dog, thrashing its tail and barking loudly.

At that point the phone rang and Rose picked up.

'Some chap named Thomas, says he wants to go for beer.' Rose handed the phone to Greg.

He spoke for a few moments and then leaned over to Rose.

'Any chance of a pass out this evening? I know I've only just come back from my trip, but it's that guy I mentioned. Could be worth looking into.'

'You're on,' she laughed. 'But you owe me. Big time.'

'Great,' he replied.

'If he's a friend, like he says he is, then why not invite him to stay over?'

'We'll see. I'm sure he has a hotel room booked but I'll offer.'

At seven o'clock that evening Greg and Thomas met in front of the grandiose Kilkenny Castle. The light breeze of earlier had strengthened and blew cold spray from the fountain onto the last few remaining tourists posing for photos.

'How about a stroll?' Thomas said. 'The castle grounds would be better than the pub for a private chat.'

'But pub later, right?' Greg asked.

'Right.'

They completed two circuits of the one mile Castle Park during their hour long discussion.

From what Greg could gather, Thistlethwaite's employer wished to fund Greg's team, develop the prototype to a production model and make direct use of the final product. It was a fast track method for them to implement some infrastructure projects of key international importance. His project would be a key technological element.

Greg would receive a handsome executive salary, performance related annual bonuses and expenses for a contract period of five years. A share participation scheme would be open to all his team and he'd have substantial personal share options.

Full development, project and production resources would be supplied against a business plan that Greg had to submit for approval by the backer. Funds were effectively unlimited. Some five billion dollars had been budgeted for the infrastructure projects through to completion of an ambitious twenty installations within eighteen months. Further installations would follow if successful.

The project would be floated as a public company at the end of the five year term and the team members would likely become very wealthy as a result. Greg would retain the patent in his name and continue to receive licence fees.

It all sounded too good to be true. Maybe he was having one of his dreams. Walking into a tree branch overhanging the footpath, Greg realised from the very real pain in his eye that it wasn't a dream; he was very awake. And he badly needed a drink.

They walked to Langton's bar on John Street and drank to the future.

At two in the morning the two men found themselves out on the pavement as the bar closed up for the night.

'Greg, I'm not going to kid you. It'll be five years hard work. But your team will be contributing to the development of some of the most disadvantaged countries in the world. And you'll be a good catch for any woman with the money in your pocket.'

'I have the girl of my dreams.'

With a wave of the hand, Greg turned and started the uphill walk to his house where Rose was still waiting up for the news.

Thomas Thistlethwaite walked past the hotel entrance and turned up a side road, produced a key from his pocket and opened the front door of a three storey Victorian townhouse, singing a tune under his breath.

Tall and tan, and young and lovely, the girl from Ipanema goes walking, and when she passes each one she passes goes - ah.

The power within

One and a half weeks later the Special Projects Board of the Central European Bank watched Greg Marshall's business plan presentation with interest. Several sharp questions had already revealed weaknesses in his proposals.

'You need more work on your business concept, Mr Marshall,' one gentleman commented in a French accent.

Greg felt downcast. It had been a long time since he'd formulated a business plan.

'Luckily for you,' the Frenchman continued, 'we are more interested initially in bringing your technology to the implementation stage. We will help you with the business concept in due course. So please summarise again, for the board, the unique technical advantages of your project and the implications of these prototype tests.'

Greg took a deep breath and outlined the key points.

'We've perfected a prototype miniature electrical power generator. The module is small, about the size and shape of a... of a...cucumber.'

There were some chuckles from the board members. Greg tried to focus, recalling the prototypes he had placed in Itaipu and the Iguassu Falls, the resonance effect of the Guggenheim sculpture and those strange results from the Lissafjord.

'The unique piezoelectric components enable power generation from two renewable, environmentally friendly and natural sources. Water flow is the primary energy source. Change in pressure is the other. Prototype tests confirm each module is capable of generating an output power of one thousand Kilowatts, which is a million

Watts, enough to power ten thousand light bulbs of one hundred Watts.'

Greg looked around the table for approval but saw a few blank faces. They weren't all switched on yet. He persevered.

'Five hundred modules can be arranged in a formation covering an area of five hundred square metres. That will generate up to five hundred Megawatts, which is half a billion Watts. A superconductor loop is used to harness this power and feed the transmission grid.' There were a few shakes of the head that indicated lack of understanding. Surely it obvious to them by now?

'Mr Marshall, Greg, what is the production cost of each module?' an attractive Englishwoman asked.

'Around fifty thousand dollars. A formation of five hundred will cost…'

'Yes, twenty five million dollars. We are *bankers*, Mr Marshall,' a distinguished looking gentleman said.

Unperturbed by the bankers, Greg continued. 'With the superconductor loop and all necessary ancillaries, which unfortunately have to be conventional technology, we come to an additional cost of forty five million dollars. Estimating five million for civil works we can put half a Gigawatt of power on the grid for a total of…'

'Seventy five million dollars. That's one seventh of the price of any other kind of existing power technology. Stunning!' another board member said.

The room erupted into excited conversation.

Greg took the chance to survey his audience more closely now they were distracted. There were some twenty board members, eight of them women.

The chairman cleared his throat and the hubbub subsided.

'Mr Thistlethwaite, are these facts verified to your satisfaction?'

'They are, Mr Chairman,' Thomas said with a smile.

'In that case, Mr Marshall, we confirm our financial offer. You will receive our formal contract by the end of next week. We're sure you will find it very satisfactory for both yourself and your project team, in line with the preliminary discussions you have had with Mr Thistlethwaite. Your services are invaluable to our social plans. The river runs deep and strong at the foot of the garden of Africa, Mr Marshall.' The chairman glanced at the clock on the wall and concluded. 'We welcome you onboard. Thank you for your time.'

The board members showed their approval with a unified drumming of their knuckles on the surface of the massive walnut table.

Greg stood to leave and tried to execute a bow in his confusion. The secretary opened the door for him and Greg exited together with Thomas.

They took a seat on the marble bench in the corridor.

'Well, Greg, you pulled it off. Congratulations. After you've signed the contract I would advise you to take a month's holiday with your family because you're going to need it.'

At that moment the board secretary passed by, heading back to the boardroom. Greg looked up and saw the board members in a queue, rolling up their sleeves and waiting to wash their hands and wrists in a washbasin at the far end of the boardroom.

'What's that all about? MRSA? Compulsive cleanliness disorder?' Greg asked.

'No,' Thomas replied with a strange smile. 'Prayer time.'

Death comes creeping in

'How was the holiday?' James Conway asked Greg as they settled into their seats for the flight to Nairobi.

'Very relaxing. A leisurely coastal tour of the west, some time with the family and a bit of work on the house. Just in case we decide to rent it out.'

'Ah. So your wife still wants to come with you. As I said before, best to assess the lie of the land before you agree to that. You'll see what I mean,' Conway said.

James Conway was the Central European Bank project leader for Kenya. They had selected Kenya for the pilot project and that suited Greg very well. He hoped to get to see a lot more of his parents in their new home.

'Have you been to Africa before?' Conway asked.

'Only Egypt. Very different to sub-Saharan Africa, I guess?'

'Quite right. You'll be in for a big surprise.'

The flight was completely full. It wasn't what Greg had expected. The passengers didn't all look like European tourists going on a safari holiday. Couples of various ages and some entire families, all exuding nervous excitement. It seemed his parents were not the only immigrants destined for this part of the New Commonwealth.

On approach to Nairobi airport Greg could see the stunning snow-capped heights of Mount Kenya. He found it difficult to believe there were glaciers in East Africa.

The plane landed and opening the aircraft doors introduced a first smell of Africa, a heady mix of unfamiliar scents. Greg felt a thrill. A new life, totally different to that before. A brave new world. He could understand the attraction.

The passengers disembarked, cleared customs and proceeded to the luggage hall, all at a leisurely pace induced as much by wonderment as the climate. In the arrivals hall Greg noticed there were many Kenyan porters. All wore brown uniforms with a plastic envelope hanging from the breast pocket.

'What's all that about?' he asked Conway.

'Certificates. Each must display his or her certificate in order to work in the airport.' Noticing Greg's confusion he explained further. 'HIV certificates. Each worker must be certified free of HIV. The certificate is valid for one month. Big business these days, HIV testing.'

Greg felt his first misgivings. He'd heard the incidence of HIV in Africa generally was pretty high but hadn't really expected it to be such a visible issue in Kenya.

One of the porters brought their cases to the pre-booked hire car. Conway tipped the man with a hundred Kenyan shillings, a little over one US dollar.

'That's why these airport jobs are prized, why they keep themselves clean. They can earn more in a day in airport tips than the average monthly Kenyan salary.'

The tone of Conway's comment made Greg uneasy.

'Why didn't we take a taxi?' Greg asked.

'Not many of them around these days. Most of the able-bodied adults are working on the infrastructure projects. Much better pay than taxi driving. Also many of our new arrivals elect to drive themselves, they're used to it.'

Greg looked around at the traffic and realised Conway was right. About ninety percent of vehicles were being driven by Europeans and the predominantly Japanese brands were all current models, as was their four-wheel drive rental.

Within a couple of minutes the climate control of the big Mitsubishi had stabilised at twenty-two degrees and Greg sank into the leather upholstery, drifting into sleep. He awoke some time later with a start and thought it must be a dream. The modern buildings of Nairobi had given way to a strange rambling assortment of wooden structures lining both sides of the road.

'We're in the townlands outside Nairobi,' Conway said, noticing Greg had woken.

'And those boxes,' Greg said, indicating the many different coloured long wooden crates that stood upended against the buildings. 'Are they…'

'Coffins? Yes. This is the undertaker townland for the northern sector. Still a brisk trade at the moment, although business is dying off.'

Greg stared wide-eyed out of the window. Vendors and customers were in conversation on the front porches of the buildings. White seemed to be the most popular colour of coffin. Some of the designs were quite similar to those favoured in Europe. Others were simple, plain rectangular boxes.

After a few minutes they passed out of the undertaker townland and through what looked like squatter areas and slum lands. There was no sign of life.

Without warning a shadow flew at their vehicle from the side of the road. Conway was unable to avoid hitting whatever it was and the car shook from the impact. Greg watch in horror as a human form rose up over the bonnet, hit the windscreen and rolled back over the roof. Conway stopped the car.

'Shit!' said Conway. 'Look at that!' He pointed to the crack in the windscreen. 'Good job we have those bull bars on the front or we'd have had some damage to the headlights as well. Can't drive this road at night without lights.'

Greg was clambering into the back seat, trying to see what had happened to the pedestrian. When the dust cleared he saw an inert form lying on the ground behind their Mitsubishi. It was a boy of perhaps fifteen years old, sparsely clad. Blood pooled on the tarmac next to the boy's head and his legs were a tangled mess. Greg reached for the door handle but the central locking was on.

'For God's sake open up! We have to see if we can help!'

'This is Africa, Greg. Nairobi townlands. That boy ran straight at us with a death wish. Getting near his blood is not a good idea. Hold on, I'll make an emergency call.'

Conway pulled out his mobile phone and started to drive away. They'd gone half a kilometre before the call was answered.

'Sanitary department please. Yep, northern squatter camp, just outside the undertaker townland. Teenage boy hit by vehicle, appears to be dead. Okay, thanks. Bye.' He finished the call and turned to Greg who was shaking his head in disbelief. 'Greg, things probably look pretty bad to you right now. You'll adapt through necessity. It won't be like this forever.'

Greg wondered what he had got himself into.

They drove on, occasionally meeting other vehicles, all four-wheel drives moving at deadly speed. Greg was in shock. He'd seen accidents before. One time in Istanbul a small street urchin had been knocked down by a car on the motorway. The child's home bordered the carriageway and children routinely ran across the traffic. On that occasion the vehicles had come to a halt and the driver involved was clearly distressed, as were the onlookers, where the child lay motionless on the tarmac as if fallen asleep. That he could deal with, life had some value there. But here was different.

As the dark night streamed past the car window he envisaged some kind of Orwellian nightmare in which Kenya had an underclass of HIV sufferers whose lives were devalued, forfeit even.

An hour or so later they entered the limits of a small town some sixty miles north of Nairobi. Conway consulted his written directions and found their way into a leafy suburb with handsome houses on large plots.

The long gravel drives of each house were gated and they pulled up at one of them. Conway pressed a button and spoke into a microphone panel. Greg could see a security camera scanning their vehicle. There was some dialogue with the loudspeaker and the gate rolled back behind a hedge. Conway drove inside and towards a Kenyan who was standing illuminated by the soft glow of lamps in the entrance porch.

Their luggage was unloaded from the car by the Kenyan. Greg noticed the guy also wore a certificate on the chest.

'Your mother's a doctor, I understand,' Conway said to Greg as they walked up to the house.

'Yes, retired.'

It had been more than a year since Greg had seen his mother and father. They looked tanned but tired. There were embraces and kisses that overstepped the boundaries of normal British reserve. He sensed some tension in his mother's shoulders. His father, on the other hand, seemed slightly drunk. Greg introduced Conway.

'Nice to meet you, James. Please call me Derek,' Greg's father said.

'And I'm Bernie,' Greg's mother added. 'Thanks for safely delivering our son.'

'You're welcome,' Conway replied. 'And thanks in advance for letting me stay in your house. It's a very convenient stop en route to the project site.'

They went inside to escape the mosquitoes buzzing hungrily around their ears. Derek led them into a large, cool sitting room furnished with dark green leather chairs and sofas.

'Can I get you a drink?' he asked.

Greg requested a gin and tonic, Conway a malt whisky with water. Derek reappeared shortly with a tray.

'Kenneth prepares the drinks but your father prefers to serve them to new guests on the first occasion,' Bernie said.

Greg and his mother were old drinking buddies. But he was astonished to see his father take a whisky with soda.

'Dad, I don't think I've ever seen you drink spirits before. What's going on?'

'Quite a few things have changed here, Greg,' Bernie answered for her husband. 'You'll be surprised at how different our life is now.'

The group exchanged idle chat about the day's journey and weather developments in Scotland. Greg's suspicion about his father's drunkenness was confirmed when, after the first drinks were finished, his father made his excuses and staggered off to a bedroom. Conway also expressed a desire to get some sleep and Kenneth showed him to a guest room.

Calmed by his gin and tonic, which contained a very generous amount of gin, Greg settled down for a chat with his mother. Kenneth disappeared to fetch more drinks.

'Tell me, Mum. How do you like life here in Kenya?'

'Still in the process of settling down,' Bernie replied.

'But you've been here for nearly a year now. Tell me about the differences between life here and Scotland.'

'Well, one major difference is your father enjoys the occasional drink these days which, as you know, he never used to. That's his way of coping.'

'Coping? Coping with what?'

'Coping with death.'

'What do you mean?'

'The AIDS situation here. It's totally out of control.'

Bernie took a swig of her gin and tonic.

'But I thought HIV here was a decreasing problem?'

Greg knew, as he said it, that what he'd seen already in Kenya suggested otherwise.

'Current official HIV prevalence amongst Kenyan adults is *twenty* percent,' his mother said, ever the doctor. 'That's just counting people who go for treatment.'

'Why wouldn't people get treated? Aren't the retroviral drugs free?'

'The drugs are free but treatment isn't. One injection costs one month's salary for the average Kenyan. A lot of people just can't afford treatment.'

Greg thought back to the car accident earlier that night, the poverty of the township and Conway's take on the value of life there.

'So what's the real picture then, Mum?'

'Pretty grim. Real HIV prevalence is estimated at over forty percent. In some sectors of society it could be eighty percent. Even allowing for the high birth rate, they're losing twenty percent of the indigenous population each year. It's risen to this rate over the past five years. The total population of native Kenyans is down fifty percent compared to the turn of the century. Another couple of years of this and they'll be a small minority in their own country.'

'Blimey! How many Europeans are here now, then?' Greg asked.

'Your father estimates about one million, mostly British. Greg, it's not just that…'

'What, Mum?'

'They're dying in front of us, every day. People fall down dead on the street in front of you when you walk through town. In the slums they're piled on barrows.'

'Are you at risk, you and Dad?'

'All British subjects are prescribed prophylactic medicines to prevent accidental contraction of HIV. We have to inject ourselves daily, your father and I. But the worse thing of all is HIV positive lives mean nothing here. Absolutely nothing. After one year I'm numb to it but your father still gets upset. Last weekend we hit another one with the car. That's the fourth time.'

'Oh, Mum, I had no idea.'

'We came here in the twilight of our lives at the suggestion of the British government. There are incentives, you know, generous incentives for pensioners to emigrate here. But we're surrounded by death.'

'God, how awful. I admired you both for making the decision to come here. I really had no idea.'

'Most of the men have taken to drinking. Your father spends a lot of time at the local bar with his new cronies and nothing would get done around here if it wasn't for Kenneth. In a couple of years I'm sure it'll settle down but Kenya will have changed so much. It's not what I wanted, Greg,' she sobbed. 'It's supposed to be a brave new world, but it's not what I wanted.'

He reached out and hugged his mother. 'A brave new world, Mum,' he whispered gently. 'A brave new world.'

Power flows

Peter Abrams, President of Kenya, stood on the bank of the Nzoia River, surveying the men at work on the power project. He had a frown on his face.

Greg and Conway stood either side of Abrams and wondered at the excavations for the project. An area of one thousand square meters had been turned into what the men called the dry dock. They could see the sandy river bed from their vantage point. On the far side of the dock the river's diverted waters rushed through an alternative channel of forty meters width, excavated for the purpose.

'When we were developing the micro-generators I never envisaged I'd actually get to see this,' Greg said.

They descended a ladder down the inside of a fifteen foot steel wall. Greg stamped his feet on the dry river bed. He reached down and grasped a handful of the sand. The top surface was dry but there was moisture below. Greg looked up and saw four bodyguards had stationed themselves close to the President.

'We have pumps below the sand to keep out the water,' Conway explained. 'We're several meters below the water table here. It'd refill like a giant swimming pool within seconds if the pumps were to fail. Already happened five times and we lost men. Most of the workers can't swim.'

Greg and Abrams looked at each other and then at the bodyguards.

A number of thick metal posts protruded from the sand. The river bed itself was marked out into a thousand squares of one meter each.

'Those are the supporting posts for the superconductor loop. They're fixed into the bedrock. Each of these meter squares will also have a mounting rod for its individual micro-generator. We're trying out different alloys for the rods to get the right combination of flexibility and durability as they'll be subject to considerable stress.'

The walkie-talkie on Conway's belt crackled a message.

'We have to go,' he said, leading them back to the ladder. They started to climb without further encouragement.

As Greg reached the top of the ladder a warning siren sounded. He looked down and saw the dock begin to fill with water at an alarming rate. It flooded up out of the sand like a giant filling a bucket.

The last of the bodyguards was caught by surprise and nearly swept away by the swirling eddies of water in the dock. He had to be hauled out by his colleagues, black suit wrinkled and dripping wet, clinging to his body.

Conway continued with his discourse as if nothing had happened.

'This pilot installation is expected to generate one Gigawatt of electricity. That's more than enough for the region at present rates of consumption, so we'll be able to put up to fifty percent of the power onto the new national power grid for use elsewhere in the country, mainly the capital of course.'

Abrams turned to Greg and spoke in a perfect English accent.

'Mr Marshall, your invention is enabling us to produce this power at an amazingly low cost. I just want you to know how much we appreciate your work.'

'Please, Mr Abrams, call me Greg. It's a pleasure and an honour to be able to contribute to your country's development.'

'You may call him *Mr President*,' a dark voice spoke quietly into Greg's ear.

Abrams held up his hand. 'They're very particular about forms of address. It comes from so many years of autocracy. I have to play the lord a little from time to time to satisfy them. *Professor Abrams* will suffice.'

Greg had the distinct impression he was conversing with an African university professor rather than a head of state.

They bid Abrams farewell and the presidential cavalcade left the compound.

~

The presidential limousine charged down the road in a cloud of dust, preceded and followed by two large black SUVs. After some ten miles the convoy was passing through a deserted looking squatter town when a popping sound came from one of the wheels of the limousine. The SUVs pulled to a halt and a bodyguard, jumping out and quickly inspecting the tyres of the limousine, gestured to the limousine co-driver that a change of wheel would be necessary.

The President's guard, eight in total, positioned themselves in formation around the vehicles and kept a nervous watch. Sweat broke on their brows above the mirrored sunglasses as their black suits absorbed the midday sun's heat.

The wheel had just been removed when a commotion arose from the front of the convoy. Several street urchins had approached two of the bodyguards and were pleading for money, cigarettes, anything. The rest of the President's bodyguard looked around nervously. It was an AIDS squatter town, known to be inhabited by former development project workers who had failed the monthly HIV test and been discharged from the payroll.

Things started to get ugly with the urchins. Blows were exchanged and one of the boys produced a bladed weapon, slicing into the buttock of one of the bodyguards. The men moved to support their colleagues at the front but the one who had instructed Greg on the correct address for the president barked a command, making them hold ranks. He alone moved to the front and sent the boy with the blade sprawling with a well aimed kick to the chest.

At that moment the squatter camp erupted. Men and women poured out from underneath makeshift roofs, streaming towards the halted vehicles. The head bodyguard took immediate action and shouted instructions, withdrawing a machine pistol from a holster underneath his jacket and repositioning himself next to the presidential limousine. The others followed example and drew their firearms.

A curtain of bullets felled the attacking squatters in waves. Bodies fell twitching on top of one another. At the front of the convoy a machine pistol jammed in the bloodied hands of the man who had been sliced with the weapon and several assailants lunged for him, only to be cut down in mid stride by the pistol of another bodyguard. But it wasn't enough to cancel the attackers' momentum and they fell forwards. The body of one crashed into the injured guard, knocking him face down onto the ground and landing, blood gushing, on top of him.

All was quiet around the cavalcade. The wheel of the limousine had in the meantime been replaced. A groan emerged from the front of the convoy. The bodyguard who had fallen picked himself up and was staring at his own suit, drenched with the blood of the squatter who had felled him. Then he held out his hands and let out a scream. His own blood and that of the squatter were indistinguishable on his hands, jacket and trousers, on his wounds.

The head bodyguard moved forward to his injured colleague. Everyone knew the rules. There could be no incidence of HIV or AIDS permitted within the presidential sector of Nairobi or within five hundred meters of His Excellency whilst travelling. Members of the

President's Guard remained personally clear of HIV on pain of death. Considering all the blood and the open wound, it was inevitable the injured man would now be infected.

With a sob, the blood-soaked man dropped to his knees and bowed his head. It was the bodyguard who had nearly drowned in the dry dock. Each of the others clasped their hands together and bowed their heads in respect.

'Patrick, we will look after your family. You go to meet your ancestors. Lord have mercy on us all.'

The head of the Presidential Guard raised his machine pistol and fired a single shot into the top of the kneeling man's skull.

Within thirty seconds the cavalcade was speeding onwards to Nairobi. Professor Peter Abrams shivered in the back of the air-conditioned limousine. The head of the President's Guard handed him a blanket, glanced down and noticed, with disgust, that the President of Kenya had once again wet his pants.

Perimeter

A row of four small TV screens showed the front and rear entrance to the property and two views of an eight foot high fence.

'The top of that fence is electrified with six kilovolts. The main body of the fence is connected to low voltage so the system can detect any breakage.'

There was a single red bulb flashing amongst a bank of twenty or so lights on a control panel.

'We had a breakage in the fence yesterday and it needs repair. The company can't come out until tomorrow so we need to be extra vigilant tonight.'

A further row of TV screens showed a panning view of the external walls of the house taken from the upstairs balconies.

'There are motion sensors which detect any moving heat source within ten meters of the main building. That will sound the main alarm. It's fairly basic stuff but the retina recognition on the access gates makes it state of the art.'

'Very impressive, Dad,' Greg said.

'You're probably thinking it looks like we're preparing for a siege.'

'Well, yes. It all looks a bit like overkill to me.'

'Greg, your mother and I, well, we appreciate a little extra security these days. There are still a few unsavoury characters out there and, until the government has rounded them up, we need a few extra precautions.'

'You'll find this fairly typical in the suburbs,' Conway interjected. 'The general consensus is it'll cease to be necessary within a year to eighteen months.'

'Now I see what you mean about perhaps waiting a while before bringing over Rose and the kids,' Greg said.

They moved out onto the veranda where Bernie was enjoying her gin and tonic in the twilight. Insects chirped a soothing African chorus in the gloom.

An intermittent buzzing sound from the security room went unnoticed by them, but not by Kenneth. He took a look at the TV screens and ran upstairs, grabbing something from a cabinet behind the door.

Then the main alarm went off. There was no ignoring it, the siren howled and floodlights lit up the lawns surrounding the house. Greg saw a silhouette just beyond the edge of the light and was stunned by the retort of two consecutive shotgun blasts from the balcony above. The silhouette lay prone on the grass.

As Kenneth reloaded, another shadow emerged into the floodlight and came running straight towards them, wielding the ubiquitous machete. Without hesitation, Conway drew a pistol from beneath his jacket, took quick aim and fired three times. The attacker fell to her knees then pitched headlong into the grass.

At the same time shots were heard coming from the balcony on the other side of the house. Kenneth had run through the bedrooms to deal with the incursion there.

Greg hadn't moved from his chair, but his parents were nowhere to be seen. He found them inside, his mother wrapped in his father's arms.

'It's not the first time, Son,' Derek said.

'What the hell were they after?' Greg asked.

'Who knows?' Conway said, coming in from the veranda. 'Thieves? Supporters of the last president? Or maybe just desperate AIDS victims looking for food and money. Anyway, problem solved. The security company will be here within half an hour. Emergency callout.'

'I'm sorry, Greg,' Bernie said, pulling herself together. 'It's not the killing. I just can't get used to the sound of gunfire.'

Greg looked at his parents. These were not the meek and gentle people who had emigrated from Scotland. He had an idea.

'Mum, Dad. How about a trip to Ireland to see your grandchildren?'

Flood gates

Two days later they landed in Dublin. It was the early hours after a long delay in Frankfurt. Greg's old Honda was parked at the airport and they were soon hurtling through the darkness down country. At that time of night he could cover the eighty mile trip in less than an hour, thanks to the new motorway link.

Greg listened to the radio. Weather news predicted a high tide at the weekend. The new Dublin tidal barriers at the mouth of the River Liffey wouldn't be ready for another eighteen months, some thirty years after London's flood barriers had first been erected.

Bernie dozed in the back of the car, lulled to sleep by the soothing hum of the engine. Derek talked incessantly. He was pleased to be away from Kenya and was holding discourse on the relative merits of Saab and Volvo turbo engines when Greg interrupted him.

'Dad, why exactly did you and Mum decide to move to Kenya?'

'Quite a number of reasons. Twenty years of retirement in Scotland and it was getting colder every year. Floods in the good weather, snowed in during the winter. It all affected your mother's sinus problem and made her life miserable.'

'How's that new tidal barrier on the River Clyde holding up?'

'A great improvement. It's only needed during extra high tides but the barrier stops coastal roads flooding. The motorway was actually closed for two days last year due to floods. That's certainly a twenty-first century phenomenon.' Derek liked to talk about the good old days of last century.

'But why didn't you just move back down south?'

'Well, the weather there isn't really much better these days. Then there's the price of property; we couldn't afford a shoe box in the south. East Anglia would have been a nice, cheap place to retire but the fenlands are mostly under water these days and all those pretty coastal towns we used to visit, when you and your brother were little, are pretty much wiped out. There are no coastal roads left. All of that was always just a few feet above sea level.'

Greg remembered those coastal towns and fenlands when he was a child. Sometimes the car park at the quayside would be knee deep in water for days and the holiday caravan park would become a massive shallow lake in which the static caravans stood raised up on concrete blocks.

'Well, you can put up barriers on a river mouth but you can't build a barrier along an entire coastline.'

'I don't see why not,' Derek said. 'The Dutch did it with their polders and dykes and what have you. Most of their land was reclaimed, although I know they've lost a lot again in the last five years. No, I think those English coastal areas were considered dispensable. Very few people lived there and the holiday trade had gone abroad decades earlier.'

'Well, how about the places you considered when you first retired?'

'You mean sunny Spain or the south of France? The Mediterranean is no guarantee of good weather these days. Even the oranges don't grow properly in Seville any more.'

Rain lashed the windscreen and Greg switched on the wipers.

'So how did this holiday trend towards Africa start?'

'With all the growing interest in the environment, people started to go on discovery holidays. I remember the ads on the TV starting up. Energetic types hiking up Kilimanjaro. Then there were retired folks enjoying an idyllic lifestyle with wild animals in the background. All the low cost airlines offering direct flights to Tanzania and Kenya, two countries that both speak English. They even have the same electrical plugs as we have in the UK. It was easy.'

'Colonial habits die hard,' Greg said .

They exited the motorway. The rain had stopped but the wind outside had risen and it buffeted the car as they snaked around the bends on the link road to Kilkenny city.

'Okay, so the climate was enticing, the scenery was scenic and the animals were wild. But what about the poverty and what about the HIV situation?'

'Well, you don't see poverty and HIV when you take that type of holiday.'

'And how did you afford the move?' Greg asked as they pulled up in front of his family home. He knew his parents weren't wealthy. Their early retirement had been at the expense of a very modest pension and he was surprised they could even have afforded African discovery holidays.

'Ah, that,' Derek said and let out a sigh. 'Well, how can I put it? They virtually paid us to go. First they gave us the holidays. Free for pensioners. Next they gave us the house for nearly nothing, and then they paid us to move our lives there.'

~

In the morning Derek and Bernie slept in late in the guest bedroom. When Rose and the kids returned from church the children bolted up the stairs and jumped all over their grandparents. Greg could hear them from his home office next door. He didn't go to mass, it wasn't his thing, and he had a bit of household administration to take care of before the business trip the following week.

'Grandma,' Kate said, 'why didn't you come to see Holy God? You usually do!' Kate was indignant with her septuagenarian grandmother. Greg was eavesdropping. Originally his parents were Catholic but they had been non-denominational since soon after retirement and wouldn't normally miss a Sunday visit to a Christian church of any persuasion.

'Katherine, darling, Grandma and Grandad don't believe…'

'Grandma and Grandad were too tired this morning,' Derek interrupted. 'I hope you said a prayer for us.'

'Of course I did,' Kate said. 'Dear God, please keep Grandma and Grandad alive for ever,' she said, hands pressed together.

'An Jeesus, don't let 'em die at all!' little Pete added, jumping knees first onto his grandfather's chest.

Down in the breakfast room Greg decided to probe a little. The kids were happily watching TV in the sitting room and Rose was taking a turn around the garden.

'So, what's the story with the church thing, Dad?'

'How do you mean?' his father replied.

'Well, in all the times you've visited, today's the first time you missed church with the kids. And I know you were both up early because so was I and you were spotted doing your Tai Chi form in the sitting room.'

Bernie looked at Derek and he cleared his throat.

'Your mother and I, well, we have different beliefs now. Beliefs that don't need a fixed religious denomination.'

'Something you picked up in Africa?'

'No, it started before we left. It's an irresistible truth, full of promise,' Bernie said.

Greg found her answer disturbing as sincerity was not one of his mother's regular traits.

'Right, well, um, you'll have to tell me more sometime,' Greg said, seeing Rose on her way back in from the garden.

'There's plenty of time,' Derek replied. 'You'll see it yourself, soon enough.'

Rose entered the breakfast room.

'It's chilly out there. So the reason you guys didn't join us at mass is you've taken up Kenyan voodoo, right?' She beamed a smile at her in-laws.

No, not voodoo, Greg thought. Something far more dangerous.

Down by the banks

Reto Hersperger looked around him and saw an elite.
Private banking organisations from around the world were
represented by the financial equivalent of aristocracy.
Some of them actually carried titles of nobility. Their
future lay in the hands of the austere bureaucrats seated on
the other side of the massive walnut boardroom table.

'Gentlemen,' a small, elderly Belgian man said, turning
to look each of the private bankers individually in the eye.
'As you know, we are a pan-European organisation set up
by EU legislation with the prime objective to redistribute
wealth in underprivileged countries, the victims of
systematic corruption.'

His audience nodded and each felt the scrutiny of
twenty pairs of eyes from the other side of the table.

'You have been the custodians of this diverted wealth
and I congratulate you on the prudent handling and
investment of the funds. The nature of your advice to your
clients has been, so to say, in the interests of maximising
those funds within your care and, as such, you have served
all parties well.'

There were a few politely raised eyebrows amongst the
elite. Who would expect any other kind of custodian
behaviour from the bankers of Luxembourg, Switzerland
and Lichtenstein?

'Needless to say, the transfer of the bulk of these funds
to our Central European Bank has depleted your reserves
and we have made guarantees to ensure your creditors do
not call in their notes.' At this the faces on the other side of
the table became grave. 'And, now, true to our word, I can
confirm the funds will be returned to your stewardship

forthwith and we would ask you to administer the funding of new infrastructure projects that have been initiated in those disadvantaged countries.'

There was a murmur of assent from the bureaucrats' side and one of relief from the group opposite.

'We ask you to continue in your prudent investment approach with these funds, of which we are the legal guardian. There will be high-return investment opportunities in the infrastructure projects and growth benefits for all.'

A few crooked smiles cracked the faces of the elite.

'We must remember it has not been a painless journey and there may have to be further sacrifices before we reach a situation of financial and political tranquillity in the disadvantaged states.'

Many in the room closed their eyes in reaction to this statement. Reto alone could claim a hand in the death of twenty men in pursuit of justified repatriation of funds.

'Let the blood be shed of the unjust who oppose our search for tranquillity, and may those who let the blood not be castigated,' the Chairman recited.

'Let them not be castigated,' the bureaucrats echoed.

Some of the elite exchanged momentary perplexed glances. Reto, however, was not fazed. He understood perfectly well what was going on. But he found no absolution in the mantra.

Zurich, four hours later. The board of Reto's private bank gratefully received his personal affirmation that the funds would be returning to their care. Just a small matter of some two hundred billion dollars, representing the combined extracted wealth of the New British Commonwealth States in Africa.

Reto exuded confidence to his patrons. He had never doubted the Central European Bank would continue their relationship. There had been personal assurances from key individuals in the British administration. Nevertheless, he felt some relief his lavish lifestyle and sensational financial bonuses would continue.

Simultaneously, comparable meetings were being held at other locations in Zurich, Geneva, Lichtenstein and Luxembourg. The scale of the wealth involved was astounding. It gratified Reto the financial investment expertise of the private banking elite would continue to be utilised. This time, however, the product would be a programme of essential African infrastructure projects instead of a procession of luxury limousines, yachts and palaces for the exclusive use of murderous dictators and their families. So why didn't he feel good about it?

After the meeting Reto took a walk around the town to clear his head. He was mulling over the new, altruistic aspects of private banking when, distracted, he walked straight into a man standing in his path.

'You're getting a little careless, old chap.' Thomas Thistlethwaite placed a hand on the shoulder of his friend's immaculately tailored suit. 'What say we make a little visit to your friend Svetlana?'

'Ah, Thomas. Exactly what I had in mind.' In fact Reto had not seen Svetlana for nearly a week and was missing the company of his Transylvanian lover. So much so, he'd been seriously considering extricating her from the Prince's Club and installing her in a luxury apartment as his mistress. He shared this thought with Thomas.

'For God's sake man, you're married with kids,' Thomas said. Secretly, he was envious of the income that enabled such an idea but it also offended his old fashioned English sense of marital fidelity.

'Thomas, I love my children deeply. But you know very well that Jacqueline and I, well, it was to bring the families together. We've never really had anything that would resemble what you had with Natalie.' Reto looked at his friend's face. Reminding Thomas about his family was rarely a good start to an evening. 'In fact, Jacqueline has been having a liaison with her Austrian friend for some time. We tolerate each other. Nothing more.'

How the other half live, Thomas thought. His envy was rapidly diminishing.

At the Prince's Club they found Svetlana to be in an agitated state. It didn't bode well for Reto's proposal.

'Darling, you're far too dangerous a man to be exclusively associated with,' the tall Romanian said in a husky voice.

Reto considered other people to be the dangerous ones and told Svetlana so.

'No, honey, you misunderstand me. There have been bad men in here during the last few days, looking for you and your Englishman.'

'They were Nigerians,' Sophie added as she slipped onto the couch next to Thomas. Despite himself, Thomas couldn't deny a tingle of electricity as the tall South African ran her finger along his thigh.

'Thanks for your concern,' Thomas said, 'but it's probably just a misunderstanding about a small sum of money.'

'Well, we had the Polizei run them out of here,' Sophie said. 'Those kind of Africans carry something more deadly than guns and we don't take that kind of risk.'

The champagne arrived and the mood started to lighten, at least for the girls.

'Anything to worry about, Thomas?' Reto said, leaning over to toast his friend.

'Possibly. We need to increase our vigilance.'

Thomas was concerned. He hadn't received any information of Nigerian operatives on the prowl in Zurich. Somehow they had slipped through the net. Or else they had already left the country again.

Several bottles of champagne later, the girls had given up trying to lure Thomas upstairs, although they came close. Sophie could be very persuasive.

The two men left the club, stepping out towards the river and across to the Altstadt where Reto's second apartment was located. It served him as a kind of bachelor den.

Reto had a feeling they were being shadowed and said as much to Thomas who indicated everything was under control.

Once in the Altstadt they turned up a steep cobbled alleyway and their pace slowed with the gradient. Thomas glanced up the hill and, seeing two silhouettes outlined against the moonlit sky, steered Reto into an adjacent side alley. Behind them hurried steps could be heard in pursuit.

They pressed up against the stone wall. Thomas held a finger to his lips. A few seconds later two large African men moved swiftly past them down the narrow street.

Emerging from the doorway, Reto and Thomas turned back to the original steep alley and continued up the hill. They were near the top when they heard movement again and, glancing behind, saw three Africans starting to run up the alley towards them. The faces of the men weren't visible but they moved with menace.

Reto was now regretting the third bottle of champagne and wondered if Thomas was sharing this feeling of helplessness. They faced back uphill and contemplated flight, only to find the first two men had circled around and were standing at the top of the alley. One of them pulled a firearm from inside his jacket, the other a long bladed weapon.

'Thomas, I guess you have some bright ideas at this point?' Reto said. But he was surprised to see his friend in an apparent trance.

Thomas could see Natalie, Hannah and Matt in silhouette. They were waving to him, the same wave as the last time he saw them on that final blood-soaked day in Uganda. Then they faded away.

'Thomas, don't leave me now.'

In one swift movement Thomas pulled his pistol from his holster, took careful aim at the two shadowy figures at the top of the alley and felled them both with two gentle retorts from the silenced barrel of his weapon.

Reto was still looking at the bodies when he heard a sequence of muffled shots behind him and turned to see the three pursuers below slump to the ground.

Blue lights flashed briefly at each end of the alley and, within seconds, the bodies were lifted into waiting police vans by men emerging from the shadows.

Reto let out the breath he had been holding unawares. Thomas clapped him once again on the shoulder.

'Reto, you're precious to us, to me, my friend. You need have no fear, we're always watching out for you.'

Twenty-five souls, Reto thought.

Heart to heart

With Bernie and Derek still staying in Kilkenny, Greg and Rose took full advantage of their offer of baby-sitting to go unwind and release some of the tension that had been building. A stroll downhill in the mild evening air brought them to a new hotel bar they had been meaning to try out.

Rose ordered a glass of white wine and Greg went for a pint of Smithwicks.

Their drinks had the relaxing effect they sought and the expected topic of conversation arose.

'Just how happy are your parents in Kenya?' Rose asked.

Greg's parents hadn't opened up to her on the way their lives had altered but she sensed from the tense demeanour of her normally mellow in-laws that something had changed radically.

He contemplated how to deal with the conversation. On one hand he didn't want to alarm his wife with the true account of British immigrant life in Kenya. On the other he guessed she would propose the family join him over there during his project work.

'Well, they're not entirely happy. To be honest, I think they've made another one of their mistakes with this move to Kenya. It was probably too early.'

'What do you mean?' Rose said. 'What's too early? They're in their seventies and life's too short for waiting.'

Life's too short Greg thought. He had no desire to bring his family into a country where death of a stranger on the bumper of your car or in your back garden was commonplace. At the same time he didn't want Rose worrying about his personal safety during the project.

'Let me put it this way.' Rose narrowed her eyes, sensing he was about to be economical with the truth. 'Kenya is still pretty unstable, like a lot of other African countries at the moment. Well, that's what Thomas tells me. Kenya needs to establish a new constitution and further develop their infrastructure in order to have the standard of living I would want for our family.'

Greg had hit the right spot. Rose was keen on a reasonable standard of living and would trust his judgement.

'Well, I guess, your parents did live on a boat for three years. I could never have done it. So me and the kids won't be coming over just yet then,' Rose decided.

'Not for a while yet,' Greg said. He thought of his recent experiences in Bilbao and then Nairobi. How could he reconcile them with the innocence of Pete and Kate. And, for that matter, Rose.

'They'll tough it out,' Greg said. 'If the Scottish weather didn't kill them then the Kenyan climate is unlikely to do so.'

The barman served and they raised their glasses to each other once again.

'What I am concerned about, however, is the religion thing.'

'You? Concerned about religion?' Rose tittered into her wineglass.

'Not me personally, but Mum and Dad's change of attitude. Something Dad said the other day, sounded positively evangelistic. But I can't quite pin it down.'

'Perhaps they've joined some kind of religious cult for retirees? It wouldn't be the strangest thing they've ever done.'

'Very true.'

Greg was wondering if he should share some of his own strange recent experiences with her when a familiar face appeared at the door.

'Hey, Thomas! Fancy meeting you here. What a coincidence!'

Rose eyed her husband. It looked like their night out together was turning into a business meeting.

'Thomas, allow me to introduce my wife, Rose.'

Thomas Thistlethwaite took Rose's hand. For a moment it looked like he would kiss it. Rose's eyes took on a predatory slant.

Greg reconciled himself to an evening of Rose's famous flirting. At least he was off the hook regarding their 'chance' meeting.

'Rose, delighted to meet you at last,' Thomas said. 'I must apologise for dragging your husband out of the country so often, but he's really rather a clever chap and slightly indispensable, if you'll forgive the oxymoron.'

'I forgive the oxymoron on a regular basis,' Rose said, looking at Greg.

Greg couldn't decide whether to respond to the flattery or the insult, or to just interrupt the intercourse. However, what happened next diverted his thought train.

A cool breeze entered the bar from the door, causing them all to turn. A tall, slim woman approached with a gentle, unconscious shake of her long dark hair. Her face had an eastern European look and there was something very knowing in the glance she gave first to Greg and then to Thomas.

'Allow me to introduce my friend. Rose, Greg, this is Svetlana,' Thomas said.

'Is she a *vampire*?' Rose whispered to her husband.

'Svetlana, great to see you again.' Greg leant forward and gave the girl three kisses on alternate cheeks in the Swiss style.

'A friend of Lars,' he whispered back to Rose, whose arms were crossed.

Rose took a deep breath and, with a sly wink at Thomas, reached forward and enveloped Svetlana in a friendly embrace that teased the men. 'Svetlana, welcome to Kilkenny.'

'Right then, where's dinner?' Thomas said.

They enjoyed a further drink at the bar and headed for Pordylo's restaurant in the Butter Slip.

Champagne and oysters, two beautiful women and the best Mediterranean food in Kilkenny. For a couple of hours Greg managed to forget the blood-soaked townlands of Africa.

On the run

They awoke in separate beds. The first thought that went through his aching head was it had been a great night. Then he recalled stumbling home through the cobbled streets of Kilkenny, Svetlana leaning on him and sometimes he on her.

He could still sense the delicious, pungent perfume she wore. *Light Blue* by Christian Dior. The same perfume favoured by Rose.

But the pillow next to him was untouched and the bed looked like he had slept alone without moving all night.

The sound of a running shower running came through the door. He swung his legs out of the bed and reached for his dressing gown to preserve his modesty. Just at that moment a dripping Svetlana walked into his room, completely naked.

'Thomas, where do you keep your towels?'

She stood nonchalantly, hand on hip.

'Um, in the airing cupboard. I'll get a couple of them for you.' He opened a door into a walk-in linen cupboard.

'Thomas, you have a very nice bum,' Svetlana giggled.

'Don't you let Reto hear you say that.' He turned and handed her a bath-towel and a smaller towel for her hair.

'By the way, we didn't get up to anything last night, did we?' he asked.

'No such luck. You're the perfect gentleman! Reto certainly has a very loyal friend.' Svetlana gave a wide smile.

In five minutes they were both dressed and sitting in the kitchen. Thomas prepared a pot of tea and some toast.

'So, Svetlana, to what do I owe the pleasure of your unexpected visit here in Kilkenny?'

Thomas was surprised when she had turned up the previous evening but he'd cruelly enjoyed putting Greg on the spot in the bar.

'Well, I'm sure you remember the last time we saw each other. Some bad guys had been looking for Reto and I believe they found you both in the Altstadt.'

Thomas's eyes narrowed.

Svetlana knew even more. 'There have been a couple of other similar occasions.'

Thomas was aware of this; his contacts had been kept quite busy with ensuring Reto's safety.

'Reto was becoming very concerned,' she continued. 'He wanted to get away and asked me to go with him but, a couple of days ago, he vanished from Zurich. So I'm fulfilling my promise to him that, if he disappeared, I would come to Kilkenny and find you.'

'But why not tell me all this as soon as you realised they'd got him?' Thomas was angry. Perhaps he could have had a chance to save his friend.

'No, his instructions were clear. I was to come here and wait one night before contacting you.'

Thomas was thinking it all sounded rather queer when the doorbell rang. A few moments later he returned with Reto Hersperger in tow.

Svetlana let out a surprised cry and ran into the arms of her lover. Reto looked over at Thomas with an enquiring raise of an eyebrow.

'No, no. I'm not as degenerate as you Swiss guys. Your lady is intact.' *Well, as intact as a girl from the Prince's Club can be*, Thomas thought.

Reto quickly put them in the picture. He'd found the cat and mouse games of recent weeks rather tiresome and come close to serious injury when a bunch of thugs had surprised him and his family on Lake Greifensee near

Zurich. The entire family nearly drowned in the water and, as a consequence, Reto's wife had fled with the children to her mother's house in Austria. Fearing the next incident might finally cost him his life, Reto had taken flight and hung around in the shadows of Kilkenny until Svetlana put in her appearance.

'So, darling, we're together at last. You're so clever.' Svetlana tangled herself around Reto.

Thomas gave a chuckle and raised his hands. 'Listen, you two, I have to go out for a while so why don't you make yourselves at home. In fact, it's a good idea if you don't go out before I return.'

Svetlana planted a wet kiss on Thomas's cheek and squeezed his shoulder as he passed by them and out the door. The five point security bolts slid home as he turned the key in the lock from outside. The door couldn't be broken down without demolishing the entire wall of the house.

He headed across the river towards the Castle Park where the grounds afforded some guaranteed isolation for use of his mobile phone. The sun was shining strongly and warmed his back but a cool breeze swept across the meadow, rippling the grass like waves on the sea.

A few phone calls confirmed his fears. Svetlana had been followed to Zurich airport by mercenaries from Zimbabwe and they had boarded her flight. Fortunately, or perhaps by Reto's design, she had taken an indirect route via Amsterdam and not checked in the second leg until arrival at Schiphol. Thomas's Dutch colleagues had intercepted the assassins and dealt with them.

The only tail on Svetlana after that had been Thomas's own people and the Kilkenny location was still secure. Thomas resolved to have a little word with Reto when a suitable moment arose. He was under strict instructions to keep Greg away from such trouble. Much as he hated to admit it to himself, it looked like his good friend Reto was becoming something of a liability and it might fall upon him, Thomas, to remedy the situation.

On his return to the house around two hours later, however, it appeared the liability had been removed. The front door was closed but the deadbolts were disengaged. Fearing the worst, Thomas drew his pistol and crept into the kitchen, steeling himself for the expected bloodshed.

Instead, he found a note in Reto's characteristic neat hand on the grey granite breakfast bar.

Dear Thomas, I appreciate our sudden appearance in Kilkenny ran the risk of jeopardising your position here. For that please accept my sincere apologies. However, I think you would agree the time has come for a parting of our ways. Svetlana and I have made good our escape from Switzerland and are moving on to pastures new. I wish you well in your future endeavours and hope you find the tranquillity you deserve. Your true friend, Reto.

P.S. we left almost immediately, it's not necessary to change your bed linen!

Svetlana had signed with a lipstick kiss.

Corridors of power

A warm breeze wafted gently in from the garden, bringing a fragrance of mixed roses into the Jacobean drawing room at Chequers, the British prime minister's official country residence.

They were known as Old Europe. Numbering eight sovereign nations, they formed the core of the old former colonial masters.

A ranking existed amongst them in this forum, equivalent to their historical colonial influence in Africa. Britain and France were equal first. Belgium and Portugal were equal second. Spain, Italy and Germany were equal third and the Netherlands brought up the rear.

Infrastructure Projects in Africa was the name of the forum. Other European countries had peripheral involvement but these eight made the decisions.

The eight heads of state gazed at a map of Africa projected onto a screen. Thomas Thistlethwaite pointed out areas of interest on the map with a red laser pointer.

'We have six territories secured in the Eastern Region.' Thomas indicated Uganda, Kenya, Tanzania, Malawi, Zambia and Zimbabwe. 'In the Western Region we have five territories secured.' The laser moved over Cameroon, Nigeria, Ghana, Sierra Leone and The Gambia.

The Spanish Prime Minister, Rafael Santacruz, spoke up. 'And by *secured* what do you mean?'

'Secured means misappropriated funds have been placed under our control in trust for the country of origin, corrupt leaders have been deposed and forward thinking leaders have been retained or assisted into power.' Images of the unconvincing Winston Cunningham and Peter Abrams waltzed through Thomas's mind.

'Would you please clarify for the group the key issues regarding those secured areas?' Anthony Goolden, British Prime Minister, asked.

'Certainly,' Thomas replied. 'There are incursions on the Zimbabwe / Botswana and Zambia / Angola borders. This is primarily due to South African sponsored activities but they're weakening.'

The audience nodded, appreciating Thomas's frankness.

'In Nigeria we're facing substantial manpower issues due to the population size.'

There were murmurs around the room. At the commencement of the programme Nigeria had a population nearly double of any nation represented at Chequers.

The President of the French Republic, Charles Lorin, spoke up: 'Can you share with us the actions taken to mitigate the key issues you describe?'

'Certainly,' Thomas said. 'The Zimbabwe / Botswana and Zambia / Angola borders are being monitored by high altitude Sentinel surveillance aircraft and we have continuous jet fighter coverage. Rapid response ground forces are pushing back the insurgents and inflicting heavy casualties. Since the UN resolution and sanctions passed against South Africa last week, it's expected the South African support will be withdrawn and the insurgents will go to ground. At that point we'll secure Botswana and we expect our Portuguese colleagues to do the same with Angola.'

The Prime Minister of the Portuguese Republic, Carlos Ramirez, nodded in assent.

Thomas continued. 'The scale of the task in Nigeria will require coalition forces to be deployed for six months until the numbers are more manageable. A motion will be tabled to you later this afternoon. The expectation is for the coalition force to come predominantly from Spain, Italy, Germany and the Netherlands as the ground engagement of these members is currently at a low level.'

'We will have no problem with that,' Kurt Waldshut responded, Chancellor of the Federal Republic of Germany. 'Stabilisation of Nigeria was always going to be one of the biggest challenges. They were unexpectedly successful in treating their HIV for a period of time and the population has remained substantial.'

'Very good, Thomas.' Anthony Goolden gave a tight lipped smile and the crow's feet at the corners of his eyes deepened. 'Now please inform us how the British contribution to infrastructure is proceeding.'

Thomas indicated the location of power generation projects on the map. Kenya was identified as the pilot and nearing completion. Further projects in the other ten territories secured by the British were planned to commence before year end, together with additional projects in the ten major territories secured by the French, the three Belgian territories and Mozambique for Portugal. Smaller territories would be supplied cross-border electricity through the new transmission grid. New technology solutions for power generation and the transmission grid were on budget at around ten percent of the cost of traditional systems.

Anthony Goolden thanked Thomas for his informative presentation and handed over to the French President. A similar explanation of French progress followed, given by their project leader Patrice Poulin. French contribution to infrastructure consisted of high speed rail links. Innovation in track-laying technology would enable them to install the major rail infrastructure within eighteen months and a complete integrated system within five years.

Belgium and Portugal followed with information on the few territories under their jurisdiction and joint progress on infrastructure for broadband communications.

Germany and Spain had no secured territories but were fully involved in two massive infrastructure projects. The Germans were directing local manpower in construction of the new highway network. Spain was dealing with the issue of water supply and had a new technology available that extruded massive sections of water main on-site. In those countries where surface water was in short supply the water would be piped from natural underground reservoirs in a similar fashion to the Great Man-Made River Project in Libya.

'Gentlemen,' Anthony Goolden concluded, 'we are returning the sovereign riches of Africa to those fertile gardens.'

'Beneath which rivers flow,' Charles Lorin said.

'Beneath which rivers flow,' the other guests chanted in unison.

Murphy's law

Greg spent much of the next three months in Africa and Switzerland. Serious problems had arisen with the pilot project.

When the first fifty micro-generators were installed they had been tested during a period of heavy rainfall. The flow of water was close to the maximum expected in the Nzoia River during the course of a normal year but the generators had only reached fifty percent of their generating capacity. After three days at this level of flow the units began to overheat and malfunction. Within a week all fifty units had ceased to function and it was back to the drawing board in Switzerland with the micro-generator design.

Greg had leased design offices close to the research centre of his previous employer in order to make the transition as easy as possible for the team members who had moved with him. Further work on thermal modelling and running simulations of conditions identical to those in the Nzoia River revealed the problem was related to an aluminium alloy used in the micro-generator construction. A titanium alloy with higher heat dissipation was introduced into the simulated design and the results were astounding. Potentially, the micro-generators could run at one hundred and fifty percent of original rating. However, this was of academic benefit as the maximum expected flow of the Nzoia River would only generate fifty percent of capacity. The decision by Greg to proceed with an over-engineered redesign of the micro-generators would come back to haunt him before the year was out.

After three weeks in continuous liaison with the Swiss manufacturers, the first batch of fifty units with the new titanium alloy design was flown to Kenya on the same aircraft as Greg.

James Conway had the replacement micro-generators installed within a couple of days. The dry dock was flooded again and testing recommenced. After one week of running up to half capacity, all units were functioning perfectly. Greg took one last look at the fifty generator icons flashing on the control screen of the power station and headed over to his parents' house just north of Nairobi, accompanied by a bodyguard who had been his shadow since returning from Switzerland.

Kenneth was keeping the house and gardens in perfect condition, awaiting the return of his employers. Greg set up a video call between Kenneth and his parents during which they explained their extended stay in Ireland had to do with some special family celebrations for the grandchildren. Greg himself knew this was a white lie and Kenneth was nobody's fool.

'Your mother was looking very happy, if you don't mind me saying so,' Kenneth said later that evening. 'And your father, he was rather lively. The Irish air must be agreeing with them both.'

'Yes, quite.' Greg was wondering how Rose was getting on with his happy and lively parents in Kilkenny after nearly three months of cohabiting.

Greg stayed over the weekend at his parents' house as there was nothing for him to do at the project site. The remainder of the one thousand micro-generators were being installed so he had decided to give domestic life in Kenya another chance.

Kenneth devoted a lot of time and effort to showing Greg around the town and pointing out improvements that had taken place over the past few months. New sports and social facilities had been completed together with a couple of medium sized shopping centres. Marks and Spencer had a store as did Selfridges and Debenhams. Car showrooms included Jaguar, BMW, Lexus and Mercedes, and the prices were very favourable compared to Ireland and the UK.

Back at the house Kenneth pointed out the finer details of the domestic appliances and the herbaceous variety of the carefully irrigated gardens. He also delicately addressed the issue of security and pointed out there had been no events of concern since Greg's last visit.

Reassuring Kenneth his parents would soon return, Greg left for the project site and found himself later that day staring in awe at an array of one thousand micro-generators in the dry dock. Conway gave the signal, the dry dock was flooded and the dock walls were retracted. A hum filled the air, emanating from power station transmission equipment connected to the generator array.

In the control room a five metre square wall flashed with one thousand indicators showing the generator array beginning to function. Although the river flow was not at its greatest level, the micro-generators were running at forty percent of capacity. Each unit appeared to be functioning correctly and was producing two hundred kilowatts on average, totalling two hundred Megawatts, the equivalent of an average sized power station in most western European countries.

The project team clapped each other on the back and shook hands. Conway and Greg made sure they had thanked all the team members before heading off to their hotel in a townland some half an hour away, in the opposite direction to the squatter camp. They indulged themselves to excess with the local beer but that was as far as Greg went. He didn't join Conway on a jaunt to a local club popular with visiting European engineers of all ages and persuasions.

Next morning, a little bleary eyed, the two Englishmen arrived a little later than usual at the scene of their previous day's triumph only to find the project team in a state of despondency. Puzzled, they entered the control room and noticed immediately that power output was down by ninety percent. Only one hundred or so units were flashing on the display wall.

Conway moved over to a large LCD screen display for the positioning system.

'Look at this, Greg,' he said.

The one hundred units still generating were exactly where they were supposed to be. But the other nine hundred were dispersed up and down the river, a large number of them in a cluster on the river bank downstream.

Greg and Conway walked out towards the river to find out what was going on and were greeted by a gory sight. Ten Kenyans stood around in a circle, three of them holding marksman's rifles. One was kneeling and, with some evident difficulty, disembowelling a large crocodile. As the stomach was slit open the group leaped back from a gush of partially digested matter including what looked like a man's leg. Reaching into the putrid mess, Conway extracted and held aloft the titanium body of a micro-generator.

'They came in after we removed all the equipment and pontoons,' explained one of the Kenyans who had been on the night shift. 'They came straight through the safety nets.'

One of the other men handed a pair of binoculars to Greg and indicated downstream. Looking through the lenses, Greg could see a number of hippopotami lying motionless on the river bank.

Later that afternoon they discovered an adult hippopotamus can consume up to fifty micro-generators in a single sitting but with fatal consequences.

It took Greg's team one month to come up with the solution to their wildlife problem. One of the Swiss borrowed an idea he'd heard about whilst shark diving in South Africa. Most creatures can be repelled by certain sound frequencies and patterns. Zurich Zoo reluctantly allowed the team to run tests on their crocodiles and hippopotami, and a combined solution was identified. Adding the sound repellent to the micro-generator design was not problematic but the retrofit to existing units would have to be carried out in factory conditions. As nine hundred micro-generators had been consumed by the Nzoia River fauna, Greg decided one thousand units would be manufactured to the new design.

Three weeks later the second redesign of micro-generator was installed in the Nzoia River power array and successfully tested. Power generation again reached two hundred Megawatts. No further titanium micro-generators were consumed and no further animals were harmed. However, unwelcome clusters of crocodile activity were experienced upstream and downstream of the power array.

Two months over schedule and one hundred and fifty percent over budget, the pilot installation was completed. Greg returned to Ireland and his family.

You're barred

It was an error of judgement on the part of Thomas. He knew a gang of hired assassins was in the country and looking for him. This would be the second attempt of the Kano family to revenge the murder of Nigeria's late president. Thomas's contacts had not reported any suspicious new arrivals in Ireland and so he'd assumed it was safe to go ahead and rendezvous with Greg in town.

A man seated at the bar nursed his pint of lager. He had a closely shaven head in a style favoured by men with receding hairlines. The barber would call it a number two cut. He wore a pair of blue jeans and a patterned shirt over a white tee. On his feet was a pair of heavy boots. From the hairstyle, the choice of drink and the clothes it could be guessed he was a typical Kilkenny man in his late twenties, probably not yet married and involved in some kind of sport. He looked fit enough and not the kind of guy to pick a fight with.

Thomas Thistlethwaite took in the rest of the clientele. He immediately regretted this choice of venue. There were too many close cropped heads and too few women at that hour. So they would have a swift pint to show their mettle and then head off somewhere else, no problem. Thomas had driven direct from Dublin airport and found himself in need of the toilet. He followed the sign into a dark corner at the back of the room.

Greg arrived at the World's End bar almost immediately after Thomas had gone out the back. Seeing no familiar faces he assumed himself to be the first to arrive and ordered a pint of Smithwicks. Greg felt ill at ease. His own hair, clothes and choice of drink characterised him as a married man in early middle age who was not too bothered about his appearance. But the beer was a higher priority than his discomfort and so he settled onto his stool at the bar and drank deeply from his glass.

Greg was very happy to be back in Ireland. He took a look around. It was a real man's bar of the old school. The décor likely hadn't changed much in thirty years or so.

Wondering how he himself would look with a number two cut, Greg's eyes lit on the shaven headed man Thomas had noted earlier. The man looked up and their eyes met. He had irises of a very light grey colour, so light they were almost indiscernible from the whites of his eyes.

Those curious eyes and the Slavic facial features suggested the man was from Eastern Europe. It was nothing unusual in modern Ireland to meet many Czechs, Poles, Latvians, Lithuanians and other immigrants. They had come in their thousands to supply the labour required for the Celtic Tiger economy of the early twenty first century. But they didn't frequent the same pubs and restaurants the Irish and British inhabitants preferred.

Greg realised he was staring and in return received a slight smile and an inquisitive look from the grey-eyed man.

A slight commotion issued from somewhere behind the toilet door and the man rose sharply from his bar stool, heading in that direction. Two other men seated at a small round table also stood up and moved towards the toilet. They were clearly all together.

Intuition told Greg he should follow.

Behind the door was an alley with two doors marked *Mná* and *Fir* leading off it, the Irish words for *Ladies* and *Gents*. The *Fir* door led into a small courtyard where five shaven headed men had cornered Thomas. This was no ordinary street fight or mugging. Blows were being exchanged but there were no shouts, just grunts of exertion and pain from the protagonists. Thomas was in deep trouble. Two men grabbed him from behind. He was able to wriggle out of his jacket and throw one of the two men over his shoulder. The assailant landed on the ground, his head whipping onto the cobblestones of the yard with a crack, and he lay still.

Greg had the advantage of being unnoticed in the courtyard. One of the men was directly in front of him and Greg aimed a front kick in the middle of the shoulder blades. As the kick impacted, he tensed his body against the recoil and leant his full bodyweight into the kick. The man was propelled into the solid stone wall across the small yard. Dazed, he turned and Greg leapt at him, drawing back his fist and swinging his bent arm in a short hook that brought his elbow into smart contact with the side of the man's head. The man crumpled to the floor.

One of the three remaining men reacted quickly to this and landed a kick in Greg's ribs.

Against the far wall, Thomas was locked in mortal combat with the other two assailants. He had drawn a small knife, just some three inches long with a groove along the length of the blade. There was something in the groove with a bluish red hue and it didn't look like blood.

Greg rallied himself, despite his possible cracked rib, and spun around, stamping down with his entire weight into the back of his attacker's knee. The man fell into a crouch and, lifting the man's head sharply with two hands – he had to grasp him by the ears as there was no hair – Greg snapped the head back down, simultaneously driving his knee upwards. That was the end of him.

The remaining two men had produced knives much larger than Thomas's. He feinted a knife strike and simultaneously threw his left foot in an arc, connecting with the wrist of one of the knife holders. The evil looking, jagged edged knife clattered to the ground and skidded across the cobbles towards Greg who picked it up. Having no idea what to do with a knife and fearful of having it ripped from his hand by the attackers, he threw it over the wall of the yard into a neighbouring garden. A dog that had been barking furiously let out a yelp of pain.

The remaining knifeman made a slash at Thomas. He managed to block the blow and push the man away in the direction of Greg, who decided to have a go at the knife himself. Raising his left foot as if stepping up onto an imaginary stairs, Greg threw his body upwards and kicked out sideways, making heavy contact with the man's upper arm which was not exactly his intention. It did, however, disable the knifeman's arm and Thomas, lunging forward, easily took the knife from the dangling hand, floored the man with a solid punch to the face and slashed with his small knife for good measure.

As Greg's left foot came back down onto the cobbles it was whipped away from under him by the remaining assailant, the grey eyed man. Greg landed awkwardly on the side of his damaged ribs and, with a groan, passed out.

Facing each other, amidst groaning, writhing and motionless bodies, Thomas and the grey eyed man took stock of the situation. Thomas had no doubt he could overpower and, if necessary, kill this individual. But he had to think quickly. This was Kilkenny, where Greg lived, where he also lived on and off. There could be no murder here.

He slashed at the grey eyed man with his small knife, drawing blood in a couple of shallow wounds across the shaven head. He landed a flurry of kicks and punches that put his opponent into a stunned defensive posture. The other four assailants began to rouse themselves and would soon rejoin the fray. Thomas made a decision and bolted back inside the pub, leaving Greg unconscious on the floor of the yard.

As he reappeared into the bar through the toilet door, Thomas glanced over his shoulder and saw all five shaven heads were following him with varying degrees of mobility. The pub was now quite full. Thomas let out a roar of pain and headed towards the bar. Clutching his chest he launched himself over the bar and landed at the feet of the surprised landlord.

'Call an ambulance, I think I'm having a heart attack,' he rasped through gritted teeth.

The landlord, alarmed, grabbed his mobile phone to summon the emergency services. Out of the corner of his eye he noticed five men shambling out of the door and onto the street.

When the ambulance arrived it was Greg and not Thomas who received treatment. Thomas had staged a miraculous recovery from his suspected heart attack. Greg had sustained two cracked ribs and a bruised hip where he had landed on the cobblestones of the pub's backyard. Nothing serious enough to require a trip to the hospital.

As the paramedics escorted Greg from the pub, the landlord came out to them.

'Fighting in my back yard? This is no place for the likes of you two! Consider yourselves barred!'

They returned to Thomas's Victorian townhouse and set about a bottle of Lagavulin single malt scotch.

Greg subsequently explained away his injuries to Rose as the result of a drunken fall in Thomas's back yard, which was sufficiently close to the truth to be convincing.

But the overall situation was becoming untenable for Greg's conscience. There was a growing gulf between what Rose knew and what was happening in his life. He had to deal with it and soon.

~

The following week Rose pointed out to Greg a curious story in the local newspaper. Gardai had been alerted to a rented house after neighbours noticed a strange smell. On forcing entry Gardai found the decomposing bodies of five men believed to be of Eastern European origin. The state pathologist reported the corpses exhibited minor injuries including shallow knife wounds, consistent with a pub brawl. However, the toxicologist's report confirmed they had all died from poison found in a deadly fungus that grows in the woods north of the city. Once again a public warning was issued against picking wild mushrooms.

Full disclosure

'Rose, we need to talk. I have to share some things with you.'

'Yes, honey' she replied, 'I think you do.'

It was midday on Sunday and the children had gone to the cinema. The Kids Club was running an animated adventure story Pete and Kate were keen to see. Greg's parents took them along and planned to give Greg and Rose a couple of extra hours by following up with a visit to SuperMacs and the Castle Park playground. Derek and Bernie had seen the look on their son's face and knew some space was needed.

Rose took Greg by the hand and led him down to the summer house at the bottom of the garden. It was secluded, still shaded by the apple trees, always the last in losing their leaves to the November fall. The air was unseasonably mild, a warm spell before the cold, wet and blustery winter to follow. A bottle of Pinot Grigio was cooling in a bucket and two glasses stood ready on the small wooden table. Greg poured the wine and raised his glass to toast Rose.

'Slainté,' Rose said.

'Slainté mhaith,' Greg replied. He didn't quite know how to start his story. So he started at the beginning, which for him was the occasion of his identity theft on the return flight from Brazil some months earlier. Even to him, the tale sounded far fetched.

'So they stole your fingerprints, scanned your retinas and took a mould of your face?' Rose was incredulous. 'I suppose Thomas can verify all this if I ask him?'

'Sure, but that was just the start.' He proceeded to tell her about his surviving a mid-air assassination attempt and the subsequent bomb explosion in the Norwegian fjord.

Her incredulity turned to horror as he recounted the deadly encounter in the men's toilet at Bilbao airport.

'You actually killed someone? You, Greg? I don't believe it.'

'Rose, it really was a matter of life or death, me or them. If it hadn't been for Thomas then I wouldn't be here now and you'd be drawing a widow's pension.'

'But, how could this happen? To you, of all people? Nothing like this ever happens to you, to us!'

Greg explained how Thomas was the real target. He was some kind of British government agent and had been targeted several times.

'I knew he was a dark horse, that Thomas Thistlethwaite, from the first moment I saw him,' Rose said.

'The reason I got wrapped up in this was the project work with the last company. Thomas and his colleagues resorted to some extensive subterfuge in gathering details about my work, and it seemed quite unnecessary as the company released me and the patent anyway. But, on reflection, I think it was all manipulation and our friend Lars had a hand in it.'

'Sounds to me like some very dodgy industrial espionage. What the hell have you got involved in?'

'It's huge. This project is just one of several massive infrastructure developments in Africa. And everything is funded by recovered assets. The whole thing is approved and controlled by the European Union; it's even a part of the G10 millennium goals!'

Rose wasn't impressed.

'So, what about these nightmares then? And what's the story with your parents? I love them and everything, don't get me wrong, but they've been here for over four months now. Will they ever return to Kenya?'

This was the truly hard part to disclose. Greg took a deep breath and explained the current state of life in Kenya as he had seen it. The exclusion of HIV and AIDS victims from the workplace, the human cost of the development projects, worthlessness of life in the HIV townlands, and a shoot to kill policy with intruders.

Rose was silent for several minutes. Greg refilled her wineglass and tried to read her expression but Rose averted her gaze.

Finally she responded.

'I suppose I should be grateful to you for not dragging us over there. Is there no way out of this? There must be. Your parents can't go back there, can they?'

'Actually, they seem to have acclimatised, in more ways than one. Terrible cliché but it's true; after one killing you become rather numb to it. And the situation over there does seem to have settled down a lot in the last few months. Is it really so much worse than Dublin with all its gangland murders, or even Kilkenny?'

'Well, you certainly paint a picture of Africa as a whole heap less desirable than Ireland. For me and the kids it's not an option.' Rose folded her arms across her chest. 'In fact, I'm not even sure how I feel about you going back to work there.'

'It's as safe as houses for me,' he replied, perhaps trying to convince himself. 'And probably pretty okay for Mum and Dad as well. But let's not rush them back. Please?'

'Okay,' Rose agreed. 'We'll let them make it their choice if and when they go. But if they decide to stay then we'll need a bigger house.'

Greg smiled with relief. Rose always found a way to turn things to her advantage. She'd been angling for a bigger house for some time but, until Greg had started the new project, they just couldn't afford it. Now it was a possibility. He nodded in acquiescence.

Millennium Goals

'In the year 2000 the G8 countries subscribed to achieving the millennium goals across the planet by the year 2015. When 2005 came to pass it was recognised Africa was the only continent not on track to achieve any of those goals. Lasting peace and prosperity were the sum aim of the goals and Africa was way behind expectations in the areas of conflict, health, education and infrastructure.'

Kurt Waldshut, German Chancellor, paused and assessed his audience's engagement. He had their attention and so continued.

'It is only fair to say there had been advances made in the areas of democracy and economy. Inflation was coming under control, growth was occurring and democratic elections were becoming widespread, if rather unorthodox in some respects.'

Anthony Goolden gave a slight nod.

'At that time the G8 countries made commitments to international aid, amounting to some billions of dollars. But, in truth, it was known this would not be adequate to make the massive investments required by the African states in order to achieve the Millennium Goals for 2015. There was hope that private investment by wealthy philanthropists would bridge the gap but they required, in general, an equal contribution from the G8 and we did not have the desire, courage or ability to dig so deep into our pockets.'

Some of his audience appeared humbled. Others, including James Burden, President of the United States of America, folded their arms defensively.

'When we welcomed China and Brazil into our club in 2009, and became the G10, it was clear our new colleagues were also unable to provide the necessary resources. But further consideration pointed to a logical solution within our control.'

The guest from Switzerland, Christo Schwarz, shifted in his chair. Waldshut continued.

'Article 14(f) of the Gleneagles Communiqué, together with ratification of the UN Convention Against Corruption, enabled us to *establish effective mechanisms for the recovery of assets including those stolen through corruption.*' Waldshut pronounced the second part of the sentence in a slightly high-pitched voice. The British premier had to suppress a snigger.

'This procedure was not without considerable personal risk to those involved and I take this opportunity to thank special guests here present.' The German Chancellor indicated a section of the audience with a gracious sweep of his hand, at which a gentle ripple of applause emanated from the rest of the attendees.

'Let us not forget, however, those who lost their lives during these brave efforts to return the riches of Africa to the very soil of mankind's creation.' Waldshut clasped his hands in front of his chest, closed his eyes and bowed his head. The European G10 members and most of the audience followed suit whilst the American, Russian, Japanese, Chinese and Brazilian panel members looked around in some confusion.

After about one minute of silence, Waldshut continued. 'We, the G10, supported by the African Union, have succeeded in the return of some three hundred and fifty billion dollars, administered by the Central European Bank. This has enabled massive development relief for post-conflict countries and commencement of the Pan-African Infrastructure and Health Development project that will help attain the goals by 2015.'

Thomas Thistlethwaite, seated in the special guests section, twitched his mouth in a lopsided smile of irony. He knew very well some of those post-conflict countries had been pre-conflict before the colonial powers decided to reassert their authority. On the other hand, he couldn't argue with the idea that returning such fabulous wealth to unreformed African states would be to merely place the riches in the pockets of a new set of corrupt leaders. He had taken many lives based upon this rationale.

The German Chancellor resumed his speech.

'Our renewed interim goals are as follows: the African Union will have two hundred and fifty thousand trained peacekeeping troops; all children will have access to free local education up to the age of eighteen and access to third level education within their own province, and all education will be of a Western European standard; all inhabitants will have access to basic healthcare within their area of residence, either at no cost or as regulated by the health sponsor country; universal treatment for chronic diseases and conditions will be available to all those who have entitlement.'

Thomas considered these promises. *Entitlement* to treatment for HIV, *entitlement* to treatment for AIDS. He had seen on the ground in Africa what the interpretation of *entitlement* was.

Waldshut began to wrap up. 'As outcomes we can expect the following: the thirty million orphans in Africa will be fully cared for.'

Thirty million? A conservative estimate, Thomas thought.

'No children will die from malaria and no one will die from tuberculosis; fresh water and affordable electricity will be available to all settled citizens of Africa; infant mortality and death of mothers during childbirth will be reduced to the same rates as Western Europe; polio will be eradicated; there will be equality of access to health, education and employment regardless of sex, race, colour or creed. These are our commitments to the African Union. We stand proudly together and look towards a future of equity, peace and prosperity in the fertile garden of Africa.'

The audience section containing the leaders of the African Union stood and smiled towards the panel.

'Beneath which the rivers flow,' came the murmured response from the audience and European panel members, all of whom stood and began to applaud.

The premiers of Japan and Brazil also stood and applauded but in slight confusion. Russia, China and the USA gradually stood and clapped a little awkwardly, the three of them exchanging fleeting glances that did not escape the watchful eyes of Thomas Thistlethwaite, Anthony Goolden and several others.

Legacy of Zimbabwe

Robert Mugabe became president of Zimbabwe in 1987. He had been the country's effective ruler since official independence from the United Kingdom in 1980.

Rhodesia, as the country had formerly been known, was a relic of white supremacy ruled by a man named Ian Smith and the world welcomed Mugabe's subsequent liberalisation and populist approach. An African country ruled by Africans, for Africans.

Twenty years later and the world clamoured for the removal of Mugabe. Zimbabwe was still a land rich in minerals and agriculture but decades of social and economic mismanagement had resulted in deforestation, soil erosion, land degradation and air and water pollution. Poor mining practices had led to toxic waste and heavy metal pollution. Even the most visible of natural resources had been decimated. The black rhinoceros herd - once the largest concentration of the species in the world - had been almost eliminated by poaching.

There was also a toll to be paid by the people. Prevalence of HIV had risen to thirty percent of the population and average life expectancy for Zimbabweans dwindled to thirty-nine years.

Thomas Thistlethwaite had spent some time in the country at the start of the century, ostensibly in the role of news reporter for the British Broadcasting Corporation. He played the part rather well and found it to be very good cover for his presence at major events during the country's development, or rather deterioration.

In fact, he was operating as a British agent within a team that had the brief to move moderate leadership into power in Zimbabwe. This was proving a rather difficult task, bearing in mind Mugabe, throughout his reign, had effectively quashed all opposition.

It was Mugabe himself who sowed the seeds of his downfall. A chaotic land distribution campaign, launched in 2000, sent the white farmers into flight and the country's agriculture began to fall into disarray.

Any African with a claim to have fought in the war of independence was entitled to squat on the huge farms and claim acreage. Initially this was an annoyance to the white farmers, with dubious claimants squatting on productive land and reducing it to an unsustainable subsistence method of farming.

As the land redistribution gained momentum, things took a more sinister turn.

It was August 2005. Thomas had travelled with his family to a farm in the north of the country that consisted of lush and fertile lands leading down towards the Zambezi River on the border with Zambia. Their host was a white farmer named Arthur Shipley, a tall and tanned man of English origin and in his fifties.

They sat gazing across the golden fields. Arthur's wife, Emma, provided them with tea on the veranda of the sprawling farmhouse. Although they had an extensive serving staff, it was Emma's custom to personally serve refreshments to visitors.

Arthur was of Yorkshire stock and his family had moved to what was then Rhodesia two generations previously. During their conversation Thomas noticed a slight accent and some curious turns of phrase that betrayed those roots.

It was in the role of BBC reporter that Thomas had made the visit and he sensed deep concern in the otherwise stoic demeanour of Arthur and his wife. That morning they had been stopped on the road across their own land as they returned from a shopping trip to the nearest town. A group of squatters had blocked the thoroughfare, demanding land and issuing threats. This was not the first time such an event had occurred but it was the first time the would-be squatters were clearly not from Zimbabwe. The land distribution programme had reached such a level of chaos that opportunistic immigrants were able to simply wander across the border and demand their share of a white-owned farm.

Arthur had taken the approach that had proven successful thus far. His armed escort had made a show of force and then he had delegated two of his agents to lead the claimants to a far corner of the farm where other squatters had established their smallholdings.

On return the agents had expressed their concern. The new squatters were quite different to the Zimbabweans. They appeared to be a unified community of some fifty or more people but were strangely constituted. The women were all young, little more than girls, although most of them carried young babies. The men were also very young, barely men, with the exception of one who was about twenty-five and obviously led the troop. Also there were no obviously ill group members, no apparent AIDS sufferers.

The agents, who had served in the Zimbabwean military contingent in the Democratic Republic of Congo, said the group formation reminded them of the child armies of the Rwandan Patriotic Front. Arthur asked the advice of his men and they concluded a daily patrol of the smallholdings area would be a sensible precaution.

The following morning two agents headed over to the area occupied by the new squatters at around nine a.m. By midday there was no sign of them returning and this raised concern as the round trip should have been less than two hours including patrol of the smallholdings.

In addition to the Thistlethwaites, Arthur's extended family was also visiting. After lunch, the women and children made their way down to the fields near a small wooded area. A stream flowed along the bottom of the field and the children began to paddle in the shallow water. Arthur, his two adult sons and Thomas could hear the tinkling laughter of the boys and girls as they splashed each other, punctuated by the mock scolding of the watchful mothers.

Thomas's wife, Natalie, had a natural light bronze colour to her Brazilian skin but the hot African sun had also toned the skin of Arthur's daughters-in-law. From a distance the families were almost indistinguishable from one another, bare footed and golden, running around the field and traipsing through the water.

Two of the larger children had crossed the stream and were making a foray into the woods. They were only out of sight for a minute or two before shrill shouts of terror issued from within the trees. The children, a boy and a girl, came bolting out of the wood and straight across the stream.

It was too far away for Thomas to hear what the children were shouting but he acted on instinct and went straight to the cab of his pickup truck where he fished out two Kevlar vests and an Uzi sub-machine gun from a locker beneath the dashboard.

Throwing one of the bullet-proof vests at Arthur, Thomas donned his own and, weapon in hand, ran down towards the children. Arthur and his two sons ran inside the house and soon reappeared, armed with hunting rifles.

Arthur's oldest grandson, the boy who emerged from the wood, had by this time run up the field towards the house. The girl was being comforted by one of the women at the side of the stream. Thomas met the boy half way down the field and managed to understand the gasping words.

'Dead men, Grandfather's men, hanging in the trees, two of them, on ropes.'

Thomas looked up from the boy and could make out Natalie, Hannah and Matt crouching together by the stream. Beyond them were a group of childish figures emerging from the woods. Each carried an assault rifle held diagonally across the front of the body.

As yet there had been no shots fired. Thomas thought there was a good chance of bringing the women and children to safety. Just at that moment, on Arthur's instruction, his sons released a volley of warning shots into the air above the approaching boy soldiers.

Their reaction was immediate. The advancing line took aim and fired. One of Arthur's sons, John, went down. Thomas felt a bullet pass alarmingly close to his unprotected head. A shot hit Arthur square in the chest and knocked him off his feet. But he was soon back up again, the Kevlar vest proving effective.

Down in the field the women and children had begun to race back to the house. They were half way between the two sets of armed men. Another volley of shots issued from the squatter soldiers and a woman fell to the ground with two children, a small girl and a smaller boy. Thomas scanned the field. He couldn't see Natalie and the kids, they were gone.

'Get down, now!' he screamed at the top of his voice. All the remaining women dropped to the ground, dragging the children with them. So too, stupidly, did Frank, Arthur's remaining son.

Running at full speed, Thomas raised his weapon and let loose a spray of bullets in a repeated sweeping motion. He was unaware of anything around him. Several of the boy soldiers were able to release shots and one grazed Thomas on the thigh, another creased his temple. There were retorts from behind him as Arthur and his son took careful aim. Thomas didn't stop until the magazine of his Uzi was empty. To him it seemed to take for ever but in fact the complete discharge of the weapon only lasted a few seconds.

As the dust and smoke cleared, the full picture became apparent. Seventeen young African men lay bleeding in the field. Their wounds were horrendous. Not all were dead but all soon would be.

One solitary man of around twenty five years of age remained standing, looking around at the bodies, mouth agape. Then, face twisted in fury, he raised his rifle and aimed at Thomas's heart. Thomas closed his eyes. There were two loud retorts, one after another, followed closely by the sound of large calibre bullets ripping through flesh. The bullets from a hunting rifle. The leader of the boy soldiers crumpled and fell.

Arthur and Frank were soon at Thomas's shoulder and shaking him. 'You mad bastard!' Arthur shouted. 'Exactly what kind of news reporter are you?'

Thomas didn't answer. He looked towards where his wife and kids had fallen. Natalie stood up and pulled the children with her out of the grass. Thomas found himself standing next to them, with no recollection of having moved towards them. He knew he was in shock.

'It seemed like a good idea to hit the ground when the shooting started,' she explained.

Thomas placed his hands around her shoulders. 'Jesus, Nat. You're brilliant! I thought I'd lost you, all of you. Go on up to the house with the others, we'll be right up.'

All the women and children were unscathed, unlike John who had a nasty bullet wound in his shoulder.

The men walked amongst the soldiers. All the males in the troop were accounted for. Two of them were still conscious. Arthur didn't hesitate to place a bullet in their skulls.

'Get your JCB and start digging,' Thomas instructed Frank. 'We need to get all of them buried as soon as possible. And John, get yourself to the nearest doctor with that shoulder wound. Hunting accident.'

Before nightfall the seventeen boy soldiers and their leader had been buried behind the woods.

During the course of a bottle of good malt whisky Arthur, Frank and Thomas discussed with their wives how best to handle the aftermath. John was sedated and being cared for by his wife in a quiet room at the far end of the house.

They concluded the authorities need not be informed. The new squatters originated from across the border and Mugabe's men would have no interest in their welfare. However, the remaining women and children would have to be humanely cared for and Arthur undertook to build shelters for them and support them in development of their smallholdings. It was far from ideal but the best anyone could come up with.

Next morning Thomas, Natalie and the kids bade the Shipleys farewell and headed back towards their rented house in Chinhoyi, north of the capital Harare.

And so it came to pass

'Thomas, we have to leave this country.'

Natalie had made her decision. They would return to Bedfordshire, England on the next convenient flight which would be in two days time.

Thomas nodded in agreement. He was still in a state of mental shock. The stinging pain of the dressed wounds on his thigh and temple were the only physical feeling he had.

'Of course, darling. It's become really insane here and I should have sent you all safely back before now. I'm sorry.'

They both knew the previous day could have so easily ended very differently for all of them.

After the long drive to Chinhoyi the children raced out into the garden to play, cabin crazy from several hours in the car. Their adventures of the previous day were all but forgotten. Thomas and Natalie sneaked off for a little adult time in the large and cool bed of their simply furnished room.

'I love you so much, Natalie.'

Her eyes were a dark hazel, an irresistible colour that fills the beholder with an involuntary sensation of warmth.

'Thomas, you're so brave. But don't become careless! We need you, Hannah, Matt and I. It's becoming too dangerous here for you as well.'

'I won't let anyone or anything hurt you or the kids. In two days you'll be back home and I'll follow within the month. I just need to...' but Thomas didn't finish his sentence.

There were shouts and screams from the children in the garden. Grabbing his pistol from its holster, he flung back the curtain and vaulted naked out of the window, weapon raised. But it was an overreaction. The children were shouting and screaming in delight at the local market being erected behind their house. Thomas had forgotten the weekly event.

A few startled stallholders looked anxiously at the pistol wielding naked Englishman before he leapt back in through the bedroom window and landed laughing in the bed.

Natalie smoothed Thomas's hair and, kissing down the inside of his arm, removed the pistol from his grip, placing it on the floor beside the bed. Her soft, warm kisses had reached his stomach when a loudhailer in the street started to blast out some repeated slogan.

The market was not the only thing they had forgotten. Thomas had jointly organised a white farmers' protest march through the town. With a deep sigh he lifted his wife's head with two hands, kissed her on the lips and rose from the bed to dress.

Out in the street the turnout was impressive. Around one hundred white farmers had congregated with placards and pickup trucks. There were numerous press representatives and a global network TV crew. Most of the townsfolk not at the market had also lined the streets.

As expected, half a dozen military vehicles were positioned at the far end of the street. This would make good news coverage, Thomas thought. There might be a few injuries to add some spice, but nothing worse. The protesters were unarmed, as he had taken pains to ensure.

The troops formed a loose formation and approached the farmers. Thomas stood to one side with other members of the media. At a distance of some ten metres the captain of the military contingent halted his men. He was a large man in his forties with a shambling gait and a slightly glazed look in one eye. He kept his left hand in the pocket of his bullet-proof jacket in the regal style of the King of England, former Prince of Wales.

'You farmers, go back to your farms. You are not allowed to gather and demonstrate here, you have no permit.'

The farmers' leader stepped forward and proudly raised his chin.

'We are citizens of Zimbabwe. There is no law to prevent this march, it is a peaceful process.'

The captain lost his temper. Waving his arms wildly, he shouted at them. 'Disperse immediately! I am instructed by the government to use any means at my disposal to stop this unauthorised opposition gathering!'

The farmers, to a man, stepped forward threateningly and the captain stepped back. He shouted a command and the fifty or so troops raised their rifles at the farmers.

Thomas was alarmed. Things seemed to be escalating out of control. His training caused him to step back and take in the surroundings a bit more carefully.

The street was lined with two storey houses and most of the street-facing windows were open. He caught a glimpse of reflected sunlight on a gun barrel from a second floor window just before a series of shots rang out. Two of the farmers dropped to the ground.

Drawing his pistol, the captain barked another command and the troops opened fire. Most of the shots missed the farmers, the troops aiming into the air above the heads of the white men for whom they had mingled feelings of respect, fear and envy.

Even a warning shot has to fall to ground somewhere. Several volleys of bullets from the troops sailed high into the air. Screams came from behind the houses lining the main street and Thomas realised with horror they were coming from the local market. He gave up the journalist pretence and bolted towards the screams, just as the troops took fresh aim at the farmers.

The unarmed protesters had already begun to disperse into the side streets. Most of them were making good their escape, but the captain led his troops in pursuit of the farmers' leader and a few others.

They ran behind a house and directly towards Thomas. Thomas could see several market stalls were in disarray and bodies lay across them and on the ground. Near the back garden of his house he saw Natalie, Matt in her arms and Hannah holding onto her skirts. Blood coursed from Natalie's forehead and down her golden neck onto Matt's little trousers.

Thomas was felled from behind by a blow from a rifle butt and rose slowly and painfully to his knees. He was just in time to see the captain and troops spray the fleeing farmers with a hail of bullets. The farmers fell like toy soldiers. Natalie, Hannah and Matt were caught in the hail. When he reached them they were already dead. Natalie was still cradling the body of her little boy who had been killed outright when the first stray bullets hit the market. She had a look of shock on her face. Hannah looked peaceful in her eternal sleep.

Rage swept up in Thomas Thistlethwaite. He rose from his dead family and marched directly to the captain, reaching for the pistol in his own holster. The pistol and holster that still lay on the floor of the bedroom.

Impotent, incensed, he struck the captain with an insulting open handed blow across the face.

With a look of distaste, the captain shook his head to dispel the momentary dizziness and spoke with a snarl. 'So, Mr BBC Reporter. You have seen how the government of Mr Mugabe handles its enemies. Go and tell your viewers, your readers, your listeners that we will not be intimidated by degenerate, capitalist colonial oppressors.'

The last thing Thomas remembered before he was beaten unconscious was the missing ring finger on the captain's left hand.

Rebirth

The light on the TV camera flashed red. Anthony Goolden adopted his characteristic smile and then let it drop into a more serious expression.

'I was brought up in a religious family, as a Catholic. A religious minority in a secular society. Growing up in Britain I saw that minority wane and felt nations across Europe cast themselves adrift from any discernible beliefs.

Then came Islamic fundamentalist terrorism. New York 9/11. London 7/7. War on terror, Afghanistan, Iraq, Lebanon, Palestine. To a secular state there is nothing more terrifying than an unseen enemy prepared to die in the name of religion.

The fundamentalists had a power, a driving force we lacked. They believed in something. They found refuge, support even, amongst those with related, if less extreme, beliefs. Amongst us, the people of Britain, the people of Europe.

Madrid, Paris, Munich, Milan, Zurich. They couldn't be stopped. And what did they want? This faceless enemy couldn't be appeased, couldn't be fought by powerful nations who had lost their own sense of identity, who had no shared beliefs.

We cut the terrorists' support, dispersed their sympathy, revealed their refuge. Then we opened our arms, embraced them, discussed our differences, impressed them with our sincerity and understood theirs. And so it came to pass. We found our belief.

At the highest levels we promoted our faith and stopped ourselves persecuting the non-secular states. We recognised the strength of our financial and military capabilities in the European Union of States and gently rejected the evangelical dogma of our allies without creating new enemies.

And it bore fruit; we reaped the rewards. The terrorism abated; we have a harmonious society. All denominations in this country are engaged.'

Anthony Goolden paused, quite out of breath. The passion of his own words had his pulse racing.

'We are now, at last, able to turn our efforts on the impoverished nations of this world and return what is rightfully theirs. Of course I mean Africa, that fertile garden beneath which the rivers flow. That dark continent which we have so shamefully neglected in our previous quest for power and domination. Ex umbris, in veritatum. Out of darkness, into truth!'

The red light on the TV camera flashed and went out. An assistant wiped the Prime Minister's perspiring brow as the TV crew packed up their equipment. Goolden exited the brightly lit conservatory with its backdrop of English roses, a few blooms still braving the onset of winter, and entered a luxuriously furnished drawing room. A lone man turned from the large television screen where he had been viewing the live broadcast to the nation.

'Quite a speech, Mr Goolden. I can see now how you have risen to such popularity. You have the common touch. Quite so. And I do not delude myself regarding the reduced importance of my ecclesiastical role in our, in your, new society. I take you at your word that the monarchy remains a British institution.' Charles spoke with perfect politeness but his stony expression and sharp stare would have turned a lemon sour.

'Thank you and yes, of course, your assumption is correct, your majesty,' Goolden replied.

The King excused himself with a slight bow and left Chequers in his chauffeur driven Bentley. It was the first time he had ventured out of his Cornwall estate for two years.

Waters of life

Dead fish were floating on the surface of the Nzoia River in all directions. It reminded Greg of the herring massacre in Norway. So much for minimal environmental impact. He couldn't understand what was killing the fish. And it wasn't just fish. He could see birds feeding on a carcass at the riverbank. It looked like the remains of a young hippo.

Greg strode off towards the control centre. Just as he reached out to open the door of the building, a slight tremor in the ground spread up through his legs. The carrion birds lifted up off the carcass and flew into the air. Glancing at the surface of the river, he could see strange eddy patterns in the water despite the fairly strong downstream current.

A chorus of loud cheers emanated from the control room, adding to his confusion. Inside, the display screens showed an amazing story. The trend display of power generated showed clear peaks more than five times the previous maximum achieved. On closer inspection, Greg determined the latest peak coincided with the tremor he had felt outside.

'What the hell is going on?' he asked.

Conway turned to face him with a look of delight. 'Greg, you won't believe what we've found!'

'Some new way of eradicating wildlife?'

'Well, yes. That does seem to be an unfortunate side-effect. But we've found a way to boost power output in an emergency. Depth charges!'

'And how on earth did you discover that?'

A woman's face turned from the control screen towards Greg. He immediately recognised her as the dazzling

Simone Buettiker, from his Swiss research team. They had long since kissed and made up after the Blindekuh.

'By studying the data from your prototypes, Greg. The fifth unit displayed some amazing results, and we were able to surmise some kind of shockwave had occurred. So I had the idea to simulate a shock wave, combined with the normal flow of a river. The result was massive power generation of duration up to one minute.' Simone was wide-eyed.

Conway picked up the story. 'We built a device that enables us to feed depth charges into the middle of the generator matrix. It's a bit crude. No doubt the explosive effect is not doing the micro generators much good, despite their ruggedness.'

'Sure,' continued Simone. 'So we're developing a pressure pad to be installed on the bed of the river. We'll be able to pulse at one-minute intervals and achieve the same effect without risk of damage to the generator matrix. It probably won't save the wildlife though.'

'A little mad, but well done!' Greg was impressed with his team's innovativeness. 'James, you'll need to find a way to let the wildlife bypass the matrix without losing the through flow for the generators. Otherwise we'll wreck the ecosystem!'

Conway and Greg sat down together for a further hour to finalise the details. Greg then jumped into his rented jeep and headed off to see his parents.

Bernie and Derek had been back in Kenya for a month. Kenneth had maintained the house and grounds in perfect condition during their absence. More importantly, the local police had implemented a 10 kilometre HIV exclusion zone around the town and Greg's parents no longer had anything to fear on that score. Old fashioned robbers still posed a risk but, as that category of villain was not particularly prone to suicidal attacks, the comprehensive intruder alarm system was sufficiently effective.

The Marshalls enjoyed a relaxing evening together and Greg headed off to Nairobi airport early the next morning.

After check-in he went looking for kids' presents. The toy shop in the new airport shopping mall was full of model car brands Greg recognised from his childhood; Corgi, Dinky, Matchbox. A retro collection of British cars from the 1960s and 1970s caught his eye. Several different incarnations of the Ford Cortina, a Morris Minor Traveller, even a Hillman Imp estate car called the Husky. He remembered his father buying the full size version of that car; it had been a total disaster.

Absentmindedly, he read the description on one of the boxes and was amazed to see 'Made in Kenya'. Picking up other cars of different brands he found nearly all of them were Kenyan made. One or two were Tanzanian.

Greg emerged from the shop, clutching a bag of toy cars, and went on a hunt around the shopping mall. He found only a few items of non-African origin, mostly Chinese. They were mainly big-brand, complex electronics. All basic electrical items were made in Kenya or Tanzania.

He boarded the plane in a state of slight confusion. When had all this happened? It had seemed the same story a few years ago when everything was suddenly made in China. But in a way he was happier with this development. For Africa to have a modern and competitive manufacturing base would be a great foundation for finally developing a twenty-first century society on the dark continent. He saw a glimmer of hope; perhaps his parents had really made the right choice after all.

That evening, on his return home to Ireland, Greg drove his wife half-demented by picking up every item in the house and trying to establish its source of manufacture.

'For goodness sake, Greg! Whatever are you looking for?'

'Ah!' he said, waving a cordless phone in one hand and a pair of hair straightening tongs in the other. 'When did you buy these?'

'Last week. Why?' She was annoyed, recalling a time in the not too distant past when they had to watch every expense. That was before the project moved to Africa and Greg's income had taken a huge leap. 'Have I been excessively extravagant?'

'No,' Greg said. 'Look!' He pointed to the back of the two appliances. 'Made in Africa!'

Rose smiled. 'The gardens of Africa, beneath which the rivers flow.'

She looked at her husband's perplexed face.

'It's the advert on TV. You know, the one for holidays in Africa.'

'Yeah, Dad! Can we go to Africa for our holidays next year?' Kate and Pete chorused. 'Please, Dad, please?'

Greg felt like work was chasing him home to Ireland. 'We'll see. Maybe we could visit Grandma and Grandad.' He threw a wide-eyed look at Rose.

'Greg, they make it look so peaceful, so tranquil there in the advert. Not like here, no storms and flooding. No winter, biting winds, no greyness. Lush, colourful. I can almost smell the flowers and trees.'

'Hmm.' Greg scowled at the blaring television set. 'Maybe we should have a TV free weekend again.'

~

Up country, in Dublin city, the River Liffey flowed strongly under Heuston Bridge by the railway station. A tall, heavy man stood gazing downstream. There was nothing tranquil about this river. A deep and dirty, muddy swirl pushed down through the city, dragging at discarded shopping trolleys and old tyres partially submerged in sludge at the edge of the water.

He had a good vantage point, high above the Liffey. The sides of the river consisted of sheer stone walls and this was one of the parts of the city where there had not been any flood alerts despite the rise in sea level of the last decade. But he found the scene to be very alien. The Liffey is a tidal river and the seagulls squawked as they swooped down to what they thought might be something edible at the water's edge. This man was used to very different rivers.

He turned away from the flow, thrusting hands in coat pockets. The Irish weather didn't agree with him. Did it ever stop raining in this country? Why had he come here of all places? Then he remembered the woman and the money, and a smile cracked across his broad face.

In the railway station he purchased a return ticket to Kilkenny. The lady at the counter couldn't help staring at the man's hands as he fumbled with the unfamiliar euro notes and coins.

There weren't many people on the platform and the train was quite empty. The man noticed again a scruffy looking individual whom he'd seen earlier, sitting cross legged on Heuston Bridge with a coffee cup on the ground in front of him. Not having any sympathy for beggars, the man hadn't placed any money in the cup. Had he done so, or waited a few minutes until the next passer by had done so, he would have been surprised to find the cup was, in fact, full to the brim with tea.

The man saw the beggar take a seat further down the carriage. He was unshaven, wore a woolly hat above comically large black framed glasses and appeared to be singing to himself. Probably more of an eccentric than a beggar. The man sensed, rather than smelt, the odour of unwashed body and over-worn clothes.

Two hours later the train pulled to a final halt in MacDonagh Junction, Kilkenny. It was shortly after 6 pm. The man managed to locate a gift shop in the new shopping centre and made a few small purchases. Two action figures and three Barbie dolls. Looking at the boxes containing the cheap toys he smiled as he read the words 'Made in Africa'. The woman had some of his children living with her. They wouldn't know he was their father but it was worthwhile turning up with presents just for the goodwill.

At the back of the train the scruffy individual stepped down from the carriage and sauntered off down John Street in the direction of the River Nore. There were no CCTV cameras on the bridge and no risk of the Garda coming to move him on, unlike in Dublin. His hands fumbled in the pockets of the old greatcoat as if looking for keys or perhaps some change to buy a pint.

Up at the station, the tall, heavy man determined his own direction and walked steadily to a housing estate on the north eastern edge of the city. There were hundreds of houses, indistinguishable from each other but, trusting to his natural instincts, he eventually found the right building. It was an anonymous duplex on the second and third floor of a newly built block. A shiny new BMW saloon parked in the allocated space looked conspicuous amongst the ageing Japanese cars and commercial vans. So, she had already spent some of his money. But there was plenty, it wasn't a problem.

The children were won over by the presents. Three girls and two boys; he had remembered correctly, although the names escaped him. It was the job of a real man to father many offspring and this wife had proven the most fertile of the four his rank and reputation had blessed him with.

When the excited children were in bed, the parents sat down together for the serious business of the evening. She produced a rucksack packed with high value euro notes totalling five hundred thousand, perhaps only half of the total sum. This he balanced with the acceptance of obligation towards this wife and children whom he might not see again, at least not for some time.

An hour later, the woman lay sweating on the bed. He was still a man of passion and energy. She rose and slightly parted the drawn curtain, watching her husband walk away with the rucksack on his back. A glance at the clock and a smile flashed across her dark, attractive face. In twenty minutes her lover would arrive home from his shift at the brewery.

MacDonagh Station was at the top of the hill and, now knowing his way a little better than before, the tall man reached the railway station in just twenty minutes. The train timetable showed him there wasn't another train to Dublin for over an hour and a half. Time enough for a refreshment, he thought.

John Street led down the hill from the station towards the river. He stopped and looked at the decrepit sign for the World's End. A dark doorway led back from the street to a bar the Guards themselves would rarely visit. Intuitively, he knew it was a place where no questions would be asked or entertained.

The barman looked like he could have done with a good meal or a good night's sleep.

A couple of days in Dublin had taught the visitor the way to order a beer. 'I'll have a Guinness,' he drawled.

The barman gave a slight nod and reached for a three quarter full glass behind the counter, to which he gave a top up. Consumption of stout was at a high rate in the World's End and the custom was to keep the delivery line flowing.

The barman went so far as to raise an eyebrow when he was given a ten euro note and told to keep the change. The few Africans in Kilkenny were very careful with their money but this one had obviously had a windfall. The barman gave a cough and a small group of shaven headed men in the corner raised their heads to survey the situation.

Noticing the interest he had aroused, the tall African walked directly towards the men in the corner and the air of menace he exuded was more than enough to dampen their mood. They sensed something about him that turned their stomachs; the unspeakable odour of death and corruption.

In a dark corner sat another stranger, unshaven and in a heavy coat. He was approached by the barman, who wanted to turf him out, and begrudgingly ordered a large whiskey. The barman had delivered the drink, for which the apparent vagrant paid with a handful of change. During the course of the next hour he proceeded to discreetly top up his own drink from a bottle concealed within the greatcoat.

The African drank swiftly. He'd worked up a thirst in his wife's bed. With each new pint he raised a toast to the room, the other customers ignoring his words and the strange grip of his left hand on the glass. He left in a relaxed state a little over an hour later, swaggering slightly as he hoisted the backpack. The time was around nine in the evening and the last Dublin train would depart in thirty minutes. It was already dark outside and a slight drizzle was falling.

He turned downhill to look at the river. Reaching the bridge he heard a splash. A small bundle of flowers was floating downstream, the current strong after the heavy rain of the past month.

This was the moment he had worked towards. Anonymity, money, safety. He had escaped from a nightmare and would build a new life based upon better values. He grasped the handrail of the bridge and inhaled the cool, damp air.

There was a hissing crack in the night air as the Taser gun found its target. The African's hands locked onto the handrail. Although the African weighed well over two hundred pounds, the man in the greatcoat, woolly hat and glasses easily lifted the captain by the ankles and levered him over the edge of the bridge towards the dark waters below, complete with backpack.

For a tantalising moment the African's hands continued to grip, the left hand missing a ring finger, and then the weight of the body prised the fingers from the handrail

'Spend your money in hell.'

Thomas Thistlethwaite watched the inert body float downstream and then turned, shuffling up John Street.

There's more to life

Rose pointed out the story in the local newspaper. 'What kind of idiot drowns himself with a backpack full of money?'

Greg took the offered paper and studied the article. Drowning wasn't rare; Ireland's small, fast rivers could be treacherous, but this particular death caused a lot of interest due to the money. Gardai suspected the man of being a major player in the drugs business.

'Do you remember that Columbian guy - imported clothing soaked in cocaine solution? Then he chemically extracted the stuff in the back room of his house?' Greg said.

'I remember. Didn't he run off when they let him out of prison to do some charitable painting and decorating?' Rose said.

Greg smiled. Kilkenny and its local crime were a world away from the crazy world of his friend Thomas.

The phone rang and Rose picked up.

'Hello?'

Rose handed the phone straight to Greg. 'It's your drinking pal.'

'Hi, Thomas. How's it going?'

'Just fine, thanks. Listen, we need to get you over to the UK for a few days. Can you leave on Monday?'

'Sure. I'll fly from Waterford. What about you? Where are you now?'

'I've just arrived in Kilkenny.' Thomas paused and Greg said nothing. 'I need to meet first for a little chat, if that's okay with the missus?'

Greg posed the question to Rose.

'Oh yes, business is it?' She put on her *I know better, you don't fool me* face. 'Sure, go ahead. Just mind you sleep in the spare room if you come home. I don't want you waking me up from my beauty sleep at all hours. And *no* fighting!'

They arranged to meet that evening.

~

At nine o'clock, after reading the kids a bedtime story, Greg sauntered down the hill and into Syd Harkin's pub where he found Thomas sitting in a dark, quiet corner.

Greg went straight for the jugular. 'So I suppose you're assassinating African despots in Kilkenny these days?'

'Shhh!' Thomas said, his eyes darting around the clientele. For a second he toyed with the idea of coming clean with Greg but decided against it. 'He was a small guy in a bigger scheme. My colleagues were hoping to talk to him when he panicked and jumped off the bridge.'

'How come he was here in Kilkenny? Can I be sure it had nothing to do with me or my family, or you for that matter?'

'Yes, it was just a complete coincidence he came to Kilkenny.' *At least this part of the story is true*, Thomas thought.

'And the mushroom-eating Czechs, were they also here by coincidence?'

'Slovenians actually. That was unfortunate. They were looking for me. Somehow we missed them when they entered the country.'

Greg took a deep breath. 'Thomas, I can't live like this. My family and friends are here. I can't knowingly surround them with this sort of carry on.'

'I know and I understand. I'm the problem. That's why I'm going back to England for a while.'

Greg looked glum. He had come to count on Thomas as a good and true friend. Their nights out in Kilkenny were fast becoming legendary. But Thomas was right. Instead of protecting Greg from danger he was dragging him into it.

'Hey mate, cheer up!' Thomas raised his glass to Greg's. 'Next week we'll have a laugh over in England together. In the meantime, let me introduce you to a colleague of mine who will be staying in my house for a while and act as your new local liaison. Here comes Terry now with more beer.'

Greg stood and turned, expecting to see some kind of male bodyguard. Terry was a girl in her late twenties, wearing a vest top and jeans. Pretty, tall and slim, not what he expected.

Greg offered his hand. 'Nice to meet you, uh, Terry.'

'You too, Greg. Heard a lot about you from your man here.' Terry's voice was melodic and gently Irish. She took Greg's hand but held it rather than squeezed it. Her hands were slender and he could see the muscles in her arms flex as she passed Thomas his Guinness.

'Here's to life.' Thomas raised his glass.

'To life,' Terry said with a grin.

'Life,' Greg said quietly. He knew he was heading in for trouble.

The evening passed by. Terry matched the lads pint for pint and joined in the banter. Greg learned she had been working with Thomas's team for five years and distinguished herself in anti-terrorist activities in Britain.

'I guess you can fight as well as Thomas?' Greg said when Thomas had left to go to the toilet.

'Sometimes they put up a fight, but I always get my man. Would you like to see me in action?'

Greg laughed nervously, feeling slightly out of his depth. 'I promised my wife there would be no messing tonight.'

Thomas returned and sensed an energetic atmosphere developing. He whispered something in Terry's ear. She laughed, throwing back her head.

Greg imagined kissing her throat. That was one of several imaginings he had enjoyed that evening. When Terry finally took her turn in the bathroom, Greg broached the subject with Thomas.

'Thomas, listen. I'm not sure I can work with Terry. How could I explain to Rose my new liaison is so gorgeous! I know I'm fifteen years older than her but I won't be able to avoid making a fool of myself. It'll all end in disaster.'

Thomas laughed and toasted Greg's glass. 'Listen, mate. Terry always gets the same initial reaction from blokes. It's not just how she looks but the way she behaves. But scratch the surface and you'll find something else altogether.'

~

They landed at London Heathrow and were in the car within fifteen minutes of touching down. The drive to Bedfordshire took around half an hour. There was very little traffic on the motorway and Thomas drove his Biopower Saab fast. Several speeding cameras flashed at them but he was unperturbed.

'This licence plate has a special dispensation. I don't receive any fines or points.'

Greg just nodded, slightly scared by the speed of the bioethanol engine and Thomas's flagrant disregard for the rules of the road.

They rounded the M25 motorway and headed north on the M1. Greg noticed the carriageway looked unusually dark. Thomas flicked his headlamps to main beam and the super bright lights lit up a safe distance ahead of them through the approaching twilight. It reminded Greg of a breakneck journey he once made on the unrestricted Autobahn between Nuremberg and Munich.

'Another power cut in this section,' Thomas said. 'They're getting a bit frequent now.'

Greg had heard the UK was experiencing power cuts. It had come to the same point in Ireland a year ago, just before the first Irish nuclear power station was put into service.

'What's the story with the power cuts?' Greg asked.

Thomas focused on the road ahead for a few seconds before replying.

'We've a massive new nuclear program in consultation phase at the moment. But it's meeting a lot of objections on environmental grounds, as you'd expect.'

'And wind power, I guess you have the same problems as we do in Ireland.'

'Yep. Increasing number of storms producing winds that are too strong. Wind turbines shutting down automatically in the gales, it's just not the workable solution it used to be.'

'Well then, what about our new micro-turbine technology?'

'That could be a solution. We've no shortage of fast flowing rivers these days. But your Kenyan project is the proving ground. We need proof of concept first before it can be proposed here.'

'So why didn't we set up a pilot here?' Greg was finding the situation hard to fathom.

'Africa's need is greater. The benefits for them will be huge. What we have here is a slight inconvenience we can quickly remedy with your micro-turbines when we've finished our job in Africa.'

They entered a stretch of motorway where the lights were working. It had been several years since Greg had travelled in England. He was impressed by the new drainage system with massive concrete storm drains parallel to the motorway. Flood barriers along the banks of rivers had given them a more man-made aspect. The country had learnt some expensive lessons when weather patterns changed in recent years.

Thomas took a slip road off the motorway and they were soon thundering along the country lanes of Bedfordshire. A fog descended upon them but Thomas didn't moderate his speed. Greg shut his eyes against the hedges and bends in the road that appeared through the fog.

After about ten minutes Thomas slowed the car and they entered the outskirts of a small village. The road opened out onto a village green, looking eerie in the drifting fog. Thomas indicated a thatched cottage fronting onto the green.

'The King's Arms. We'll pop in there a bit later. Nice pint.'

Thomas took a lane off the green and they were soon at the edge of the village again. They bumped up an unmade road through overhanging trees to a set of old iron gates. The driveway to Thomas's house was better made, gravel crunching when they came sharply to a halt.

Greg looked at the old house, probably originally the country home of a well-heeled Victorian city dweller. It was exactly the kind of home he and Rose had always dreamed of.

Thomas unlocked the car doors and they stepped out, jaded from a long day of discussion and travel.

The two men carried their flight bags from the car. Thomas led Greg in through the front door and showed him up to a guest room on the first floor.

After a shower in the en-suite bathroom Greg wandered downstairs.

Everything was clean and tidy but didn't feel homely. A beautiful, bronze skinned woman featured in several framed photographs, sometimes with two small children. There was a timelessness to the photos, suggesting they were something from the past. Greg knew Thomas had lost his family but had never heard the details.

'My wife Natalie and my children, Hannah and Matt.' Thomas had come up quietly behind Greg.

'Yes, they're very beautiful.'

'I miss them, every day.'

Thomas walked out to the kitchen. 'Put on some music if you like,' he called out.

Greg found the music system and switched it on, then searched through several shelves of CDs. Something was already in the system and a tune started to play; *The European Female* by *The Stranglers*.

I thought she was a feline, she moved with ease and grace...The European female's here, we'll be together for a thousand years.

He and Rose would be together for a thousand years. It had to be hard for Thomas without Natalie.

Thomas returned with a couple of bottles of Michelob, handed one to Greg and they toasted.

'Michael's knob.'

'Michael's knob,' Greg said. It was Rose's favourite beer pun.

After just a few swigs they both began to feel relaxed and lay back on the dark red leather sofas.

The Stranglers continued to play. A timer sounded in the kitchen and Thomas disappeared, returning a couple of minutes later with two large pizzas and another couple of beers.

'You know,' Thomas said between mouthfuls, 'I thought about moving away, forgetting the past. I was very down for a long time.'

Greg said nothing, a little uncomfortable with Thomas's openness.

'But then I found new hope. There is hope, Greg. There's a bigger scheme of things. I'll be with them again.'

'You mean the afterlife?'

'Yes. I didn't really believe in anything before. But now I've found a belief that justifies some of the questionable things I have to do.'

Greg knew first hand the nature of some of these questionable things and suspected there was much more.

'I just want say our trials and tribulations, both here in Europe and in Africa, are in a good cause. We're on the side of justice and freedom.'

'Justice and freedom,' Greg toasted, pulling a face and downing the rest of his beer.

'Okay, I get the hint. I'll stop evangelising. Time for a proper pint.'

They left Thomas's house and sauntered down the leafy lane to the village pub. Through the darkening gloom Greg could just make out small dark rabbits hopping over grassy mounds in the fallow fields. The evening air was heady with the scent of country and a moistness that promised heavy morning dew.

The King's Arms was warm and welcoming. Their arrival produced a few nods and one or two greetings. A blonde barmaid began to pull a pint of bitter as soon as they entered and Greg nodded in agreement as she waved a second glass in his direction.

They talked animatedly for the whole evening. Whenever the beer ran low, a mere glance in the direction of the bar brought the barmaid or the barman over with two more pints. Despite his love of Ireland, Guinness and Smithwicks, Greg realised just how much he missed English bitter.

After the third pint Sue, the barmaid, sat down at their table and joined in with some banter. She quite took Greg's fancy.

'So, Thomas, who's your handsome friend?'

Greg felt his colour rising.

'He's just some poor lost soul who needs redeeming.'

'Well, redemption can be had. But it doesn't come for free.' Sue squeezed Greg's thigh and, with a cheeky grin, she left them and returned to work.

'Very hospitable, the natives,' Greg said.

'Yep. Sue's noted for her hospitality. In a small village like Flitley you're a potential addition to the gene pool, so watch out.'

Greg laughed. He glanced over at the bar where Sue was pulling pints for some late arrivals. She bit her lip as she met his gaze.

By the time the lads had finished another two pints it was closing time. They'd set the world to rights and no stone had been left unturned.

Rising unsteadily, Greg felt a hand around his waist and looked up to see Sue close to him, already wearing her jacket.

She leaned in closer and whispered in his ear. 'You've pulled, lover boy.'

Thomas laughed heartily. They bid the barman goodnight and he gave Greg an overt wink.

Sue walked between the lads, arms linked. They took a short cut across the village green and down a dark track that led through an ancient graveyard.

'So, what have you fellas been talking about all evening then?'

'Oh, the nature of local hospitality, for one. And the natural beauty of the English rose.'

Greg had intended flattery, but merely managed to remind himself of his wife back in Kilkenny.

'And how about exciting tales of daring do in faraway lands? Like what Thomas is always trying to impress me with.' Sue gave Thomas a playful dig in the ribs.

Greg looked at Thomas.

'Sue is on the team, Greg. She doesn't just pull pints. Sue looks out for me, don't you, darling?' He planted a kiss on her cheek.

'That I do, someone has to!' Sue gave an infectious laugh that had them all in fits.

They reached the house and Greg collapsed on a sofa. Thomas went to fetch more beer but Sue called for vodka.

'I think I've a bit of catching up to do!'

Thomas switched on some music then sat on the other sofa. Sue took the red leather chair.

Thomas gave Sue a proper introduction. As well as being Sue the Barmaid she was Thomas's local liaison officer. This meant she kept surveillance on both the house and Thomas himself when he was around, and arranged for domestic details to be taken care of.

As the drink flowed their conversation flew off at tangents. Greg was amused and intrigued by Sue. The dizzy, cheeky barmaid act was clearly just that.

When Sue had left the room to go to the bathroom, Greg decided to quiz Thomas. 'You must surely have had your evil way with the sexy Sue?'

'Surprisingly, no. Honest. Too close to home and other memories. So feel free.'

'Feel free?' asked Sue, catching them out with a quick return. 'With me? Thomas, if only you had. Well, you missed your chance mate. Tough luck.'

With a little laugh Thomas rose and announced he was retiring to bed. A little unsteady, he headed for the stairs and up to his room.

Sue sat herself down on Greg's sofa and pressed a button on the music remote control. A strange, atmospheric tune emanated from the speakers.

He inhaled Sue's scent and she leaned into his body, relaxing to the music. Vodka had done the trick for her and they were at a similar level of inebriation. Her soft blonde hair smelled like straw and he felt her hand on his thigh.

Turning her head up to him, Sue smiled and blinked. Her milk and honey complexion was delicious and Greg longed to taste it. He lowered his lips to hers and they met in a soft, warm kiss. Then she pulled away and looked at him.

'Sue, you're really gorgeous, but…'

Sue sighed. 'Thomas told me you're married. Story of my life. You're a really nice guy, Greg. Too nice for your own good.' She straddled him and gave him a deep and lingering kiss that almost broke his resolve. Then she stood up, ran her fingers down his cheek and bade him goodnight.

Greg woke half an hour later, still on the sofa. His beer bottle was lying, empty, on its side on the deep pile carpet. With a smile on his face, Greg took the stairs and was soon sleeping the sleep of the innocent.

The origin of species

A smell of bacon frying wafted up the stairs and slowly brought the lads back to consciousness. By the time they struggled downstairs, Sue had a full cooked breakfast and mugs of tea on the table for all three of them.

'Sue, you're an angel,' Greg said through a mouthful of toast.

Thomas cut and sliced his way through the sausages, bacon, black pudding, tomatoes and mushrooms.

'Hey Greg, how do you fancy finding out some more about AIDS in Africa?' Thomas asked.

'Sure, what do you have in mind?'

'There's an AIDS activist meeting in London this afternoon. They have a guest speaker who's supposed to be really good and I've been briefed to attend.'

'I'll drop you two down the station,' Sue said. 'There's no way I'm letting either of you drive with the skinful you had last night.'

After breakfast and a shower, Greg stepped out the back door and took a stroll around the garden. He saw a small, neglected orchard of apple and plum trees. Some children's playthings in the far corner of the garden looked forgotten, weathered and broken.

He took a walk around to the front garden. A couple of riders trotted past on horses in the lane and he waved a greeting which they returned. He took a stroll into the village and returned half an hour later.

Sue dropped them at the station just in time for the 11:30 train to St Pancras and they were walking the streets of London by midday. The meeting was to be held at a hotel in the West End.

Thomas carried a small brown leather case which, combined with his smart casual attire, gave the impression of a country doctor come up to the capital for a conference.

They turned onto Kensington High Street and Greg saw a shadow fast approaching out of the corner of his eye. A cyclist appeared from behind them with a swoosh of tyres and a hand reached out, grabbing Thomas's case.

With lightning reaction, Thomas tightened his grip on the handle of the case and braced his legs. The cyclist was pulled from the saddle and landed heavily on the pavement. Thomas reached down, took the wrist of the mugger with one hand and gave it a sharp wrench. Then he then kicked the toe of his shoe sharply into the side of the man who lay on the floor. There was a crack of bone.

They walked swiftly on, leaving the failed thief writhing on the ground amidst a small crowd of concerned onlookers. Greg turned and saw a youth run across the street, hop on the bicycle and ride off.

Within a few minutes they were at the hotel. Thomas reached into his bag and withdrew a pair of severe looking spectacles. They suited his assumed character well.

A notice board in the hotel lobby indicated the *AIDS in Africa* meeting was being held on the first floor.

They walked up the stairs and found an open buffet for guests of the meeting.

At 2 p.m. the attendees were called into the meeting room. Thomas held Greg back until nearly everyone else had entered and, as a result, they had to stand at the edge of the room. Despite this they had a good view of the podium and the rest of the audience.

A small panel of speakers was arranged onstage and the chairman introduced each panel member to small applause. Finally, the guest speaker was introduced. Martin Knox, Professor of International Studies at Leeds University, took the podium to rapturous applause. He raised his head from his notes and the audience became quiet.

'The most likely scenario goes something like this: in 1930, or thereabouts, a hunting party pursued their quarry in the jungles of Southern Cameroon in West Africa. The hunted was a monkey, a red-capped mangabey. The hunters were chimpanzees, *Pan troglodytes troglodytes*. The red-capped mangabey was caught, dismembered and devoured on the spot by the troop of *P. t. troglodytes*.

In the next few days or weeks or months, another hunt followed. The hunters were the same troop. This time their prey was a greater spot-nosed monkey. Once again, the quarry met with a bloody fate.

In each case the troop bathed in the blood of their victim. In each case the victim was a carrier of a similar, but slightly different, virus. Both viruses were a simian immunodeficiency virus, SIV. At least one chimpanzee absorbed both viruses from the blood of the quarry, probably through open cuts or wounds the chimp had sustained in the course of normal jungle life.

The infected chimpanzee acted as host to these viruses which evolved into a new simian immunodeficiency virus called SIVcpz.'

The Professor looked up and surveyed the audience. They waited for him to continue.

'But Chimpanzees are also hunters' quarry, the quarry of man. A group of human hunters caught and killed the infected chimpanzee and came into contact with SIVcpz. One or more of the hunters became a host to SIVcpz, which then adapted itself to the human body and became HIV-1.

Fact : one of the earliest known instances of HIV-1 is contained in a plasma sample taken in 1959 from an adult male human living in what is now the Democratic Republic of Congo. Analysis of the virus in the sample suggests it had evolved in the region some decades earlier.

HIV was then transmitted between humans from Southern Cameroon to nearby regions of Africa and subsequently beyond the continent. This probably occurred in the body of guest workers from the Caribbean, onwards to America and internationally through the increasing prevalence of air travel.

Lifestyle has doubtlessly been a major factor in the resulting HIV pandemic. Because HIV is a lentivirus, by its nature taking a long time to produce any adverse effects upon the body, the spread of the virus had gone global by the time AIDS was fully recognised as the outcome.'

Professor Knox paused, took a drink of water, and held up his palms to the audience.

'Forgive me, I know the story I've just told you is old news but I wish to set the scene. Having done so I will journey even further back into the realms of Thomas Malthus, that old English doomsayer of two centuries ago, and I quote: "*The power of population is so superior to the power of the earth to produce subsistence for man, that premature death must in some shape or other visit the human race*".

Natural disasters befall the human race on a regular basis. Earthquakes, drought, famine, disease. Malthus maintained this was a necessary and unavoidable evil.

Then we have man-made disasters, war and genocide. The phenomenon of famine can also on occasion result from the actions of man due to neglect and bad husbandry. Theory suggests these occurrences are the result of human behaviour regulating the population in a subconscious manner.

Consider the Shaanxi Earthquake of January 23rd in the year 1556. The most deadly earthquake in recorded history, it destroyed the artificial caves in the Loess cliffs of the Shaanxi province of China, killing some 830,000 people. Sixty percent of the local population was destroyed.

A modern comparison can be made with the Asian Tsunami of December 26th in 2004. A massive movement thirty kilometres below the earth's crust, underneath the Indian Ocean, devastated the seaboard communities of the region. An estimated 230,000 people perished.

In both of these natural disasters the population's lifestyle made them vulnerable to the planet's intrinsically violent nature. Humans could do little to mitigate such disaster.'

Greg was horribly fascinated by Knox's speech. He recalled television pictures of the Asian Tsunami sweeping away homes and families.

'Instances of severe drought have been known to lead to death through starvation or disease. The 20th century had several droughts that resulted in the death of millions: India in 1900, where up to 3.25 million died; a drought in the Soviet Union in 1921 to 1922 caused death by starvation of up to 5 million; and China in 1930, 1936 and 1941, resulting in a total of over 10 million deaths.

We easily forget, or may not even have been aware of, these events of yesteryear. Latter-day, the great media and charity machines of the late twentieth and twenty-first centuries have tapped our consciences in attempts to alleviate the great African famines of *our* time. The 1984 famine in Ethiopia took the lives of up to 1 million. Arguably, media and charity efforts are futile as the causes of these actual and threatened famines are not only natural drought but the policies of the local governments.'

At this point there were murmurs of assent. Greg could tell Knox was probably preaching to the converted.

'Disease is a most natural phenomenon, but let's leave that for a moment and now consider crimes against humanity.

The Armenian Holocaust of 1915 to 1917 eliminated up to 1.5 million people. Some historians have claimed this was a holocaust of negligence but we should not allow the suggestion to belittle the issue. An entire race was virtually eliminated.

When Hitler prosecuted his *Endlösung der Judenfrage* the world saw genocide on an unprecedented scale. Between 1938 to 1945 some 9 million people were wiped from the face of the earth, of which 6 million were of Jewish origin.'

At this point a small commotion occurred towards the back of the room. A smartly dressed young man stood up and called out. 'The British National Party refutes the occurrence of any alleged wartime *Holocaust* in Germany and Poland.'

Jeers and general shouts of ridicule from the audience induced the young man to shrink back into his seat and Knox continued.

'There are other instances of genocide, though not always recognised as such. USA bombings of Khmer Rouge sites had, by 1973, killed an estimated 800,000 Cambodian civilians. The subsequent genocide of Pol Pot's Kampuchean regime murdered a further 3 million people between 1975 and 1979.

Now we move to Africa and the Rwandan genocide in 1994 that took the lives of some 1 million people in just 100 days.

Of longer duration but even more deadly was the Second Congo War involving eight African nations. It wasn't a clear genocide as many of those who died were soldiers but civilians were also subject to wholesale slaughter. 3.8 million died in the Congo between 1998 to 2003. That's a conflict worthy of mention as it turned out to be just a taste of the death to come in the region.'

The audience knew Knox's main talking point was close now Africa had been mentioned.

'Now we turn to disease, the history of which is even more horrific. The modern sciences of medicine and hygiene have eliminated many of the human race's bacterial and viral predators. Let's take a quick tour through the large-scale pandemics of the last two millennia.

In the second century the Antonine Plague killed up to five million.

The Plague of Justinian from 541 to 750 was bubonic. It eliminated some fifty percent of the total European population.

Into the second millennium and the Black Death revisited Europe. In the six years leading up to 1354 a total of twenty million died, between one quarter and one half of the population of Europe depending upon the region.

Cholera stalked the planet during the final two centuries. In 1852 the third of eight pandemics was the most devastating, killing over one million in Russia.

Influenza was the biggest killer of the twentieth century. Between 1918 and 1919 the Spanish Flu appeared, unusually virulent and deadly. Within six months twenty-five million had died, seventeen million of those in India. Amazingly, the virus disappeared completely within eighteen months.

We should acknowledge Old World diseases were also responsible for the death of millions during periods of colonisation. Further, terrible diseases such as the sixteenth century *English Sweat*, reputed to have killed virtually on contact, have eluded the establishment of their etiology.

At this point, a few short years ago, we would have been speculating about possible future pandemics. Ebola virus, MRSA, SARS, HIV and Avian flu all had their time in the limelight. However, we are now undeniably in the grip of an HIV pandemic, predominantly on the African continent.

Taken in the context of the natural disasters, genocides and pandemics that I have recounted, HIV and AIDS are having a startling impact in Africa.

By 2005 some forty million people globally were living with HIV and twenty-five million of those were in Africa. Twenty-five million people had died of AIDS over the previous three decades.

By 2006 Africa was effectively experiencing an Asian Tsunami every month with some quarter of a million people dying of AIDS on a monthly basis.

The current statistics are uncertain, except they are undoubtedly understated. Many African countries have upwards of a quarter of the population living with HIV. There are now fifty million AIDS orphans in Africa, living and dying in poverty. Let us not forget the equivalent grandparents who die destitute and lonely, robbed by AIDS of supporting adult family.

So, it's clear. HIV and AIDS are the biggest killers in recorded history. Bigger than natural disasters, genocide or other pandemics. Granted, the Black Death and Spanish Flu had a greater intensity, but their total impact was less. Hopefully, AIDS will never claim lives at the annual rate of the Spanish Flu, which was equivalent to fifty million. If it does, the African race will be eliminated from its homeland even quicker than I fear.

There has been one event that has had a bigger impact than HIV and AIDS. World War II caused the death of around fifty million, give or take ten million. It is expected HIV and AIDS will take this dubious title away from WWII within the next year. This was my first mention of military conflict, except for the Second Congo War. So, where am I going with this?

The position I propose here today is HIV in Africa, the second biggest disaster in human history, is an act of genocide. The perpetrators are the former colonial powers. In collusion with the leaders of the G10 world powers, the United Nations and the African Union.'

Professor Knox paused for another drink of water. The audience remained attentive; they had anticipated this accusation and awaited his explanation with baited breath.

Thomas leaned over to Greg and spoke into his ear. 'He's got it wrong. The G10 and UN have nothing to do with it.' Looking around the room at the audience, Thomas gave a barely perceptible nod in the direction of the rear of the room.

The Professor continued. 'We've had an effective vaccine for HIV available for two years now. Antiretroviral drugs for the treatment of HIV have also been developed that can delay the onset of AIDS. The annual cost of these medicines is less than you or I spend on our individual mobile phone bills. Despite this great advance in science, the indigenous population of Africa continues to contract HIV, develop AIDS and die. How can that be?

The answer is clear. A stranglehold is in place upon the nations of Africa. They're controlled by puppet governments installed by the former colonial powers of Old Europe. HIV vaccine is only available to European immigrants in Africa. Antiretroviral drugs are strictly controlled and used by the regimes to determine who lives and dies. The poor populace die. A pan-African HIV-based apartheid system is in operation, excluding sufferers from contact with the healthy.

South Africa, previously a dominant military influence in post-colonial times, has lost its teeth. In 2006 seventy-five percent of the South African military were HIV positive. Their army is sick and dying. In an attempt to deal with this long neglected situation, the country has broken patent law and gone ahead with unlicensed production of antiretroviral generics. The UN has intervened with a pharmaceutical embargo to thwart the export to the rest of Africa of these *illegal* drugs.

The Central European Bank has recovered substantial African assets previously stolen through corruption. Attempts by the USA, Russia, China and India at financing change in Africa have been dwarfed by the enormous infrastructure development projects initiated by the Central European Bank. As a result, these non-European G10 and UN member countries have given up their attempts to influence the region.

Money, power and influence are no hindrance to the people who are really in charge of Africa. But it appears they've decided to let the sick simply die. Tens of millions have died already and up to one hundred million more will die. This is genocide on an unprecedented scale.'

The audience were hushed. Greg noticed then, for the first time, another man and two women were wearing the same spectacles as Thomas. Sensing something was afoot, he decided to stay put.

Professor Knox, clearing his throat, pursued the theme. 'Some cynics would say this is simply typical of negligence displayed towards the third world when the media does not have a new and interesting issue under the spotlight. But it's something much more sinister. African leaders have deliberately ignored, even denied, the HIV pandemic. The media has been continuously redirected to military conflict and famine in areas of total turmoil such as the Sudan. I put it to you this is a concerted and coordinated campaign. Those who have attempted to disclose the truth about HIV in Africa have been silenced! Eliminated! Most famously, Lady Diana Spencer!'

Thomas turned to Greg and said 'Now he's lost it.'

The similarly spectacled man and women appeared to hear Thomas's hushed words from across the room.

The audience murmured. Knox continued.

'Lady Diana Spencer was the most vociferous proponent of her time for the AIDS cause. In the same way she raised the worldwide profile of the landmine issue, she brought home the real threat of the AIDS pandemic. So she had to be silenced and she was. Diana was murdered by the security forces of Great Britain and France!'

The murmur grew into a buzz. Greg saw Thomas touch the side of his glasses and speak quietly, nodding towards his bespectacled colleagues. An object was thrown at the podium from that general direction and hit the professor's microphone. A member of the audience turned and attacked the smartly dressed young man from the BNP who had interrupted earlier, assuming him to be the source of the missile. Pandemonium ensued. Greg was reminded of a Wild West bar room brawl and had an urge to participate. He started edging towards the melee but then felt Thomas's hand take his arm and they left the room.

A few seconds later, Professor Knox followed them, escorted by the man and two women Greg had concluded must be colleagues of Thomas.

'Well, Professor Knox, you certainly made an impression.' Thomas smiled.

'Yes, um, not exactly what I expected. But where are the press? Did anyone see them in the audience?'

Greg hadn't thought about the media. Professor Knox was right, they were conspicuously absent. One of the women smiled at Thomas.

They whisked the professor, and his two colleagues who had subsequently escaped the melee, out of the hotel where they flagged down a taxi.

Once the professor's team had left, Thomas's colleagues handed him their spectacles which he placed inside his bag.

~

One hour later Thomas and Greg found themselves in a first class carriage on the train back to Bedfordshire.

'So, Greg, what did you make of the Professor's *discovery*?' Thomas made his scepticism clear.

'Well, I always went for the conspiracy theory on Diana's death, but the rest? I mean, it's hardly credible, is it?'

'Truly incredible,' Thomas replied.

Greg looked out of the window at the passing countryside. Although the weather since his arrival had been fine, the previous fortnight had brought heavy rain and storms. The rivers once more threatened to burst their banks and inundate England's country garden of low lying towns and villages.

~

Greg slept fitfully. His dreams were like a confused jigsaw with pieces from different puzzles. He couldn't fit them together; the sizes, shapes and colours were incompatible.

He woke with a start. The bedside clock showed 3 a.m. and his throat was dry and he felt thirsty.

~

Martin Knox's powerful Jaguar ate up the miles on the M1 motorway between London and Leeds. He was grateful for his teetotal colleague Tony who was driving. The carriageway was empty and Tony pushed the enormous engine a little harder.

Greg went downstairs for a cold drink and noticed the light on in Thomas's study. He headed across the hall to chat with his friend, but could see Thomas was engrossed in some kind of work on the computer. Just at that moment the telephone rang and Thomas picked up on speaker.

'Hi. What's the latest?'

'Just past camera thirty-seven north of junction fifteen, rural area, no other vehicles on the carriageway. Device in place. Power cut in this area in ten seconds and counting. Over to you.'

'Okay, will do.' Thomas hung up. He counted aloud. 'Six, five, four, three, two.' Picking up the phone again he dialled a number and hung up.

~

236

At the wheel of the speeding Jaguar Tony wasn't disturbed by the power cut that switched off the carriageway lights. He flicked the headlights to full beam and pushed the V12 engine harder, having fun in trying to outrun the reach of the blue xenon beams.

The engine roared and surged. Tony took his foot off the accelerator but it stayed depressed and he began to panic.

'Martin. Martin! How do you turn off the cruise control?'

Then the headlights went out and they were in total darkness, hurtling through the remote countryside at over one hundred and thirty miles per hour, and still accelerating. Surely the engine limiter would cut in. Tony tried the brakes to no effect whatsoever. He held onto the steering wheel grimly, peering into the dark night through the windscreen and trying to see by moonlight. Then the steering wheel began to turn under his hands.

'My God!'

The wheel spun violently to the left, breaking both of Tony's thumbs. The Jaguar went into a roll and tumbled across the lanes and over an empty field.

Next day the press reports weren't overly sympathetic about the single vehicle accident. The outspoken Professor from Leeds had made serious and unfounded allegations at an extremist gathering in London, from which he had for some reason excluded the media. Having then indulged in alcohol, loose women and drugs, he had driven at reckless speed on the motorway, endangering the life of three other people in the car, including a prostitute from an erotic dance club. The car had gone out of control and crashed, killing all on board.

In defence of their safety record, the Jaguar Car Company released a statement saying even twelve airbags could not guarantee passenger safety at an impact speed of one hundred and seventy-two miles per hour.

My sweet Lord

A misty Bedfordshire morning greeted Greg when he arose the next day. Thomas persuaded him to postpone the return to Ireland until the evening. Sue had risen early and left the two men to fend for themselves in the kitchen.

'So, how much of what Knox said was accurate, in your opinion?' Greg asked between mouthfuls of toast and marmite.

Thomas took a slurp from his mug of tea. 'Well, he gave a fairly neat description of the most widely accepted story for the origin of HIV and AIDS. Monkeys, chimpanzees and then viral transfer to humans, *zoonosis*.'

'And the state of Africa, is it really so bad?'

'It's true HIV and AIDS are pandemic on the African continent, on a scale that dwarfs any other human catastrophe. India and China are also suffering to a lesser extent.'

'But what about his accusations of African genocide through European negligence?'

'Well, I have to say that was difficult to swallow. As you know, I'm working on projects in several different African countries. What I've seen is truly appalling. I've seen many cases of neglect, even denial of the HIV situation by autocratic and often dictatorial leaders.'

'But we can't deny the existence of these massive African infrastructure projects, led by Western Europe. Sure, I'm working on them myself.'

'That's right,' Thomas said. 'The Central European Bank *has* finally taken action and confiscated the stolen wealth from Swiss bank accounts. That wealth has to be returned, and not just to the pockets of a new set of swindlers. And it's true the scale of it dwarfs the aid previously subscribed by the G8 and G10. So we've unapologetically taken the initiative. But it's damned if you do and damned if you don't. For decades we exhibited neglect, we just have to face the criticism of sceptics now we're finally doing the right thing by Africa.'

'And how about puppet governments and the elimination of Lady Diana?'

'Well, I don't think the world would stand idle whilst *Old Europe* re-established its African colonies, do you? As for the Diana accusation, all that's been investigated and reinvestigated ad nauseum. Plus there are numerous other high profile AIDS and famine campaigners alive and kicking, most of them knighted and still playing music.'

Over the rest of breakfast and a walk around the edge of the village, Thomas filled Greg in on the scale and progress of the other infrastructure projects. Having grown so familiar with his own micro-generator technology, Greg took the importance of his own work very much for granted. To hear that his was just one of many leading edge developments being piloted in Africa left him with mixed feelings. He had thought his project to be somehow unique. But it was fascinating to hear there were other innovative technologies being employed and he resolved to find out more about them.

By late morning the reason for his extended stay approached and, with some trepidation, Greg entered the old village church with Thomas. A thanksgiving service, Thomas had called it.

The small Norman church had brass plaques inlaid in the floor, bearing images of knights in armour, and the sun shone a medley of colour through stained glass windows depicting bible scenes in a style long forgotten.

Greg wasn't a particularly religious person but he would often wander into a cathedral or a quaint chapel on his travels to seek a few private meditative moments. He could usually determine the creed of worship by visual clues but the denomination of religion this church currently served wasn't clear. There were mixed messages.

The entire village seemed to have turned out for the service. Greg and Thomas took a seat in a wooden pew half way down the aisle. Not long after they arrived the place was so full that latecomers were restricted to standing at the back.

The minister, preacher or priest or whoever he was greeted the crowded audience with open arms and a broad smile. The themes of the service were thanksgiving for peace and prosperity, for the safe hands of the country's current ecclesiastical and governmental leaders, and for brothers and sisters in Africa whose circumstances were currently less fortunate.

Songs were sung in a cheery vein. Greg, ever the cynic, was on the alert for the catch. To his great surprise the service felt honest, heartfelt and uplifting.

Thomas gave Greg a look that said *I told you so*. Many entire families were present, although there were very few elderly people. Folk at the back of the church were catered for with flat screens and loudspeakers relaying the service. In fact there were screens discreetly placed at intervals throughout the building, everyone had a view.

A few members of the congregation stood in turn in the midst of the people to read excerpts of ecclesiastical texts Greg only partially recognised. This puzzled him as, having endured and later cast off a very religious upbringing, he considered himself au fait with the Bible, old testament and new. One of the readings about rivers and gardens made his mind flash back to something he had once read on a plane.

Thomas gave him a dig in the ribs and said 'You'll enjoy this bit.'

Everyone rose to their feet as guitars began to strum together. Greg made out the unmistakeable introduction to

George Harrison's classic, *My Sweet Lord*. When they reached the chorus Greg felt his hands drawn across his body. Sue had appeared to his left and squeezed his hand in hers. Thomas had stepped aside and another woman Greg recognised from the baker's shop took his other hand.

My sweet Lord, oh, my Lord, I really want to see you....

Greg filled with warmth. He was cool with it, found it uplifting, freeing.

I really want to see you Lord, but it takes so long, my Lord...

There was no saccharin sickly sweetness, no disturbing evangelism. The congregation sang as one, some with eyes closed, some smiling, others serious.

My sweet Lord, Hare Krishna, my sweet Lord, Allah Akhbah, oh my Lord, Jesus, Yahweh, Buddha Dharma, Vahiguru, my Lord...

Greg heard the mixed denominations but it seemed right. He looked around again, smiling. The congregation were cosmopolitan, even in this small village.

My, my Lord...

The crowd repeated the chorus like drunks who won't get off a karaoke machine, even when the song is finished. Greg wondered how it would end. He followed Sue's gaze and looked up at the nearest display screen showing a gathering at another, larger venue. On screen a well-dressed man in the middle of the front row broke ranks with a gentle laugh and held his hands forward in supplication.

Oh my Lord thought Greg. The smiling face of Anthony Goolden beamed out benevolently upon the people of the United Kingdom.

Enraptured

'Is he sincere?' Greg asked as he enjoyed a last pint before leaving Flitley.

'Absolutely,' Thomas said. 'I've met Anthony about a dozen times through work and he's totally genuine. An amazing individual.'

'The Prime Minister of Great Britain, an evangelical leader? I'm surprised the public would go for it, to be honest. Look at Tony Blair back at the start of the century. The temptation must have been immense but he resisted any reference to being driven by religion. Blair knew it would have spelt immediate political suicide.'

Thomas nodded in agreement. 'You're quite right. And remember George W Bush? He made no bones about it, saw himself as God's weapon in the fight against terrorism. A thinly veiled Christian crusade against Islam. Millions of American Christians embraced his theology but billions worldwide rejected and resented it.'

'So how has it happened?'

'No, I think you misunderstand. Anthony didn't lead the country into this. It evolved. His chosen role is to acknowledge and endorse it.'

'But it is a religion, right? A new religion?' Greg felt excited. He hadn't been spiritually moved for years in the way he had been that morning.

'No, it's not a religion per se. More an accommodation of existing religions. You could say it's the logical outcome of a cosmopolitan secular society. When the different religious groups reach an equilibrium regarding shared aims, values and aspirations then a kind of harmony can break out.'

'And if they don't reach equilibrium?'

'Well, mostly they don't, that's true. The Islamic terrorism we experienced here a few years ago, the race riots in France, ethnic persecution, they're alternative outcomes.'

'So how has it come about?'

Thomas paused to collect his thoughts, taking a deep draught of his beer.

'I think it's a lot to do with a climate of tolerance engendered by nearly two decades of fairly liberal government. Extremists marginalised, their support undermined. It really gathered momentum after the July 7th London bombings of 2005.'

'So Goolden's administration is the custodian of harmony,' Greg said with a grin.

Thomas laughed. 'It sounds corny but that's about the size of it. Public opinion polls put the morale of the nation at an all time high. And all those churches, once empty, are back in use for celebration. The individual religions maintain their momentum; Christianity, Islam, Hinduism, Buddhism, Judaism, Shinto, you name it. And, of course, agnosticism, which is really the majority of us.'

Greg nodded. He considered himself agnostic.

'What's the story elsewhere in Europe, do you know? I heard the Swiss finally managed to push through a referendum against any mosque building a minaret.'

'Yes, that's right,' Thomas said. 'Switzerland is beyond the pale regarding religious harmony. Christo Schwarz and his party make sure of that. France, Germany and Spain, on the other hand, are in a similar position to us. Italy is a little more problematic because of the Vatican but they're making steps in the right direction.'

'And there's nothing weird going on like *the Rapture* or anything?'

Greg and Rose had long been into conspiracy theories and one of their favourites was the rapture. Evangelical

Christian fundamentalists had long anticipated a second coming of Christ would raise the righteous from the earth's surface and deal apocalyptic devastation upon the remaining unbelievers.

Although ex-President Bush never explicitly referenced his foreign policy to the language of Rapture, he had the support of millions of evangelical Christian Americans who expressed firm belief in it. One conspiracy theory proposed that American foreign policy was designed to bring about certain events in the world, particularly in the Middle East, events that literal interpretation of the Bible had named as prerequisites before the rapture could occur. There was even a movement identifying Tony Blair as the Antichrist, leading a European super-state and acting as a catalyst for the Apocalypse.

'No. No doctrine whatsoever. Simply live and let live. But it's not without its challenges.'

Greg could tell from the look on his friend's face that Thomas had been involved in those challenges.

'Well, I say cheers to harmony.' Greg raised his glass.

'This green and pleasant land,' Thomas said as rain lashed against the pub windows.

Five minutes later Greg was running through the wind and rain to a taxi, dragging his suitcase behind him. The threatened storm had broken and the car's radio informed of flood warnings across the lower lying counties.

Where were you?

'Do you remember where you were and what you were doing when the King died?'

'Sure, I was preparing my paper round in Charlie Watkins newsagents at six in the morning. I read the headlines - *The King is dead.* Nearly cried. Which is funny because I never really liked Elvis Presley. I loved that paper round though. Must have been about twelve years old.'

Greg took his turn with a question for Rose. 'Twin Towers, 9 11. Where were you?'

'I was walking through the Glattzentrum shopping centre in Zurich and I saw it happen live on the TV. Then I called you on your mobile.'

'That's right. I was on that business training course in the mountains. How about John Lennon?'

'No, I don't remember. Asian Tsunami?'

'That's easy. We were here in Kilkenny, relaxing in front of the TV on Boxing Day. How about…how about Lady Diana?'

'Yeah, I remember that was our first summer in Switzerland. Your family phoned and told us before it hit the news over there.'

Greg went quiet for a few moments.

'A penny for your thoughts,' Rose said.

'I was just thinking, I had no idea or interest at the time about what Diana was doing. She seemed a strange figure to me, much too young to be Prince Charles's bride and quite a shy girl.'

'And now you think differently.'

'Yep. She was probably the last high profile figure to draw attention to HIV and AIDS in Africa. Since then it's been famine, war, refugees, debt cancellation and pop concerts.'

'You're so cynical. So I guess you're back on the Diana conspiracy trail?'

'Yep, but with a new twist. You wouldn't believe what I heard in London this week, and the guy who told the story has since died mysteriously!'

Greg recounted to Rose the events of the week in England. They both loved to cook up conspiracy theories and would take it in turns to play devil's advocate. This story was Greg's so Rose tried to pull it apart.

'So, what you're saying is persons unknown eliminated Diana to stop her drawing further attention to the AIDS situation in Africa? Who would want to do that and why?'

'Well, it could have been one of the African countries who didn't want further attention. You know, one of the crazy guys who denied HIV and AIDS were a problem or maybe one of them who developed a *magical herbal cure*. Where was that?'

'Gambia, I think.'

'Yeah. Or even, if the European intervention part is true, one or more of the former colonial powers.'

'Well, about that part,' Rose said, 'I have to say it's just too far fetched. The massive reinvestment of ill-gotten gains in infrastructure projects is genuine, right?'

'Right. As we know.'

'Right. So why would Europe be making positive interventions on the one hand and committing genocide on the other?'

'Point taken.'

'Another weakness in the argument is the way the other superpowers are just sitting back and letting it happen. I thought Russia, China and the USA were all heavily involved in different African countries.' Rose smiled and crossed her arms. *The prosecution rests.*

Greg held out three fingers of his left hand, palm up, and began to count them off.

'Russia had post-colonial military interests in several African countries but that pretty much died off after the Cold War ended and the USSR broke up. China had some similar military interests that have faded and more recently had oil interests in Angola. Those have diminished since the oil fields have been subject to sabotage and now China has found oil reserves in its own provinces.'

Rose put on a face of comic annoyance.

'As for the USA, military engagement is virtually zero since their Somalia and Sudan experiences. They've worked hard to reduce domestic oil consumption to match domestic reserves. And, of course, they have continuing conflict in the Middle East and more than a little trouble at home at the moment. I rest my case.' Greg refilled Rose's wineglass with a triumphal flourish.

'Not convinced, not convinced,' she retorted. 'It all kind of makes sense except for the AIDS genocide part.'

'And Diana, was she murdered in a conspiracy?'

'Of course she was. Not all princess stories have a happy ending you know.'

'Indeed they don't.'

~

On the other side of the Atlantic Ocean the *little trouble at home* was once again manifesting itself.

It had started around one year earlier with sporadic confrontations in predominantly rural communities. Evangelical Christians, confident of redemption in the ever imminent final reckoning, became increasingly interventional with their preaching and attempts at conversion. A backlash was unavoidable amongst other religious groups. Entire communities became polarised and the few liberals were left in an uncomfortable middle ground. And, it being a constitutional right, most of the antagonists were armed.

Initially, a few serious injuries had occurred and one or two deaths due to gunshots, but nothing remarkable. Certainly insignificant compared to the routine levels of muggings and murders in the cities. It was this comparative insignificance that allowed the situation to escalate virtually unnoticed.

Whilst Homeland Security had its eyes and ears finely tuned to the terrorist threat in the big cities, America was caught with its pants down when sectarian violence spilled onto the provincial streets and country roads of the heartland.

~

Two soldiers in camouflage stood manning a roadblock on the outskirts of Bland, West Virginia. The Blue Ridge Mountains made a scenic backdrop but the troops were tired of looking at it. An hour ago they had heard the retort of rifle fire echoing up in those mountains.

'Hey, Jake?' asked the younger of the two.

'Yeah, what's up?'

'You come from round here, right?'

'Yup.'

'What's the population of Bland then?'

'About seven thousand souls.'

'Hey, that's a pretty small city.'

'Nope, that's the county. Bland County, man. Bland city is about three thousand.'

'Like I said, pretty small.'

'Of course, it's only the half if you don't count the penitentiary.' The older man spat tobacco juice on the ground.

'Well even with fifteen hundred persons and a prison, how come there's only you and me on this roadblock?'

'Shit, man! How many towns do you think this goddamn country has? And how many soldiers we got available with what's going on all around the world? I'll tell you, we ain't got enough. Nowhere near enough.'

The younger man kicked his boot in the dust, regretting starting the conversation.

'What's more, this ain't the only road into town. We've got about a dozen other buddies sitting on weapon watch. We're spread thin, it ain't our fault.'

'Okay, Jake, okay. Sorry I asked. Jesus, shit.'

'Hey, Todd, quit the blaspheming. Just 'cos everything is going to hell doesn't mean we can take the Lord's name in vain.'

God, thought Todd, I bet he dances with snakes in that evangelical church in Bland on Sundays. But he just said 'Sorry, Jake. Sorry, man.'

Their attention was drawn by the sound of an approaching vehicle. A large pickup could be seen approaching along the hazy blacktop road. The soldiers took up their positions. Jake moved into the middle of the barrier and Todd moved to one side so they would have two angles on the truck when, hopefully, it came to a halt.

The muscled Japanese vehicle slowed on its approach and they could see the cabin and bed of the truck were bristling with armed men. The pickup was a medium blue colour and sported an amateurish logo on each door that read *Bland Militia*.

Shit, Jake muttered under his breath. Every man in the truck was armed as well as or better than the soldiers. They had assault rifles, grenade launchers, high velocity sniper rifles. But none of the arms were aimed at Jake or Todd, at least not yet.

The driver pulled up short of the barrier but didn't turn off the engine. Jake suspected the guy was smiling but there was too much beard to be sure.

'Hey, what you boys up to out here?' Jake asked.

A tall man stood up on the bed of the truck. 'We just had us a little bit of hunting up there in the mountains and we're on our way home.'

He was brandishing a type of rifle Jake had only seen in more expensive gun catalogues. Jake glanced down at his own inferior weapon.

'Any luck with the hunting?' Todd asked, looking suspiciously at the bed of the truck.

'Not to speak of,' the man replied. 'Now, you boys let us through. My wife'll be mighty angry with me if I'm late for dinner and this here gun's no match for the wrath of a woman. Gotta be there when food's on the table.'

Jake signed with his left hand and Todd picked up the signal, moving casually towards a small military fast response vehicle parked at the side of the roadblock.

'Listen boys,' Jake said. 'I'm a Bland boy myself and I don't seem to recall seeing you all around here before.' He took one hand off the muzzle of his rifle and casually indicated the truck's license plate where the town name Roanoke was clearly visible. Even Todd knew Roanoke stood on the other side of the Blue Ridge.

'Well to tell the truth, sir, we was just gonna visit our cousins here in Bland.'

There was a sound of oiled mechanisms moving and clicking from the pickup. Jake raised his rifle and pointed generally at the truck from his waist. 'This is the United States Army, you are refused permission to pass this roadblock. Return immediately to your domicile.'

For a few uneasy seconds Jake felt like a hunter's quarry as he saw upwards of a dozen weapons move to point in his direction.

'Private Todd here is waiting for you to comply with my command.' Jake indicated with his non-trigger hand at Todd. Turning to look, the Roanoke boys saw Todd sitting comfortably behind the bullet-proof shield of a machine gun mounted on the back of the military fast response vehicle. He looked ready and willing to try it out.

'Okay boys, let's go,' the tall man said, sitting back down into the back of the truck. The driver floored the gas and turned a tight circle, disappearing back towards the mountains in a cloud of dust that settled slowly over the two soldiers.

'Good work, Todd,' Jake said. 'Last week a soldier was killed at this checkpoint, right there. Probably the same Roanoke rednecks. Planning on a prison break or evangelical cleansing or some such.'

He pointed to where he'd been standing, targeted by a dozen guns. Todd could just make out an ugly dark dry stain on the blacktop.

'No kidding! You're one brave soldier,' Todd said. As he clapped Jake on the shoulder he noticed a small wet stain in the crotch of Jake's camouflage trousers.

'Ain't nothing,' Jake said. 'A soldier's gotta be piss scared every now and then just to keep his joy of being alive.'

He reached inside his jacket and pulled out a piece of chewing tobacco, offering it to Todd. They were now on the far side of the barrier, away from their vehicle.

The sound of crows was what saved them. The birds took off at a distance, cawing at the disturbance at the point of launch. Jake threw himself into a ditch at the roadside, pulling the unaware Todd with him. There was a slight whistling sound and then the impact. Their vehicle was pushed a few meters down the road, on fire and mangled.

'Lucky shot,' Jake muttered, watching the pickup retreat into the distance.

On the road again

She awoke in a motel room to the droning sound of an air conditioning unit. It was a box-like bedroom with a windowless bathroom at the rear.

A draughty window next to the entrance door spanned the entire wall. Zero privacy unless the room was kept in dusty curtained gloom.

Through the wall she could hear a couple enjoying their waking moments together. Everyone has their favourite time of the day. Hers used to be predictable, purely a matter of business. But these days she preferred the spontaneity of her lover and that could be anytime, anyplace, anyhow.

He lay covered by a single sheet on the enormous bed. The motel diet wasn't doing his waistline any good. She could see a spare tyre developing where previously his small waist had been lean. But that wasn't all bad, the last few years she'd had her fill of skinny, over-groomed men. And she'd rounded out a little too.

It wasn't easy to keep a svelte figure with takeaways, diners, planes and cars. They had a Toyota Camry parked outside, another nondescript hire car that made her want to puke. He'd said they would hire a pickup or an SUV at the next change.

He let out a groan and she knew the long succession of cloned motel rooms wasn't doing it for him either. Rolling over on top, she managed to take his mind off it. They added their own harmony to the dawn chorus coming from the other side of the wall.

He grabbed some donuts and a cup of coffee in the motel lobby. She took some sugary breakfast cereal with milk in a polystyrene bowl and ate with a plastic spoon. What a classy establishment. The sign by the *breakfast buffet* boasted it was included in the price. She would have paid the price of the motel room just to have a *pain au chocolate* and a cup of English tea.

They set off in the Camry along the highway, the car set to cruise at the speed limit. The road undulated like a sea with a long, deep swell and the cruise control of the Japanese vehicle surged each time they crested. Out of South Boston, Virginia, they headed for the wilds of the Blue Ridge Mountains.

After about forty minutes they had to start looking for petrol as the tank was running low. The large engines in the USA certainly guzzled gas in comparison with European models. She was at the wheel and soon spotted a Mobil station. They exited the highway onto the station forecourt.

In keeping with most of the filling stations they had encountered, and there had been many, this one had a range of alternative fuels. He filled up the tank with bioethanol. Being a domestic product, it decreased the reliance upon imported oil. As he tanked up he recalled a friend who also had a bioethanol engine in his car and claimed, rather unbelievably, the fuel was somehow derived from milk.

The cashier was intrigued by his accent. He spoke English well with a trace of the continental European. As always, he paid cash, untraceable. Carrying a brown paper bag of soda cans and potato chips he returned to the car.

She'd once again attracted unwelcome attention. A pickup truck with four men had pulled in alongside the Toyota and the driver was in conversation with her. She'd got out of the car to get something from the boot. Being so long, tall, tanned and lovely, she always caught the eye and he got a kick out of it, but sometimes her admirers wanted to do more than look.

Something the pickup driver said obviously caused offence and she gave the guy a slap in the face. The other three men jeered their friend but at the same time stepped out beside the driver. They were four very large men.

It was a dangerous situation. Two of them were holding rifles and he could see a pistol in the driver's waistband. Drawing the pistol, the driver pointed it at the girl and gestured behind the filling station. A glance at the building was enough for the cashier to bury his head in his newspaper. See no evil.

The four men had noticed she wasn't alone and her companion found himself rounded up at gunpoint on the way across the forecourt.

'Little lady of yours gotta learn some manners. Don't know how to return a civil greeting from an American gentleman. 'Bout time she learns we don't take no shit from some European slut and you're gonna have the pleasure to observe the proceedings. Watch and learn, little man.'

The tallest man started to unbuckle his belt. The riflemen had their weapons aimed at the Europeans but were watching the ringleader.

At first it looked like he was just going to beat her with the belt, but he continued to pull down his jeans.

'Jesus Christ almighty, Vern, you sure gonna hurt the girl with that there monster,' one of the other rednecks said.

'Don't mean to hurt the slut, only pleasure. Best way for her to remember this little lesson is to enjoy it.'

Fighting the urge to make some comment, the girl looked across and caught the eye of her boyfriend with a barely perceptible nod.

As Vern's trouser dropped to his ankles, and he wasn't wearing any underwear, the armed men lowered their rifles slightly. Two well aimed kicks sent the weapons out of their hands and sailing through the air. While he ran to retrieve the weapons, she slammed a hard fist into the stomach of one of the disarmed men and landed a sharp kick in the groin of the other.

Vern tried to reach down to the ground where his pistol was in his belt but only succeeded in falling flat on his face in the dust. The butt of a rifle landed with a crack on the wrist of his searching hand.

The fourth man had no firearm but drew a large Bowie knife from his belt. He was unceremoniously despatched with a rifle shot to the left shoulder and dropped the knife to the ground.

She walked over to the rifle owners, aimed the pistol she'd taken from Vern's belt and shot a bullet into the calf of each man.

There were groans of agony but no one was going to die today. Experience told them it was necessary to incapacitate otherwise they'd be pursued. These guys would simply fade away, licking their wounds and too ashamed to tell the true story to anyone.

She wanted to take the pickup but he insisted they continue in the hire car. To steal a car would clearly be a crime. On the other hand, a shoot out with unauthorised militia was pretty much an everyday occurrence. He did allow her to put a bullet in each tyre of the pickup.

They left Vern and friends moaning behind the filling station. Vern didn't look such a monster anymore, sitting naked from the waist down in the dust.

The rifles were pretty neat, much better than the standard Swiss Army issue Reto had in his cellar at home. He stashed them in the luggage compartment. Svetlana placed the pistol in her handbag. On the road again.

As ye sow, so shall ye reap

'The President of the United States is on line two, sir.'

Anthony Goolden looked at the flashing light on his desk. It was a conversation he didn't want to have. But matters hadn't yet progressed to the stage where he could seriously contemplate refusing to take a call from James Burden.

'Mr President, how are you today?' Goolden forced his face into a smile and the tone of his voice automatically became warm and friendly.

'Prime Minister. Anthony, I'm having a bad day. The United States of America is having a bad day. Give me some good news and tell me you've persuaded your cabinet to authorise military support.'

'James, you overestimate my influence as an individual. I'm not in a position to dictate to the cabinet; it's not the way we work here anymore. And even if cabinet were to agree, which they don't, we have no troops to send. Three quarters of active service personnel are currently engaged in ongoing overseas operations.'

'Africa. What the hell are you doing in Africa anyway? They're not the terrorist threat, they don't have strategic trade importance, they don't control fuel supplies. They're nothing. You and your pals are wasting valuable resources out there.'

'With all due respect, James, that is for the sovereign state of the United Kingdom to decide. We are rising above self interest, for once, and the African Union requires our support during the infrastructure development programme. As you're well aware.'

'That's very noble but what we're doing in the Middle East is the Lord's work. Surely you, of all people, can understand. The Christian world has to stand united in the face of global terrorism. We have a role to play. I, personally, have the duty to lead America in pursuit of God's work. And I believe you and your country are essential allies in our quest.'

'In your crusade? Which isn't sanctioned by the United Nations and doesn't have governmental or popular support in any other G10 country? You have one million troops on the ground in a military stand-off with Iran. On the verge of a land war with a country that can call twelve million men to arms. A country with which you've had no discernible diplomatic dialogue for twenty years. Even if I had the power to divert our soldiers to Iran, which I don't, I couldn't in all conscience send them on a suicide mission.'

'How can you say that? Every one of our men is worth ten of theirs! We have the best military machine in the world, technology so advanced even I don't fully understand it and, most importantly, God on our side. It's a righteous venture and we will triumph.'

'No, it's not, and I'm afraid you won't.' Goolden let the words sink in. The telephone line remained silent at both ends for thirty long seconds. Goolden slowly started to replace the receiver and had nearly hung up when the American eventually resumed in a reconciliatory tone.

'Anthony, we need your support here. You know our domestic situation. It's placing strains on our resources. We have half a million personnel deployed around our own towns and cities. If you take a lead in Persia then others will follow. We need to at least match our forces in Iran, man for man, with an allied contingent to have any chance of success.'

'James, you'll have to back down. There's no way any of the European Union countries will follow the USA into

Iran. You're taking the part of unprovoked aggressor against an Islamic state. We will not be a part of that again.'

'I cannot back out. It has to be Europe that comes into Persia with us. China or India has the power but they're not intended to take part. It has to be this way. It's our destiny.'

'It may be your destiny but it's not mine, it's not the destiny of the UK. It's not the way forward, James. I'm absolutely convinced. The way forward is peace, not confrontation. We learned the hard way in Iraq. Why can't you see that? Why do you have to force this apocalypse scenario? Do you see yourself as the Gatekeeper? Iran sees its position as defender of the faith. Can't the doctrine be wrong? Isn't it possible you've misinterpreted the scriptures? They will fight to the last man, woman and child. James, examine your conscience and call a halt to this now.'

'What? How dare you challenge our chosen path? You, of no faith, of every faith, peddler of platitudes and mediocrity!'

'Really, James, there's no need to get offensive.' Goolden thought he may have gone a bit too far. A second silence ensued but it was briefer than previously.

'Anthony, I will *show* you, I *will* convince you. Europe has a part to play.'

'Not in Iran.' Goolden was now desperately looking for a way to conclude the conversation without hanging up. At that moment his communications advisor, Ron Wildman, came through the office door with a concerned look on his face, tapping his wristwatch.

'Listen, James, I have to address the nation in the next few minutes. Come and see me at Chequers. Soon. We can talk further.'

'Okay.' Burden hung up.

Wildman raised an eyebrow and Goolden found himself trying to fight off a sudden migraine.

'Time for our daily session, Anthony. Had you forgotten? Shall I order tea?'

Wildman sat down in an armchair, resting the ankle of his right leg across his left knee. As ever, Goolden felt at first slightly intimidated by the penetrating gaze of his communications guru, and then calm as if absorbing Wildman's aura of self confidence.

'Ron, we need to be quite clear on the expected role of Europe. James Burden is spinning me a yarn to try and pull us into Iran. He'll be here within a fortnight and I need you to tutor me further in whatever fundamental Evangelical Christian beliefs the Whitehouse is promulgating.'

Wildman looked so intense when he replied that Goolden thought those grey blue eyes might bore straight through his skull.

'Well, of course we can't go to Iran because we're rather busy in Africa at the moment. But I can tell you right now Burden had no real expectation of your agreement.'

~

In the Whitehouse the President turned to his team and smiled with satisfaction.

'Europe will not follow us into Persia. It is as anticipated.'

The people in the room exhaled as one and a murmur of voices arose.

'So, gentlemen, we have to take the agreed next steps. Place the emergency military conscription bill before the senate this week.'

Turning to his presidential aide he spoke in a lowered voice. 'And get the Israeli Prime Minister over here by Thursday.'

On the trail of the lonesome pine

Twenty of them entered the country via different routes. A further thirty were already there. None knew of the name or location of any of the others outside their own cell.

Their targets were a selection of the multitudinous Christian fundamentalist communities spread right across the United States of America. The infiltrators were well briefed, educated in the scriptures and able to exhibit a convincing evangelical fervour.

In some cases they became a little carried away in their role and engaged in skirmishes with antifundamentalist forces. One such incident had proven fatal for the agent concerned and it was deemed necessary to send a short term replacement. Looking for fresh adventure, Thomas Thistlethwaite volunteered and was accepted for the job.

He chose to fly via Dublin as one of the airports where US immigration control was carried out at the point of departure. Sporting a convincing facsimile disguise, Thomas boarded and arrived a few hours later at Atlanta, Georgia with immigration pre-clearance. He connected under another identity via domestic flights to Roanoke, Virginia where a rental car sat waiting for him.

From the outset Thomas had problems with his accent, the reason he hadn't been in the first wave of agents. The car rental attendant frowned at his flattened vowels and he had trouble being understood by the waiter at the restaurant where he stopped for a spot of lunch. A sense of foreboding crept up on him. He was well used to adopting disguise and could speak several other languages fluently but successful adaptation of his native tongue to something American was eluding him. The hire car at least was innocuous, so he thought, but in fact it marked him out as a tourist.

The first army road block on the outskirts of Roanoke confirmed part of the briefing he'd received. All routes into and out of towns and cities would be under military observation. What Thomas wasn't ready for was the militia roadblock at the foot of the Blue Ridge Mountains.

'You transporting weapons?' a young man asked. He wore a light blue shirt with a 'Roanoke Militia' emblem on the breast pocket. The young man himself was well armed and Thomas could see the shirt was lined with Kevlar.

'No, I have no weapons,' Thomas said.

'Sir, I would advise you not to proceed unaccompanied and unarmed into the mountains. You could be at some personal risk.' The militia man indicated back towards Roanoke with his rifle. 'There's a gun store back down town or you could wait and travel in convoy with our next patrol.'

Thomas's smile didn't reach his eyes.

'Thanks for the advice. I'll be especially vigilant.'

The militia man shook his head and turned to a colleague. 'Goddamn tourists just don't take this situation seriously. We could lose another one today.'

Thomas drove on.

He had picked up a set of weapons from a left luggage facility close to the airport. A machine pistol under the driver's seat, a small pistol in a holster strapped to his right calf and a pump action shotgun in the trunk of the car.

The road climbed via a long series of sweeping bends and he lowered the car windows, enjoying the mountain air. The only traffic he saw were one or two wrecked vehicles at the roadside along the route.

Near the top of the ridge he pulled over at a picnic area to take in the view. It was the same stop he and Natalie had made several years ago before the kids had come along. On that occasion they'd taken a keepsake of a quartz crystal he'd found poking up through the soil. This time there were empty bullet cases lying on the ground.

A few shots came from somewhere west of where he was standing. It sounded like a hunting rifle. Returning to the car, Thomas removed the shotgun from the trunk and placed it on the passenger seat before continuing on his way.

The road became narrower as it descended down the other side of the mountains. Another volley of shots rang out and he slowed, rounding a tight bend to see two vehicles in the road, one of them partially blocking the way. Two men stood laughing and one of them took aim with his hunting rifle into the woods bordering the road.

It seemed a strange way to go hunting, shooting at game from the roadside. Thomas followed the trajectory of the bullet with his eyes and saw a red lumberjack shirt disappear behind a tree at a distance of a couple of hundred meters. The prey seemed to have escaped this time.

The hunter, a tall man, turned to the jeep parked at the side of the road and blasted the nearside tyres with his rifle. 'Hell, that guy's sure got a long walk back to Bland,' he laughed.

The two of them turned and noticed Thomas with some surprise. They'd been so focused on the elusive driver of the jeep they had failed to hear Thomas approach and get out of his car. He stood facing them with the pump-action shotgun hanging lazily from one hand.

It was a strange picture to their way of thinking. A tourist type in a hire car but armed. When Thomas addressed them they became even more uneasy.

'Open season on lumberjacks?' he asked, making little effort with his accent.

The escaped driver of the jeep, who was now presumably charging head down through the forest, had been Thomas's intended escort to his destination of Bland. He wasn't amused by the antics of these rednecks.

'Well, what do we have here?' the tall man said. 'A limey?'

The two of them walked towards Thomas who kept his shotgun hanging down. He was preparing to take them out when stars exploded in front of his eyes and his mouth filled with dust. He fell face first into the dirt.

Thomas's assailant, a third man, let out a yell from behind Thomas and stepped forward to place a hearty kick in his ribcage as Thomas lay unmoving on the ground.

'Hey Bob, why did ya wanna go and Taser him for?' the second man said. 'He wasn't aiming his gun at us or nothing!'

'Goddamn English! Those sons of bitches left my brother to die in Iraq. And thousands more are gonna die in goddamn Iran because the yella bellied cowards won't face up to the Ayatollah! Goddamn it!' He swung his leg right back and landed a kick on Thomas's shin that hit the pistol in Thomas's calf holster and caused Bob some pain himself. 'Shit!'

'Hey, keep ya wits about ya Bob,' the second man said as he came forward and removed the shotgun from Thomas's clenched hand. 'He's starting to come around.'

Thomas pulled himself up to his knees just in time to receive a kick in the head that might have broken his jaw had Bob been a little more cold blooded and a little less incensed. Nevertheless, it sent Thomas spinning.

He took the opportunity to reach for his pistol but found the calf holster had been damaged by the previous kick and the pistol was stuck. Luckily the rednecks didn't see the weapon otherwise they would probably have sunk a bullet into him without further ceremony.

Bob had himself fallen with the badly aimed kick to Thomas's head. The tall man stepped forward and brought

Thomas back down to earth with a blow from the butt of his hunting rifle.

Not feeling in very good shape for hand to hand combat, Thomas decided to try again for his holstered pistol. The redneck holding Thomas's confiscated shotgun saw what he was doing and, stepping forward, aimed the weapon and discharged it at close range. A scalding wave swept over Thomas's face as the cartridge fired. He shut his eyes and felt his eyebrows burn off.

'What in hell's name?' the second man exclaimed.

What in hell's name? thought Thomas. He'd been provided with blank ammunition.

'I got him, I got him,' the tall man said, swinging round his hunting rifle, but found the chamber of the weapon to be empty. Thomas made a charge before the rifle could be reloaded but was crushed under a flying tackle from Bob. Winded, the two men struggled to disentangle themselves as the tall man leisurely reloaded the rifle. The second man still stood gazing stupidly at the ineffective shotgun in his hands. Behind him Thomas heard the wheels of a vehicle crunch on the rough road surface.

Thomas scrambled to his feet just as the rifle was aimed. He grabbed Bob and launched the unwitting redneck towards the tall man as the shot was fired. Bob took a bullet in the face and fell like a slaughtered beast.

'Jesus, no! Bob!' The tall man dropped on one knee to comfort his friend but the life had already left Bob's eyes.

Seizing the chance, Thomas lunged towards the rifle but the tall man reacted swiftly and let loose another shot that knocked Thomas backwards off his feet, clutching his chest.

'Make peace with your maker, boy,' the man said, taking aim for a headshot. Thomas closed his eyes. The Kevlar vest had saved him from the last shot but now he needed a miracle.

The finger closed on the trigger but Thomas didn't hear the single retort. He heard a continuous burst of fire. An automatic rifle. Opening his eyes, he saw the bodies of all three men lying prone. Those of the tall man and the other were riddled with bullet holes and lay in spreading pools of blood.

He looked up to his saviour and met the smiling eyes of Svetlana.

'Oh, Thomas. What a fine mess you've got yourself into.' She hugged him and he groaned from his injuries.

Reto sauntered over with the automatic weapon in his hands. 'I never thought we'd see *you* here, in the Blue Ridge Mountains of Virginia.'

'Me neither, Reto, me neither.'

They drove the two cars on down from the ridge, Reto in Thomas's Chevrolet and Svetlana following in the Toyota. Thomas himself lay across the back seat of the Camry, recuperating from his ordeal.

As they rounded a hairpin bend a red blur flew towards them from the trees and both cars slammed to a halt. A man in jeans, a lumberjack shirt and baseball cap rolled across the Camry's bonnet and landed in a crumpled heap on the ground. Reto was quickly out of the driver's door and, rifle in hand, approached the man who was struggling to his feet.

'Good to see you, Graham,' Thomas said from behind Reto's shoulder. He stood on one leg and was holding his ribs with one hand. The other he extended in greeting.

'You too, Thomas. Any chance of a lift to Bland?' he said to Reto.

Reto handed over the Chevrolet to Thomas's escort and they headed on, Reto and Svetlana together in their own car.

Graham filled Thomas in on the assignment. They had no problems at the checkpoint entering Bland and the soldiers on duty were more than pleased to hear Bob and friends might have met a sticky end somewhere up in the mountains.

The Bland medical centre doctor diagnosed Thomas as having two broken ribs and a possible hairline fracture to the jaw. This gave Thomas hero status amongst the local evangelical community and eased their acceptance of him as a newcomer. However, after a few days they were becoming suspicious of the strange accent, which he still didn't have under control. So he became a man of few words for the remainder of his stay. That suited him well as he was there to watch and listen.

Thomas found Graham had thoroughly penetrated the local evangelical movement. In addition to the expected services of worship and stirring sermons, most of the families in Bland were actively involved in preparation for the Rapture. Teams of teenagers kept an internet vigil for signs of the approaching apocalypse and coordinated with national and international Rapture organisations.

There was undeniably something in the air and constant discussion was the norm in chapel, bars and restaurants on the topic of whether Bland would be honoured with any representation amongst the first chosen few. Most able bodied adult males were considering volunteering for military service in the Middle East and they assumed a distinct connection with what was happening there and the Rapture.

It was a successful but uncomfortable assignment for Thomas. He left the country within the week, information gathered according to the brief, but with pride hurt and bones still aching.

Reto and Svetlana bade Thomas a fond farewell at a small local airfield in Wytheville.

Thomas knew Reto had saved his life. He'd lost control of the situation up there in the mountains and looked death in the face. He hadn't shared with anyone but, when he'd shut his eyes waiting for the final bullet, Natalie had appeared in his mind's eye together with Hannah and Matt. They'd held out their hands and he'd been ready to meet them.

On return to the UK Thomas submitted his report, one of the last. It had taken just over one week for Ron Wildman's network to build a current and accurate grass roots picture of American Christian fundamentalist sentiment.

Kill or cure

The air in the boardroom was perfect. A constant twenty-two degrees Celsius, forty percent humidity and full of positive ions. The far wall of the room soothed the air as water trickled down a solid rock face, extracted from deep within the Swiss Alps.

Three men and two women were spaced evenly around a granite table, seated in leather chairs that made the occupant feel like a million dollars. An amount equivalent to around one month's salary for each of these captains of the pharmaceutical industry. A sixth person sat at a desk in the corner, ready to make notes on a computer.

'Firstly, let me say for the record we will not discuss relative price levels or market allocations. There will be no suggestion in any respect of any kind of cartel. We must make this clear statement as it is the first time our five companies have met together on this subject. This is the first gathering of the Pharmaceutical Industry HIV Collective. Our purpose is to ensure we align our duty to mankind with our duty to shareholders.' Stefan Westman looked around at the other members and took in their nods of assent at his grandiose opening.

The group went on to discuss their individual organisations' progress in the areas of HIV vaccine and antiretrovirals.

Westman's corporation, based in Germany, had been the first to make a breakthrough with the vaccine. Each of the others had followed suit within twelve months with a different vaccine patent. They all had a stable full of antiretrovirals which had various side effects, generally diminishing in inverse proportion to the cost of the drugs.

John Thurlby, of the UK based member, explained their progress with vaccine supplies to the UK government, predominantly for ex-patriots in Africa. They had endured protests during shareholder meetings regarding the non-supply of antiretrovirals to Africans. Thurlby explained no funding had been forthcoming from any African governments, aid agencies or G10 members to purchase antiretrovirals for sub-Saharan African countries.

Piers Newland II, of the American based member, confirmed his company was in a similar position. They were supplying the American armed forces with vaccine and had a substantial antiretroviral business in North and South America, although patent infringements in Brazil were problematic. There appeared to be no commercial market in Africa.

There was a voice of slight dissent from Nicole Thierry, the head of the Swiss pharmaceutical giant. Her board of directors had made a proposal to shareholders that a fund could be set up to pay for antriretrovirals for use in some of the harder hit African countries such as Zimbabwe and Kenya. However, a lobby group had successfully vetoed the proposal. They had shown the proposed size of fund to be inadequate and that ongoing commitment would be detrimental to shareholder return.

Conversation turned to the issue of patents and Francois Gilet, of the Franco-German member, expounded his company's view that continued UN sanctions against South Africa and Brazil were justified. 'The very fabric of the prosperity of each of our organisations is based upon the sanctity of patents we have earned through our product development pipelines. To flout these patents is to undermine the multi-billion investments we each make every year in development of potentially life saving drugs.'

All were in agreement on this item and took the statement on the record verbatim.

Nicole Thierry brought them back to the subject of the scale of the HIV pandemic in sub-Saharan Africa.

'I would like to share some statistics for discussion,' she said, opening her laptop computer and beckoning the assistant from the desk in the corner.

The assistant had Thierry's computer connected in a few seconds and a large picture on the wall revealed itself to be a flat-screen display unit.

'We estimate the number of HIV cases in sub-Saharan Africa, excluding South Africa, to exceed one hundred and fifty million by the end of this year. Consider that, depending upon the stage of HIV development, the cost of treatment per case ranges from two hundred and fifty to two thousand dollars per year to treat with antiretrovirals. Even if the situation were addressed with our cheapest antiretrovirals, those with the most severe side effects, then the current annual cost of drugs would still be in the region of one hundred billion dollars.'

The other members of the collective nodded seriously.

Thierry continued. 'The lobby group at my company's shareholder meeting was correct in identifying this as an unsustainable, ongoing commitment. This exceeds, by a factor of more than ten, the available funding. Available funding means AIDS foundations that are willing to address this issue. As already mentioned,' Thierry waved towards Thurlby with her left hand, 'African governments, general aid agencies and the G10 are not willing to address these costs.'

'So these people will all be left to die?' Westman asked.

'The rate of infection is at a peak,' Thierry replied. 'Numbers will decline as those who are most vulnerable go on to develop AIDS and die.'

Gilet interjected. 'There will come a point where the cost of treating the HIV positive population will become manageable for the governments and the G10. The financial strength of the aid agencies is negligible by comparison.'

'That time will come, a time when even our shareholders will find the philanthropic cost acceptable,' Newland added.

Westman summarised. 'We recognise the issue, Africa is dying. None of us is in a position to make a useful intervention at this time. The power of intervention lies with the African governments and the G10. It is our contractual duty to our shareholders that we maintain their financial returns and protect our patents. It is our ethical duty to the people of the world that we draw an appropriate amount of attention to their plight and prevail upon those in power to intercede when their conscience sees fit to do so.'

The collective agreed upon the wording for the press release and each member departed in their chauffeur driven limousine, comfortable in the belief they had done as much as humanly possible to satisfy the interest of their shareholders and alleviate the suffering of mankind.

Evil Empire

Rose was still in her dressing gown although it was one o'clock in the afternoon. She sat on a breakfast stool by the granite island in the kitchen, eating a fried egg sandwich and drinking from a mug of tea whilst surfing the internet.

'Hey, don't get egg on the keyboard!' Greg had got over a lot of his compulsive cleanliness hang-ups but fried egg yolk on the laptop keyboard was crossing the line.

'Wow, things are really looking bad in the Netherlands,' she said. 'They've declared a state of emergency and the military are trying to keep out the seawater. It makes our weather problems look trivial.'

Greg looked out of the patio doors at their quagmire of a garden. It was the third episode of extended rainfall that year. There hadn't been a totally dry day in over a month. The garden was thriving, everything was growing unseasonably well, but it had a manic feel to it. The boggy ground prevented cutting of the lawn.

'There've been marches in Berlin, Madrid and London against the proposed American invasion of western Iran. The US President is meeting with the UK Prime Minister at a secret location this week. Well, everybody knows what that's about. What do you think, Greg? Should the UK go into Iran?' Rose held out her empty mug and Greg poured from the pot.

'No way. That would be insane. Both the USA and Iran think they're on the verge of a holy war. It's way out of control and not something to get involved in.'

Rose slurped her fresh mug of tea and held up her empty plate with a puppy dog pleading look. He started to make another sandwich. It was their patent hangover cure - fried egg sandwiches with salted butter on white pan.

Rose had been out with the girls the night before. They'd met up in Syd's and ended up in Langton's. It had been a predictably outrageous night, made even more so by Terry's antics. Rose found Terry to be a pretty amazing individual in more ways than one. That didn't mean she'd forgotten Thomas Thistlethwaite. She missed him dearly.

Rose continued to click around the BBC news website.

'More power cuts across Europe. Tell me, why aren't they building power stations all over Europe with your micro-generators, if they're every bit as good as you say they are?'

'That, my dear, is a very good question. I get different answers from different places. Thomas tells me the UK is committed to nuclear power and there are delays in the public consultation process. Anyhow they don't really have the big rivers needed for my technology.

Germany has over-committed to wind power and the gales and storms of the past couple of years have been too violent for the wind turbines to handle. That puts them in a spot because they're totally anti-nuclear.

Ireland and Spain have the same issue with wind power. Looked like wave power was going to be their alternative solution until last winter's hurricane carried the first commercial wave generator array off into the sunset. Last seen somewhere off the coast of Iceland.'

Rose laughed. 'And anyway, you're busy enough in Africa, right?

'Sure. We couldn't really take on any additional projects for a couple of years. The amount of titanium and other special metals we need for the micro-generators and superconductor loops is absorbing most of the capacity of the mines and processing plants in Burundi, Kenya and Mozambique.'

'But in a way that's good news, right? Because when all the power plants have been built in Africa, then you can concentrate on Europe and continue to keep me in the style to which I've become accustomed.' Rose slipped her dressing gown aside and ran a hand down the voluptuous silk underwear that clung to her sporty contours.

Greg sidled up to his wife and placed his hand over hers. 'So, feeling a bit better after the cure?'

'Feeling a lot better, after your cure.' She reached up and pulled him towards her.

~

In Zurich the rain blew horizontally across the runway. All other air traffic had been put in a holding pattern and passengers on the ground were experiencing extensive departure delays. Air Force One taxied down the main runway and towards a massive hangar surrounded by bloated looking black jeeps with darkened windows.

Anthony Goolden fought to repress the contempt he was feeling. It wasn't the kind of low profile, discreet arrival favoured by the Europeans. If he was any kind of terrorist he wouldn't need any more clues to know who was bestowing the honour of a visit upon Switzerland.

Goolden and his small team sped away in a large Mercedes limousine, quite unobtrusive in this land of the rich, famous and infamous. He didn't want to be in convoy with the American arrivals for a couple of reasons. If there was any attempt on the US President's life he wanted to be a safe distance away. Additionally, travelling together would be sending the wrong signals to several parties.

The driver of the Mercedes pressed a button and a black glass privacy divider slid up between the front seats and the rest of the limousine. Goolden turned to his team and took the briefing. Ron Wildman held them captivated with his synopsis of the situation. Thomas Thistlethwaite felt highly privileged to be there and wasn't quite sure why he was. Air Chief Marshal Sir Edward Norman, Chief of

UK Defence Staff, found himself simultaneously horrified and enthralled by Wildman's interpretation of the USA position and his proposal of how to proceed.

'Most excellent, Ron. Good work from your team, as always. So, you propose we give them what they're looking for?' Goolden looked like an eager schoolboy asking his teacher for advice.

'Absolutely. But first you draw them over the hot coals. Question their motives. Give them the chance to reveal their true motivation. And they'll feel good about it, as will we. This is the Day of Justification. Each of us will end this day feeling vindicated and ready to walk in verdant pastures.'

'Beneath which the rivers flow,' the response came from all. They shared a smile.

~

The cavalcade of black jeeps drove deep into the mountains. There was snow on the ground but the road surface was clean, dry, and impeccable as always.

The British contingent, having already arrived, observed the approaching vehicles. Thomas looked up from the road, towards the peak of Mount Santis.

'Thomas, you've travelled a troubled road,' Wildman said to him. 'We've asked you to commit terrible acts for the sake of your country. Be assured our motives are pure. I want to tell you your conscience can be clear.'

Thomas nodded at the absolution. Goolden placed his hand on Thomas's shoulder.

An aide entered the room and informed the Prime Minister that the US President had arrived.

'Very good,' Goolden thanked the aide. 'Very well, gentlemen. Let's go and give President James Burden the surprise of his life.'

A few moments later Goolden was leading Burden towards the doors of the designated meeting room. The President's bodyguards moved ahead to ensure the room was safe, secure, free of assassination risk. Goolden was familiar with this ritual lack of trust but intercepted the bodyguards and went ahead of them.

The meeting room was gloomy with thick curtains across the far wall.

'What the hell?' Burden exclaimed.

'Mr President,' Kurt Waldshut said. The heads of government of Old Europe greeted the American.

'Goddammit, Anthony! This was supposed to be a USA UK summit!' Burden was incensed.

'James, we are as one. What you have to say to me you can say to our colleagues here. Please, take your seat.' Goolden indicated a row of seats lined up along one side of a large square table and facing the curtains.

Goolden took a seat with his back to the curtains and was joined by the chancellors of Germany and Austria and the prime ministers of Sweden, Norway, Denmark, Spain, Portugal, Netherlands, Luxembourg, Italy, Ireland, France and Belgium.

'Firstly, let me express our thanks to our Swiss hosts,' Goolden began.

Christo Schwarz of the Swiss Confederation stepped forward with a slight bow. He waved a hand and the curtains behind the European contingent were drawn.

There was an involuntary gasp from the Americans. The panorama from windows on three sides of the room gave the impression they were balanced on the very tip of Mount Santis.

'The view, gentlemen, is symbolic,' Schwarz said. 'You see before you the lands of seven different countries. These countries are part of the United European Union of States. Switzerland, of course, remains outside the union but as a full ally.'

Burden and his team murmured. The United European Union of States was a new designation.

'Very well, gentlemen,' Burden said. 'As we are all here we can all face the issue of the day together. The United States government requests the support of its trusted and honourable European allies in the battlefields of Iran. We have righteousness on our side. Iran has foresworn us as their enemy and battle looms. We'll be victorious but, with your participation, the victory will be quicker, cleaner, more humane, less costly. I call on all here present to repay your historical debt, now in our hour of need.'

It was charismatically delivered. Burden was a top class orator. Thomas could feel the draw of his words, a fervour that commanded disciples to follow.

Charles Lorin of France cleared his throat and became the focus of attention. 'Monsieur Burden, would you say America is a secular society? Think carefully before you respond. If your answer is yes then we cannot believe you as your country is clearly on a fundamentalist Christian crusade against the second largest religion in the world.'

The rest of the Europeans nodded their assent.

Burden responded. 'This is a war against a nation that has vowed to destroy Israel, vowed to destroy the United States. A war against a nation whose leader names himself as the Gatekeeper of the Apocalypse. Yes, this is a holy war, if you like. Iran sees this as a holy war. And we, I, have been given the task by God to make war and defeat this enemy of freedom. We are the righteous, we will triumph!'

Michela Lombardi of Italy rose and spoke. 'Italy is the home of Christianity, the home of the Vatican See. Mr Goolden has already told you, we will not make war on an Islamic state because of their beliefs. Your aggression is unjustified. Iran poses no threat.'

Burden rose from his seat. He was a tall man and towered over Lombardi but the Italian wasn't intimidated.

'Who am I speaking to here?' Burden turned to face the Europeans individually. 'We are the most powerful nation on earth. Where we lead others follow for their own good. If you spurn us now in our hour of need then you are like Peter denying Jesus. Or even Judas!'

Goolden rose to his feet and, following his gesture, all the other European premiers also stood. 'Mr President, you are being addressed by the first President of the United European Union of States. The most powerful entity on this planet economically, militarily and spiritually. We are a peaceful union and we mean you no harm. We cannot follow you in this venture and urge you to desist, although it's not expected you will take our advice in this matter. Your nation is following a fundamentalist religious doctrine that will be ruinous to the people and economies on both sides of any conflict. You are on your own.'

Goolden sat back down and the others followed suit.

Burden was left standing alone. 'I acknowledge the strength of your Union and I regret your stance. But it is foreseen. Your destiny is darkness, Anthony.' He turned to the others. 'You follow him into oblivion.' He turned on his heels and marched straight from the room, his bodyguards struggling to keep up with him.

Wildman closed the doors behind them. 'It is foreseen.'

'Indeed it is, Ron, indeed it is. Gentlemen, the presidency rotates every two years, as agreed, commencing today?' All nodded in assent.

'Very good,' Lorin said. 'Now we can forget about them for a time and continue with our good work in the gardens of Africa.'

Power to the people

Greg was reviewing the project publicity material, at Thomas's request.

Early in the first decade of the third millennium the economies of Western Europe were thriving. Spiralling property values and increased disposable income gave the man and woman in the street a feeling of well-to-do. This spread right across the social spectrum in a way that had never existed before. Normal people in normal jobs felt empowered to reach out and touch the lives of poor, sick and dying people. The media reliably informed them such people lived, and died, in Africa.

Aid agencies proliferated. Celebrities adopted would-be orphans from some of the poorest sub-Saharan countries in a blaze of publicity that often rejuvenated ailing careers. It became fashionable to present friends with a Christmas or birthday present of a certificate confirming the shipment of a live goat from Ireland to a small named village in Burundi or Malawi as a source of cheese and milk. The traditional student year out before university was increasingly spent in a large 4x4 vehicle, speeding between Christian parishes in Uganda to deliver a 'wet feed' of vitamin enriched porridge to children.

It took until the end of the decade, when the economic boom had begun to subside, before honest feedback from the aid recipients began to filter through:

- *When you take one child and spend millions of dollars on that child, you could have treated the entire district's HIV problem;*

- The goat's milk and cheese was malodorous but the goat itself was delicious, thank you, please send more live meat;

- 'Wet feeds' are not needed in our village, we already have porridge, thank you;

- We don't need a goat. We need electricity!

Greg had known in his heart this was the real need. Africa needed electricity. He was delighted to be part of bringing electrical power to Africa.

The Swiss engineer Stephan Wichser coughed and brought Greg's attention back to the meeting. A large table in the middle of the room displayed a contoured map of Africa. Wichser indicated several illuminated three dimensional models on the map with his laser pointer. They represented power stations. He pressed a button on the control panel at the end of the table and the power stations were joined by a bright green network of lines across the surface of the map.

'We've been successful in joining these four power stations in Kenya with our new transmission system. The network is laid down at a speed of five kilometres per hour.'

Wichser clicked his computer keyboard and a video clip projected onto a large white screen at the side of the room. A huge contraption that looked like a combine harvester was rolling across the Kenyan countryside at a brisk walking pace. In front of the network laying vehicle, a giant bulldozer cleared vegetation and left a deep trench. The laying vehicle deposited a continuous cable as thick as a man's leg into the trench, the cable fed from a series of huge trucks that trundled alongside.

'Every two kilometres the cable must be joined by laser beam.'

The video showed the joining procedure, the laying vehicle pausing as it swung an arm around and into the trench, placing a joining device between the ends of two cables and welding the joint in a flash of brilliant blue light.

'How long did it take to lay the network and what issues did you encounter?' James Conway asked.

'We completed two thousand miles of cable in just over one hundred days,' the Swiss replied. 'Challenges were quality of the first cable drums from the factory in Zambia and reliable surveying to ensure the route had at least five feet of soil. From the second batch onwards the cable quality was resolved. We found vegetation to be the best assurance of soil depth.'

Greg was able to see that from the video. The nightmarish convoy cut a forty metre swathe through the land like an oil super tanker sailing across the Kenyan Highlands. The result wasn't pretty but he reassured himself the landscape would readjust quickly enough. Within a year the track of the network would be barely noticeable.

'Once those issues were resolved we were able to put another three laying systems into operation and that's how we achieved such rapid progress.' The video clip finished and Wichser handed the pointer to Greg.

Greg highlighted the power generation projects with a press of another button on the control panel. By the time Conway's team had completed the first micro-generator array in Kenya, there were new projects spread across twenty countries.

'We have three further phases of development,' Greg advised the room.

An additional ten power stations lit up and were joined by luminous green lines. Two seconds later a further fifteen illuminated and then the third phase also became visible. The picture was impressive. Around a hundred power stations could be seen on the table, linked by a spider's web of transmission cables.

'Power to the people,' Greg said.

'The planned network will require additional local manufacturing facilities for both cable and machinery,' Wichser interjected. 'We are sharing machinery design with the German road network team. They will utilise much of the equipment after we are finished.' He looked to Greg for comment.

'Each of these micro-generator arrays is five times the size of our pilot installation. Titanium is the main source material for the micro-generators. Mining and processing of the metal has reached the capacity of existing facilities but should be adequate. Our main issue is skilled manpower because there has never been this number of simultaneous new power projects before. We are training up all the power engineers we can find within the Union.' Greg felt a little daunted by the scale of what he was describing.

'Excellent, Greg and Stephan, excellent!' Anthony Goolden put his hands together and the other national leaders joined in the applause.

Thomas clapped Greg on the shoulder. A buzz of conversation welled up as the group moved through to the next room to examine French progress with the pan-African high speed rail network.

~

That evening Greg, Thomas and Conway sat at a long wooden table in the Zeughauskeller in Zurich, tankards of beer in hand.

Thomas gazed around the walls at the ancient armoury's display of weapons. There were halberds from the middle ages, arquebuses and muskets, duelling pistols and early twentieth century rifles. If he'd been forced by the Zurcherpolizei to submit to a body search it would have revealed a similarly impressive arsenal about his person. The days of high daring in Zurich with Reto were becoming a distant memory but Thomas wasn't taking any chances.

As usual, Greg and Conway were oblivious to the darker dangers of their environment and discussed the coming projects with mixed feelings. Thomas decided to set some expectations.

'You guys should be aware the pilot in Kenya was a fairly tame situation. In the next phase of twenty host countries, fifteen of them are acutely poor. More than fifty percent of the people in those countries live on less than a dollar a day. Places like Burundi, Democratic Republic of Congo, Liberia, Malawi, Rwanda, and Uganda. I'm not going to lie to you. These are some of the world's most lawless and war-torn countries.'

Conway looked exhilarated. Greg was aghast.

'We'll be working in some remote areas and there'll be a lot more security at the project sites. Materials and equipment will need constant guarding.'

'These are places I've only ever dreamed of seeing,' Conway said.

'More like my worst nightmare,' Greg mumbled.

'Greg, your individual involvement at each site need not be so extensive. James, on the other hand, we'll need you to fully set up each project team before moving on to the next one. Just so you know what to expect.'

'What I expect,' Greg said, 'is less shop talk and more party!'

'Absolutely!' Conway chimed in, clinking his refilled beer glass with the others.

That's what friends are for

Greg's reluctance to engage with the next phase of projects in Africa hadn't gone unnoticed by Thomas and Conway. The next day, before they went off on their separate ways, the three of them had negotiated and agreed the roles each would play.

Thomas would take care of putting adequate security into place for each project. With his experience and contacts they should be able to avoid any serious trouble.

Greg would spend a few days during the initial stages of the first new project and then parachute in whenever issues arose that needed him. This would satisfy his desire to spend more time with the family and keep him out of harm's way.

Conway would lead the first new project and train up a team of project leaders, subsequently spending his time between all ongoing projects. This suited his mercenary spirit and, being considerably younger than Greg and without family, he had the energy and time for it.

As Greg left the Swissotel he felt he had arranged a good deal. His company was performing strongly, the money was flowing and it was getting to the stage where he could step back a little from the coalface. The train to St Gallen wasn't due to leave for another forty-five minutes so he took a commuter line into the central station for a little window shopping in the extensive underground shopping mall. A sports shop display caught his eye and he made a purchase of a garden badminton set. Of course these things could be bought at home in Ireland but gifts from overseas always had an air of the exotic about them for the family.

There were still thirty minutes to spare so he took a seat outside an underground café and enjoyed a small glass of ice cold beer whilst reading some research papers.

At ten minutes before departure he found his way to platform twenty-two, deep below the surface. The badminton set was in his carry-on luggage and he held the important papers in a leather zip folder under his arm. As the train preceding his drew in he leaned down to examine the luggage and felt the folder fall from under his arm. Reaching down with one hand to pick it up, he was unable to find it but saw the back of a man running towards the surface escalator, leather folder in hand.

'Hey, stop! *Halt*! He's stolen my folder!'

The other would-be passengers tried to avoid the shouting face of the Englishman, probably hoping he might be removed by the police for breaking an excessive platform loudness regulation or some such Swiss byelaw.

Greg abandoned his luggage, realising no help could be expected, and took chase. The thief paused at the foot of the escalator and then bounded up it like a chased rabbit.

Fuelled by adrenaline, Greg made up distance on his mugger. He shouted another appeal, this time directly at the thief.

'Stop! There's nothing in it. No money, no computer. Just some papers. Give it back to me.'

The man stood at the top of the escalator and shouted down: 'If there's nothing in it then you don't need it.'

The escalator continued its rise and Greg found himself face to face with the mugger. He was shorter than Greg, swarthy and facially scarred. There was something in his face that said *no matter how hard you beat me, I will laugh in your face. Then, at night, I will stab you while you sleep.*

Greg decided to leave it rather than tangle with a low-life mugger who would find nothing of value in his folder.

He could get electronic copies of the papers emailed to his office.

He just made it back to the platform in time as the St Gallen train pulled in. Snatching his abandoned luggage from under the gaze of an inquisitive railway policeman, Greg leapt onto the train and made his way through to the reserved first class section.

Once the luggage was stowed, Greg collapsed into his allocated seat and noticed the shakes in his hands as the adrenaline left his system. Then he realised. The stolen folder contained confidential details of the micro-generator development projects from the previous day's meeting. A sweat broke out down his back. Leaping to his feet, he ran to the sliding doors of the carriage and began to step out just as the signal sounded for doors closing. A hand grasped his shoulder and pulled him back inside as the doors closed and the train moved off.

Standing stiffly with one hand resting on the butt of his pistol and the other on Greg's shoulder, the officer was clearly not to be argued with. He gave Greg something of an interrogation and made him open his luggage. It contained the newly purchased badminton set and Greg's dirty clothes from the last five days. Having explained the circumstances, Greg supplied the officer with his mobile phone number and was advised stolen items of no apparent value usually turned up at the lost property office.

~

A colossal Italian man hugged and kissed what looked like a sack of potatoes on a railway platform in St Gallen. As the arms unfolded, a crumpled Greg was released from the embrace.

Gino Peroni loved his friend Greg like a little brother. There was a ten year difference in their ages and this put Gino in the role of something of a spiritual mentor for Greg. After a bottle of red wine, preferably Italian, Gino usually referred to Greg as his muse. They knew each other of old and met once or twice a year to right the world's wrongs.

Dinner at the Peroni household was like a UN conference without the official translators. Various guests attended and the air was full of the languages of Italy, Germany, Switzerland, France, the UK, America and sometimes more exotic tongues from places such as Greece, India or Hungary. The food was, invariably, Pasta del Gino. Wine flowed like the River Jordan and Grappa was always deemed necessary to ease the digestion. Regular agenda items included probability of life on other planets, sustainability of the ecosystem and whether or not Ché Guevara was really dead.

When all the other guests had left, Greg and Gino settled down with a glass of single malt whisky and moved onto matters more mysterious. Greg outlined his work on the project and the general direction of developments.

'You know, my friend, I have to say I have heard something of this. And I am very intrigued to know what you think.' Gino was a good listener.

'I think the scheme is admirable.' Greg counted off the points with his thumb and fingers. 'It's fair, to return the stolen wealth. It's in the public interest to ensure these investments improve the infrastructure instead of lining dictators' pockets.'

'But? Something is missing for you in all this, no?' Gino sensed his friend's general unease earlier in the evening and was pleased to have a chance to uncover and share the cause.

'Apart from the HIV situation? Yes, the electrical infrastructure is excessive. It seems oversized and over capacity for the population. A population that's dwindling.'

'But I think you already have the answer, my friend. As you told me earlier this evening, the unexploited natural resources in these countries are huge. Just think about the energy requirements for mining and producing all the titanium you're using. Have you forgotten how much electricity it takes to produce metals like copper?'

Greg shook his head. He hadn't been thinking about industrial use. It was obvious.

'That could make sense. But more things are unexplained. The new road networks, the high speed trains, the telecommunications networks. It'll be like, well, it'll be like Switzerland!'

'And the problem with that, my friend? If you were building a new national infrastructure in Ireland, wouldn't you build it to be like Switzerland or maybe even better?'

Greg looked bemused. Trains on time, high speed. Telecommunications reaching every corner of the country. The purest water available in limitless supply. Environmentally friendly electricity in such abundance that surplus could be exported. Roads as smooth as silk, tunnelling through the landscape. In Ireland? What a wonderful thought!

'Yes, I would. I would.'

They toasted with a clink of glasses.

'The fertile gardens of Africa, beneath which the rivers flow.'

'What did you say?' Greg asked.

'TV advert, haven't you seen it? Holidays in Africa. Jacqui and I, we've booked a holiday there for the family next year. Very popular with the Swiss and the Germans now. Mainly Namibia, they speak a kind of German there you know, and Botswana.'

'Two of the richest countries in Africa,' Greg said drowsily. 'And two of the highest HIV rates in Africa as well.'

'At my age and with my blood pressure I'm not likely to go chasing the local women, so there's no danger there,' Gino laughed.

'There's more than one way to contract HIV,' Greg said, remembering the African blood on the windscreen of a jeep, in the garden of his parents house, on the battered body of an African man in a toilet in Bilbao airport. 'You be careful Gino. You be careful, old friend.'

~

In the morning Greg received a phone call on his mobile from the lost property office in Zurich main station. His leather folder had been found, complete with the confidential papers.

Greg bade Gino and family a fond farewell until next time and boarded the train back to Zurich to collect his lost property before heading on to the airport and home.

He slept fitfully on the flight and, finally shaking himself awake, decided to review the project documents again. There was something odd about them and it took him a while to determine what had changed. The staples holding the documents together were not the robust Swiss type but a thinner version he'd seen before in the USA. He looked close up and could see some of the pages had additional staple holes close to the actual staple. Someone in Zurich had separated his confidential documents, probably for copying, and re-stapled them.

Only the good die young

James Conway was dead by the start of the sixth project. Thomas and Greg travelled to Uganda, Conway's final resting place. The project had a graveyard with a monument paying tribute to those who had lost their lives. Each project had one.

Conway's gravestone was the newest. Greg touched the polished surface with the tips of his fingers. It felt warm.

'There were attacks on all the project sites,' Thomas explained. 'It was a concerted effort to disrupt the programme. We don't know how they knew the project sequence or the locations because it was restricted information.'

Greg recalled the battered face of a thief in Zurich train station. He should have told Thomas when it happened.

'James was caught by a sniper's bullet when he left his vehicle, just as we're doing now.'

Greg looked around. He saw a cleared perimeter of a hundred metres around the project site with dense jungle beyond. The thunderous roar of the nearby Victoria Nile River dominated the jungle noise.

'We've taken extensive security measures to prevent a recurrence. Come over to the control room and I'll show you.'

Thomas led Greg into the dark windowed building. A row of flat screens scanned a wire fenced perimeter, beyond which a wide clearance had been cut through the forest.

'That fence encircles the project with a radius of one kilometre. We have a two hundred and fifty metre death zone beyond the fence. Take a closer look. I'll turn on the volume.' Thomas reached for a switch.

Greg examined the death zone on the screens. Animal carcasses could be seen on the ground. One of the screens showed movement and he saw an animal emerge from the jungle. Within a second there was a mechanical whirring noise followed by a volley of machine gun fire. The animal, some kind of monkey, now lay dead just outside the jungle edge.

'Movement sensors?' Greg asked.

'Yep. Every ten meters there's a sensor and every three hundred an automatic machine gun post. It's impossible for anything except an armoured vehicle to get through.' Thomas indicated another screen. 'If that happens we'll see it on the good old fashioned radar over here. We have a helicopter gunship on each project site for defence and evacuation of key personnel.'

Greg shook his head slowly. 'Poor James.'

'He wasn't the only one, unfortunately. Other projects have been attacked and sabotaged too. More than one person was mugged after the meeting in Zurich.' Thomas looked at Greg darkly. 'The French had an entire communications team assassinated in Guinea and the Germans had one of their road laying machines blown to bits.'

'Sounds like a concerted campaign. Who's behind it?'

Thomas frowned. 'The attackers were from disparate groups.'

Greg had the feeling a larger enemy was behind it and Thomas wasn't telling him the full story because he wasn't on the list of people who needed to know.

'The good news,' Thomas continued, 'is James had trained up five very capable project leaders. So you're only needed at the start-up of each project; one every two weeks for the next year.'

Greg sighed. He thought of Rose and the kids, of how little he'd seen them since he'd known Thomas. He had an idea.

'Unless I manage to develop another overall project leader.'

Greg thought over the members of his Swiss team. There were a few mercenary types in the group all right. Simone Buettiker for one.

Greg spent the next few hours making his inspection of the dry dock and river bed. The floor of the dock was covered by a pressure pad developed from Simone's leap of intuition in Kenya. Within a couple of months the pad would be pulsing and the array generating enough electricity for a small city. Fish, mammals and reptiles wouldn't be able to survive this stretch of the river. No form of life would be able to survive the security perimeter. It wasn't how he had envisioned his environmentally friendly invention in practice but he convinced himself the compromise was necessary.

When Greg had done, the two men boarded a helicopter gunship and were flown at high speed to an airfield on the outskirts of Kampala. They had the honour of joining the Ugandan President Winston Cunningham for dinner in his presidential palace.

Cunningham's frame and face had filled out and he displayed a new aura of confidence since being catapulted into leadership.

'So, Winston, how are things going?' Thomas asked.

The dining room had a very homely feel to it, more like a Scottish Victorian villa than an African presidential palace.

'Very well, Thomas, very well. We have very good relations with all our neighbours, excepting Sudan of course. Infrastructure is forging ahead. New cases of HIV are very low. Most of our armed forces are busy working on the projects and we have immigration rates of one hundred thousand per month. Exclusively from the UK.'

Greg sliced through the fillet on his plate.

'This is delicious. What sort of meat is it?'

'Venison. Specially imported from the Scottish Highlands. It's one of the few luxuries I allow myself.'

'Except for the Scotch,' Thomas said.

'Yes. It seems a very long time since Obote's boys terrorised the right-thinking people of this country,' Cunningham said. 'Uganda is now a safe and peaceful place to live. Greg, you should think about settling here with your family.'

Greg gave a polite smile in return but thought of the warm stone memorial in the jungle.

Absence makes the heart grow fonder

They had already packed their bags for the visit to Kenya. Kate and Pete had their own carry-on luggage containing favourite toys. Rose and Greg had two large suitcases; the family's clothes for the first two weeks.

Two hours later they parked Greg's new Jaguar in Dublin airport long term car park and checked in for their flight.

The route took them via Heathrow to Nairobi. The African leg was full to capacity and the passengers had a mood of expectation rather than holiday.

Nairobi's arrivals hall was teeming with porters who bore the usual HIV-free certificates on cords around their necks. Kenneth met them and, with a broad smile, loaded them all into a hearse-like Volvo with three rows of seats.

Greg noted, on the way out to his parents' suburb, that the Nairobi townlands had taken on a different aspect. There were no longer coffins on street display. The squatter areas had been cleaned up and redeveloped. Everything was very different to his first Kenyan visit with the late James Conway.

Rose eyed him curiously as they sped through the Nairobi outskirts. Although the Volvo was fitted with bull-bars there were no Kenyans hurling themselves at the vehicle and no calls to the sanitation team for intervention. He knew she suspected him of over-dramatising the dangers.

The trip from the airport to his parents' house took just an hour, thanks to the new high speed carriageways.

Derek and Bernie were delighted to see their grandchildren again after several months and played with them in the garden. The children were high spirited in the unfamiliar climate.

After a couple of hours they all settled down to enjoy Kenneth's cooking, a blend of Kenyan cuisine and English favourites. The children, tired after a long day, were soon tucked up in bed and the adults relaxed on the veranda, customary drinks in hand.

'So, Greg, how is your business going?' Bernie said.

'Going very well, thanks. A few initial snags, but the pilot site worked out well in the end and we're active across Africa now.'

To Greg's certain knowledge the *snags* included fifty-four Africans, one European, three mountain gorillas, five hippos, dozens of crocodiles and countless monkeys.

'Yes, Greg's having a great time,' Rose said. 'We've hardly seen him over the past year. I've had to find my own amusement at home.'

'Well, there's plenty of amusement to be had here,' Derek said.

Bernie and Rose exchanged a look.

Derek continued, oblivious. 'No doubt Greg told you Kenya was a terrible place, but things have improved immensely. We've good law and order, great community spirit, loads of facilities...'

'Have you seen the latest UK census figures?' Greg asked.

'No,' Bernie said. 'What's the story?'

'Average age in the UK has reduced from thirty-nine to thirty-one. Population has reduced by fifteen percent. Compared to five years ago.'

'Very interesting,' Rose said with sarcasm.

'No,' Derek said, 'it's significant and we're part of it. Most of our retired friends from Scotland have come here.'

'But it's not just pensioners,' Bernie said. 'There's that new factory down the road, making some sort of electronics.'

'Movement sensors,' Derek said.

Bernie continued. 'And the financial centre in Nairobi is flourishing, according to the newspapers.'

'Any indigenous Kenyans working in these places?' Rose asked. 'Or is it mostly ex-pats?'

'Mostly Brits,' Derek said. 'There are a few Kenyans on the shop floor in the factory.'

'What happened to the squatter towns?' Greg asked. 'When I first came to see you it was a major issue.'

Bernie and Derek looked at each other.

'I'll leave it to your mother to tell you,' Derek said.

'Mum?'

'There was a government policy of relocation, so to speak,' Bernie said.

'What does that mean?' Rose asked.

'The conditions they were living in were atrocious. Our friend Winston proposed a solution and the government put it into action. New towns were built to house those who were healthy and those who weren't were given care.'

'So where did they send them to?' Greg asked, although he suspected he knew the answer.

'The new towns are located mostly in the north of the country. They've been given employment in the new industrial developments and on the larger projects.'

Greg envisioned workers in the titanium and zinc mines feeding his projects with raw materials, and thousands more labouring on roads and railway lines.

'Those with HIV have been supplied with the latest antiretroviral drugs and comprise a large part of the Kenyan peacekeeping forces on the borders with Sudan, Ethiopia and Somalia,' Derek added.

'And those with AIDS?' asked Rose.

'Those with AIDS have been given places in custom built hospice camps where they can spend their final days in relative comfort and dignity.' Derek downed the rest of his gin and tonic in one go. He gesticulated to Kenneth, who was hovering just in the house, for a refill.

'Problem solved,' Greg laughed cynically. 'Ship the sick out to die and use the rest as canon fodder or captive workforce. Just like the old days of the Empire.'

'That's not really fair!' Bernie said. 'Before Abrams came into power there were rumours of killer squads in the squatter camps.'

'It's true.' Kenneth emerged from the shadows with a tray of drinks, ice clinking in crystal tumblers. 'Exterminating the squatters would have been easier. In the old days we didn't have the money or the will to find a humanitarian solution but now we have both.'

'There's a movement of conscience,' Bernie said. 'For those who don't find equity in this new order. A peaceful protest movement, mostly women.'

'By women with more time and money than sense!' Derek said. 'Let's not talk about that, it's not exactly supporting the aims of a government we voted for.'

Bernie was silent for a few moments. Greg recognised the situation of old. His mother wasn't defeated, she was merely letting the ripples on the pond's surface die away after a stone had been thrown. The stone had nevertheless been thrown.

Bernie made an offer to lighten the darkening mood. 'Come with us tomorrow, to the morning service. Then afterwards we have a really special treat planned for you and the children.'

Greg remembered the service he'd attended with Thomas in Bedfordshire. If nothing else, it would be interesting to compare with that welcome and uplifting experience.

'I'm not too interested in non-Catholic services,' Rose said.

'And a special treat,' Derek reminded her.

'What kind of special treat? What will we do, what will we see?'

'We'll make a journey.'

'Where to?'

'The cradle of mankind.'

The Creator's crucible

At nine in the morning, after an early breakfast, three generations of the Marshall family undertook a short walk to the local place of worship. It was a modern building, light and airy, promising day-long sanctuary from the African sun.

Greg noted the visual absence of any particular denomination, as in the old Bedfordshire church. Readings were given by congregation members from texts suggesting a rainbow coalition of religions. However, there was a contrast with the expectant feeling he'd sensed in England. These people, of cosmopolitan creed, colour, class and age, had arrived at their destination.

There were no TV screens showing Anthony Goolden in supplicant pose but the same version of George Harrison's *My Sweet Lord* did feature. It went down well with little Kate and Pete who danced in the aisles with some of the other children.

Once the service had finished, Derek solicited Rose's opinion outside the building.

'It feels a little odd to have a service without a communion rite. If I don't receive the Eucharist then it doesn't feel like mass.'

'Yes, but that wasn't mass,' Bernie explained. 'It was just a celebration, a communal thanks to the creator. Many of the people there today will separately attend the rites of their own religion. And those who are a little agnostic, like your father-in-law and I, normally repair to the pub!'

Rose gave a laugh. 'Well then, let's be agnostic for the day!'

'That would be an idea,' Bernie said, 'but you're forgetting the special treat.'

'C'mon kids!' Greg shouted to Kate and Pete who were playing chase with other children.

'We have to leave right away. Kenneth has the car ready.' Bernie waved at Kenneth who was sitting waiting in the Volvo at the kerbside.

In twenty minutes they were at a local airfield. The kids were delighted to be going on a plane again so soon.

The aircraft taxied and took off. There were around thirty passengers and Greg recognised some of them from the earlier celebration service, but all were European in appearance. He asked his father about Kenneth.

'Oh, Kenneth. He's seen this before, loads of times, no point boring him with it. We've been there just once before but I'm looking forward to seeing it again. Just you wait.'

After about one hour the plane began to descend. Rose and Greg looked out of their windows. As the fuselage was only three seats wide everyone had a good view. Kate and Pete pressed their faces up against the glass.

A massive inland sea spread below them as far ahead and behind the plane as was visible. Each caught their breath as the simmering sun reflected off the surface of the Jade Sea, Lake Turkana.

They landed on the north eastern side of the great lake and taxied sedately towards the small terminal building. An air conditioned bus was waiting and everyone disembarked without formality. Twenty minutes drive and they passed through a gate with a sign marked *Koobi Fora*. The name was somehow familiar to Greg. Rose gave him the answer before he could ask.

'Koobi Fora. Richard Leakey, Maeve Leakey. Twentieth century discoveries of the early human fossils.'

Greg nodded and smiled. *The Cradle of Mankind.* If modern day humans originated from Africa, as many believed, then this was quite likely their Eden.

The visitor centre at Koobi Fora was a wonder. The Leakey's famous display of crude rows of fossilised hominid skulls on wooden benches had been replaced with high-tech exhibits.

The Marshalls walked around a lowly lit display with the other visitors and found themselves accompanied by a number of holographic figures representative of the different historical eras in the exhibition.

The holograms gradually assumed a more erect stature, moving from Homo habilis to Homo erectus and ultimately Homo sapiens. A chart on the wall showed the different forms of man's ancient ancestors stretching back over two million years. Each hologram walked or ambled towards its allocated place against the wall and slowly faded away to leave just the skull and bones found in the area by anthropologists.

As the holograms dimmed, Rose felt a cool hand touch her elbow and a mouth close to her ear whispered, 'Your servant to command, m'lady.'

She turned to see the smiling face of Thomas Thistlethwaite.

The lights went up and the crowd gave a spontaneous burst of applause.

'Well, Thomas, something of a surprise seeing you here,' Greg said.

'A very pleasant surprise,' Rose added.

'Well, I'll see you here again in a few weeks,' Thomas replied and turned to leave.

'Hey!' Greg stepped forward and caught Thomas by the arm. 'Don't go running out on us. Come back down to Nairobi for a couple of days. My parents would love to have you stay. Right, Mum?'

Bernie eyed Rose who was working hard on an expression of indifference.

'Sure, any friend of Greg's is a friend of ours.'

'Very kind of you,' Thomas said, 'but work will keep me here for another day and then back to the wind and rain of the UK. As I said, see you here in a few weeks.'

He took his leave, giving Greg a shake of the hand and Rose a kiss on the cheek.

'Seems like a nice young chap, looks familiar,' Derek said on their way out of the building.

A few minutes later they were on the shaded deck of a newly built bar next to the Koobi Fora Visitor Centre, enjoying iced long drinks. Kate and Pete rampaged in the play area, returning occasionally to slurp chilled Kenyan lemonade through straws from glass bottles.

'*The Cradle of Mankind*,' Derek said, looking across the harsh landscape. 'If this was truly Eden then it must once have been a little more hospitable.'

'According to the visitor centre, Lake Turkana was probably freshwater at the time,' Greg said.

'Yes, but then it wouldn't have this amazing jade colour. It's all to do with the build up of salts and stuff,' Bernie said.

'I thought the actual *Garden of Eden* was supposed to be somewhere in what's now Iraq or Iran?' Rose asked.

'I've heard the same thing,' Derek replied. 'But that's taking the *Genesis* story all very literally. I just like to think this is where we probably came from and here we have returned. The Eastern Rift Valley.'

'No rivers running here, though,' Greg said.

'I'm sure even that can be fixed.' Rose looked across to the visitor centre.

Greg followed her gaze to where Thomas was standing, with a man in a hard hat, in the middle of a small garden of lush vegetation. It looked out of place in the arid surroundings of Koobi Fora.

Thomas was indicating something in the distance to the hard hat man. For a few seconds the heat haze cleared and Greg could make out a perimeter fence about a kilometre from the centre. Interspersed at intervals of a few hundred meters were what looked like viewing towers. It was reminiscent of the power project exclusion zones.

~

The party returned to Nairobi, dozing on the bus and plane.

Kate and Pete were asleep in the Volvo before Kenneth had managed to reach the house. Greg and Rose carried the children in their arms like babies and placed them gently in their beds. Pete's round little face, normally by turn white or pink, was shaded to a honey colour by the Kenyan sun. Kate's complexion was developing a delicate band of freckles across her nose. They glowed more from two days in Africa than an entire summer in Ireland.

'I need to talk to you later,' Rose said to Greg as Kenneth served their evening meal.

Bernie and Derek decided to give them some space and retired to bed soon after desert was served.

In the cool quiet of the sitting room, Rose stretched out along one of the yellow leather sofas and regarded her husband. Greg had the impression he was in for some more of her straight talking.

Greg wandered around the room, looking at photographs on the walls. There was a recent one from his parents' last visit to Kilkenny. Who had taken the photo? It had probably been Kate. She was a natural with the camera.

The picture showed Bernie, Derek, Rose, Pete and himself on the eastern lawns of Kilkenny castle. Kate always fantasised about a damsel in distress, imprisoned in the Parade Tower.

It was a happy family. His parents were ageing gracefully and Rose, several years his junior, was radiant.

He, on the other hand, looked tired. Poor posture, a slight paunch, greying hair in no particular style. Certainly not the slim and dapper young man she'd married. *Okay, so nobody is getting any younger, but maybe I should make a bit of an effort* he thought.

The next photo was a candid scene was from a bar. Rose, Terry and Thomas were raising pints of Guinness to each other, unaware of the camera. Greg remembered sending it to his parents as an example of the Kilkenny highlife.

Rose and Terry were toasting each other. They'd developed a sisterly rapport during the few months they'd known each other. Thomas could be seen stealing a look at Greg's wife. If he didn't know Thomas better he would say there was something in it.

'Greg, sit down. We need to talk.' Rose drew his attention away from the photo.

She swung her legs off the sofa and patted the cushion next to hers. He sat down obediently.

'Greg, I think it's about time we moved on.'

'But we only arrived yesterday.' He gave a look of fake surprise.

'Don't be obtuse. This is the land of opportunity. We should follow your parents and move the family here from Ireland.'

'What?'

'Why not? This is like a new Switzerland! Everything is brand new and works perfectly. There's plenty of space, sports and social facilities, schools and churches of all denominations, great employment prospects. Super healthcare and, most importantly, a fantastic climate and amazing countryside.' She spread her arms wide to express the totality of the new Kenya.

'Yeah, all true.'

'And there's something going on I've never experienced before. In Europe people talk about *the good old days* and, on examination, it's just rose coloured glasses. But these are *the good old days*, happening here and now. There's no envy, no fear, a great community spirit, and tolerance of religion and race. People here have money and it's at nobody's expense. What a great place for kids to grow up! Let's be a part of it. What do you say, Greg?'

'I'm not going to burst your bubble,' Greg began. 'I agree totally. That's the way I see it too. But it's just what I said, a bubble. A controlled environment. So, where do you think all the bad stuff is? Where's it gone and what's been done with it?'

'What bad stuff? I don't see anything. You were exaggerating. They can't have just got rid of everything you described.'

'You think I made up those stories? Desperate squatter camps, HIV positive Africans run down like road kill? An African man and woman on the lawn out there, just last year. Shot dead by Kenneth and Conway, albeit in self defence.'

Rose shook her head in disbelief. 'You heard what your dad said about the squatter camps. Everyone is employed or cared for.'

'Taken care of, more like it. Displaced, dispossessed and disenfranchised. The only thing the Kenyan government hasn't done is *disappeared* them.'

'Greg, you know I'm as big a fan of conspiracy theory as you are. But I think you're going too far. Could you imagine any better way of handling the situation?'

'A more pragmatic way? No, I can't. A more humane and ethical way, quite possibly. The dying separated from their families. The infected press-ganged into military service on remote and inhospitable borders with dangerous enemies. The healthy used as forced labour for low wages in purpose built new industrial towns.'

'For a change, my son is completely correct.' Bernie emerged from the shadowed hallway where she'd been eavesdropping. 'This is no place for you and the kids, Rose. At least, not yet awhile.'

Bernie sat on the edge of the sofa and put her arm around her daughter-in-law's shoulders. 'Whatever you might be wanting to leave behind in Ireland,' Bernie threw a glance at the Kilkenny highlife photo, 'there's a lot more about this country you have to see before making any rash decisions.'

'What do you mean for a change I'm completely correct?' Greg said.

The women ignored him. Bernie continued. 'This movement of conscience I mentioned yesterday, we're monitoring the situation and using lobby groups to pressurise the government. I'll take you to some of these places Greg mentioned and we'll open your eyes.'

Bernie eyed her son over the back of Rose's neck and gave him a gentle smile.

'Okay, I'll go but I want to bring the children.'

'No, not the children. They can stay here with Greg and Derek.' She turned to her son. 'Your father won't go, he's in denial.'

Greg nodded. He knew it would be better for Rose to make her own experience. As for him, he'd seen enough already.

~

After they'd risen and breakfasted the next morning, Bernie took Rose out to the sunroom and they sat on the rattan chairs. Bernie opened a small toiletries bag and Rose let her administer an injection in her shoulder.

'That's a one week dose of HIV vaccine. When we first came here the doses were daily. Now we can get monthly doses but the needles are a lot scarier than these.'

Rose could see Greg's concerned face peering at them from the breakfast table where he and his father were still drinking tea. She was preparing to step outside the bubble.

Seasons in the sun

'C'mon Dad! You slowcoach!'

The kids were right, he was lagging behind. His breathing was laboured and he could hear his own heartbeat.

'Dad!' The chorus of annoyed little voices spurred him on and he stepped out with longer strides down the rutted path across the field. Taking deeper breaths seemed to help and the thumping in his chest eased.

His children ran hand in hand with their mother and disappeared over the brow of the hill. They took the sunshine with them. A cloud shadow overtook him from behind, the dark edge racing at the speed of the jet stream. He knew it was the cloud of death and, when it stopped, whoever stood beneath would lose their lives.

Without the sun to warm, the breeze turned cold and raised a shiver down his back. He shouted a warning downwind to his family, but his throat was too dry to raise any volume. Not that it would have helped them anyway. Drawing on reserves of energy, he broke into a run, assisted by the wind.

He crested the brow of the hill and stood, watching the inevitable unfold. The wind blew waves across the wild grass and down into the shallow valley where a stream trickled over its stony bed. Natalie, Hannah and Matt stopped in their tracks and looked up into the cloud of death.

'Wait for me! I'll come with you! Wait!' Thomas cried. He leaned forward to run down the path to his family, but his feet had turned to clay.

There was a crack of thunder and the cloud sank to earth. Natalie and the kids huddled together in the maelstrom.

He broke free from his constraints and ran down the valley but his view was obscured by the fine mist of cloud. Another crack of thunder and he was pushed to the ground. Lightning burned the palms of his hands where they touched the earth.

The cloud began to fade. With no energy left it was simply vaporised by the sun. Thomas knew what he would see in the valley. Scorched earth. They were gone.

He woke from the nightmare. Tears ran from his eyes but he didn't try to stop or wipe them, merely rolled over on his pillow. Perhaps today, he thought. Let it be today.

In time the terrible constriction of grief around his throat eased and he came back to the realities of life. He was feeling under considerable pressure. Perhaps that was why the family had come back to him again in the nights.

So he faced the day ahead. Another unwelcome assignment.

Goolden suspected Abrams of overstepping the agreed measures and needed Thomas to check he wasn't going native. Ron Wildman needed everything in place for Koobi Fora, there could be no upsets allowed.

The brief for the assignment was observation. Low profile, no intervention. That meant concealing his presence from Abrams as the man knew very well what kind of role Thomas normally played.

He rolled out of bed and looked out between the bedroom window curtains. Birds were singing in the sky, launching themselves into air and song from the upper branches of acacia trees shading the back of the hotel. A muscle halfway up his back was in constant spasm and he stretched his right hand around and up in an attempt to rub the ache away.

A vigorous shower had a more positive impact. Thomas had noticed, in the aftermath of his near disastrous trip to the USA, his recovery time from injuries was extending. He was beginning to feel middle age creeping in. The time to seek less active duty was approaching and he resolved to pursue the matter on his return to England at the weekend.

Peter Abrams would have to be kept in line and Thomas's experience in field operations of this kind was widely known. He was the best placed team member to judge what was really behind media reports coming out of the industrial townships where healthy squatters had been relocated.

Blackgang Chine was a new town west of Nairobi, close to Nakuru. The improbable name came from an English tourist attraction on the Isle of Wight, recently disappeared into the sea following repeated seasons of severe storms. Thomas had visited the original during his childhood and the name seemed appropriate. Complicated cascades of steep steps down the walls of the open cast Kenyan mine looked very similar to the Isle's strange tourist attraction in the chalk and sand cliffs of the English channel.

One of the new regime's first attempts at dealing with the issue of urban squatters, Blackgang Chine had been a disastrous affair from the start. In subsequent developments the government had learned to build the hospices, industrial towns and military encampments at a respectable distance from each other. The problem with Blackgang Chine was location of the AIDS hospice just outside the mining town. Families who wished to continue to have anything to do with the hospice occupants, and not everyone did, were able to see how the authorities mistreated their sick and dying relatives. It didn't foster good community spirit.

Another factor was the five dollars a day earnings of township workers in the mines and factories. The government rationale was that, although Kenya was not one of the African countries within the UN's list of fifty least developed, all five of its neighbours were and that meant more than fifty percent of people living in neighbouring countries survived on less than one dollar per day. Five dollars a day put the Kenyan township workers on a higher standing.

The daily payment led to inflated accommodation and food costs, leaving the workers with little disposable income. There had been attempts to organise unions and withdraw labour for fair pay, attempted boycotts of the regulated food and accommodation, and other more recent and public expressions of unrest.

Forewarned with this information, Thomas travelled to Blackgang Chine in the company of Lieutenant Trevor Anderson, a fellow operative. Anderson had received information that Abrams's elite police were planning to set an example by putting down a planned demonstration in the township.

~

Bernie and Rose had arrived in Blackgang Chine with Kenneth that morning. Derek had attempted to prevent the trip to little effect, his wife overruling as usual.

The AIDS hospice was on the eastern side of the township and Rose, seeing the road signs approaching it, asked Bernie if they could make a stop there.

'I really don't think it's a good idea,' Bernie replied.

'Why ever not?' Rose asked. 'We've had our vaccine, so there's no danger of infection. How bad can it be? I need to know the whole picture.'

'Yes, you do. Okay then. It's something you have to see, at least once.'

The two women left Kenneth with the Volvo in the visitors' car park. He chose not to accompany them.

Rose noticed an acrid smell as they walked the footpath up the building. The hospice reception was unmanned but Bernie said she'd been there before. She leaned over the desk and signed them both in, taking two visitor badges which they fastened to their tops. Bernie picked up a clipboard and pen from the reception desk and walked to double doors on the left, touching her visitor's badge to the card reader to gain entrance. Rose hesitated and then followed.

They walked long corridors, one after another, joined by locked double doors, each requiring a card swipe. They met several African people in white coats but weren't challenged. The staff looked dejected.

'Are they doctors?' Rose asked.

'No, they're HIV positive volunteers. They do a bare minimum of training in AIDS care in return for drug treatment. There's only a handful of fully trained doctors and nurses in facilities like this. Most medical staff are assigned to hospitals in the major towns, where the European immigrant populations live.'

Bernie began to take Rose through the wards. They all looked the same; spotlessly clean but completely full of bed-ridden patients. There were adults and children of all ages and both sexes, all of them African. A few of them called out as Rose and Bernie passed. Bernie paused to hold hands here and there.

It was only after several wards Rose realised what was missing.

'Bernie, where are the drips? Where's the medication?'

'There isn't any. They don't receive medication. This is a one way journey.'

'But there are drugs available, right? To delay the development of AIDS, to minimise the symptoms, to improve the quality of life?'

'Yes, at an expense the government doesn't wish to support.'

The wards had become increasingly noisy as they progressed and the condition of the patients had deteriorated. Then it became quieter. They reached a place where all the beds were occupied by patients who looked like concentration camp victims.

'These people are in the final stages of AIDS. They haven't been fed or given water for about one week. Their journey is nearly over.'

The next ward was completely empty.

They didn't enter the ward after the empty one but stood looking through the windows at a flurry of activity. Bernie's voice dropped to a whisper.

'New arrivals. They're being bedded in, given sedatives and informed they'll stay in this ward until it's time to leave. All the qualified nurses and doctors are in here.' A matronly looking nurse glanced at the door and frowned at Rose and Bernie. 'Okay, we have to leave now before we're asked to.'

'There's a new intake every week,' Bernie explained as they walked towards the exit. 'Fifty bedded wards. Every patient stays in the same bed during their time here and one ward is emptied every week. I'll let you do the maths.'

Rose thought about what her mother-in-law said. All patients who arrived at the hospice would be dead within twelve weeks.

Kenneth opened the doors of the car for them.

'You probably smelled that on the way in,' Bernie said, pointing to a chimney behind the hospital. It emitted the grey smoke of an incinerator.

Rose said nothing for the remainder of the journey to Blackgang Chine.

The township raised her spirits. There was a holiday camp feel to the newly built single storey dwellings. Every few blocks she saw a supermarket or shop of sorts and places of worship or community buildings. Kenneth drove them straight to the centre of town at a leisurely pace although there was very little traffic on the roads. He gave the horn a brief toot from time to time to make pedestrians in the middle of the road aware of the approaching car.

They parked up outside a café. Rose and Bernie went inside and shared a pot of tea while Kenneth stayed with the car at the kerbside. He had been invited in but preferred to act as guard dog for the Volvo which had already attracted some attention.

Rose watched out the café window. Three men appeared on the street, walking down the middle of the road towards the car. They didn't appear armed but moved purposefully, unlike the other people on the streets who ambled along.

Kenneth turned towards the men. He nodded in response to their questions and indicated the teashop. The men shook Kenneth's hand and melted back into the street.

'There's a demonstration planned,' Bernie said. 'They're protesting to get fair market pricing for food and accommodation. Whatever about that, it's the secondary demonstration we're here for, protesting about lack of proper treatment in the hospice. International media has been invited.'

'Will it be safe for us?'

'Oh, we don't plan to take part, just to observe. Staying out of harm's way. Not that any harm is expected. The presence of TV crews will ensure that.'

They finished their tea and rejoined Kenneth. He drove them back out towards the township limits and parked at the rear of a block of bungalows. On the way past Rose had noticed half a dozen people standing outside a supermarket and languidly waving protest placards.

'We'll take a look inside so you can see what I mean.' Bernie led them into the shop.

Rose gazed at the mundane selection of goods on the shelves. There were no luxury foods and not many brands she recognised. Rose picked up a tin of peas labelled *produce of Kenya.* The price of one dollar equivalent didn't alarm her and she told Bernie so.

'That's because you have a monthly household budget of a couple of thousand,' her mother-in-law replied. 'Remember, these people earn around three hundred dollars per month. From that they have to pay rent of a hundred dollars, all their other bills and then buy food.'

Rose replaced the tin of peas on the shelf.

'So how do they manage, Bernie?'

Kenneth spoke up from behind her. 'They buy fresh food at markets in the fields behind the houses. I'll show you. I need to buy some food for the house, so you can see how it works.'

Kenneth took them half a kilometre in the car and parked around the back of another block right on the edge of town, this time in an open field next to several old pickups. The rest of the field was occupied by wooden folding tables, some with canvas awnings fluttering gently in the breeze.

'This is where everyone buys their food,' Kenneth said.

Bernie led them amongst the stalls. There were fresh vegetables of every description, many with the fertile rift valley earth still clinging to their roots.

Kenneth bargained with a woman for a kilo of fresh peas, still in the pod. From the same stall he also purchased potatoes, carrots and some other vegetable Rose didn't recognise. An exchange of money was made and pleasantries exchanged in a language Bernie explained was Kiswahili.

'Twenty five cents,' Bernie said. 'Less than one quarter of the price of a tin of peas.'

They moved amongst the stalls.

'The only problem is these markets have no permit. The authorities make a weekly sweep of the area and close down any unauthorised trading they find. Fortunately the locals have their sources of information and stay one step ahead.'

A man walked down between the stalls, announcing something in a loud sing-song voice.

'We have one hour and then the authorities will come and clear it away,' Kenneth explained. 'That coincides with the start time for the protest marches.'

'Well then, time for some serious shopping!' Rose said. With authentic Kenyan holiday presents for her Irish relatives in mind, she applied herself to the task.

Kenneth left them to it for a few minutes and walked off to the main street.

~

A procession of media vehicles passed the AIDS hospice ten kilometres east of the township. Military escorts formed the front and rear of the convoy, each jeep containing four armed soldiers and a driver.

Thomas Thistlethwaite and Lieutenant Anderson slowed in their jeep as they saw the procession heading away from the township. Thomas checked the time on his wristwatch. The military must have excluded the media from the protests in Blackgang Chine. The convoy was travelling east and they were travelling west. Without having to exchange more than a look with Thomas, Anderson stepped hard on the accelerator. It might already be too late.

Overhead two helicopter gunships intercepted a media helicopter hovering above the convoy. They forced the media aircraft to the ground and the convoy was halted as the civilian aircrew was loaded onto one of the news vans. The convoy then moved on and the gunships took off, heading at speed for Blackgang Chine. One of them swooped close to Anderson's vehicle and, the crew being satisfied with the vehicle insignia and a wave from Anderson, continued towards the township.

~

Kenneth sensed something amiss when the news people failed to materialise. He'd organised them to be there an hour before the demonstration and they were twenty minutes late. A couple of hundred townspeople swarmed around the main street. There were a few placards for each cause but the groups mingled in confusion, expecting their fifteen seconds of fame on satellite TV news.

A rumble from the eastern approach road caught his attention. It wasn't the high revving race of camera and sound teams vying for pole position at an event, rather the steady and heavy sound of a disciplined group of vehicles. From the dust cloud being raised, perhaps twenty trucks and half a dozen smaller vehicles.

Bernie, who had also come to see what was developing, saw Kenneth turn to the two protest organisers and take them aside for a hurried discussion. There was shaking of heads and Kenneth gesticulated towards the approaching vehicles, then at the market behind the buildings. Apparently not finding any agreement, he briefly embraced both organisers and came towards Bernie at a run.

'We have to leave now! There's been an unexpected and dangerous development. Let's get the others to the car. Right now!'

Bernie didn't question the authority in Kenneth's voice but simply turned with him towards the market.

They were both nearly blown off their feet by the downdraught of a helicopter gunship, coming in fast and low over the market. Canvas awnings were flying across the field and some stalls had tipped over. The helicopter continued on course and landed at the far west end of the high street, just as the military convoy arrived at the eastern end.

~

Anderson drove like a maniac. They nearly careered straight into the soldiers dismounting from their trucks, making a sharp turn to come to a skidding halt next to an armoured car.

'Looks like they mean business,' James said.

The troops were in full battledress. Anderson indicated a dozen army snipers who had taken up positions along the high street. The sounds of helicopter rotors, truck engines and noises of confusion from the protesters had all died away. The only noise was soldiers' boots hitting the hard ground as they took up their positions.

A sergeant stood next to an armoured car and addressed the township occupants via a loudhailer.

'These protests and this market are illegal gatherings. You must disperse immediately via the western end of the street. You have two minutes in which to comply and avoid further action.'

Anderson and Thomas moved along the pavement unimpeded, the soldiers in position respecting Anderson's rank.

The protest leaders finally appeared to heed Kenneth's earlier advice and signalled their colleagues to move towards the far end of the high street.

As the crowd began to move there was a whirr of rotors and the roar of an engine. The helicopter gunship took off into the air, hovering menacingly just a few metres above the ground, nose down and weapons pointed at the people.

Thomas couldn't tell where the first shot came from. The crowd appeared unarmed.

'Fire at will,' the sergeant ordered.

Troops and snipers opened fire with rifles and screams came from the crowd.

Anderson turned to Thomas. 'We'd better get out of here, nothing we can do.'

Thomas nodded in agreement but, as he turned, saw two familiar figures running towards the market. Bernie and Kenneth. Anderson was already on the way to his vehicle, failing to notice Thomas hadn't followed.

By the time Bernie and Kenneth reached the market Thomas was upon them.

'What the hell are you doing here?' he said and, not waiting for an answer, took them both by the arm to lead them to safety.

'Thomas?' Bernie cried. 'Rose is in the market!'

Kenneth nodded and they all scurried on towards the stalls.

From the main street a new sound arose, far more deadly than the sound of rifle fire. The helicopter gunship. Thomas felt rather than saw the shadow block the sun as the aircraft rose to spray death at high velocity along the high street. After just a few seconds there were almost no further sounds from the protesters, just screams of panic from the market.

A few stalls away Thomas could see Rose, pale and beautiful in the sun.

The cloud of death converged upon them. It moved faster than he could run but, this time, his feet were not of clay. In several bounds he was there, crushing Rose beneath his body into the ground, just as the cloud let lose its fateful lightning.

The gunship poured bullets onto the market like boiling water onto a pathway of ants. It was a miracle anyone survived.

Kenneth fell on top of Bernie to protect her. He landed with such impact it broke her right forearm and brought down two tables of melons on top of both of them, saving them from further injury.

Rose felt the first three impacts through Thomas's body, passing through the Kevlar armour he was wearing, and heard the fourth as it whistled past her ear and into the earth.

The fifth was the one that tilted his face into hers as he gave a twisted smile and said, 'your knight in shining armour.'

She met those blue eyes with her own and felt the life in them. Then the light faded, went out.

Anderson pulled Kenneth and Bernie from the wreckage. Kenneth carried Bernie into the back seat of the jeep. Anderson placed the body of Thomas in the luggage area behind the back seat, covering it with a blanket. Then he helped Rose into the vehicle.

They drove steadily across the bumpy fields and onto the road east out of the township. No one stopped them, the official insignia on the vehicle adequate identification for the VIP occupants. Thomas Thistlethwaite's field activities had drawn to a close.

·

The bubble bursts

Anderson radioed ahead for a military helicopter to meet them outside the AIDS hospice. They were whisked away to a private hospital where Bernie's arm was set and put in plaster. Rose didn't see them take Thomas away and there was mercifully little blood to act as a reminder of what had happened in the market at Blackgang Chine.

Anderson then brought them back to Nairobi where Derek and Greg were waiting, having earlier been informed of the day's events by telephone.

Greg was shattered by the news about Thomas. He hugged Rose but she was still in shock, barely responding.

Bernie was in good form, the painkillers numbing her discomfort from the broken arm.

'Sorry about the car,' Kenneth said. The Volvo sat full of bullet holes in a field on the outskirts of Blackgang Chine.

Derek put an arm around Kenneth's shoulders and pulled him into a hug. 'Greater love hath no man...'

'...than he lay on the wife of another,' Greg finished and immediately regretted it. One of his best friends had died in the act of saving his wife and mother, and all he could do was make a stupid joke.

~

Rose withdrew into her shell like a hermit crab. Despite the prescribed medication and rest for shock, she didn't speak a word to anyone for the next three days.

When Rose finally did speak again, the first words she uttered were to Greg.

'Let's get the hell out of this godforsaken country!'

Greg welcomed the return of his wife and her fiery spirit which he had feared was broken.

They packed their bags and left with the children the next day for the airport. Derek and Bernie were glum, suspecting it might be some time before they saw them again.

'Come back to Kilkenny, come back soon,' Rose said.

There were hugs and kisses all round.

They all slept on the flight back to Dublin. Greg dreamed of Thomas Thistlethwaite. He saw the Bedfordshire house then found himself floating from room to room. The dining room table was set for dinner for four. Gazing out of the kitchen window he saw the garden well manicured and the children's toys swinging to and fro. In the sitting room the framed family pictures showed Thomas together with Natalie, Hannah and Matt. They smiled into the camera. Then, like a magical picture in a Harry Potter story, they turned and walked away across a field, their figures fading as the wind sent rippling waves across the golden grass.

Greg awoke with a feeling of acceptance and, for the first time in three days, an absence of grief. Rose turned to him and he kissed her on the lips. 'We don't need to worry about Thomas, he'll be okay.'

From the sudden look of impossible hope on her upturned face he realised Rose had misunderstood but, perhaps cruelly, he left it there.

On return to Kilkenny, they took up immediate contact with Terry. She appeared at the front door soon after the kids were tucked up in bed.

Together, over large glasses of Spanish red wine, they recounted the best of times each had spent with Thomas.

'Do you remember when he told you I was a transvestite?' Terry said.

'And the time he poisoned the Slovenians with that extract of mushrooms,' Rose added.

'I didn't realise you knew about that!' Greg said.

'Didn't know you were banned from the World's End after a brawl with five eastern Europeans who were later found dead?'

'Or that either!'

'Greg,' Terry said, 'you can't move in Kilkenny without somebody knowing about it. Rose put two and two together after most of your escapades.'

'To be honest I don't think you have any secrets from me,' Rose said.

'And I don't suppose Africa has any secrets from you now, either,' Greg said.

'No. My bubble is well and truly burst there. I don't think you fully realise what a lucky escape the kids and I had, Greg. Any desire to move to Kenya has well and truly evaporated. And we've lost a great friend.'

Rose raised her glass in a toast to Thomas and the others followed.

'What I have to ask you is this,' Rose said. 'Is it right to continue with these infrastructure projects?'

Greg cleared his throat. He knew Terry would have to report back if there was any serious change in his commitment to the projects, but he decided to give an honest answer anyway.

'What I've seen in the last months and what you experienced last week makes me think the late Professor Martin Knox might not have been talking complete nonsense.'

Terry nodded and Greg continued.

'But we can't influence what the rest of the world is doing with Africa. One thing's for sure; infrastructure will be built in developing countries, regardless of their human rights status, as long as funds are available and international trade is open with those countries. Every country has an electrical system. What I'm saying is projects like mine will go on regardless. There's no point in backing out unless it's a question of safety.'

'He's right you know,' Terry said. 'Kenya and the rest of Africa are in renewal. They have humanitarian problems that have to be dealt with by governments and leaders. As long as Greg is safe then he should continue.'

'Okay,' Rose said. 'We're just little people, we sit back and let shit go on. We're powerless to intervene. What I don't understand is how the world is letting it happen.'

'From what I can see it's a long process,' Terry said. 'Power stations, roads, railways, you can build them in a year or two. Eliminating corruption, establishing democracy, disarming conflict zones, all takes longer. Africa is going to remain bad news in parts for some time, but we'll get there.'

'Well, I have to take what you say at face value because I trust you both and you know more about it than I do. Just to say, we ain't going there. Not now and no time soon.' Rose downed her glass and held it out for a refill. 'And another thing. I don't go for this phoney cosmopolitan religion stuff. *Gardens beneath which the rivers flow.* Some serious wool being pulled over the eyes there.'

The evening wore on. Thomas was reborn in their drunken reminiscences of misdeeds and comical moments.

The gathering

They answered the call when it came. Men and women of state, leaders. Elected by the people. It had been a long time in planning and they were entitled to be the first to bask in the glory.

Some political opponents were included with this band of the elite. They had shown ideological support, despite political differences, and they deserved the recognition.

Then there were the religious leaders from various denominations that had wrought unity and a sense of purpose from the chaos of the preceding decade.

These initial numbers were completed by the entourage of the faithful. Financial leaders who had taken difficult steps to fund the necessary activities. Military leaders who had shown courage in the face of public aversion to placing troops in harm's way for the greater good of civilisation. Public figures who had won the support of men and women on the street who mistrusted politicians but would follow celebrities. Industrialists who had lobbied where necessary, sailed close to the wind of industrial law and pushed their workforce hard to deliver technology, vaccines and other essentials.

In all they numbered close to ten thousand souls, this elite. Already on the ground, another one hundred and thirty-four thousand fortunate individuals had been chosen to share the return to Eden.

Across the continent they boarded their aircraft. Private jets, charter jets, commercial flights. At a predestined rendezvous all were transferred to a fleet of super airliners, designed to carry eight hundred but luxuriously refitted such that five hundred would enjoy a relaxing journey as befitted them. The instructions were clear; room for only nineteen large aircraft plus the President's, which was already near the destination. They would have to fit the fleet into a confined space.

The mood was buoyant, expectant, jubilant. Others would surely follow in their millions. They knew there would be those who would stay behind through choice, most likely to eventually perish as the natural course of events unfolded. And then there were the millions in other nations who had not been invited. Some would perish, others would find a way to survive if that was their destiny.

Such was their belief, so strong was their conviction. *A time for every purpose under heaven.*

Invasion

Air Chief Marshal Sir Edward Norman, Chief of the UK Defence Staff, addressed Goolden and Wildman in a military bunker deep beneath London.

'Gentlemen, the situation on the Iraq / Iran border is at crisis point. The USA have launched extensive air attacks on Iranian positions here,' he indicated a place just inside the Iranian border on the satellite picture, 'and here. The amassed count of four million Iranian soldiers is predominantly Basij. They are the volunteers Iran traditionally uses in potentially suicidal *human wave* attacks. Indications are of Iranian casualties already running into hundreds of thousands. The Iranians are showing signs of making preparations for withdrawal. They'll probably retreat some one hundred kilometres and make a stand.'

'What are you expecting of the Americans?' Goolden asked.

'They'll advance inside Iranian territory en masse and then send an expeditionary force of around one tenth of their numbers ahead into the desert.' The reply came from Wildman.

'Yes, quite correct.' Sir Norman had grown used to Wildman's prophetic grasp of military situations. 'It's a similar scenario to the invasion of Iraq. They anticipate the Iranian forces will crumble and yield.'

'And the Israelis, where are they?' Goolden studied the map.

'They're here, just south of the Turkish border. We don't anticipate their engagement before the Islamic Revolutionary Guard are encountered in Tehran.'

'You can forget about them,' Wildman said. 'They won't be called into combat.'

Sir Norman looked bemused but didn't question Wildman's prediction.

'So, gentlemen, what do we do now?' Goolden asked.

'Patrol our European and African air corridors. Operate a one hundred kilometre air and sea exclusion zone on our European and African borders. Prepare for post-conflict humanitarian relief as planned,' Sir Norman said.

Wildman had further advice. 'Send a final request to the USA to withdraw behind Iraqi borders and stand down their air attacks. Request Israel not to engage. Confirm our non-military support to Iran. Move for a UN emergency resolution against the USA and threaten sanctions if withdrawal doesn't occur within forty eight hours.'

Wildman sounded dispassionate, as if he was just going through the motions.

'Very well, I accept your recommendations.' Goolden studied the satellite picture once more with a frown. 'I do hope they don't spoil our party.'

~

General Bartholomew Brett, Chief of Staff of the United States Army, stood next to his operational colleague, General George Kinsaul, who was explaining the thrust of operations in Iran.

'We have inflicted heavy collateral damage of up to twenty percent in their forward positions with no losses on our side. The Basij are in disarray and the regular army are falling back. Our satellite surveillance tells us they have no missile defence systems of any consequence left intact and their air force is declining to engage.'

Brett nodded. 'It looks like you've pulled their teeth. What next?'

'We'll soften their front line up a little more with air bombardment over the next hour and then launch a major land invasion.' Kinsaul gestured forwards with his large, square clenched fist.

'Which units are going to lead the invasion?' Brett asked.

'The fifteen divisions of the President's Three Special Corps will lead the invasion.'

'And the Israelis?'

'They'll be held in reserve behind the Iraqi border,' Kinsaul said. 'We don't expect they'll be deployed. We'll spearhead the invasion with a brigade from each division of the Special Corps and our expectation is the enemy will be routed. You can tell the President we'll eat dinner in Tehran tomorrow night.'

I very much doubt it, thought Brett.

'George, if any unexpected obstacles are encountered the President and I need to be informed immediately.'

'Certainly, Bart, you can rest assured. But I'd be most surprised if anything unforeseen materialises in the desert.'

The generals shook hands and parted. Brett was on the phone immediately to the President. 'Mr President, all proceeding to plan, sir. Kinsaul has respected your wishes and the Special Corps will share our glory.'

'Thanks, Bart,' President Burden replied from his deep bunker in Iraq. 'I need you to stay with him during the first wave of the land invasion. Does he suspect anything?'

'Nothing, sir. He fully expects to dine in Tehran tomorrow night.'

'Each of us will find his own destiny, Bart. God will guide us.'

'I trust He will, sir. I trust He will.'

Return to Eden

Greg was honoured to receive the invitation to Koobi Fora. Rose and the kids understandably declined to accompany him. She said it would be a lifetime before she set foot in Africa again.

Once onboard the super airliner he found himself in illustrious company. In addition to all the key individuals currently working on infrastructure projects, the passengers included Prime Minister and European President Anthony Goolden, his communications guru Ron Wildman and a plethora of security service personnel including Trevor Anderson. In total the aircraft had a complement of some five hundred souls plus crew.

Spirits were high amongst the passengers and the eight hour flight went smoothly. The super airliner touched down at the new airport just outside Koobi Fora and taxied to pier number one of twenty.

In the air over the Mediterranean Sea a further nineteen super airliners could be seen high up in the sky. The loose formation, like a gaggle of giant migrating geese, was flanked on all sides, above and below, by fighter jets. Any other aircraft ignoring warnings to keep a fifty kilometre distance was swiftly intercepted by two of the fighters and escorted outside this mobile exclusion zone with a severe warning.

Goolden's team prepared his speech to the leaders of the European Union of States. Political, religious, industrial, military, celebrity, this would be an historic audience for what would be the event of the century, perhaps of the millennium. Cameras and additional viewing screens were put in place to bring the experience into the homes of more than half a billion people. Goolden hoped and trusted they would all take the example of their leaders and make the journey in their own time.

My Sweet Lord played out across the recently completed conference facility. Today there would be tens of thousands at Koobi Fora and millions would visit over the coming years, paying homage to the symbolic Garden of Eden, origin of Homo Sapiens, in the East African Rift Valley.

Within the next hour further super airliners began to arrive, landing from a holding pattern at five minute intervals. Greg's parents were onboard the second aircraft and a security officer escorted them to the VIP area where they joined their son. Goolden came by and Greg took the chance to introduce his parents to the premier. Goolden was joined by a Kenyan who he introduced as Milton Basila. When they had moved on Bernie explained to Greg that they had just met the new President of Kenya.

'Peter Abrams resigned soon after the Blackgang Chine massacre, ostensibly because of a scandal involving an underage African girl.' Bernie winked knowingly. 'Basila will go to the polls for reconfirmation of his electoral mandate next spring. Most of the political promises from him and the opposition are related to humanitarian improvements.'

'I'll believe it when I see it,' Derek mumbled.

'Kenneth plans to stand as a local parliamentary candidate,' Bernie continued. 'Apparently he's bigger into politics than we knew.'

'We'll have to get another bloody housekeeper,' Derek said.

~

Down in Nairobi Nurse Steevens did her rounds on long term care ward number seven. She was happy with this bunch of patients. A quiet lot, no complaints, no meals necessary. Just blanket washes and changing the drips. *No-*

340

hopers the other nurses called them but she preferred the term *sleepers*, like the Robert de Niro film.

There was one in particular who was her favourite. He had the physique of an athlete and the looks of a film star. Well, perhaps of one retired early due to serious injury. She liked to fantasise, pulling the curtains around him and giving him a gentle kiss on the lips, that he would wake and rise, take her hand and tell her he loved her, needed her and wanted to be with her forever.

It was the best thing about her *sleepers*. Fantasy was harmless, they would never wake. Even this one, he would slowly fade. The muscle tone would disappear in the arms, legs, even the face. He would gradually waste away and then, one day, the organs would begin to fail and the peace of eternal sleep would be his final reward.

Nurse Steevens wondered if the afterlife, if it existed, would be the same for all of them. And this one, whoever he might have waiting for him or whoever he would wait for, would they see each other as they remembered each other, or would one age and the other not?

Now it was quiet there was guaranteed to be no one else around. She pulled the curtains around his bed and, cupping his handsome but cruel face in her hands, placed a soft kiss on his warm lips. It always surprised her his lips were warm; somehow they should be cold. As usual, her efforts failed. He didn't wake up.

Stepping out from between the curtains, she switched on the television in the corner of the ward, put a peppermint in her mouth and prepared to watch the announcement at Koobi Fora.

The riders

General George Kinsaul looked across the information screens in his command centre.

Satellite images confirmed the Iranian forces were making a hasty retreat from the conflict zone. On request an operator adjusted the image for higher definition and the enemy could be seen in some disarray, abandoning heavy equipment and artillery.

On the air surveillance screen the squadrons of American jets were continuing their runs, leaving geometric patterns of devastation in the enemy's front line. Iran's aging air force was still virtually grounded and Kinsaul didn't expect it would be deployed to any effect.

Civilian air traffic in the greater area of Europe, the Middle East and North Africa looked to be grounded. No one was taking the risk of being mistakenly identified as hostile or getting struck by a stray missile. He did see a strange formation of airliners and jet fighters traversing the Mediterranean corridor. No doubt that was the cowardly Europeans travelling to Kenya on their fool's errand. It was a well known secret their supposedly philanthropic developments across Africa were nearing completion of the first phase. *They fiddle while Rome burns*, Kinsaul thought.

A small flurry of surprising new activity caught his eye. Around a dozen fighters had become airborne on the Iranian side of the front and were heading towards the Iraqi border. Their timing was good as they were between two waves of USA aircraft on bombing runs. *It's so easy to become complacent*, he thought. With no Iranian air activity in the conflict to date, the USA had begun to adopt the most efficient method of attack and allowed basic defensive tactics to slip.

Looking to the communications desk, the General nodded to the operator there and bursts of radio dialogue started to emit from the speakers around the room. He could tell from the different conversations all interested parties were aware of the Iranian jet fighter squadron being airborne. Anti-aircraft weaponry in the advancing land forces was at the ready and additional fighters had been scrambled to intercept the attacking aircraft, but the enemy would be upon the infantry before the USA jets could engage them.

Then a strange development occurred. The Iranian fighters split into four groups of three and flew single file between the advancing spearheads of the invasion, straight up, over and past the USA troops.

On the ground, American soldiers looked up from their personnel carriers into the sky to see the enemy jets streak over them at high altitude. Travelling at supersonic speeds, it was some twenty seconds before the troops could hear the scream of the aircraft. Exchanging looks of bewilderment, the invasion forces continued their progress across the desert terrain unabated.

Kinsaul already had an idea about the target of the Iranian aircraft and watched events unfold. Once past the USA ground invasion force, the four streams reunited and turned towards the Mediterranean.

There was a flurry of radio exchanges in Hebrew and it was clear the Israeli forces inside the Iraqi border had the same concern as Kinsaul; an attack on Israel itself was imminent. After a few more minutes it became clear this wasn't the intention. The Iranian jet squadron headed across Syrian air space and into the Mediterranean - in the direction of the nineteen passenger super airliners.

Captivated, Kinsaul instructed the operator to zoom in on the area. Strangely, no military aircraft from Turkey or

Italy had been scrambled to intercept and down the Iranians, which was what he would have expected.

Streaking over Cyprus and towards Sicily, the Iranians moved into an attack formation and each aircraft launched a missile towards the relatively slow moving civilian convoy. Within seconds each missile lost its track and fell harmlessly into the sea, mid-way between the Iranians and the convoy. Kinsaul recognised the use of anti-missile technology on the super airliners and had to admire the thoroughness of the Europeans.

Meanwhile, twenty of the fifty fighter jets escorting the airliner convoy had broken off to engage the Iranians. One by one the Iranian aircraft disappeared from the screen. Within five minutes they were all down, destroyed by the more modern and deadlier aircraft protecting their charges.

On reflection, it had been a desperate mission by the Iranian air force. Kinsaul was perplexed by what had occurred. Intelligence hadn't informed him Iran might attack the Europeans. The Union's refusal to join the USA invasion forces had put them close to being allies with Iran.

'Sir, I think you should see this.'

The general's attention was brought back to his invasion forces. An operator was zeroing in on some ground activity at the northern edge of the attack wave. About one kilometre east of the northern lead battalion a land feature appeared that hadn't previously been there; a deep indentation in the ground, some two hundred metres square.

As they watched, another indentation appeared, fifty kilometres further south and alarmingly close to the lead battalion. Then, like a row of dominoes cascading, a further five such strange landforms appeared in the desert on a line running north-south.

The American ground forces had crossed a four hundred kilometre stretch of the Iran Iraq border simultaneously and, with the border running at a slight angle to the south east, they weren't vertically aligned.

As a result, the third and subsequent indentations appeared directly underneath the advancing forces. Personnel carriers, fast attack vehicles and tanks disappeared into the sands of the desert.

'What the hell?' Kinsaul exclaimed. He grabbed an amber phone from the communications desk and spoke rapidly into it. The American advance faltered, stopped and reversed, leaving five thousand men and their equipment buried in the desert. Kinsaul made another connection and specified the coordinates for air support.

Within two minutes the lead battalions had retreated one kilometre back from the indentations. It would take another five minutes before air surveillance could try and interpret whatever was causing the phenomena. As Kinsaul waited for this, he and the others in the room looked on dumbfounded as the two hundred metre square indentations began to move towards the invasion forces.

Platoon leaders on the ground reported back visual accounts of what was being seen in the control room. Kinsaul barked an order to go to visual and fifteen television screens flickered on, showing what the platoon leaders could see from the cameras mounted on their fast attack vehicles.

The large indentations in the desert had been caused by enormous ramps dropping down below the desert surface. A dark cavernous mouth indicated an underground installation at the bottom of each of the seven ramps. Audio accompanied the images and a deep growling sound emerged from the direction of the tunnels. What the General and his staff in the control centre couldn't feel was the tremor in the ground that accompanied the sound.

Out of the desert sands, at intervals of fifty kilometres in a line running north south, something emerged simultaneously from each of the seven caverns. From the head-on perspective of the platoon leaders it appeared massive boulders were creeping up the ramps and towards them. USA fast attack mobiles were despatched to flank the ramps and it soon became clear these weren't boulders but extremely large and slow moving vehicles with desert camouflage.

Each of the vehicles was advancing at a walking pace up the ramp and out onto the surface.

Kinsaul shook his head. He'd never seen anything of the like. The stony grey dappled vehicles looked more like passenger ferries on wheels than anything military. Fifty meters wide and nearly as high, one hundred meters long and belching enormous clouds of black smoke from the rear as they climbed. But even more monstrous were the sounds and screams of the battalions that had fallen down the ramps as they were crushed by the caterpillar tracks of the leviathans.

Local tactics engaged and the lead platoons took action against the slow moving vehicles across the wide front of the invasion. Rocket powered grenades were aimed at the caterpillar tracks with some success, destroying several of the four metre tracks on each vehicle. With a sound of grinding metal and rubber, the tracks seized and the USA troops gave a cheer. Their jubilation was short lived, however, as the damaged tracks were jettisoned by the giant vehicles like a lizard losing its tail. Protective shielding folded out of the vehicle body and formed a guard over the remaining functioning tracks. *Russian tank track technology*, Kinsaul thought. The vehicles gathered speed infinitesimally.

It took five minutes for them to complete their ascent and manoeuvre onto the surface, by which time air strikes had commenced. Although the Iranian vehicles were perilously close to, and in some cases in the midst of, American land forces, the air attack was full blooded.

Modern missile technology meant a distance of two hundred meters was safe enough to avoid friendly fire.

The devastating effect of the USA air attack was unforeseen. Missiles rained down on the seven Iranian supertanks, those USA missiles equipped with the best of laser guided, satellite positioning technology to ensure accuracy. The first missile landed in the middle of an American brigade, blowing a dozen vehicles into the air and killing hundreds of USA troops.

Kinsaul knew immediately what was happening. He could see beams of red light firing out of the enemy vehicles into the sky. The Iranians were employing anti-missile lasers on the vehicles to scramble the missile onboard direction systems and deflect them. The technology looked very similar to that employed by the super airliners over the Mediterranean. Kinsaul knew of only one technology able to totally override the missiles of the USA attack jets; a French system.

Shouting commands into the amber phone, the General tried to call off the air attack but it was too late. Wave after wave of armaments cascaded down at the Iranians, only to deflect at the final moment onto the surrounding Americans. After two minutes of bombardment the Iranians enjoyed a death zone of five hundred meters in every direction. It looked as though USA forces closest to the supertanks had been flattened underfoot by giants. The enemy gathered pace.

'Shit, shit, shit!' Kinsaul held his hands to his temples.

'George, you were to inform me in the event of any unexpected developments,' a voice from behind him chided. General Bartholomew Brett stood wearing a headset at the rear of the room. Kinsaul couldn't tell how long the chief of staff had been there.

'We've just reached that point now, Bart. Please inform the President our front line has engaged with... has met with... encountered some large obstacles.' Kinsaul lamely concluded his message and realised the gargantuan Iranian vehicles hadn't attacked the USA forces in any way.

Kinsaul was on the amber phone again. 'All battalions to engage enemy with tank and howitzer. Avoid friendly fire at all costs.'

He could hear Brett talking on his headset and, by Brett's demeanour, he guessed the President was on the line.

The video screens now showed a mad battle scene resembling an army of ants swarming over something huge, invulnerable and unstoppable. Tanks fired shells into the sides of the enemy with some effect. It was like peeling a giant grey onion. The grey camouflage of the supertanks dropped off with each impact, revealing a dark green layer that looked more impenetrable. Howitzer shells easily found their target on the upper areas of the enemy vehicles and had the same effect there.

After several minutes of attack by the Americans, the Iranian vehicles no longer resembled giant boulders so much as huge shadows moving across the desert. The surfaces seemed to absorb light and gave the illusion of having only two dimensions. Without any let up in intensity the USA attacks continued but to lesser effect. The dark green armour was far more resistant. Parts of the surface slowly succumbed to the bombardment, falling likes scales from a dragon, only to reveal a further undamaged layer beneath.

'Looks like UK prototype body armour,' commented one of the operators in the control room.

'Pretty formidable, you have to admit,' Brett said into Kinsaul's ear. 'Russian transport systems, French anti-missile technology and British regenerative body armour. I wonder what else they have up their sleeves?'

As if to answer the comment a transmission was received on several frequencies. The communications operator signalled to Kinsaul and put the message live onto the speakers.

'Cease your attack immediately. You are on Iranian soil. If you fail to comply with this warning then we will return fire.'

The voice delivering the message was synthesised and totally devoid of emotion.

'Continue your attack,' Kinsaul instructed on the amber phone and then turned to Brett. 'Their body armour can't last for ever. We just have to persevere.'

Precisely sixty seconds after the warning message was received, armoured plates of several metres diameter popped off the sides and top of the enemy vehicles and gun turrets pushed out of the apertures like fresh shoots on a tree in springtime.

Large bore gun barrels emerged from the turrets and proceeded to make short work of the American tanks and armoured vehicles that had been attacking from the ground.

'No, I've never seen anything like it,' Kinsaul admitted in response to Brett's look of enquiry. He barked into the amber phone. 'Retreat and maintain two kilometres distance,' but the command was superfluous. Any American tanks and other vehicles not already obliterated by the supertank turret guns were sprinting away in the direction of the Iraq border.

The pace of the Iranian vehicles had increased to twenty kilometres per hour. Having been informed of this, Kinsaul advised the invasion force to retreat to and hold the border. Although the American vehicles were all capable of more than forty kilometres per hour, there were some mishaps during the retreat. Mechanical failures and human error left several hundred men and women at the mercy of the enemy.

Those who didn't fire upon the supertanks were simply ignored as the vast green vehicles trundled past. Those unlucky enough to become immobilised directly in the path of the enemy were crushed like ants.

Redemption

He lay on a bed of straw in the cave, tired from his exertions and waiting for it to happen, as it had every night without fail as long as he could remember.

The pool of water at the back of the cave looked cool and deep, inviting.

Outside the entrance to the cave were the sounds of men lifting heavy rocks. He had dragged those rocks there during the early evening in an attempt to keep the men out but it was futile. There were so many of them and, as a group, they were easily and quickly able to remove the barricade it had taken him hours to build. He knew his efforts were wasted but every night he was driven by an inexplicable force to try and bar their entry.

They cleared his blockade and each entered the cave with the slow, deliberate walk of the executioner.

First to reach him was the Kenyan, Joseph Kyanga. The bespectacled African came to his bedside and, reaching into a pocket of his sports jacket, produced a wriggling scorpion. The evil looking insect jabbed its poisonous tail into Thomas's neck, injecting lethal venom that brought near instant paralysis. This didn't however, stop the pain creeping up from Thomas's fingers and toes, slowly to his heart, and it took only a minute for him to die.

Kyanga looked solemnly down at the body and withdrew. As he did so, the body of Thomas convulsed and he was resurrected.

Now came the men of water - Henry Asobayire of Uganda and the infantry captain of Zimbabwe with the missing ring finger. Taking turns, they drowned him in the pool. First Asobayire stunned him with a rock and threw him into the pool, where his lungs filled with water and he lost his life. Then he woke again on the straw bed and the captain, taking him by the ankles, held him upside down in the pool until he ceased to struggle and expired. Once again he found himself reborn on the straw bed.

Then came Edward Mboto, also of Uganda. The straw became stained with blood as, body held down by others, Thomas's hands and feet were hacked off by Mboto's machete. Shock ran through his body and the blood ebbed until his sight faded and heart stopped.

Awakened on the bed, he was approached by two dark men, clearly brothers. The Bouquet family pulled him up and beat him mercilessly until his neck finally snapped, bringing a moment of deathly relief.

This was short lived as five Slovenians with shorn heads dealt him the death of a thousand cuts, the poison from their knives attacking his nervous system. He died horribly, foaming red at the mouth.

Finally, a gentle, scholarly type approached and shook him alive. He took Thomas up by the shoulders and proceeded to throw him like a rag doll across the cave, hammering his flesh and bones into the stone until his face was unrecognisable, limbs twisted and back broken. Prof. Martin Knox stood looking grimly at the wrecked body of Thomas Thistlethwaite and then, with all the others, turned slowly to leave the cave.

'Same time again tomorrow, fellas?' Thomas quipped stoically in a barely audible voice. On the bed of straw again, he was alive but the mental and physical trauma had made him into an old, crippled man.

One of the vengeful raised the back of a hand by way of farewell and then they were gone. Thomas collapsed onto the bed, his breathing that of a man in his final hours. Raising his head weakly, his milky eyes nearly blind, he could see the break of day through the cave entrance and, with a superhuman effort, he dragged himself to greet the dawn.

The first rays of sun hit his body and rejuvenated it. Thomas stood straight, handsome and proud again. He took a drink of refreshing water from the stream that babbled past the cave, and headed up the track.

The sound of his children's laughter carried through the air like birdsong. They ran down the slope of the field and into his waiting arms. Hannah threw herself into the air and landed on her father's chest. Matt jumped on Thomas's back and ruffled his hair.

Natalie sauntered down the slope, smiling wistfully.

'Oh, Thomas, if only you could stay with us. The children miss you at night time.'

Thomas kissed his beautiful wife and they walked on, hand in hand, the children running ahead to the stream and hopping across the stepping stones. They crossed to the other bank and sat a little way up on the lush grass, already warmed by the morning sun.

At this age the children were a complete delight. Hannah was so graceful, forever acting the princess and gently teasing her younger brother into chases. Matt was fast and agile but, when he finally caught his sister, gentle in play and still with a touch of the puppy about him.

Thomas didn't feel any regret that the children would never grow up. He felt only contentment that the family was together in such perfect circumstances, harmonious with each other and nature.

Later Natalie produced a picnic from a bag. The parents drank Champagne and the children gorged on oak-smoked salmon. Fresh salad and cheeses were accompanied by different types of roast and cured meat and rustic bread. The meal reminded Thomas of the first time he and Natalie had made love in the Brazilian countryside. She read his thoughts and gave him a tender kiss that made his heart leap.

Thomas was experiencing a cumulative delight from each day spent with his family. It soothed all desires and let him face the day feeling refreshed and full of optimism.

Natalie knew what her husband experienced at night. He had explained this to her and, strangely, neither of them felt anguish or fear. It was an accepted part of the conditions placed upon Thomas's presence there. Nevertheless, Natalie did ask if he didn't want to find a way to stop the night activities.

'I have to endure it,' Thomas said. 'These are my worst deeds and it seems there is no walking away from righteous retribution.'

'No, you misunderstand,' Natalie explained in her Brazilian accent. 'The men you speak of, I have seen some of them in the palace during the evenings and nights. They are not exacting revenge. That is not part of their existence here. What you experience is for you alone.'

'But this is it now, Natalie. Unless there is to be a fixed duration to my night time sentence, this is how it will be. I accept it. In perpetuity.'

'No, Daddy,' Hannah said, taking her father's hand. 'There's a way for you to be with us. The man told us.'

Thomas looked at his daughter and felt his heart would burst.

'Thomas, the door isn't closed for you. We both know you've committed terrible acts in the name of freedom and country. There have been things you did after we left you. To kill without any justification. To take the wife of another man.'

Thomas felt a sudden, certain knowledge he truly had no secrets from his wife.

'Are you saying there is a way to redeem myself?' he asked.

'Yes, darling,' Natalie said, smiling. 'I don't know what you have to do but I've been told it's possible. You're granted a chance to right things. Will you take it? Take it now, Thomas, and come back when you're ready to be with us.'

He took his wife's hand and that of his daughter. Matt stood by, pulling on his father's trouser leg. Thomas kissed them and closed his eyes.

'I seek redemption. My sweet Lord, I will gratefully accept this second chance.'

The grip of his family loosened and he fell through the cosmos.

~

His bed was warm and clean. The straw gone, replaced by a firm mattress covered in fresh cotton bed linen. He could feel softness under the palms of his hands.

Thomas sensed pain in his limbs. A heaviness restricted his breathing and he had a strange feeling in his head as though part of his skull had been removed. And he could hear a strange, regular panting noise nearby, like someone engaged in a repetitive, strenuous exercise. *My Sweet Lord* played in the background.

He took stock of his situation. Senses of touch and hearing were intact. Smell – there was a smell, not unpleasant, but pungent. He realised it was a perfume. And taste, he could taste peppermint. There was peppermint on his tongue. In fact, there was a tongue on his tongue. He moved his tongue against the invading tongue.

When Thomas regained his final sense, that of vision, Nurse Steevens found herself eye to eye with her patient. She withdrew from his mouth in great surprise and involuntarily dismounted onto the floor in a faint.

With a glance at Nurse Steevens, the thought occurred to Thomas that his journey to redemption had begun inauspiciously.

He reached out to the curtain around his bed, pulled it back and saw the smiling, benevolent face of Anthony Goolden looking down from a TV screen in the corner of the ward. It was time. Koobi Fora, return to Eden. Thomas had been asleep for four weeks.

Then there were four

One hundred thousand American troops stood stock still on the Iraq Iran border. Behind them, across a strip of land one hundred kilometres wide and nearly one thousand long, a million battle-ready colleagues awaited their instructions. They expected a mass invasion of Iran, to crush the enemy underfoot, to subjugate a civilian population that, according to USA politicians, considered them to be the Devil's spawn.

The seven huge Iranian vehicles were now approaching across the desert at alarmingly high speed. General Kinsaul was consulting with General Brett in the control centre regarding his plan of action.

'What is the ETA of the Iranians at the border,' Brett asked his peer.

'At current speed, about twenty minutes,' Kinsaul said.

Brett moved away and spoke into his headset, apparently receiving instructions in return.

'Lay a bombardment in their path to slow them down, the engagement must not happen for another forty five minutes. Orders from the President.'

With a look of slight confusion, Kinsaul relayed the order and howitzers began to pummel the landscape in the path of the Iranians.

Air surveillance showed missile impact reshaping the contours of the desert. The massive caterpillar tracks of the vehicles managed the shifting sand landscape but at a slower pace.

Brett received further instructions and asked the air surveillance operator to zoom in on the supertanks, one after another. Kinsaul could see large emblems on the back of the vehicles. He didn't recognise the symbols and assumed they were in the Iranian language of Farsi but each was unique and of a different colour.

'Target those with yellow, purple and blue emblems,' Brett said, again relaying orders from on high.

'General Brett,' Kinsaul growled, 'if you have material intelligence of which I'm not aware then I advise this is the time to share it.'

'That's what I'm doing, George,' Brett replied.

Kinsaul directed artillery against the three identified vehicles as ordered. After some ten minutes the vehicle with the blue emblem ceased to move and, stuck halfway up a steep dune, showed no signs of resistance. The two others marked with yellow and purple symbols were soon in a similar position, apparently disabled and immobile. Further south, the four remaining Iranian vehicles continued their charge towards the border.

Kinsaul began preparations for a deadly assault. He was lining up the old faithful B52 bombers to drop their deadly cargo in the way of the supertanks when Brett advised him again.

'They'll stop at the border. Cease attack and withdraw one kilometre inside Iraqi territory. Maintain the main body of our forces at a distance of twenty kilometres.'

Bemused by what seemed to be a giant chess game, Kinsaul complied and noticed the enemy vehicles slowing on their approach to the border.

'It's time to get going,' Brett said. 'George, the President requests your company.' He turned to the door of the control centre and indicated they should leave. Two adjutants in full dress uniform held the doors open and Kinsaul let himself be led out after officially delegating command of the control centre to his second.

Outside the centre a jet helicopter whisked them away and within fifteen minutes they were at a long landing strip some fifty kilometres from the border and in the middle of the main USA forces.

Looking around the airbase Kinsaul found that, despite his many years of active service, he was still impressed to be in charge of such superlative military strength. Everywhere he looked there were troops and equipment being made ready for battle.

Morale felt high and, despite the strange events of the day, Kinsaul still felt sure he would dine in Tehran that evening or else very soon. He knew they had flown to the location of a deep military bunker but he was nevertheless surprised to see President James Burden emerge from heavily armoured double doors that seemed to swing up out of the sand.

'Mr President.' Kinsaul saluted Burden who returned the gesture.

'George, we have a day of great honour ahead of us. It's part of our destiny and you've been selected to join us.' Burden took Kinsaul by the arm as he strode with his entourage towards a large aircraft hangar. The huge doors slid open to reveal the President's own super airliner, the latest incarnation of Air Force One.

Once onboard the aircraft Kinsaul realised he was in very illustrious company. In addition to the President and close political allies there were two former presidents and several other current and former military leaders. He also recognised a number of USA celebrities of global fame and the heads of several state agencies including the FBI and the CIA. It was contrary to convention to have so many key individuals on one aircraft, thought Kinsaul. Especially in a war zone. He concluded the President must have some PR stunt up his sleeve.

Outside on the runway fighter jets took off in rapid succession. Air Force One soon trundled out of the hangar and made its own journey up into the atmosphere, joining the protective escort circling above.

Once the aircraft levelled off, Brett led Kinsaul into an area at the rear of the aircraft. It was a smaller version of the control room he had previously occupied on the ground. They had access to the same information – satellite aerial images, video and sound relayed from ground forces, and radio transmissions. The four Iranian supertanks could be seen taking up positions close to the Iraq Iran border.

On one wall of the control area there was a large whiteboard with extensive notes in different colour pen and some statements written boldly and enclosed in squares. Kinsaul stepped over to take a look. Today's date and a time some twenty minutes hence were in one box. Another contained the same three symbols Brett had identified on the enemy vehicles to be attacked. A bigger box contained the symbols borne by the four remaining supertanks and corresponding words in English of four colours – white, red, black and green.

Kinsaul moved back to the system display screens and had another surprise. Air Force One had reached cruising altitude and risen into pole position of a formation of twenty super airliners flanked by a protective sheath of some sixty jet fighters.

'Gentlemen,' announced President James Burden, 'today will be a great day in history. We are privileged to embark upon a unique journey together. This is the culmination of all your work, your faith and your dedication. Our return to paradise.'

An audience of millions

Nurse Steevens picked herself up from the floor of the long term care ward. For the first time one of her *sleepers* had woken up. She had mixed feelings about the miraculous event, considering her compromising position, but concluded he could well be brain damaged and would almost certainly remember nothing of his waking moments. She sat down in a chair next to Thomas's bed to watch the ceremony at Koobi Fora.

Thomas was happy to be alive but a little disappointed he wasn't personally attending an event that marked the culmination of so much effort by Europe in Africa over the past few years.

The camera panned over the audience and he recognised many faces from the projects, colleagues from the agency and, could it be? Yes, that was definitely Reto Hersperger, fattened by an American diet, and his girlfriend Svetlana. Trevor Anderson was also there. Next to them stood Greg Marshall's parents, then Greg and the androgynous Terry. With a pang Thomas realised there was no sign of Rose. Had she survived Blackgang Chine?

Returning to the stage, the TV screen again showed Anthony Goolden engaging in handshakes and hugs with various key members of the British and French governments. The dignitaries transmitted an unmistakable atmosphere of jubilation to the audience at Koobi Fora and equally to those watching remotely across Europe and Africa.

~

Greg felt a shiver run across his shoulders. The mood was electric. Surrounded by friends, family and colleagues, he spared a moment's thought for Rose and the kids, regretting he hadn't talked his wife into coming over. And poor Thomas, lying immobile and wasting away in a hospital bed in Nairobi. They'd received news of his survival just a couple of weeks ago. Rose had somehow been even more devastated than when she thought he was dead.

Anthony Goolden now moved to the stage centre and waited patiently as the large crowd in the conference hall quietened down.

He spoke quietly, humbly, with his hands clasped and eyes cast downwards.

'Ex umbris, in veritatum. Out of darkness, into truth.'

Goolden's very breathing could be heard by his audience of millions.

'Africa has suffered terribly at our negligent hands and those of our forebears. Missionary zeal. Slavery. War and genocide. The AIDS pandemic. We have thirsted for the continent's resources, its gold and diamonds, its flesh and blood. We have turned a blind eye to corruption, funded dictatorships and allowed children to be orphaned.'

The crowd was silent. They hadn't expected castigation.

'Our brothers and sisters here in Africa are not without their share of the guilt. Fellow men have been bought and sold. The less privileged have been exploited. Women have been dehumanised. Life has been taken cheaply. Mother Earth has been plundered, neglected.'

There were many Africans in the audience and they shared in the general discomfort.

'But there is good news.' Goolden lifted up his head and faced directly into the camera, his piercing blue eyes gripping those hundreds of millions who were watching via TV and the live audience gazing upon massive screens around the conference centre. An irresistible fervour began to fill the air at Koobi Fora.

'God loves a sinner. More so one who repents. And we have repented. You and I. And where better to repent than here, in Koobi Fora, Kenya. The Crucible of Mankind, the Garden of Eden, beneath which the rivers first flowed.'

Beneath which the rivers flow murmured the audience unconsciously in the pause Goolden left for them.

'Here, where we took our original burden of sin, we have begun to make good our debts. Here in Africa, on a scale the world has never seen before, the States of Europe have united with a purpose. The twenty-first century has arrived across this continent, funded by the repatriated riches of a land which now has the world's best water supplies, roads, electricity, buildings and every modern technology.'

Images of infrastructure projects appeared on the screens. A land transformed. In the hospital ward in Nairobi a happy smile spread across Thomas's face. A smile echoed by Greg and his family in Koobi Fora and by hundreds of millions of others across Africa and Europe.

The camera returned to Goolden and he held out a hand to Charles Lorin, President of the French Republic, who walked from the side of the stage towards the microphone and began to speak.

'Children of France, children of Great Britain, children of Europe, children of Africa. This land awaits you. God has told us to build a home for all his children. It is time to return to Eden, from whence we came.'

A great cheer erupted from the audience in Koobi Fora and spread simultaneously across the European and African continents. The screens in the conference centre showed cheering crowds gathered in the major cities of Europe.

Goolden and Lorin embraced, kissed each other's cheeks, shook hands and were quite carried away with the emotion of the moment.

Goolden moved to the microphone and his voice now boomed out.

'During my presidency we will take special measures to ease your journey. All school leavers who embark upon further education will receive this free if they choose to study here. All those in retirement will be provided with accommodation as part of a European state pension. And for the rest of us I can say every job occupation in Europe has been recreated here. Africa is becoming a global source of manufacturing and commerce. God is smiling upon his children. This is Africa. This is our future!'

In the wings Ron Wildman gave the signal. George Harrison's *My Sweet Lord* began to fill the air.

Greg thought he would burst with joy. Everyone around him was smiling, dancing, hugging. It was a mass hysteria of the kind he had only experienced once before, in London's Trafalgar Square on the Millennium New Year's Eve. For a few seconds he remained above it, conscious of it. And then he let it wash over him, cleansing, uplifting..

In Paris, London, Berlin, Madrid, Rome and numerous other European cities the mood was effervescent. Images of Africa's scenic beauty flashed across the screens, broadcast from Kenya. A familiar phrase in ornate script gradually began to materialise across the bottom of the screen. *Beneath which the rivers flow.*

Wildman gave another signal and the main camera switched to the dry ancient river bed surrounding Koobi Fora. Deep under the deserts of Saharan Africa the Spanish water supply systems were activated. A wave of water bore down towards the northern reaches of Kenya along a pipe so large it could have accommodated a double-decker bus.

Wildman, Goolden and Lorin exchanged glances of sublime anticipation and stared at the image of the dry Koobi Fora river bed on the screens. Across Europe the heads of state, religion and government expectantly watched the televised images in their home cities.

Nothing happened. The river didn't flow.

End game

The formation of super airliners set itself in a holding pattern just inside Iraqi airspace, high above the surface of the earth and circling in a tight stack with a diameter of twenty kilometres.

General Kinsaul was relaying instructions to ground command, issued to him directly from President Burden.

'Pull forward all fifteen divisions of the three Special Corps to engage the enemy,' the President instructed. 'How many men are left in that force?'

'Around one hundred and twenty-four thousand, sir,' Kinsaul replied.

'And the Israelis, where are they now?' Burden asked.

'The Israeli forces have been further withdrawn to a distance of five hundred kilometres from the battle zone,' General Brett said.

'Good, good,' the President murmured. 'I want an immediate all-out attack on the four remaining enemy vehicles, using land forces at close quarters. Send them in waves of a brigade at a time, one brigade on each enemy target.'

'Mr President, I have to point out that's tantamount to a suicide attack,' Kinsaul said. 'The Iranian reaction earlier today doesn't suggest we would gain anything by such an action.'

'Oh, we'll gain plenty, General,' Burden replied. 'Trust me, our rewards will be great.'

The President of the United States and his two generals watched as events unfolded below them on the surface of the planet. Within a few minutes the first wave of Special Corps fell upon the Iranian supertanks like a marauding hoard. As previously, the American firepower was ineffective and a warning was issued on the airwaves in the same synthesised voice, totally devoid of emotion.

'Cease your attack immediately. You are on Iranian soil. If you fail to comply with this warning then we will return fire.'

Kinsaul looked at the President but received no instruction to withdraw. They stood and watched as four brigades, consisting of twelve battalions, some fourteen thousand men, were mown down and obliterated by the gun turrets of the enemy.

Even before the last men and women had fallen, Burden instructed Kinsaul to keep up the momentum and move the next wave into attack. Kinsaul objected.

'Is this really necessary, Mr President? These are American service personnel with families at home and we're sending them to certain death!'

'Theirs is a worthy sacrifice, General. The enemy must be provoked for us to succeed. Trust me, I'm well informed.'

Kinsaul looked across to Brett and saw the many faces in the airborne control room turned towards him. He had the feeling he was the only one who didn't know what was really going on.

It took an hour for the Special Corps to be completely annihilated. After the first three waves Kinsaul became numb to the slaughter. He wasn't oblivious, however, of the growing sense of elation onboard Air Force One.

At the end of the hour Brett spoke. 'Mr President, your Special Corps is gone. We are ready for the final attack.'

Burden placed a hand on the shoulder of each general and gave his instructions.

'General Kinsaul, commence bombardment of the enemy with all the artillery you have. We have a little surprise lined up for them with our fighter escort.'

'These fighters are equipped with special missiles that can evade all anti-missile systems,' Brett explained to Kinsaul. 'But we only have enough armaments to attack one target successfully.'

Burden beckoned the generals over to the whiteboard where the Iranian symbols were drawn. The rest of the people in the room congregated around them.

Burden raised a finger and placed it on the red symbol.

'This is the one.'

'Are you certain, Mr President?' Brett asked.

One of the gathered people stepped forward and began to talk animatedly. Kinsaul recognised him as an evangelical Christian figure he had once seen on TV back in the USA.

'This one here, the green, means pestilence in Farsi. That will be carrying biological weapons. Not much use to us.' The man of religion moved his finger across the board to the black symbol. 'This is famine and will be carrying chemical weapons, same applies.' He then indicated the white symbol. 'This is conquest, victory. This vehicle contains nothing bad.'

Brett moved to the board and placed his hand over the red symbol. 'Yes, this *must* be the one. The red of war. We know they have only one nuclear weapon, supplied by the Europeans, and this must be it.'

'All agreed?' the President asked the congregation.

'All agreed,' they responded in unison and returned to their posts.

The display screens showed a chaotic scene with heavy shells exploding on and around the four Iranian supertanks. Despite some surface damage, the vehicles were moving steadily towards the Iraqi border. They had retracted their gun turrets and once again looked like dark green shadows moving over the surface of the desert.

'Commence the air attack,' the President instructed.

Kinsaul had no command over the fighter jet escort and listened as the Air Force General gave instructions. He could feel through his legs and ears that Air Force One had also left the holding pattern and was in descent.

The President turned his attention to the radar screen and watched as their escort of sixty jet fighters streamed away from the formation of super airliners and down towards the Iranians. It looked like a swarm of wasps flying out from their nest to sting an aggressor to death.

Kinsaul could see from the satellite aerial images that a furious onslaught had been initiated upon the supertank with the red symbol, identified by Brett as symbolising war. The other Iranian vehicles continued to be bombarded from a safe distance by ground artillery.

Each jet fighter carried two missiles and was instructed to launch one of these at the red supertank on the first attack. By the time fifteen of the first twenty missiles had successfully found their target, the red vehicle was smoking heavily and showing signs of material damage for the first time during the day's engagement.

The communications channels were affected by the mayhem on the ground but once again a familiar message came through, although this time delivered with Iranian inflection in a voice that carried significant emotion.

'You have attacked the Islamic Republic of Iran. Cease your aggression immediately. You are on Iranian soil. If you fail to comply with this warning then God will be your judge.'

They had answered the call when it came. Men and women of state, leaders. Elected by the people. It had been a long time in planning and they were entitled to be the first to bask in the glory. Some political opponents were included with this band of the elite, religious leaders from the various denominations that had wrought unity and a sense of purpose from the chaos of the preceding decade. Financial and military leaders, public figures, industrialists. In all they numbered close to ten thousand souls, this elite, airborne and determined. Already on the ground, another one hundred and thirty-four thousand fortunate individuals had already embarked upon their journey.

President Burden indicated to the Air Force General to continue their attack in the agreed formation.

'Target their periphery,' Brett instructed. 'Don't kill the target!'

Kinsaul saw from the radar screen that Air Force One retained pole position in the formation of larger aircraft. Fifteen jet fighters led in front of the super airliners, accelerating towards their goal. He could feel the steep descent of the aircraft and, moving to a window, saw the surface of the desert bathed in the glow of the evening sun. Air Force One descended towards the ground and levelled off at an altitude of just one and a half kilometres. Plumes of smoke could be seen in the distance and the airliner was headed directly towards the source of the smoke.

'What is our ETA and distance?' Burden asked.

'One minute and five miles precisely sir,' the Air Force General answered.

'And the device range?' the President continued.

'Two miles, Mr President.'

'Excellent. Full attack, but peripheral,' Burden said.

The formation moved steadily towards the Iranians at three hundred knots, now just one kilometre above the desert terrain. Around them the American fighter jets screamed past, aiming their deadly load at the enemy.

From the satellite image Kinsaul could see the red supertank was now rendered immobile, its caterpillar tracks destroyed. Laser beams flew in all directions as the Iranians desperately attempted to disarm the incoming missiles. As he watched, the top of the vehicle appeared to bulge and form into a dome. Foreign language filled the airwaves, a rhythmic incantation Kinsaul assumed must be a religious verse.

'Brothers and sisters, the time is nigh,' the evangelical preacher began. Ten thousand souls onboard twenty super airliners listened in rapt attention. 'The Lord is our shepherd. We shall not want. He makes us down to lie...'

Kinsaul glanced out the window and saw they would soon be directly above the red Iranian vehicle of war. His own worst fears were confirmed. He was an unwilling sheep for this shepherd.

'in green pastures...'

The dome of war pulled back its cover like a giant eyelid and released its message upwards. Kinsaul watched in horrified amazement as he saw the projectile rise and seem to hover just a few hundred meters away.

'He leadeth us the quiet waters by,' the preacher continued, then bowed his head, clasping his hands. Ten thousand faithful followed suit, except for Kinsaul. 'We are ready, Lord.'

On the airwaves an automated voice, devoid of emotion, announced, *'Dire retribution is visited upon our enemies.'*

Kinsaul looked out of the window and saw the light.

The air split. Desert was rent asunder. War did not leave even the blood of its enemies upon the battlefield. No burials would be necessary for the ten thousand who had died in the air, nor for the one hundred and thirty-four thousand who had died on the ground. All were vaporised.

Burden and his throng had misjudged the content of the other Iranian vehicles. Each had contained nuclear weapons and all had detonated, two in the air and two on the ground. No one would tread this wasteland again for a long time to come.

Beneath the earth's surface old fault lines were strained by the explosions. Eastern spurs of the ancient Rift Valley passed their energy back along to their roots and the planet quivered.

~

In Africa the jungles stilled to a sudden silence. In the Sahara desert dunes collapsed and moved. A great roar and a hot wind spread across the land mass. All along the East African Rift Valley the land creaked and groaned like the protesting timbers of an ancient vessel at sea.

Anthony Goolden felt the tremor. He threw a glance at Wildman who nodded. The expected event must have taken place in Persia. There was consternation amongst the audience as the conference centre at Koobi Fora seemed to move on its foundations. Elation turned to uncertainty as family members gathered their arms around one another. Greg hugged Bernie and Derek protectively, wishing he were home with Rose and the kids.

Lorin, Goolden and Wildman were deep in agitated conversation. Perhaps the Americans were going to spoil the party after all.

Rock strata under the Saharan desert realigned in response to the strain of events in Iran. The movements were small, just a few feet, but enough to close up the chasm down which the waters intended for Koobi Fora had until now disappeared. In a great shudder the giant water pipes were realigned, correcting the engineering mistake.

Wildman recognised the change first. The tremors desisted and were replaced with the roar of a powerful river in full flow. A miracle was seen to appear on the TV screens of Europe and Africa. The dry river bed of Koobi Fora filled with the ancient waters.

And they will enjoy tranquil and verdant gardens, beneath which the rivers flow.

Epilogue

There were many repercussions from the events on the Iraq Iran border.

Other, lesser fault lines experienced local tremors. One such line ran underneath the foundations of a cold and desolate churchyard in the south west of England.

In an old and neglected crypt in Bath Abbey the tremor caused some local damage. A crack appeared across the stone sarcophagus of a man long dead. An unassuming clergyman of the nineteenth century, a man with a hare lip and unpopular views on the capability of nature to deal with overpopulation. The bones and dust of John Malthus fell through the cracks of his stone coffin and onto the dark floor.

Mother Earth felt her burden suddenly lighten in Persia and let out a sigh of relief. It wasn't enough, however, to compensate for recent developments in Africa. They came again into her garden, these *Homo sapiens*, in ever increasing numbers. She placed her measures upon them and still they came.

And so I must try again. Something winged. My little angel of death.

Contact Ruby Barnes

Connect online:

Email: ruby.barnes@marblecitypublishing.com

My Blog: http://rubybarnes.blogspot.com

Twitter: http://twitter.com/Ruby_Barnes

Facebook page: Ruby Barnes

Facebook person: RubyBarnesBooks

Author biography:

I've pedalled the pushbike of life through the Shires' rolling hills, along the folded rocks of Scotland's lochs and out west to the fractured reaches of North Wales. Love found me in the MacGillycuddy's Reeks of Ireland. The Swiss Alps cured me of obsessive compulsion and yielded progeny.

Misfits, rogues and psychopaths take form in Peril, The Baptist and other works. Their voices, they speak to me. I plead with them, but the demons are real. I've carried them on my back across Scandinavia, through the Mid-West, Eastern Seaboard and Deep South of the USA and to the borders of Argentina, Brazil and Paraguay. We teetered together on the brink of the Iguassu Falls and came back.

My writing is dedicated to the memory of my late grandfather Robert 'Ruby' Barnes.

Other books by Ruby Barnes

If you've enjoyed The Crucible then try **Peril**, the first novel from Ruby Barnes.

A contemporary crime thriller set in Dublin, Ireland.

Full of sharp wit and realistic characters, this book does exactly what it sets out to do - take readers on an adventure and leave them wondering what could possibly happen next.

Ruby Barnes has taken a character's life and spins a web that keeps you reading until the very end.

Ger is an anti-hero, the lad all the lads want to be, the guy all the girls love to hate but just can't bring themselves to. Scrape after scrape, he trundles through life with all the awareness of a rock, and yet you just can't help rooting for him...

Like nothing I've ever read before. The story is well written with a fast pace, intriguing plot twists and a good balance of dark humour and human drama.

You won't want to put it down... it twists and turns like a twisty turny thing.

A fantastic read, one of those rare books that keeps you guessing.

Gerard Mayes is in a bind. He's committed most of the seven deadly sins and is trying to avoid paying the price.

'I balance on the precipice of life. Friends and family have turned their backs on me and walked into the shadowland. Police and thieves are shouting Jump, Ger. Do it.'

Ladies, don't let your man read this book. You don't want him getting ideas on how to misbehave.

Fellas, keep your copy of **Peril** well hidden.

Ruby's second novel is **The Baptist**, a psychological thriller set in Kilkenny, Ireland.

Tight writing, very atmospheric. A chilling tale of real evil.

Dark and disturbing, but oh so good.

Dark and dingy, hot and steamy, everything you need from a novel in one swift download.

Well written and totally convincing, it provides an absorbing insight into the minds of some very strange characters. It's not without humour albeit of the dark kind.

Compelling and very, very different.

I was hooked right from the start and loved the dark and sinister quality of this tale.

He's clever, calculating and uncatchable. If you hear a knocking on your door don't let him in. John Baptist is cleansing a path for the Second Coming.

To deliberately drown your brother in a bathtub is a terrible, if clean, thing. Might it not be excused, if he is the manifest son of Satan? But that wasn't the view of the Authorities, when they committed John to Fairfield Mental Institution. It wasn't all bad; they let him keep his hair long and he met Dirty Mary. Like an institutionalised Bonnie and Clyde, they roamed the Victorian asylum and grounds, fulfilling their deluded fantasies. There were casualties.

John and Mary loved, lost and left. Thank God for Care in the Community.

When God shines a light, it burns.

The last prophet must wander, cleanse.

I am not the One. I am merely sent to prepare a way for the One.

I am **The Baptist**.

For aspiring writers - **The New Author** by Ruby Barnes

A beginner's self-help guide to novel writing, publishing as an independent author and promoting your brand using social networks.

There are three reasons why you should read and digest this book:

1. you want to be an author;
2. you have already written a novel and want to publish it as an ebook;
3. you want to promote yourself as an author.

With foreword by Jim Williams, author of the Booker Prize nominated *Scherzo*.

The New Author is available in ebook and paperback format from all major online bookstores.

www.ingramcontent.com/pod-product-compliance
Lightning Source LLC
Chambersburg PA
CBHW051317250626

47155CB00007B/2355